Love Me

&

Let Me Go

Love Me

&

Let Me Go

by
Trudy Harvey Tait

UNITED STATES ADDRESS
Harvey Christian Publishers, Inc.
3107 Hwy. 321, Hampton, TN 37658
Tel./Fax (423) 768-2297
E-mail: books@harveycp.com
http://www.harveycp.com

BRITISH ADDRESS
Harvey Christian Publishers UK
11 Chapel Lane, Kingsley Holt
Stoke-on-Trent, ST10 2BG
Tel./Fax (01538) 756391
E-mail: jjcook@mac.com

Printed in USA
First Edition 2012

ISBN: 978-1-932774-75-7

Cover Design by
Randall Bennett

Printed by
Lightning Source
La Vergne, TN 37086

Dedication

I wish to dedicate this book to:

Every young person in the process of discovering their true identity in Christ Jesus.

Every parent caught in the painful process of allowing their children to become who they truly are in Christ.

Every friend on the brink of sacrificing a cherished relationship on the altar of some self-imposed ideal.

Acknowledgments:

Warm thanks to my son and daughter-in-law for their constructive criticism and to Ottie Mearl Stuckenbruck, Margaret Smith, Jean Ward, and Anna Lee Tull for their help in proof-reading.

Special thanks to my very dear husband who has laughed, cried, and prayed with me as I went through the process of producing this book. Without his patience, love, and constant encouragement, *Love me and Let me Go* would still a fanciful dream instead of the book I now present to all my readers in the hope that they will read, enjoy, and be blessed!

Trudy Harvey Tait
Hampton, November, 2012

Contents

Contents Cont.

Part One

Chapter One

Cherry: Dad always wins!

I can't believe it! For the first time ever, I've hung up on my dad! I stare blankly at the receiver in my hand. Relief, guilt, anger, confusion—all these emotions and others I can't quite define—surge through me as I slowly and deliberately replace it in its cradle and flop into the nearest chair.

"Cherry, have you heard?" I hear a voice at my elbow and give a start. I hadn't realized that Allie had entered the apartment we share together.

"Heard what?" I mutter sullenly.

"That the Arabs have attacked Israel, and on their Day of Atonement, too!"

"Oh, really?" I mutter again. "I'm afraid I'm not very interested right now."

Allie gives a long sigh. "Well, you ought to be. Any Christian should be interested in what happens to Israel."

It's my turn to sigh. "I suppose so," I agree. "But I can't think of anything else right now except what's going on between my dad and me. It's a sort of war, too."

Allie's eyes open wide. "So?" she asks, as she perches herself on the arm of my chair.

"So I got mad at Dad," I mutter. "I hung up on him."

Allie stares at me in disbelief. She simply adores my father, just like nearly everyone else I know, including myself, of course.

"Don't look at me like that!" I explode. "You make me feel guilty. Just like Dad does! I just can't please him anymore. His latest gripe is over where I worship, though it's really none of his business. Isn't it just between God and me?" I pause for breath. Allie looks thoroughly shocked now. "He wants me to find another house church," I continue, in the vain hope that maybe she'll understand me just a little.

"You could come with me to my church," Allie puts in hopefully. "I think that would make him happy."

"No way," I retort. "I wouldn't last there a week. I need something different, Allie—a real church, with steeple, and stained glass windows, and liturgy."

Allie shakes her head in despair. "No wonder your dad is upset, Cherry. I can't blame him."

"You wouldn't!" I mutter. "He's Saint Dennis to you."

She opens her mouth then shuts it again. I know I've hurt her and feel terrible. "Can't you understand me?" I plead, trying to sound piteous. "I'm not doing anything terrible, am I? I am trying to follow Christ, Allie, honest I am. Only I can't do it like you do, or Dad does, or anyone else for that matter. I'm me, Cherry McMann. And I'll follow God the way that meets my needs. What's so unreasonable about that?"

I ought to feel better for having let it out like this, but I don't. Allie's large brown eyes look into mine accusingly. It's no use. We'll never understand each other, though maybe I ought to give it one more try.

"Dad says he'll come up and help me find somewhere suitable to worship," I go on more calmly. "Somewhere that suits *him*, he means. Meanwhile, he pretty much ordered me to attend Pendleton Mission this Saturday. Some missionary is going to show slides of his work in Malawi."

"So?" Allie asks.

"So I just lost it," I explode. "I love my dad to bits; you know that, Allie, but when he treats me as if I'm a juvenile delinquent on probation, well, it sends me up the wall."

Allie frowns. I brace for another lecture. Then I see her expression change, and I'm not quite prepared for the pain in her voice as she says slowly, "I'd give anything to have a dad like yours, Cherry, even if he did act as policeman. You just don't know how lucky you are."

She's right, of course. She's always right. She dresses right; she studies right; she prays right. That's why Dad was so keen that I share this apartment with her. She and her mom attend our home fellowship back in Meadow Creek, NC, where I've lived for the past twenty years. She has just transferred to Blackmore College where I attend. She's two years older than I am, but we're both juniors. That, and our church background, is about all we have in common.

Suddenly, I burst into tears. I feel Allie's hand on my shoulder. I brush it off, bolt into my bedroom, and slam the door behind me. I don't need her comfort or advice. I just want to be alone to recover. I've never ever talked to Dad like I did a few moments ago and I suppose I never will again. It's not worth it. I feel so miserable.

"Sorry, Dad," I find myself saying half an hour later. "I shouldn't have lost my cool like I did. I'll go to Pendleton Mission on Saturday if it means so much to you."

"That's my girl!" he exclaims. I can hear the triumph in his voice and I cringe. He always wins and he knows it. "We have great hopes for you, Cherry," he goes on. "Your mother and I have just been reminding ourselves of how, before you were even born, we dedicated you to be a missionary."

I stifle a groan. I know all about his hopes for me—that's just the problem. It takes all I've got not to hang up on him again. I clench my knuckles tight. "That's all very well, Dad," I manage to say after a long pause, "but I've got to feel called myself, haven't I, to be a missionary, I mean?"

"Of course you have to feel called," he booms. "And that's just what we're praying for." There it is again. Dad's prayers! They're powerful. I know that only too well.

I'm still thinking about those prayers a few days later as Allie and I pull up in front of a square, brick building in the center of Pendleton, a town ten miles from Blackmore. A stocky young man with a mop of unruly, sandy colored hair greets us at the door. We shake his hand, return his smile, and make for two empty seats at the back of the hall.

"You'll see much better if you sit nearer the front," the young man advises. "It's going to be pretty crowded tonight."

Allie rises and follows him down the center aisle. He looks around to see if I'm coming. "You'll see the slides much better from here," he whispers, as I slip into the third row from the front.

I nod my thanks, but inwardly I'm fuming. First Dad almost makes me come here and then this man, whoever he is, doesn't even let me choose my own seat.

"I think he's the pastor here," Allie whispers a few moments later, as this same individual mounts the platform steps and sits down beside a middle-aged gentleman who, I take it, is tonight's speaker.

I shrug. I'm not really interested‾ not in him, nor in the missionary, nor his slides, nor in anything else in this place.

"Look at that girl's hair!" I hear a boy muttering behind me as the lights are turned off a few minutes later and we settle down to watch the slides. "It almost glows in the dark."

I hear giggles all round. I know the little scallywag is talking about me. No one else has hair like mine, at least, that's what I'm told about a hundred times a month.

"I like her hair," I hear another boy saying. "It's so curly and awfully thick! She's probably very pretty. I wonder what her face is like."

"We can soon find that out," the first boy says.

"SShh," a woman's voice cautions. It must be their mother. "Your dad is speaking now. So be quiet!"

Their dad! Allie and I exchange glances, but the first slide is on the screen now and I find that I'm interested in spite of myself. Strange, faraway places always fascinate me, and I've never known much about Malawi.

It seems as if Reg Stanton, that's the speaker's name, is in charge of Ngavi Mission Station in Northern Malawi, high up on the Central African Plateau and about two hours' drive from Lake Malawi. I stare at the smiling, shining black faces on the screen and wonder what missionary life is actually like. Is it really the utopia Mr. Stanton is making it out to be? And are all those converts genuine? And what about the missionaries? Are they as saintly as they look, or are they real, live, flawed human beings just like me?

"This is our farm manager," Reg Stanton is saying, pointing to a balding, middle-aged, gentleman. "He is leaving the mission-field on account of his health, and so we are praying for some able-bodied young man to take his place."

"Good job it's a man they want," I whisper to Allie, "otherwise Dad would arrange for me to be shipped off to Ngavi tomorrow."

"Stop whispering!" Allie orders, grinning in spite of herself. She knows that I've helped Dad on our farm for years—that I can drive a tractor, ride a horse, milk cows, feed hens, help with the lambing, and….

The picture changes and I stare, fascinated, at the figure of a little girl of about nine years old. Her large, liquid brown eyes hold me like a magnet.

"This is Joy Mkandawire," Reg is telling us. "She's the granddaughter of Rhoda, our station housekeeper and cook. Joy's mother died a few years ago, leaving the child in Rhoda's care."

"That's my girlfriend," I hear the boy behind me comment. "Isn't she gorgeous?"

"She's not your girlfriend, Guy," the younger boy counters. "And she never will be. Dad won't allow it. She's not white, so that's that!"

I look closer at the girl in the slide. No, she's not white, or black. Her skin is a light tan and her wavy black hair is long and glossy.

"She *is* my girlfriend," the first boy says firmly. "And I'm going to marry her when I grow up."

"Sshh," I hear his mother caution once more.

At last the meeting is over. I slip out into the aisle, but not before I hear the boy called Guy whispering to his brother, "I've seen her face, the girl with the red hair, I mean, and she's not a bit as pretty as my girlfriend. Her nose turns up too much."

I try to act as if I haven't heard a word, but it's no use. Talk about my nose, and you're asking for trouble!

"I think she *is* pretty," the younger boy counters. "I like turned-up noses. They're cute. Besides, her hair makes up for everything."

I catch a glimpse of the boys out of the corner of my eye. The oldest is an absolute charmer! He meets my gaze and sticks out his tongue. His mother gives me an apologetic smile as she yanks her son in the opposite direction. I turn away in disgust. Missionaries' kids should at least know how to behave in public. I push back a stray ringlet that has escaped its band and give a sigh as I make for the door. Who am I to criticize? I'm a preacher's kid, too, and know only too well what that means!

"I hope you enjoyed your evening," the sandy-haired young man tells us a few moments later.

"We certainly did," Allie exclaims warmly. I say nothing.

"I'm Angus Campbell," he announces with a grin. He looks about the happiest, most contented guy I've met in a long time.

"And I'm Cherry McMann," I reply. Our eyes meet for just a moment.

"We have services here every Sunday evening," he goes on. "You are welcome any time."

"Thanks," I mutter, and escape into the darkness of the balmy, September night.

Chapter Two

Cherry: The annoying question.

It is a gorgeous evening in early October. The sun will set any moment now⁻ my favorite time of day. Two weeks have passed since I went with Allie to Pendleton Mission. Dad rang soon afterwards and wanted to know all about it. I didn't tell him much. I just couldn't. I mean, what would he think if he knew that I can't forget those large sad eyes of little Joy Mkandawire. They seem to be calling to me, asking for help, wanting me to love her as a mother would have done. Dad would say it was God calling me to devote my life to the children of Africa, or something like that. I suppose if he weren't so persistent about all this missionary business, I might be tempted to at least consider it.

Actually, I couldn't choose whether I would become a doctor or a journalist when I first came to Blackmore, so I opted for a double major— biology and English. But recently, I've decided that being a doctor would signal, to my parents at least, that I might very well become a medical missionary one day, which is definitely their dream, not mine. So I've decided to become a journalist when I graduate. After all, I've written stories ever since I was able to hold a pen. I'd love to write a bestseller one day, not that I've told anyone my dream. And besides, I'd never last long on the mission field. I'd lose my temper before I'd been there a day! Still, I'm not dropping biology. I love it and who knows? It just might come in useful one day.

A breeze rustles the leaves in the branches above my head. I'm sitting curled up under an old oak tree down by the river, doing my best to cram for a test tomorrow, but with little success. My mind is too full of missions and dark-eyed children with no mothers.

I give myself a shake. I'm getting morbid as I often do since my brother Paul graduated and moved to Chicago. And that reminds me. Why hasn't he phoned me in a month? I miss him terribly. If it hadn't been for him, Dad would never have let me come up here to Blackmore, hundreds of miles away from my family. But with steady, responsible Paul by my side, Dad thought I'd be fine. And I was, at least until last November, when my brother went for an interview to the University of Chicago and came back talking about nothing else but some librarian who seems to have completely bowled him over. What else would make him forget his little "Carrot Top" as he calls me, and spend all his free time miles away from me with some girl I've never met? Thing is, he's resisted the prettiest girls at Blackmore for years, so this librarian must be something else!

But it's not really Paul who worries me. It's myself—Cherry McMann! I'm growing more and more confused every day when I think about home. Sometimes I never want to see it again, and the next moment I'm dreadfully homesick. Maybe....

"Hi," says a deep voice just behind me. I nearly jump out of my skin. "Sorry to startle you," the voice continues. "You must have been miles away."

I look up into a pair of merry gray eyes. "I was miles away," I admit, blushing to the roots of my flaming red hair.

Angus smiles. Yes, it's Angus all right. I'd know his smile anywhere. It's warm and lights up his whole face. "You're Cherry McMann, aren't you?" he asks. He has remembered me, too, of course. I say of course, because who could forget the girl with the incandescent hair!

"Yes, and you're Angus Campbell," I tell him, holding his gaze for a moment.

"So we've at least remembered each other's names. That's a start." He smiles again. "Mind if I sit down beside you?" I shake my head, blushing again in spite of myself.

"You're a freshman?" he inquires, as he leans back against the tree and folds his arms.

"Actually, I'm a junior," I inform him, trying to camouflage my chagrin. I sit up a little straighter and push back an unruly curl that has escaped its clasp.

"I didn't mean to insult you," he says defensively, "but I thought you looked...."

"As if I'd just left home for the first time," I interrupt.

"I wouldn't put it that way."

"You're too polite. And you look like a grad student," I tell him, studying his face. He's not nearly as handsome as my brother, but then, few men are.

"Well, I'm a sophomore," he announces almost proudly. "How about that!"

I can't believe my ears! He looks twenty-five or older. "But you've probably got at least one degree under your belt," I comment, plucking a blade of grass as I speak. I can't believe I feel so comfortable with Angus.

"One or two," he admits. "But right now, I'm studying at the agricultural college in Pendleton, learning how to become a good farmer. It's a two-year course."

I stare at him for a moment. My dad is a professor turned farmer, well, farmer-preacher to be more exact, so I suppose I shouldn't be surprised.

"I want to help unfortunate youngsters by bringing them close to Mother Earth," Angus explains. "Maybe I'll start a rehab center, or something like it. I was a wild sort of guy until I met Christ two-and-a-half years ago. It was on January 6th, 1973. I remember the date because that's when my life really and truly began!"

He pauses a moment and I look at him wistfully. It must be rather comforting to know the exact date when you first met Christ. Actually, though, I've experienced quite a few important moments in my life, spiritual moments, I mean, so I guess I shouldn't be envious of someone like Angus.

"Now I want to spend my life helping others to meet Him too," he tells me, his eyes bright with hope, "either here or in Africa. That missionary who showed slides the other night made me think a lot."

I stare at him again, thinking how much he seems to be enjoying life. I feel envious. I catch his eye and wonder what he's thinking about me. He's the sort of guy I'd like for a friend. Suddenly, I wish that my hair wasn't such a shocking red, and that it hung in graceful waves around my shoulders instead of being so unmanageable I can do nothing but yank it into a pony tail and even then, it won't do as it's told.

"And what about you, Cherry? What do you want to do in life?"

"Me?" I ask, startled. I can't understand why anyone would want to know much about me.

"Who else?" he retorts with another grin. "I mean, what are you studying? Art? Music? You seem the artistic type."

"Oh I do, do I?" I ask, blushing again. That's three times in the past five minutes! Guys always make me blush. And the more I try to stop myself, the worse it gets, so I've given up trying.

"I meant it as a compliment," Angus says apologetically. My cheeks are flaming now. I'm just not at home with the opposite sex and I blame Dad for that. Maybe if he hadn't tried to protect me so much, I'd have learned how to cope with compliments from charming young men. And Angus *is* charming, at least his smile is. If it weren't for that and his very expressive gray eyes, he'd be pretty ordinary looking. Oh, and his hair! It's very thick and light brown, and there's one wayward strand that keeps falling down over his forehead.

"Thanks," I finally mutter, wanting to keep the conversation going. "And you're right, in a way. I'm majoring in English. I'm going to be a journalist when I graduate."

Angus nods. "That's great! Writers have done a lot to influence the world's thinking." There's a long pause. I'm curious about him. Studying farming so that he can help troubled kids? I wonder if I'd be willing to do that sort of thing.

We both are silent for a long time, looking out over the river and beyond. The sky is pink and gray. I pull my sweater tighter around me. Then, out of the blue, Angus asks me the question I always dread to hear. "By the way, Cherry," he begins, "where do you go to church?" I was just beginning to feel relaxed, but now his question gets under my skin, just as it does when my dad asks it nearly every time he calls.

"Why do you want to know?" I ask sharply.

Angus frowns for the first time. "Well," he says slowly, "isn't that the question Christians ask when they want to get to know each other better?"

"If it is, then it certainly shouldn't be," I retort.

"But haven't you ever been asked that before?" he persists.

"Hundreds of times! I hated it the first time I was asked the question and I still hate it."

"But why? I mean, I asked you what you were majoring in and you didn't get offended, did you?"

"Of course not! That's absolutely different."

"How is it different?" he asks, his grey eyes probing mine.

"Well," I begin slowly, winding an errant strand of hair around my fingers as I speak, "what you study describes you as a student, but what church you attend should not define you as a Christian."

"Agreed! And it doesn't, at least, not for me. But still, I really don't know why you're so touchy on the subject."

I glare at him as I stand up and grab my backpack. "Sorry, but it's getting late, and I've got to go now."

Angus springs to his feet and starts to follow me as I stride along the path that skirts the river. "I'm sorry to have upset you, Cherry," he calls after me.

I turn round. He's standing in the middle of the path, looking very much like a dog that's been chastised. I take a few steps towards him, ready to apologize for the way I've spoken, and then I notice the expression on his face. For some reason or other, it's pretty clear that he actually pities me!

"Bye!" I say abruptly, turning on my heel as I speak.

"Typical redhead!" Angus mutters as he also turns and heads in the opposite direction.

Chapter Three

Angus: *That irascible redhead!*

Midnight already! I'm usually asleep long before this. I hate to admit it, even to myself, but it's that redhead. I can't get her out of my mind. Maybe it's that hair of hers; it's not pure red, more red-gold like the leaves on the oak tree outside my dorm window. But what a temper! I should have been warned, though. Most redheads I know fly off the handle at the slightest provocation.

I smile to myself as I turn over for the hundredth time. Then my smile turns sour. Talk about rude! She had no right to react the way she did to my simple, innocent question. She's upset me; she's annoyed me; and yet, let's face it, she's fascinated me ever since she walked into our mission the other night. Thing is, I haven't even looked at a girl for months. And why should I, after pursuing them shamelessly for years! I'm a different guy now. And when I do settle down, I want a good Christian woman, one who doesn't want me for my money¯ someone steady, reliable, even-tempered¯ definitely not someone like Cherry McMann. Whoever marries that girl will be marrying a hurricane!

I close my eyes and count sheep. It doesn't work. I begin to think of farming and of my dreams for the future, but that redhead just won't go away! I'd really like to help her, though helping a girl like Cherry McMann might be risky for a guy like me. Something is eating her up. She's quite obviously a Christian, but she doesn't seem at peace with herself. I can at least pray for her. Prayer sounds safe enough, and it's amazing how quickly I fall asleep when I pray. Sounds awful, but it's true.

And so I begin to pray for the girl with the incandescent hair and a personality to match. Before I know it, the sun is streaming in through the window opposite and a new day begins, then another, and another. The days merge into weeks. Classes for hours on end, work on a nearby farm on a Saturday, helping out at the mission on a Sunday evening—all this and more gives me little spare time. But then, I'm happiest that way.

And then one Sunday, I wake up wondering where I should attend church that morning. Usually, I need the time to prepare my sermon for the evening service at the mission. But today, I have a Sunday off. So where should I go?

I stroll into town, thinking that I'll try out the Methodist church. I've heard that it's pretty evangelical. But on the way, I pass St. Asaph's Episcopal Church. I pause a moment on the sidewalk and stare at the quaint stone building.

"Like to join us for worship?" I hear a voice behind me saying.

I turn around. It's the priest himself. He looks as if he really wants me to come to his church. Sincere—that's what he seems⁻ so I accept his invitation.

"I left something in my car," he explains as we walk up the flagged stone path to the church door. "Maybe providential, don't you think?"

Now that's what I like—the missionary spirit. In spite of my prejudice against Episcopalians, I follow him to the door of the church. I say prejudice—that's because I was brought up Episcopalian and it didn't do much for me, or help my mother stay away from the bottle, or prevent my father from divorcing her. And it didn't show me the way to Christ. Then why on earth do I follow this total stranger through the arched doorway and into the church vestibule? Maybe it's because I'm still, officially, an Episcopalian.

Whatever the reason, I nod to the priest as I slip past him and into the church. I enter and sit on the back pew. The organ music, the smell of incense—all bring back a flood of memories. I almost wish I'd never come. As the service begins, I give a start. There, sitting five or six rows in front of me, is the girl with the red-gold hair.

We stand to sing but it's hard to concentrate. "Providential!" the priest had called his meeting me this morning. I tend to agree with him. I've been trying in vain to put this girl out of my head for the past month, and now I almost bump into her in an Episcopalian church! She isn't like any Episcopalian I know—long, thick hair tied back in its usual ponytail, simple white cotton blouse, three quarter sleeves, and long floral skirt. Simplicity personified! Hope she never changes!

The priest is reading the collect for the day, but my mind wanders again. I know now why she didn't want to answer my question. She probably thought that a radical evangelical like me would frown on her Episcopalian roots. Little did she know! I grab the prayer book and begin to intone the familiar words, but inside I'm thinking, "Lunch? The China King on Main Street? Will she come? Who knows? I can only ask, can't I?"

Chapter Four

Cherry: At St. Asaph's.

I'm finally getting the hang of this service. It's my first time at St. Asaph's, though I've passed it many times on the way to the mall and wondered what it would be like to attend there. Something has always held me back, even though I knew that a church like this has it all—steeple, stained glass windows, and liturgy. But I couldn't get away from Dad's advice to me before I left home two years ago. I can hear his words yet: "Don't get mixed up in worldly churches, especially the Episcopalian Church." And when I asked why, I could see he was appalled at my ignorance. "It's Romanism dressed up in Protestant clothes," he had informed me loftily.

I couldn't forget his words, not that I ever forget what my father tells me, but when Angus asked that question the other week, it made me think. I need to have a church I could call my own. That's what I have longed for ever since I left home two years ago. But any advice from Dad tends to evolve into some law I must follow, so I attended a home fellowship in a nearby town for two years until it became so divided over petty issues that it eventually broke it up. Now I make do with the Intervarsity Fellowship and a monthly non-denominational Bible Study as my means of worship. But after that incident with Angus Campbell, I realized that I can't keep on being ashamed of having no church to belong to.

I'm brought back to the present as the lady next to me hands me the prayer book open at the appropriate place. She met me entering the church and introduced herself as "Kathy." I'm glad I'm sitting next to her, though she's definitely not my type—elegant, sophisticated, and extremely made-up. But she's friendly, and that means a lot to me right now; in fact, it means everything!

I do exactly what she does except cross myself. That would be going too far. I smile a little. Dad would have a fit if he knew where I am this morning. Then the smile dies on my lips. I am actually doing something he would not approve of and doing it deliberately. I give a shudder. How dare I go against my saintly father? Maybe God's curse will fall on me, because Dad is saintly, isn't he? No one I've ever met prays from morning to night like he does, or preaches his heart out until the congregation either loves him or hates him, or saves every penny to give to missions, or.... His virtues seem endless. My lips tighten as the choir prepares to sing. Problem is that I secretly doubt if any saint, past or present, has been able to control his family as effectively as my father does.

I push such thoughts from my mind as the choir begins to sing. My minor is in music and I have joined the college chorale, so I flatter myself that I know real music when I hear it. And this is, without a doubt, real music. That's another thing about house churches. They usually don't have choirs, at least, not one like this.

An elderly gentleman sitting in front of me rises and makes his way to the reading desk and begins to read from the Old Testament. I like that. Involving the congregation in worship is something I didn't expect in a church like this. After a few more prayers, there is another Scripture reading and another. Three in one service! That would please Dad— plenty of Bible to chew on. And now Father Andrew Price, for that is the priest's name, is beginning his sermon. I can't quite make him out. His hair is as white as my grandma's was when she passed away three years ago. But his face is young, and his eyes are blue as the sky. He must be in his mid-thirties, no more. And he looks so spiritual! Well, maybe mystical is a better word to describe him. But he wasn't always that way, or so he's telling us. It seems as if he has had an experience something like St. Paul's on the Damascus road which completely transformed him. He holds me spellbound. He's every bit as earnest and as eloquent as Dad is and a lot better looking.

"And this experience is for each one of us," he is saying, and his eyes seem to meet mine as he speaks. "It need not be as dramatic as St. Paul's. It might come through the verse of a hymn, a collect, or a friend's prayers for us; but we must all realize that the God of glory is ever ready and willing to reveal Himself to His creation and to fill every life with the sweetness of His presence, leading them individually in the way that they should go."

The sermon is over now, but I'm still thinking about Father Andrew's closing words when I feel Kathy nudging me.

"It's time to take the Sacrament," she whispers, as, row by row, the worshipers make their way to the communion rail.

"Is everyone allowed to take it?" I ask timidly.

"If you've been baptized and believe in the Real Presence, you can," she assures me.

Yes, I've been baptized all right—by Dad in the river behind our house. That was four years ago and I'll never forget it. But the Real Presence? I'm not at all sure what that means. "I won't go this time," I whisper to my new friend.

"That's OK," she says reassuringly, patting my shoulder. "Now, if you'll let me pass."

I look longingly as Kathy receives the bread and wine and am just beginning to regret my scruples, when a stocky young man with an unruly shock of light brown hair makes his way past me up the aisle and stands reverently at the rail. I watch as he holds his hand out for the bread. Yes, it is definitely Angus Campbell and it's obviously not the first time he has visited an Episcopalian church. I am still in shock as we file out some minutes later into the warm, October sunshine.

"This is my new friend, Cherry," Kathy tells the priest as I shake his hand.

"A student?" he asks smiling. I thought Angus' smile was extraordinary, but this man's is almost mesmerizing!

"Yes, I'm a junior at the college in town," I mutter, blushing to the roots of my hair.

"Then welcome to St. Asaph's. I trust you have enjoyed our service."

"Yes, very much," I find myself replying.

"I hope to see you here again." His voice is gentle and kind.

"I hope so too," I murmur as he turns to greet the lady behind me.

Chapter Five

Angus: Lunch with Cherry.

"Fancy seeing you here!" I didn't mean it to come out like that, but I had to say something, or the tall and very sophisticated lady who sat beside Cherry during the service would have whisked her right past me.

"I could say the same about you," Cherry murmurs, blushing.

"An old friend?" the older lady asks.

Cherry seems flustered and is silent. "Not exactly old friends," I put in, smiling. "But friends, nevertheless, or at least I hope so."

The lady smiles politely. "Well, you two friends have a wonderful day," she tells us as she gives Cherry a hug and whispers, "Remember, I hope to see you next week!"

"Thanks," Cherry mutters. "Till next week!"

"Till next week!" her friend echoes, then turns on her heel and leaves us alone.

After a moment's silence, we find ourselves walking together towards the church parking lot. "I think I see now why you reacted that way to my question," I comment, as the gravel crunches beneath our feet.

"I don't understand," Cherry says, looking totally confused.

"Well, you probably thought...." I pause. Now I'm in hot water. When will I ever learn to think more before I speak!

"Are you trying to say that...." Cherry stops abruptly. She doesn't know how to go on and neither do I.

We stand, stock still, and stare at each other for a few moments in silence, each as confused as the other. Then we both burst out laughing at the same time.

"Let's go where we can talk better," I suggest when we come to our senses. "It's obvious we both need to do some explaining. How about the China King in Pendleton?"

Cherry's brown eyes open wide. I can see she wasn't expecting me to say that.

"You're asking me to...," she stammers, not able to finish her sentence.

"I'm asking you to have lunch with me, but maybe you've got somewhere better to go?"

"Like the school cafeteria?" she suggests with a grin.

"Then it's settled. Let's go in my car and I'll drop you off here when we return."

She nods her thanks, looking a bit uncertain but pleased at the same time. The silence is rather awkward between us as we speed along the Interstate towards Pendleton. I'm not sure why I'm doing this and, quite obviously, neither is she.

"You're not used to this, are you?" I blurt out suddenly.

"Being chauffeured to lunch by a young man?" she asks, blushing furiously. She blushes a lot, I've noticed, not like most girls I know. "No, I admit I'm not used to this," she continues. "My dad never allowed it. He always saw to it that I was chaperoned."

"I see."

"But I'm my own boss now," she says defensively. "Only...."

"Only you're wondering if he would approve." I finish the sentence for her.

Her face darkens. "How did you guess?" she mutters.

Well, how did I guess? I'm getting in this up to my neck now. Not only am I out of practice with girls, but in all my twenty-six years, I've never met one quite as naïve as this redhead. I glance at her out of the corner of my eye. I see that mentioning her father has hit a sore spot and think it best to change the subject.

"Well, I'm not used to this either," I tell her awkwardly. "Taking girls out to lunch, I mean."

She looks surprised. I suppose I strike her as being very worldly-wise. "To be absolutely truthful," I admit, reddening a little, "I've not always been this way. I led a pretty wild life until about two years ago."

She looks at me curiously. "Tell me about it," she urges.

I hesitate a moment. I don't understand myself this morning. First, I ask a girl I hardly know out to lunch and before we've driven five miles, I find myself about to tell her my life history. I give her a quick glance. She's waiting, expectant.

"I don't think you'd want to hear most of my story," I begin. "It's the familiar tale of a guy seeking fulfillment in anything that satisfies his desires and hurting himself and those he loves in the process."

"You don't look that type," she comments. "You look as if you've been a Christian all your life."

Her comment confirms the fact that she's utterly and completely naïve. I'm quite aware that I look no saint, not like the priest of St. Asaph's at any rate.

"I've been an Episcopalian all my life," I confess after a moment's pause, "but certainly not a Christian."

"So Episcopalians aren't Christians?" she asks a little sharply.

"I didn't say that," I counter. "But *I* certainly wasn't. Up until a few years ago, I partied every weekend, drank a fair bit, and, well, did pretty near everything I wanted to do. And I'd probably still be living that kind of life if I hadn't met a chaplain three years ago who helped turn my life around."

"Chaplain?" she repeats. "You were in the forces?"

"Yes. I served in Vietnam for two years," I reply. "From 69-71. I don't talk about it much. It was…terrible."

"I'm sorry!" Her eyes are full of sympathy now. "I remember hearing about it on the news, day after day. And to make it worse, when you came home, you weren't exactly received as heroes, were you?" she comments.

I grimace. "Not exactly, but still, if I'd never gone to Vietnam, who knows where I would be today. One thing's for sure, I'd never have met Chaplain Kerry—the only man who had the courage to tell me to my face that I was heading straight to damnation."

"He said it just like that?"

"Yes, just like that. And then, by his life and his fatherly counsel, he pointed me in a totally different direction."

"He must have been something else," Cherry mutters. "I wish I could do that for someone."

I stare at her for a moment or two. "You probably have already without knowing it," I tell her softly.

She shakes her head decidedly. "Me? No, I've never done something like that. I have enough trouble keeping my own life in order." She sees I'm about to make some comment or other and says hastily, "But let's get back to your story."

I nod. "Well, although this chaplain's words and life had already gotten through to me, I doubt if I'd have really changed my lifestyle if it hadn't been for his death."

"His death?"

"Yes." My voice chokes. "He died saving other lives—went too close to the enemy and...." I can't go on for a few moments. Talking about Chaplain Kerry brings back so many vivid memories.

"Before he died," I continue when I've gotten myself in hand once more, "he said these words to me: 'Angus, I'll tell Father his prodigal is coming Home. Don't disappoint Him or me, will you?' And then he closed his eyes and passed into eternal life leaving behind a completely changed guy. After all, I couldn't disappoint him or 'Father' as he always called the Lord, could I?"

I think I see a few teardrops in Cherry's dark brown eyes. But I haven't quite finished my story. "I came back to the States soon afterwards," I go on, "and found that my parents had divorced. I knew it was coming to that. Mom had been an alcoholic for years. Dad died of cancer shortly afterwards, but I took care of him for six months and had plenty of chances to tell Him about the God Who had done so much for me. I was at my dad's bedside when he died and feel sure he made it to Heaven."

"And your mom?" Cherry wants to know.

"At first, she would have nothing to do with my new religion as she called it. She was an Episcopalian and that was that. But what had it done for her or for me?"

"You are a bit hard on Episcopalians, Angus," Cherry says pointedly.

"Sorry, I didn't mean to offend you. I suppose it's only natural for you to defend your own church."

"My own church?" she echoes. "So you think I'm Episcopalian?"

Now she's really bamboozled me. "What else am I to think?"

"And you concluded I was ashamed of being one when I reacted to your question the way I did the other day?"

"You've hit the nail on the head, Cherry. That's what I was trying to say to you a few moments ago."

I'm not sure whether she's amused or offended. Then she begins to laugh again. "Oh, goodness!" she exclaims as we pull up in front of the China King. "What a muddle!"

"Want to 'un-muddle me' then?" I ask as I turn off the engine and we both get out of the car.

"Fair's fair!" she says, grinning. "You've told your story so now it's my turn."

I hold open the restaurant door to let her enter. She smiles her thanks. "But you didn't quite finish yours, Angus," she reminds me.

"No? Well, I was only going to explain why I'm not that keen on the Episcopalian Church. You need to understand that I had gone to church all my life and didn't see it doing much for my family or for myself. Taking the Sacrament seemed a license to live as I liked the rest of the week. And I wasn't the only one who thought that way. Besides, the chaplain was a Pentecostal and had given me a taste for something different."

"So you're Pentecostal now?" she wants to know.

"No. Officially, I'm still an Episcopalian, but I spend most of my Sundays at the Pendleton Mission." I give a short laugh. "I'm not in charge or anything like that—just helping out while the pastor is recovering from surgery."

"I see. But your mom?" she asks, as we are ushered to a table set for two. "Is she still an alcoholic?"

"Well, she's been off the bottle for six months now. She finally consented to attending AA. I went with her at the beginning till she made some good friends."

"So she's cured?"

I see the concern in Cherry's brown eyes and smile a little. "I can't say for sure. I'd feel better if she'd had some conversion experience such as I had—been changed overnight so to speak, but God works differently in all of us. And Mom has been praying a lot lately, so I can only hope that her life is being turned around, just like mine was."

I push her chair in for her and take my seat opposite. The waitress brings us a menu and two glasses of iced water. We decide to choose the buffet bar. As she rises, Cherry accidentally knocks over her glass. Water cascades in all directions.

"I was born clumsy," she mutters as we leave the waitress to mop up.

"You're just nervous," I tell her. "Who wouldn't be? I make even my mother nervous."

I see her lip tremble for a moment and then she gives me an impish grin. "Yes, Angus, I believe you would make any mother nervous."

Something sings within me as we make our way to the lunch bar. I wanted to help this girl from the first time I saw her. And I do believe I am helping her to—relax maybe? Get used to being with guys? Maybe I'll regret that some day, but right now, I'm having the time of my life!

When we've filled our plates and returned to our seats, Cherry says abruptly: "And now it's my turn."

"To tell your story?" I ask.

She nods. "But first I owe you an apology for the way I treated you a few weeks ago."

"You're forgiven already," I assure her.

"Thanks, I appreciate that. But I need to tell you why I lost my cool when you asked me that simple question."

"You don't need to explain," I interrupt.

"Yes, I do. At least," she adds, blushing, "I can't let you think that I acted that way because I was ashamed to be an Episcopalian. That wasn't true. In fact, today was the very first time I'd entered the door of an Episcopalian church."

"Really?"

"You're surprised?"

"Not exactly," I answer truthfully. "I could see from the way you handled the prayer book that you weren't used to the liturgy."

She gives a wry smile. "I'm not," she admits. "And I know I don't fit in very well at St. Asaph's. I'm not a bit sophisticated. I'm a country girl, brought up in a home fellowship, and used to either making my own clothes, or hunting for something decent in a Goodwill or Salvation Army Thrift Store."

I grin back. "Thanks for your honesty. And may you stay as you are as long as you can."

She blushes scarlet again. I didn't intend to embarrass her so I go on hurriedly: "I mean that I hope you don't adopt airs and graces and try to be someone you're not just to impress those around you."

Her face breaks into a smile. "Well, I guess I did feel rather out of place in this blouse and skirt."

"I like you just as you are," I find myself saying. The words are out before I can stop them. What I said was true, very true, only I've made her blush again. Not that I regret that. She's very pretty when she blushes, but I'm going to have to watch my step with this young lady. She's getting through to me more than I care to admit.

"I'm sure your story is pretty different from mine," I tell her, trying to put her at ease.

"It sure is," she agrees. "I've never been a member of any church. My dad runs a home fellowship, thinks traditional churches are mostly apostate, and tries to follow the worship of the early church as nearly as possible."

"Sounds like an admirable goal!" I can't help exclaiming. In fact, I make a secret note that this seems the kind of church I'd like to belong to.

"It might be admirable but it's certainly not practical," she replies firmly. "We're not in the first or second century anymore and have hundreds of years of tradition behind us as Christians, a fact my father deliberately chooses to ignore."

"So you think your home fellowship is a far-cry from the original form of worship?" I ask, sitting back in my seat and folding my arms.

"I'm no judge," she answers defensively. "How can I judge someone like my dad? I mean, I'm, well...."

"A rebel?" I suggest.

She shrugs. "Yes and no. Dad would say I'm full of rebellion. But," her lip quivers now, "he doesn't understand. I honestly love him and respect him and...."

She can't go on. I hate to see her upset like this. Personally, I'd love to get my hands on this dad of hers.

"Sorry, Cherry," I apologize. "I shouldn't quiz you like this when I hardly know you."

"It's OK, Angus," she reassures me, raising her eyes to my face. "It seems as if I've known you a long time."

"And that's just how I feel about you," I answer, feeling as if I had been given a thousand dollars.

We smile at each other. And then, to my surprise, her lip crumples and her eyes fill with tears. It's funny how vulnerable most girls look when they cry.

"Sorry," she mutters. "It's just that I'm rather emotional right now. I love my dad to death, but yet we just don't agree on so many things. His form of worship doesn't satisfy me anymore. I'm tired of being out on a limb." Her voice rises now and her cheeks are flushed. "And how can I tell people that I belong to a church that isn't really a church, which has no membership role, and no history to speak of? I need to find a church that feeds me."

"Like St Asaph's?" I can't help asking.

Cherry's deep brown eyes meet mine. She gives a faint smile as she replies slowly and deliberately, "Yes, Angus, exactly like St. Asaph's."

Chapter Six

Cherry: *A shopping spree.*

"There's a super sale at Penny's," Allie announces over breakfast, as she thumbs through the local newspaper. "And Sears!"

"Great!" I exclaim. "I need something decent if I'm going back to St. Asaph's."

Allie frowns. "Does your father know you went there?" she asks pointedly.

"No," I admit with a grimace. "He asked me if I had gone back to the Pendleton Mission and I told him I hadn't."

Allie looks thoughtful. "I've been back several times. That sandy-haired guy is a good preacher—down-to-earth and practical. You should give the mission a try, Cherry."

I'm suddenly seized by a desire to hear Angus preach. Is he as good as Father Andrew, I wonder? "I'll go back again one of these weeks," I assure her.

Allie gives a long sigh. "Why don't you come with me to the Independent Free Church? They've got a superb choir. You'd enjoy that, at least. A lot of students go there."

"You've told me that at least three times already," I pout.

"Well, I keep hoping you'll change your mind and come with me one of these Sundays. I worry about you."

I scoop up my cup and cereal bowl and deposit them in the sink. "Well, don't, Allie. And if you think Dad will blame you for any mistake I make, then you're wrong. He won't. It's not your fault that I'm stubborn and confused and everything else he doesn't want me to be. Now, if you don't mind, I'm off to that sale. Coming with me?"

Allie shakes her head. "No, I need to go to the practice room at college. I have a midterm recital on Monday."

"And I should be practicing for my voice recital or cramming for my English Lit exam, but that'll have to wait till this afternoon," I tell her, wishing for the thousandth time that my roommate wasn't so terribly industrious. She always makes me feel guilty, just like Dad does. "Bye,

Allie. Good practicing!" I shout over my shoulder as I make for the door.

"Bye, Cherry. Don't go on too much of a spree. You can't afford it. And don't buy anything your father wouldn't approve of."

"There she goes again," I mutter to myself as I make my way to the car. "Just because she's two years older than I am doesn't give her the right to lecture me all the time. And she doesn't always need to act like Dad's chief lieutenant." I'm secretly glad Allie decided not to come with me this morning. She's so over-bearing most of the time. Now I'm free to buy what I like with the hundred dollars I've saved up from working all year in the college library.

I feel unusually light-hearted as I speed towards the mall. Kathy, my new friend at St. Asaph's, has invited me to lunch with her tomorrow after church. I wonder if Angus will be there again. Probably not. He usually has to be at the mission. He's been on my mind all week. I wonder if I've been on his mind, too. Oh, I'm not thinking of him romantically. Just as someone I'd like to know better. His optimism is so contagious and what I need right now. And we do get on so well together, though I think we'd have some good arguments if we knew each other better.

Quarter of an hour later, I push open the swinging doors of the mall and wonder where to begin. Dad would think me terribly wasteful to even think of buying new clothes. All my life I've either lived on other people's castoffs or visited the local thrift stores. My mother was the world's best bargain hunter and I had always thought our family pretty well-dressed, until recently, that is.

I make my way towards the sale racks in Penny's, but soon turn away in frustration. I don't need more tops or pants. I need a few smart Sunday outfits. At last, the salesgirl directs me to another corner of the store. "Try this," she urges, handing me a pale green dress. "The color will suit you perfectly."

I take it to the dressing room and soon discover she's right. Green has always suited me. I eye myself in the full-length mirror and gasp. The dress has transformed me. But the sleeves are sheer and the neck just a little plunging. I close my eyes and see my father's face. "Modesty, Cherry, is the first priority for a Christian woman," I hear him say. And Angus' words echo in my head: "I like you as you are, Cherry."

I stamp my foot in frustration. "Please, both of you, give me a break!" I say aloud, glad no one can hear me. "I want to look and feel like a well-dressed, modern woman for once."

I shake my head. I'll have to stop talking to myself like this. Then I glance at the price tag. "Seventy-five dollars!" I give a gasp as I hand the dress to the cashier. I need a few outfits and this one item has nearly cleaned me out. But I'm going to take it, even if that's all I buy today. Nothing I have ever worn has suited me better.

"Taking advantage of the sale, Cherry?" a voice asks at my elbow.

I spin around and find myself staring into a familiar pair of smiling gray eyes. "Angus!" I gasp in surprise.

He grins. "Didn't expect to see me here, did you? But it's Mom's birthday tomorrow so I thought I'd try to hunt up something appropriate. Any ideas? I've spent the last hour wandering around without any success."

His grin has faded now and he looks really frustrated. Maybe I should offer to help him. Besides, I rather like the guy.

"What about a purse?" I suggest. "Or a blouse? They're on sale, I've noticed. Or maybe cosmetics?" I color a little as I add, half apologetically, "Not that I've much idea of cosmetics. But...."

"You don't need makeup, Cherry," he tells me quietly. I blush more furiously this time. "And I've no idea what Mom uses," he goes on hurriedly seeing my confusion. "But maybe some nice powder and perfume, or something like that would suit her fine."

I nod mutely and lead the way to the cosmetic counter. I find Angus is very easily satisfied and extremely grateful into the bargain. It doesn't take much to make him happy. Before I know it, he's made his purchase and invited me to lunch at the food court where we spend the next half hour chatting together over soup and a sandwich. I tell him all about our farm back home.

"So you're a regular farm girl?" he asks, laughing.

I nod. "Yes, tractor, horse—I can drive them all."

He studies me curiously. "I couldn't have guessed, Cherry," he says after a long pause.

"No?" I ask, feeling both relieved and embarrassed at the same time.

"No. I suppose I have some mistaken idea of what farm girls look and act like."

I grin but say nothing. "How about coming with me some Saturday to the farm I'm working on as a project for school?" he asks out of the blue. "Maybe I can learn a few things from you. I'm really a novice at farming, or was, until I started agricultural school."

I can't believe my ears. This guy actually wants to get to know me better! That, somehow, makes me feel good. I know Allie will not approve, but the idea of helping Angus on his farm appeals to me. I'm still a tomboy at heart. "Sure," I say. "I'll come."

"Then how about next week?"

"Great," I agree as we rise from the table.

"So I'll pick you up next Saturday at...?" he pauses, realizing he doesn't know where I live.

I give him my address, say good-bye, and make my way to Sears. I still have twenty-five dollars to spend. I shake my head as I push open the swinging doors. I keep bumping into Angus Campbell. What is happening to me? I've only ever had one boyfriend, and that ended disastrously owing to Dad's interference. This time, I won't let Dad, or Allie, or anyone else interfere. Not that Angus is really my boyfriend...yet!

The sale at Sears yields me wonderful returns—a dressy, cream pant-suit, a gorgeous floral skirt, and pale blue blouse. Of course I have to try everything on once I get home.

"Hmm!" Allie exclaims as she whirls me around in front of the full-length mirror in the hallway. "What on earth would your dad say, Cherry?"

"I can't stick to dresses and skirts all my life, not in the twentieth century!" I protest.

"I do."

"I know, and so did I for years, except when I worked on the farm. But I'm tired of it, and besides, it's easier to wear pants sometimes, and warmer in winter, too."

"But a woman should not dress like a man," Allie says reproachfully.

"That's exactly what my father would say," I grumble. "You think like he does, and that's why he thinks you'll be a good influence on me."

Allie looks a little wistful. "I do wish you'd like me just a little, Cherry. I mean, if we're going to spend at least a year together, we need to learn to get along, don't we?"

There she goes again. She knows how to make me feel awfully guilty. "Then don't keep preaching at me, Allie," I beg. "You just seem to be Dad's echo half the time."

"Can't help it if I've sat under his ministry for at least ten years, can I?" she retorts hotly. "I still don't understand why...." She stops abruptly and then forces a smile. "I have to admit, Cherry, in spite of what I just said, that outfit suits you."

"Thanks," I tell her, smiling. "And that means a lot because I know you've got good taste in clothes." I'm not just flattering her. It's true. Even though she's terribly conservative, Allie always looks nice in an ordered, clean, fresh sort of way.

"Neckline is too low," I hear Dad's voice in my ears as I slip on my new green dress the next morning. Will I ever be able to drown out that voice, I wonder? And do I want to drown it out? If I ever do, which voice will replace it? That is a question I can't answer, not yet, at any rate.

I enjoy my second visit to St. Asaph's even more than my first. I'm getting used to the liturgy, and Father Andrew's sermon is as challenging as his first had been.

"We're glad you decided to visit us again," he tells me smiling as he shakes my hand.

"I'm not used to this kind of a service," I admit, "but I find myself drawn to liturgical worship."

"That's what I like to hear," he says encouragingly. Maybe it is his vestments, maybe his title, "Father," but I almost feel it is sacrilege to even shake his hand.

His eyes seem to rest a moment on my green dress. Actually, I think he likes it, judging from what just might be a hint of admiration in his eyes. Well, I think I do look good today. I've done up my hair on top of my head, and this outfit makes me feel pretty confident. But, I tell myself, Father Andrew is far too holy to notice what the young women in his congregation are wearing.

"I hear that Kathy is taking you to lunch," he continues.

"Yes. She's very kind."

"She is. And I'll see you next week, I hope?"

"Yes, Father." I said the last word hurriedly as if I'm afraid that Dad will overhear. Then I smile to myself. He is ten hours' drive away. I have nothing to worry about.

Over lunch, I find that, before I know it, I am telling my new friend all about myself—about my parents, their home church, my strict upbringing, and my ambition to become a writer. I'm hoping, in turn, that I'll learn quite a bit about her, but I'm mistaken. And I'm still too shy to ask if she's divorced, or a widow, or single. And Father Andrew, I wonder about him too. I noticed that Kathy is very friendly with him. But then, she is friendly with everyone.

"You'll be a real asset to our little church," Kathy tells me as she drives me back to St. Asaph's where I've left my car. "We need young folks like you—sincere, intelligent, and willing to learn."

I am still thinking about her words when I enter my room fifteen minutes later and find the phone ringing. I pick up the receiver. It's my brother. I've not heard from him for weeks and I suppose he's feeling guilty. After all, he did promise Dad when he began his grad studies that he would continue to keep an eye on his little sister. "A two-hour drive is nothing," he had assured us all.

"How's it going, Sis?" I hear his familiar voice asking.

"OK."

"Ready for mid-term break?"

"I guess so."

"Going home?"

"No, not if I'm going at Thanksgiving. Can't afford to."

"Me neither. So what about spending the weekend with Madeline and me? We're thinking of renting a cabin by the lake." I stare at the receiver in my hand, unable to say a word.

"But...," I stammer. Then I stop. What exactly am I going to ask him?

"It's OK, Sis," he reassures me. "We'd never think of spending a weekend alone. That's why we want you there."

"As chaperone?"

"Well, sort of. And I didn't want you to spend your break all by yourself."

"I'm not sure if I want to come, Paul," I begin slowly. "I don't know this girl of yours and I'm slow in making friends."

"Oh, but she's dying to meet you. You'll love her. She's so out-going. Oh, come on, Cherry, don't spoil it for everyone."

"OK," I concede reluctantly. "I'll come."

"Great! So two weeks from this Friday I'll see you in Chicago unless you phone me otherwise."

"But Paul," I protest, "does Dad know?"

"Dad? Are you kidding! Of course he doesn't know."

"But you will tell him?"

Paul gives an exasperated sigh. "Eventually, if it's necessary. Right now, Madeline is a casual date."

"Casual!" I exclaim. "You've been going with her for nearly a year!"

I hear him laugh sarcastically at the other end. "Yes, and it's been the best year of my life. We were brought up to avoid nearly everything that's fun and enjoyable, Cherry. Besides, Dad has long ago ceased to be my father-confessor."

"But he thinks you're a saint, Paul. You hide so much from him."

I can tell I have made my brother angry, but it can't be helped. Dad has always thought of him as the good guy, the son who is going to fulfill all his dreams, the spiritual giant in the making. Paul has no right to deceive him. He hasn't gone to church for months now and yet attends every service when he's home, even taking part. I never thought my brother could be such a hypocrite!

"Look, Cherry," Paul is speaking again. "You and I have separate lives to live and we're each doing what we feel is best under the circumstances. So let's trust each other to do what's right. Now, get your work done so that you can relax and have a wonderful weekend with me. Bye for now."

"Bye," I repeat mechanically, my heart in turmoil. I love my brother to death, but I've long since lost respect for his religion. In fact, I doubt very much if he has any religion at all anymore. But as he says, that is his business, not mine.

Chapter Seven

Cherry: A memorable weekend.

I stare in dismay at the large three-storied house in one of Chicago's ritzy suburbs. "You didn't tell me that your girlfriend is so rich," I exclaim. "I wish I hadn't come, Paul."

Paul opens his car door and steps out into the driveway. "Madeline's parents aren't exactly poor," he admits with a grin, "but Madeline isn't a bit stuck up."

"I hope not."

"But she is pretty upbeat," he adds truthfully.

"It's OK, Paul. I've a fairly good idea what she'll be like," I tell him, hoping I'm right.

He bites his lip but says nothing. I can tell that he thinks I don't have a clue about his girlfriend.

I watch as Paul walks up the path, rings the bell, and disappears through the front door. Ten minutes later he reappears, arm in arm with the most beautiful blonde I have ever seen, in real life, that is. She's taller than I am and very shapely. I try not to stare at her bright orange hot pants, or her skin-tight top that leaves nothing to the imagination. I jump in the back seat, wishing I'd never agreed to come on this crazy outing.

"This is my baby sister, Cherry," Paul begins, avoiding my eyes as he speaks. "And this, Cherry, is my girlfriend, Madeline Cummings."

"Aren't you cute!" Madeline coos, eyeing me up and down. "Real cute, though you don't look a bit like your brother."

That's true enough. He's tall; I'm short. He's dark; I'm a redhead. He can fit in anywhere and has loads of self-esteem. I'm clumsy and insecure. Anything else?

"I hope you'll let me play with your hair, Cherry," Madeline remarks as she hops into the front seat. "I can do wonders with it."

I say nothing. She turns around and pats my hand. "I do want to be friends," she whispers. I look into her blue eyes and think I might like her after all.

It's an hour's drive to the cabin on Lake Michigan. I say little as we speed along. There is no need. Madeline and Paul keep up a running conversation. They discuss everything from the last movie they watched together to the new sports car Madeline has just bought. I wonder what the gorgeous gal in the front seat would say if she knew her boyfriend has been foreordained by his honorable father, if not by the Almighty Himself, to be a revival preacher! I'm still smiling over that one as we pull up in front of the most darling cabin I have ever seen.

"Here we are," Paul announces, as he helps us carry our bags into the vestibule. "Now, let's see. What we have here? Yes, two bedrooms, just as I thought. Mind sharing, girls?" he asks, as he opens the door of the largest and points to two twin beds.

"Of course we don't mind, speaking for myself, that is," Madeline replies. "I hate being alone at night."

I stare at her in surprise. "I had a twin sister," she explains softly. "She was killed in a car accident when I was twelve."

"I'm so sorry," is all I can say.

"So I've been looking for another sister ever since. And now I think I just might have found one."

Paul gives her an odd look and then shuts the door and leaves us alone. Madeline turns away so I can't see her face and begins to unpack her bag. The more I see of Paul's girlfriend the more I understand why he's so fond of her. She might not meet Dad's dress code, but she seems to have a very big heart.

Then, suddenly, she pulls out a pair of skintight jeans and a very see-through top. "Here," she exclaims," holding them up to me. "I'd love to see you in these. And your hair! I'm dying to get my hands on it."

I look alarmed. The girl laughs merrily. "Don't worry," she reassures me. "I only mean that I'm a pretty good hair-dresser and all that. You've no idea what you'll look like when I've finished with you."

I groan inwardly. I hate people messing with my hair and this girl is practically a stranger to me.

"Come on, girls," I hear Paul's voice in the hallway. "I'm ravenous. Let's find somewhere decent to eat before it gets too late."

I wonder, as we drive to the nearest town, who is paying for this weekend. I know my brother has very little spending money. But I keep my questions to myself. After a sumptuous supper, Madeline suggests that we go to the movies.

Paul glances at me apprehensively. "I'm tired," I say, yawning. "Why don't you two go and have the evening to yourselves."

Madeline makes no objections. It is midnight before I hear her slip into the bed by the window. The next morning I'm up hours before the others. I have taken a long walk by the lake, made a pot of coffee, and had my devotions before Paul joins me in the kitchen.

"What do you think of Madi?" he asks when he has downed two cups of coffee.

"She's different," I reply. "I don't think Dad would approve of her at all."

"So what? He doesn't approve of a lot of things."

"I know, and I quite like her, Paul, only Madeline is a bit...." I pause, not knowing how to explain what I really mean.

"A bit what?" Paul wants to know. "She's the best thing that's happened to me in a long time, Sis. Much the best!"

"Talking about me?" a breezy voice asks from the doorway.

Paul reddens a little as Madeline glides into the kitchen and puts her arms around his waist. "Of course!" he assures her, still looking extremely embarrassed. "Who else would we talk about?"

Madeline cuddles in closer. "I'd love a glass of orange juice," she coos. "After you've given me a good-morning kiss, that is," she adds, giving me a wink.

Paul stoops down and gives her a peck on the cheek. Madeline pouts. "Call that a kiss?" she complains, as Paul, looking extremely uneasy, untwines her arms and makes for the refrigerator.

I slip out of the kitchen wishing for the hundredth time that I'd never agreed to come here in the first place. I make my way to our room, fish out a book from my case, and throw myself on the bed. But it's not long before Madeline enters, sits down on a chair by the window and eyes me curiously. I'm conscious that she is focusing on my hair.

"You'd look fabulous if you'd let me have a go at that hair of yours," she says suddenly.

"I don't want to look fabulous," I murmur, keeping my eyes on my book.

"Course you do," she persists. "Every girl does. Oh, come on, Cherry. You don't know how I enjoy fixing hair. I miss it ever since Ruby died. She had hair something like yours."

"So you weren't identical twins?"

Madeline shakes her head. "No way! We were pretty much opposites. She was as good as I was wicked—too good really. I suppose that's why God took her."

Tears fill her beautiful eyes. My defenses are crumbling. "So please let me do it, Cherry. Just this once."

Her voice is so pleading, there is no resisting her. After all, I figure, I can soon go back to being just me once this weekend is over.

Two hours later, Paul gives a gasp as he sees me emerge from the bathroom, and no wonder. Madeline has blow-dried my hair, rolled it, set it, and now it hangs in soft waves over my shoulders.

"There," she announces, whirling me round in front of my awestruck brother. "What do you think of your baby sister now?"

Paul gives a long whistle as he eyes my white lacy, see-through top and tight Levis. Then he goes into his room and comes back, camera in hand.

"Don't, Paul," I plead. "If Dad sees me like this, he'll kill me."

"Is your dad like that?" Madeline asks in a whisper. "I can't believe it!"

"Well, he wouldn't kill me, of course, but he might excommunicate me for life," I tell her with a grin. Then I grimace. Paul has snapped three shots of me before I can make my escape. I only hope he doesn't take those photos anywhere near home.

"Now, gals, let's go swimming," Paul suggests.

"You can borrow one of my bikinis," Madeline offers, as I fish out my swimsuit from my bag.

I shake my head. "No thanks," I say decidedly. This time, she's not going to win out, I tell myself.

We go for a swim and I'm embarrassed for Paul's sake. I'm wondering what he's thinking as men's eyes follow his girl wherever she goes. All I know is that if I were him, I'd be plain angry. I can't quite make out what he thinks of Madeline Cummings. Of course, he can hardly keep his eyes off of her himself, and when they go for walks together, his arm is tightly wound around her waist. But sometimes I catch him looking at her as if he is trying to decide who she really is—an angel in disguise, or a siren sent to lure him onto the rocks.

Then, our last night in the cabin, we have a conversation that really surprises me. "I like you a lot, Cherry," Madeline tells me as we get ready for bed.

I stare at her in surprise. "And I really like you, too, Madeline; it's just that we're so different."

"Different?" she repeats. "We're not that different. Well, maybe in some things, our upbringing for example; we're poles apart there," she concedes. "But we're both very attractive young women, only you don't make the most of yourself. You should be very proud of the way God made you." I think that one over for a while.

"By the way," she asks out of the blue, "do you have a boyfriend?" I blush scarlet. What do I say? I have had two meals with Angus Campbell and spent most of last Saturday with him on the farm. It was great. I laughed more than I've laughed in months. But a boyfriend?

"I've recently become pretty good friends with a student from the agricultural college in Pendleton," I answer, "but I'm not sure if you'd call him my 'boyfriend.'"

Madeline's eyes twinkle. "You mean you haven't kissed or cuddled yet?" she asks archly.

I nod, but say nothing. I'm not sure I like where this conversation is headed. "That'll come," she assures me. "In time." I blush again and wish this girl of Paul's wouldn't be so blunt. "But to change the subject," she goes on, becoming serious all of a sudden, "do you think your brother could ever fall in love with someone like me?"

I think a moment before replying slowly, "I know he's attracted to you, that's obvious."

Madeline's lip curls. "Every male I meet is attracted to me, but I want something more than that, Cherry. I want the kind of love someone like your brother can give me. And I've made up my mind," she lowers her voice to a whisper now, "that I'll make him love me if he doesn't already."

"Make him?" I ask dubiously. "But how?"

Madeline reaches over and turns off the lamp by her bed. "What I mean is that I'll do anything it takes—change my life-style, dress differently, whatever, and if that doesn't work I'll...."

"Yes?" I persist.

"Oh, never mind," she says with a sigh. "Just pray he loves me soon, that's all, for both our sakes. And when I'm with you, Cherry, I feel I want to get back to church again, go to mass and all that."

"To mass?" My eyes open wide.

"Yes. Didn't Paul tell you I'm Roman Catholic? But our family only goes to church at Christmas and Easter. And, to tell you the truth, I think I'm being a bad influence on your brother. He doesn't go anywhere on Sundays now."

"I know."

"So I do want to change for his sake." I hear her give a long sigh as she turns over in bed. "Good Night, Cherry."

"Good Night, Madeline."

During our ride back to Chicago the next afternoon, I wonder if our conversation last night was a dream. Madeline is her usual irresistible self. And if even *I* come under her spell at times, how on earth can my brother resist her? But now, as she gets out of the car to say good-bye, she flings her arms around me and holds me tight.

"Please be my friend, Cherry, even if I shock you to death at times," she pleads. "I need you in my life, I really do." I can still feel her tears on my cheeks as I mount the stairs to my room several hours later. Why, oh why, I ask myself, has God created people so complex? It isn't only Madeline I'm thinking of. As usual, my dad is never far away from my thoughts. He is so devout, has so much love to share with everyone and yet.... There is always that "and yet" lurking in the background of my reasoning. How can someone so sincere be so controlling, so sure he is right all the time, so unbending? Maybe I will never ever find an answer to my questions. Maybe I don't even need to know the answer.

I brace myself for a lecture as I mount the stairs to our apartment. I know Allie is at home because her car is in its usual parking spot below our bedroom window. I also know she will not approve of my new hairstyle.

I turn the key in the lock. "I'm back," I exclaim as I deposit my bags in my bedroom, take off my coat, and begin to make myself a cup of hot tea.

There's no answer. "Allie," I call. "I'm back."

Still no answer. Maybe's she's fallen into one of her deep sleeps, I tell myself as I settle into my favorite chair and sip my tea. But when there's still no sound coming from her room over an hour later, I tiptoe to the door and call gently, "Allie, you all right?"

"Leave me alone," I hear a voice mumble. "I need some space, Cherry."

I don't understand. She's had space enough for nearly three whole days. This doesn't seem like Allie but then, what do I know about my roommate? We've only lived together for six weeks.

"OK," I answer. "I'm going to bed. See you in the morning."

"See you in the morning," she echoes.

But in the morning she's still in bed when I leave for college. I know she has no classes till ten, but sleeping in like this isn't at all characteristic of Allie Jordan. I worry about her all day and worry even more when I return home and find her stretched out on the sofa, sobbing her heart out.

"What on earth happened when I was away?" I want to know as I sit down beside her.

"I'm so depressed, Cherry," Allie sobs. "I just can't stand it. I think I'll give up college and go home."

"But why?" I demand. I just don't understand. I'm seeing a totally different side to my roommate and it worries me.

"Something's wrong," she whispers, pulling herself into a sitting position and pushing back her long, straight hair from her face as she speaks. "I don't really know what it is."

"Do you often get like this?" I ask gently.

"I never used to, but I have recently."

"Does your mother know?"

Allie grabs my hands and looks wildly into my eyes. "No, and you mustn't ever tell her or anyone else, promise?"

I don't answer for a long time. And then I say slowly, "I'll promise for just now," I begin, "but if you keep getting these spells, then you'll need to get professional help, Allie."

I know I've blown it as soon as the words escape my lips. "I thought I could trust you, Cherry McMann," Allie retorts angrily, getting to her feet and stalking towards her bedroom. "But I was mistaken. I thought you'd understand, but you don't. You think I've got a psychological problem or, well, who knows what else you're thinking. Anything but the truth!" She disappears into her room and slams the door behind her.

That night I toss and turn wondering how I can help the girl I'm stuck with for a whole year. Secretly, I'm glad she's not as perfect as she seemed at first, and yet I'm also scared. What's she going to be like tomorrow, or the next day, or the next?

I suppose I needn't have worried, for the next morning Allie is up at the break of dawn and acts as if yesterday had never happened.

"What have you done to your hair?" she asks over breakfast. "You're dad would have a fit if he could see you."

"Madeline, Paul's girl, tried her hand at hairdressing," I manage to answer.

"I'd have to say it improves you," Allie admits. "Is she pretty, Cherry? I suppose she must be for your brother to fall for her." I hear a catch in her voice and then the penny drops, or at least I think it does. Has my weekend with Paul and Madi anything to do with her mood swing yesterday? I thought she had gotten over her crush on my handsome brother who has never given her a second look. Now I'm not so sure.

"Madeline's, well, she's...," I hesitate, not knowing how much to say.

Allie tosses her head. "Oh don't worry about me. I know that brother of yours. He only falls for the fabulous, sexy girls."

"That's not a bit fair," I explode. Then I see her lip tremble and my voice changes. "Well, he is a bit of a softy for good-looking blondes," I admit. "And Madeline is pretty fabulous and I suppose you would certainly call her 'sexy' though I hate that word."

"But is she nice?" Allie persists. Glamour girls are often unbearable."

"She's adorable."

Allie shakes her head in disbelief. "Then has she no down-side?" she persists.

"Of course she has, like everyone else," I retort, setting down my bag by my dresser.

"You mean she's stuck-up? Or a know-it-all? Or a nag?"

Now I feel like screaming and my pity for Allie flies out the window. "If she's stuck-up just a little, she's every right to be that way. She's the most gorgeous young woman I've seen in a long time. And," I go on, unable to resist an urge to thoroughly shock my room-mate, "before the weekend was up, I couldn't help thinking that she just might be an angel in disguise."

Allie's mouth falls open. "But she can't be both sensual and angelic at the same time, Cherry," she says in disbelief.

I shake my head. "No, you're right, she can't. And yet, somehow or other, she just is. Now, I'm off to school. Are you sure you're OK today, Allie?"

"OK?" she asks, trying hard to sound puzzled but failing miserably.

"Yes, well, I mean..." I stammer.

"Oh that!" she says contemptuously. "That was nothing. We all have our lows as well as our highs, don't we? I certainly notice that you do. Your mood swings nearly every day. So if we're going to live together, we'll just have to put up with each other, won't we?"

She throws me a warning look as she grabs her bag and slips on her sneakers. Then her expression changes. She lets her bag fall to the floor with a thud and throws her arms around me. She clings to me for a moment and then, without saying a word, she pushes me away, and bolts out the door.

Chapter Eight

Dennis: *That shocking photo!*

"What do you think of our kids, Dennis? Are they doing well, or not?"

My wife Rachel has a knack of asking such questions just when I feel least like answering them. Paul and Cherry have left fifteen minutes ago after spending Thanksgiving with us and I feel as if I need a little space.

"Paul seems OK; I'm more worried about Cherry," I answer cautiously.

"As you always are," Rachel retorts. "But to me, Paul isn't himself."

"No?" I ask. "Well, he did refuse to speak at the fellowship on Sunday, but then, he seemed dead beat and he is in the middle of his thesis."

"Yes, but he can't meet my eye like he used to."

I give a long sigh. "But Cherry? Didn't you see the change in her? I mean, look at her hair—it's not natural anymore and she's actually wearing slacks now."

Rachel gives a faint smile. "But that's all on the outside, Dennis," she tells me. "What about inside our children. What's going on in there?"

I shake my head in frustration. "Only God knows," I admit. "But there are telltale signs, aren't there?"

"Yes, like Paul's silence when we talk about spiritual things."

"And Cherry's," I add defensively.

"Yes, but she's always been that way. Paul hasn't."

She's got a point there. Cherry has never been one to talk much about her relationship with God. But Paul has. He's been preaching ever since he was fourteen when it was obvious that he had a call to the ministry. So even when it looks as if he is mighty slow in fulfilling that call, I've always got faith that it'll happen in the end. But Cherry! She's the rebellious one. Not that we didn't dedicate her at birth just as Hannah did with Samuel.

"Remember when we both got a confirmation from the Lord that our daughter would become a missionary?" I ask suddenly.

Rachel nods. "How can I ever forget?"

"But she doesn't look or act like a missionary candidate," I protest. "I've been too lax with her. I should never have let her go to college, Rachel."

My wife shook her head. "We couldn't have kept her caged in here forever, Dennis. We did what was best and can leave it to God."

I'm still not persuaded that we did do what was best. We did, in fact, what we were expected to do—let her loose in the world which is growing more licentious every minute. And caged in? That's ridiculous!

"We never kept our daughter caged in, Rachel," I remonstrate. "She's traveled more for her age than most young women have. Whatever are you talking about?"

Rachel grimaces. "Well, I used the wrong expression. 'Tied to our apron-strings,' I should have said. Sure she traveled, but we were always with her, weren't we?"

"Of course we were. And that was only right and proper. She's a precious gift to us, Rachel, a very precious gift and we had to treat that gift with care."

My wife gives a very long sigh. "But she's a woman now, Dennis."

She gives me one of her "Rachel" glances as if to say, "There, you can't deny that one, can you?" And of course I can't. That's the problem. My darling little Ginger has grown into a very attractive young woman. She needs protection now, if ever she did, and she doesn't even know it.

"Where's she going to church?" I ask after a long silence.

Rachel shrugged. "She said she'd found a good one and I didn't ask where."

"It's probably some Methodist or Baptist church," I comment with a slight smile.

"She could do worse."

"And she could do better. After all our teaching, Rachel, you'd think she'd hunger for something deeper, wouldn't you?" I stop abruptly as my glance falls on something lying on the floor by the door. I go over and pick it up. It's a photograph of some girl. I stare at it long and hard and give a gasp of dismay.

"That's the kind of woman our daughter's turning into," I mutter, handing it to my wife who takes it, studies it for a very long time, and then hands it back without a word.

"It's Cherry!" she mutters, avoiding my eyes.

"Look at her!" I exclaim, my voice rising. "She's showing every inch of her body. Look at those skin-tight jeans and see-through blouse. My voice breaks. "She's like some cover-girl on a *Playboy* magazine—our daughter—our precious girl! Just look at her!"

I'm sobbing now. My worst fears have come true. What has all our teaching on modesty come to? Where have we gone wrong? My family thinks I've been too strict. Problem is, I've not been half strict enough.

I feel my wife's hand on my shoulder. "There must be some explanation," she whispers gently. "Let's write and ask her, or call her once she gets home."

I shake my head. "What explanation can there possibly be?" I ask stubbornly. I point to the photograph. "It's all there. What excuse can she give?"

Rachel reaches up and kisses me tenderly. "I know Cherry," she reassures me. "And the girl who has been with us this Thanksgiving is not the girl in the photo."

I say nothing. Secretly, I have fears that it is this persistent optimism and soft streak in my wonderful wife that may have undermined my efforts to produce godly children. I take the photo from her hands, stride over to the desk in the corner, and put it safely in a drawer.

"God allowed this to happen," I say grimly as I put on my boots. "Hasn't He said, 'Be sure your sin will find you out'?"

I see my wife is about to answer, but I don't want to hear what she has to say, not just now. I grab my jacket and rush out into the chill November morning. I'll get the chores done in record time and then devote the day to fasting and prayer. That's the only way to sort this mess out, that plus some straight talking, of course.

My eyes sting with tears as I walk to the barn. It has been a great weekend, really. It's always so good to have the kids home. But that photo! The tears are raining down on the pail of feed I hold in one hand. God forgive me! I've been such a failure as a father!

Then I look up into the storm clouds passing overhead. All storms pass eventually and so will this one. But meanwhile, I'll have to be firm, have to hurt her in order to save her. "Oh God, that I'd chosen an easier path!" I groan as I enter the barn. Then I straighten and stride towards the stalls. "No, those are coward's words. I've put my hand to the plow and will never look back not even...." I pause, fighting the tears once more. "Not even if I lose my daughter. It has to be and will always be...God first...at any cost!"

Chapter Nine

Cherry: A disturbing discovery.

"God can be everything to us." Father Andrew's words reach deep into my soul as they do most Sundays. "I discovered this," he goes on earnestly, "when my wife divorced me and I felt stranded and bereft."

I give a start. Divorced him? No one has ever mentioned to me that this saintly, kindly priest is a divorced man, and I've been coming to St. Asaph's nearly every Sunday morning for almost two months now.

I try to concentrate on the rest of the sermon, but it's no use. A divorced pastor or priest was practically unheard of in the world in which I had grown up. I'm still in shock as I shake Father Andrew's hand half an hour later.

"Going home for the Holidays?" he asks kindly.

I force a smile. "Yes, Father," I reply briefly.

"I really enjoyed your solo this morning," he tells me softly. "You have a wonderful voice, Cherry."

I blush scarlet. "Thanks," I mutter, feeling totally confused. It's my first Advent Season ever: the first season I've ever celebrated, that is. And when I sang this morning, I felt so humbled to be a part of such a celebration, but that was, of course, before Father Andrew dropped his bombshell.

He seems to sense my confusion, but probably thinks I'm embarrassed by his praise. "If he only knew!" I think to myself, as I make my way to my car. "Divorced!" I can't get the word out of my head as I drive home, nibble on a sandwich, and then throw myself onto my bed. I'm glad Allie has been invited out to lunch by some girlfriend or other. That leaves me free to think all this out in peace and quiet. But four or five hours later, I'm even more depressed and frustrated with myself. What other girl in the whole of Blackmore College, apart from Allie, that is, would let that one word "divorced" upset her so much that she would mope away an entire Sunday afternoon?

I try to face the truth as I lie on my back and stare up at the tiled ceiling. One simple word has toppled my saintly priest from his pinnacle of holiness, and, no matter how hard I try, I can't seem to do anything about it. I put my hand to my head. Maybe I've got it all wrong. Maybe Dad has got it all wrong. I need to talk out my confusion to someone who's neutral in all this, someone I trust.

And then I remember. I'm going to Pendleton Mission tonight. Angus invited me yesterday while we were milking the prize dairy herd at Pendleton Meadows. I've spent quite a few Saturdays with him now on the farm. He says I'm a big help, but I think he's being polite. I do think, though, that he rather enjoys my company, especially the gallops we have around the paddock after we've finished our chores. And then there are the discussions we generally get into over a pizza or a hamburger before he drives me home. We agree on a lot of things, argue about others, and always end up laughing. That's what does me so much good.

Why didn't I think of it before! Angus Campbell is just the person I need right now. I reach for the phone. "It's me, Cherry," I begin when I hear his voice at the other end. "Can you spare me half an hour after the service tonight?" I blurt out.

"Are you all right?" he asks, concerned.

"I suppose so, only I've found out that Father Andrew is divorced."

There's a very long silence and then I hear Angus saying quietly, "And that has shocked you, Cherry?"

"Of course! Doesn't it shock you too?"

"Not really," he answers calmly. "But we'll talk about that later. Actually," he clears his throat, "I had intended to take you somewhere for a meal this evening, but now I have a better idea, if you're game, that is."

"Yes?" I toss a curl from my forehead and smile a little. Angus' ideas are usually worth hearing.

"If we are going to discuss the problem of divorce, then we need to have access to a Bible."

"Of course," I agree.

"So why not come home with me? That way I'll be able to look up some other sources of reference. I have a pretty good library. And then, to top it all, it'll give Mom a chance to meet you."

Meet his mother! I hadn't bargained for that, at least, not just yet. I hesitate, but only for a moment. "That sounds just the thing, Angus," I tell him much more calmly than I really feel.

"Great!" I sense the relief in his voice. "I'll call Mom and let her know. She'll put on a spread in your honor, I promise. But, Cherry?"

"Yes?"

"About the service tonight. Don't expect my sermons to be like Father Andrew's. I heard him once, and he's about the most eloquent preacher I've ever heard." He pauses a moment. I'm rather puzzled. Angus doesn't sound a bit like himself. "Please remember," he goes on with a slight laugh, "that I'm just an ex-army guy turned farmer who's trying to tell Christ's story to those who wouldn't otherwise hear it."

"Don't worry," I reassure him, not knowing how to cope with this side of Angus Campbell, "I don't expect you to preach like Father Andrew so...."

"No, of course you don't!" he interrupts. "How stupid of me to even think you would." He gives an odd little laugh. "I'm just a bit nervous tonight."

"Nervous?"

"Yes, of course!"

"Because I'm coming?" I ask, before I can help myself.

I hear him chuckling at the other end and feel relieved. "Yes, Cherry, because *you're* coming, believe it or not. But I'll get over it. Now I've got to finish my sermon. See you in an hour or so."

"See you!" I echo, rather bewildered by the whole conversation. "Men are strange," I mutter to myself as I slip on my favorite green sweater and then spend half an hour or so trying to tame my wayward locks. I study myself for a few moments. Not quite up to Madeline Cummings' standard, but not bad. I wonder what Mrs. Campbell will think of me?

"Going to church tonight?" a voice asks from the hallway.

I give a long sigh as I turn round and find Allie staring at me curiously. I had hoped to slip out before she returned from her visit, but I ought to have known I'd have no such luck.

"Yes, Allie," I reply, trying to sound more civil than I feel. "I'm going to Pendleton Mission. I hope I have your permission."

"Sure," she says coolly. "Only won't you invite me to come with you?"

I groan inwardly. I should have seen this coming. "You're welcome to come with me, Allie, only you'll have to come back by yourself, I'm afraid." I blurt out, blushing scarlet. "I have something I need to discuss with Angus after the service so we're going to his mother's."

"His mother's?" She looks shocked, amused, and irritated, all at once, then her eyes narrow. "Seriously, Cherry, you'll have to tell your dad what's going on between you and Angus and do it soon. Otherwise I will."

That does it. I rise to my feet, take a step or two nearer to where she is standing and begin to let rip. She braces for the attack, but I've only gotten as far as, "You're supposed to be my roommate not my spy," when

I stop abruptly. I realize, suddenly, that my anger should be directed at a father who keeps his twenty-year-old daughter on a chain, not at this over-conscientious young woman, whose life seems to be governed by her sense of duty.

My face softens. "I'm going to tell Dad at the appropriate moment, I promise," I say gently. "And you're more than welcome to come with me tonight if you don't mind driving back alone."

Allie pushes her long, straight hair from her face and shrugs a little. "Some other time," she tells me abruptly. "I'm really too tired to go anywhere." She turns on her heel and disappears into her bedroom. "Give me a call if you're going to be later than ten," she shouts over her shoulder, "so I don't worry myself sick over you."

There she goes again, just when I was trying to be nice. "I'll call if I'm later than eleven," I retort. "Bye!"

I hear her turn the radio to her favorite classical station and give a sigh. I really want to like this girl, but we just don't hit it off. And her mood swings are getting worse. Maybe if she'd been my choice of a roommate, not Dad's, it would have been different.

I grab my jacket and purse, reach for the car keys, and make for the door. I pause a minute in front of the full length mirror in the hallway, then turn away in disgust. I'm only going to the city mission not to St. Asaph's. I don't need to dress up. I don't need....

I'm still quizzing myself as I drive downtown some minutes later. I wish I could feel as carefree as when I helped Angus milk cows, or when we planted winter crops together, or shared a pizza after a hard afternoon's work.

"Promise you'll tell me when you begin to date someone?" I can hear Dad's voice as I pull into the mission parking lot. He asked me that the evening before I left for college for the first time. I had avoided his eyes, muttered something about being over eighteen, but as usual, had said just what he wanted to hear. And after all, a promise is a promise.

I glance around as I get out of the car. The parking lot is half full. I notice a group of noisy youngsters making their way towards the back door of the mission. I decide to enter by the front door. Just ahead of me, are five or six shabbily dressed men, a few much the worse for drink. I give a sigh and wish I hadn't put on this outfit. I'll stand out like a sore thumb.

I shake my head as I slip in the door and take a seat halfway from the front. I feel totally confused, a little fearful, and surprisingly exhilarated, all in one—a rather dangerous mix, don't you think?

Chapter Ten

Angus: Meeting halfway.

The clock strikes ten. Cherry gives a start and closes her Bible. "I'd no idea it was so late!" she exclaims. "Allie will die if I'm later than eleven."

Poor Cherry! It seems that if her dad isn't controlling her then her roommate is. "We'd better call it quits, then. I wouldn't like to be the cause of your death," I say, smiling.

It's been a wonderful evening, from beginning to end and important, too. Girl meets boy's mother—that's always a date to remember. And all has gone off better than I could have dreamed. I just hope I don't blow it before the evening's over.

"I feel sometimes as if I live with a policewoman," Cherry grumbles good-naturedly.

"Then why...," I begin.

"Dad!" she interrupts. "He arranged it. He arranges everything."

"He didn't arrange tonight," I dare to remark. Joking about Cherry's dad is touchy business.

"That's why I've enjoyed it so much," she mutters with a half smile. "Now, I must thank your mother for a delicious meal and get on my way. Sorry you have to take me back to the mission, Angus," she apologizes. "I should have brought my own car."

"And driven alone all the way back to Blackmore? No way! Besides, we still haven't reached a concrete conclusion after all our discussion, have we? The ride back to the mission will give us another half an hour to do that."

"Seems you and I might need a lot longer than that," she tells me archly. "We don't come to conclusions about anything very quickly, do we?"

"Like deciding upon which is the best church to worship in?"

"Exactly! That and everything connected with worship—the liturgy, the sacraments and...."

"Going so soon?" Mom interrupts, as she comes into the room and sees us with our coats on. She gives Cherry a motherly kiss. I thought these two would hit it off. "A game of Scrabble next time you come, dear," she tells her smiling.

Cherry makes no comment on a "next time," but thanks her warmly for the meal. And now we're alone again, headed for Pendleton. There's rather an awkward silence between us for a while.

"Can we repeat this, Cherry?" I finally ask, getting up my courage. I have to know the worst, or the best for that matter.

"Our discussion about divorced priests you mean?" She's quite obviously stalling for time now.

"I think we've had enough of that to last us a lifetime," I retort. "But while we're on that subject, what conclusion shall we come to?"

Cherry gives a little laugh and then clears her throat: "Well, let's see. I think we agreed that bishops and priests, well, anyone in full time ministry, can be divorced if they are the innocent party, and that applies to everyone, not just to pastors and priests, but remarriage, well, that's another matter."

"Well put," I comment as we swing onto the interstate. "So Father Andrew is in the clear?"

Cherry thinks a long time over that one. "I think so," she says slowly. "But if he were to remarry, then, well, that would be a different story. And he probably will," she goes on with a sigh, "to Kathy."

I make no comment on her last statement. "Well, you and I agree for once," I tell her. "And it's odd, you know."

"What is?"

"That we agree on this." She looks puzzled. "Well," I go on slowly, "I was brought up to think that divorce is OK wherever and for whatever reason. You, on the other hand, were probably taught that it's never right on any occasion."

"You've pretty much hit the mark," she admits. "Although Dad would concede that there is sometimes no alternative but divorce, he's adamant that remarriage is out of the question—always!"

"Even for a lay person?"

"Yes. He makes no exceptions. And if a pastor or priest becomes divorced, then he or she should give up the ministry." She sits up a little straighter. "You know, Angus, this is one of the few times I've dared to differ with Dad on things like this. Maybe I should blame you."

"You mean you've told him your opinion on this?" I want to know. She shakes her head. "No way! But up till now, I haven't even dared to differ with him in my head."

I can't believe my ears. She reads my thoughts immediately. "You must think my dad's a monster," she mutters. "But he isn't. He's really been a wonderful father to me. Only...."

There it is again. That "only" bothers me somehow. "I need to meet this father of yours," I say quietly. "That way, I'd be able to understand you better."

"I hope you will, one day," she mutters. "Understand me better, I mean," she adds quickly. "As for meeting Dad, well, that might only make things worse."

"What on earth do you mean?"

"Only that I'd like you to know me better before you meet Dad," she mutters.

Now she is talking sense. "Nothing would please me more than getting to know you better," I reply softly. "Question is, will you give me a chance to do that?" She has opened the door now, and I don't hesitate to walk right in.

She's probably blushing furiously, though of course it's too dark to tell. "Yes, Angus," she says softly. "I will." Then she changes her tone. "Any excuse to play a game of Scrabble with your mom."

"She's good," I warn, changing my mood to match hers.

"So am I."

"I'm good too, though."

"Great! The bigger the challenge the more I like it."

"Me, too. Maybe we're more alike than I realized."

"Maybe."

"Well," I go on, changing mood again, "if we came to an agreement on divorce from two diverse points of view, then can't we do it on other things?" We've entered Pendleton city limits now and in a moment or two this drive will be over.

"You mean on things like what church to attend and how to worship?" she asks uneasily.

"Yes. It might become important to us to settle that question as we get to know each other better."

"I suppose it is important," she admits.

"It's very important," I tell her firmly. "So you'd be willing to go somewhere other than St. Asaph's?"

"Well, I might," she says cautiously. "And you'd be willing to go somewhere other than a mission church?"

"I just might."

"But, Angus, what if instead of meeting halfway in all of this, we say, 'Hi, it's been good to know you,' and then each continue on in an entirely opposite direction from the other?"

"I don't understand," I say, puzzled.

"I'm never able to express myself properly, not like Dad can, anyway."

"You always compare yourself with your father, Cherry."

"I can't help it," she says pitifully. "But, to get back to what I was saying," her voice becomes firmer now. "You've been a pretty broad-minded Anglican. I've been a very narrow-minded nondenominational Christian. Pretty nearly opposites, right?"

"Right," I agree, beginning to see where she's taking me.

"Well, you've changed, of course, and are putting all your past behind you. I'm changing too. So, sure, let's find a halfway point. But can we? That's the question."

The light is dawning now. "You mean," I say slowly, "that you'll end up a liberal Anglican and I'll become, well, like your father?"

I fancy she gives a slight shudder, but I could be wrong. "Yes, Angus, I mean pretty nearly just that."

I don't answer right away. I can't. I feel deep inside that she has a very valid point. "Maybe God has put us together to keep that from happening," I suggest hopefully.

"You could be right, Angus."

My heart gives a leap. "So, after Christmas, can we begin to try finding this middle ground, Cherry?"

A very long silence and then, "Yes, Angus. We can try. Why not?"

I brake to a halt and then we both sit in silence for several minutes. I want very much to take her hand, to tell her...well, what do I tell her?

"Thanks for a wonderful evening," she says softly, as she opens the car door.

"Ditto!" I reply briefly as I follow her across the parking lot to her car. "And see you on Saturday at the farm? It's the last weekend before the Holidays, isn't it?"

She nods. "Yes, it is. I should stay at home and cram for exams. But then, I'm not Allie."

"Thank God!" I comment, grinning.

"And, Angus?" she asks, ignoring my last comment.

"Yes?"

"Thanks for being such a wonderful friend."

She gets into her car and starts up the engine. She waits until I pull up my car behind hers and then makes for the highway. Fifteen minutes later we both brake to a halt outside of her apartment building. She gets out, locks her car, and then turns in my direction. She's standing under the streetlight now. Its rays catch the golden tints in her hair. For one moment, she seems to glow with light. Then she raises her hand and gives a wave. I wave back and watch as she disappears into the shadows and wonder if, one day soon, she'll walk out of my life as suddenly as she walked into it.

I make a U turn and head for Pendleton. There's one thing I didn't mention tonight—Africa! Reg Stanton wrote the other day and asked if I'd consider spending one year on Ngavi farm, just until he got a permanent replacement. I don't know what to think. One year in Africa might not be a bad thing, but I don't think I'm called to spend my life there. No, I really don't think I am. And has Cherry McMann something to do with all this? I suppose I need to figure that one out...soon!

"Maybe you'll stay in Africa for good," a voice inside whispers.

"I'm going to start a farm here in the States for needy kids," I argue. And then I give myself at least four or five reasons why I know I'm not called to go abroad, all but the real one—Cherry McMann. If I hadn't met her that evening nearly three months ago, maybe I would feel called, maybe leaving Mom wouldn't seem so terrible, maybe....

Well, all the maybes in the world aren't that important. Point is, I've met the girl with the red-gold hair and my life, one way or another, will never ever be the same again.

Chapter Eleven

Dennis: Talking straight!

It's New Year's Eve! Rachel advised me to wait until Christmas has come and gone before speaking to my daughter about that wretched photo. But it hasn't been easy. It's been hard to see her looking so pure and innocent and yet knowing that she must be leading a double life.

"Hi, Dad!" Cherry calls from the stable. She's just been riding her favorite horse—the one I bought for her six years ago.

She comes towards me, her hair streaming behind her in the December wind. "It's so good to be on Pebble again," she remarks, taking my arm as we stroll across the yard.

I try to smile but inside I'm choking up. I remember when I taught her to ride. We were so close then. If Cherry only knew how much I still love her and that it's my love that makes me seem so hard sometimes!

We reach the porch and sit down on the swing. I put my hand into my pocket and pull out the offending photograph. I hand it to her without a word. I watch her closely as she glances at it for a moment and then hands it back to me. The expression on her face is hard to fathom. She's obviously embarrassed, but that's not all. She's angry, too. Her eyes flash fire. I had expected to see something else in those expressive brown eyes—guilt, or remorse maybe?

"What have you got to say for yourself?" I ask sternly.

She is silent for a very long time; I think she's trying to control her emotions. Then she looks at me long and hard and asks, her voice breaking a little, "Does that really look like me, Dad?"

I'm taken aback by her question. "Of course it's you," I retort quickly, "but no, it doesn't look like you do now. You wouldn't dare come home in that outfit, would you?"

Cherry rises from the swing and stands facing me, her chest heaving, her eyes blazing. "If that's how I dressed every day at college or even once in a while, then, yes, I'd feel I couldn't come home and act the hypocrite."

"Then please explain yourself," I command.

Her nostrils flare. "I can't, Dad. Ask Paul, and if he won't explain then you can be sure I never will," and with that, she strides into the house. I hear the door bang and shake my head in frustration. Ask Paul? What can he possibly have to do with it?

A few moments later I confront my son in the living room. I hand him the photo and watch his reaction. He stares at it in disbelief for a very long time and then reddens to the roots of his hair.

"Cherry says I'd better ask you the meaning of this," I say abruptly, pointing at the photo in his hand.

I see Paul's eyes narrow and his lips go in a straight line. "I took it," he tells me, his eyes meeting mine as he speaks.

"You took it?" I repeat, my voice rising.

"Yes. Cherry didn't want me to."

"So you took it and deliberately dropped it to...." I stopped. I couldn't finish my sentence.

"To get my baby sister into trouble?" he asks with a faint smile. "Do you think I'd do that, Dad?"

"Then what on earth is all this about? Why can't I get a straightforward explanation from the pair of you?"

Paul walks over to the window and stares out at the rolling fields—the horses and cattle grazing in the nearby paddock, our faithful watchdog sunning himself on the patio steps, and I notice his shoulders are sagging. Then he turns to face me. "I asked Cherry to come with my girlfriend and me for a weekend by the lake," he says slowly, "to chaperone us, if you like, and Madeline thought she'd dress Cherry up a bit and play around with her hair. It was just for fun, Dad," he adds, dropping his eyes to the ground.

"For fun!" I repeat. "You allow some girl you fancy to transform my daughter into a sensual slut and call it fun?"

"No one could change Cherry into someone other than who she is," Paul counters, his color rising. "Don't blame her. She took the things off as soon as she could. No, blame me and blame my girl, Dad, but don't take it out on my sister. She's much better than I am, much."

"So it seems," I mutter. Then the reality of what my son has just said hits me. Rachel has been right all along. Call or no call, my son has been acting double for what must be a very long time. Now deceit is something I can't tolerate. You can't trust someone who has deceived you. And that means....

I study Paul for a very long time. He's obviously dreadfully embarrassed to be caught out like this and so he should be, and guilty, too. Waves of disappointment engulf me. But all I manage to say is, "So when are we going to meet this girl of yours? Have you got any picture of her?"

"Yes, here's one," Paul says, pulling a small, color photo out of his wallet. Blonde, shapely, modern, and very sensual—the kind of woman I used to play around with in my wild days. I hand back the photo in silence and stride out of the room.

It is New Years' Eve. A few hours later finds me conducting our usual Watch Night service. It is very hard for me to keep my focus. How can I preach to others when I've failed abysmally with my own children? Yet if I've brought them up to fear and to love God, then what they do with my upbringing is beyond my control. But this rift that's growing between us—it simply breaks my heart. Oh Lord, when will it all end?

Chapter Twelve

Cherry: Tastes differ.

For once, I'm glad to be back in college. What a Christmas holiday! Oh, there were the good times when it seemed as if Paul and I were kids again—happy, peaceful times, but that all ended on New Year's Eve. I was just going to confide in Dad about Angus when he confronted me about that awful photo. And I passed the buck on to my brother. I had no option. I wasn't going to squeal on him, but neither could I tell a lie and take all the blame. So now poor Paul tells me he is wondering if he should give up Madeline—that Dad may be right—that she just might not be a good influence on him or on me. That may be true, only somehow or other, I like Madeline and I have a feeling she really loves my brother.

"Don't do anything suddenly," I beg him.

"I won't, Sis," he says, affectionately. "I promise!"

I suppose it was the Watch Night service that was the last straw—all the heart-searching and testimonies about God's dealings in people's lives. It really gets to you after a while, so I'm not surprised it had that effect on him. Only he seems so sad. He's not used to being in Dad's bad books; not like me—it's become a part of my life now, something I have to grin and bear.

It's Saturday today, six days after my return to campus. Allie has asked me if I've told Dad about Angus. She's pretty upset that I haven't. I'm going to have to tell him very soon, before she decides to do it for me.

The phone rings. It's Angus on the other end. "Can I drive you to church tomorrow?" he asks.

"Which church?" I want to know.

"We'll start with St. Asaph's, Cherry," he says quietly.

"But...," I stammer, "it isn't exactly 'middle ground,' is it?"

"No," he concedes, "but I'm willing to give it a try. It's still a whole lot better than the liberal church we used to attend when I was growing up."

"Thanks very much, Angus," is all I can say.

The next morning, I open my closet door. What shall I wear? I decide on my long green suede skirt and tan sweater. It is January now and bitterly cold. I still can't do as good a job with my hair as Madeline did but I've come a long way in the last few months. At least, I don't look like an untamed golliwog anymore. So I must say that I'm pleased enough with the image that stares back at me from the mirror. I've lost a few pounds during the last few months and it suits me.

I slip on a white furry jacket I picked up at a thrift store for ten dollars. Then I trip down the stairs to meet my chauffeur. Angus holds the passenger door open for me. "Good Morning, Cherry," he says cheerily. Then he stops. I don't think he's used to seeing me dressed up like this. "You look like a real princess," he whispers softly as he helps me into the car.

I blush. "Thanks," I murmur. No one has ever called me a princess before. I rather like it. Then I can't help adding archly, "I thought you didn't want me to change, Angus?"

He reddens. "I meant inside, Cherry," he explains quickly. "It's not that I don't like to see you in elegant clothes, as long as…."

"I don't put on airs and graces," I finish. I'm in a provocative mood this morning, for some reason or other.

He grins. "Exactly! And I think it'd take more than clothes to really change you, Cherry."

"Meaning?" I persist.

"Stop provoking me," he orders, as he pulls out onto the highway. "Or you'll have to take the consequences."

I don't ask what he means. I don't need to. I steer the conversation into safer channels. But I must admit that I am very self-conscious as we walk into St. Asaph's together twenty minutes later, and I'm even more self-conscious when I introduce Angus to Father Andrew when the service is over.

"Think you could go to St. Asaph's on a regular basis?" I ask Angus as we stroll along the river's edge after a delicious meal at our favorite restaurant.

"I'm not sure, Cherry. It just brings back so many unpleasant memories, though for your sake, I'd be willing for that, only…."

He hesitates. "Yes?" I probe.

"I just think the Episcopalian Church stresses ritual to the exclusion of a personal relationship with Christ."

"Father Andrew doesn't," I say stubbornly. "You've heard his testimony. It's as clear as yours is."

"Maybe," he concedes. "But the very fact that he is an Episcopalian priest sends the signal to me that he thinks that the Eucharist and Baptism are at least as important as a personal knowledge of Christ."

"So you think that the Sacraments are totally symbolic?"

"Pretty much."

Inside, I'm terribly disappointed, but it's really what I expected. "So what next?" I want to know.

"Methodists?" he suggests. "They're pretty middle of the road."

"OK," I agree. "Dad thinks a lot of Wesley, though he says it's a good thing he's not alive to see how far the Methodists have degenerated. But then, he says that of all the mainline churches."

I get the feeling that Angus is only half listening. "What's bothering you?" I want to know.

"Africa!" he blurts out.

"Africa!" I repeat, puzzled.

"Yes, Reg Stanton, the missionary who showed those slides in the fall at our mission, has written asking if I'd consider spending a year on Ngavi farm, just until they can find a permanent replacement."

"And what have you decided?" I want to know.

"Nothing, without talking it over with you, Cherry. You're becoming an important part of my life."

My heart beats fast. That's what any girl wants to hear from a guy she's growing fond of, isn't it? Of course it is, and of course I'm flattered and thrilled, only....

"What is it, Cherry?" Angus asks, concerned.

"It's just that I'm not called to be a foreign missionary," I blurt out. "I'm not cut out for it, Angus."

"No?"

"No!" I say decidedly. "It's all Dad's idea." And then I tell him how my parents dedicated me before my birth to be a missionary.

"So that's the problem."

"What problem?" I retort, half angry, half mortified, and wishing Angus hadn't spoiled this wonderful day with his talk of Africa.

"Never mind, Cherry," he says gently. "I really can't understand your feelings on this. I never had a father who dedicated me to God before birth."

"Lucky you!" I explode. I see his shocked expression and go on quickly, "Oh, it's not the dedication that bothers me. It's the fact that my parents hold it over my head. It follows me wherever I go. I'm a dedicated daughter so I can't decide my own life, not where I worship, not what I do for a living, not even...." I stop, knowing I've said far too much already.

"Not even who you marry?"

I blush scarlet. We walk on in silence for a long time. "Sorry for losing it," I apologize eventually.

He stops walking and we stand facing each other. "Look, Cherry," he begins slowly, "good friends, intimate friends as I hope we're becoming, show every side of themselves to each other. I need to know this side of you, too. Thanks for showing it to me."

I look at him in wonderment. "Now," he says lightly, "I'd better get you home. I've got the service tonight."

He doesn't ask me to go with him and I don't offer. Pendleton Mission is great in small doses, not that Angus' sermons aren't pretty good—not as eloquent as Father Andrew's or Dad's for that matter, but solid, well thought out, and sincere.

"By the way, Cherry," he tells me as we say good-bye some minutes later. "I don't think I'm called to Africa either."

"You don't?"

"No, not permanently. But I may agree to go for just one year."

I feel the tension leaving my body. "I'll tell you as soon as I've decided," he promises, "and, if I do go, we can write, can't we?"

"Yes. I'm a pretty good writer," I remind him.

"And I'm a fast reader. So you'll have to write plenty."

"I will. Good Bye, Angus."

"Good Bye, Cherry."

Chapter Thirteen

Angus: *Meeting Dennis.*

"Like a gallop, Cherry, before we head back to town?"

"Sure," she answers, her eyes shining with excitement. They shine a lot these days and that makes me feel good, very good.

It's Saturday again and like nearly every Saturday for the past month, Cherry has come to help me on the farm. We get on like a house on fire. Oh, we argue all the time but we enjoy every minute of it. This past week, though, has been something else. She's told her dad about me and seems relieved. I'm relieved too. And I've finally decided to go to Africa for a year. Cherry seems pretty OK with that, and meanwhile, we're spending most of our spare time together. We're visiting many of the local churches hoping to find our "middle ground." We haven't found it yet, but that doesn't stop us enjoying our Sundays together, and Saturdays too, like today, for instance.

Cherry's even more at home than I am on horseback and she knows it. She turns around and grins as we set off at top speed around the paddock. Just then, a gust of wind tugs at her hair. The clasp snaps open and the next moment, her long thick mane is cascading over her shoulders. She tosses it back, annoyed.

"This hair!" she complains. "I can't do anything with it."

"Let it fly," I shout back. "It suits you."

But Cherry is not listening. She has reined in her horse and is staring in the direction of the stables. I rein mine in, too, and follow her gaze. Her eyes are fixed on a black Honda that has just pulled up in front of the paddock gate.

"It's Dad," she whispers as if she had seen a ghost. "See, he's getting out of the car now. Allie, bless her little heart, has told him where I was, so I suppose I'd better go and face the music."

Then her face changes and she whispers mournfully, "Now what do I do? Just look at me!"

Look at her? She doesn't realize it, but I've been doing just that all afternoon. I know exactly what she's wearing—thick blue sweater, blue jeans and denim jacket—just what any girl would wear when spending an afternoon on a farm. But she's not just any girl, not in the way she smiles, or the way she talks, or the way she thinks, or in anything else for that matter.

I watch as she tries in vain to pull her hair into some sort of knot at the back of her head. "I don't understand why you're so worried," I mutter as we trot towards the fence. "Hasn't your father ever seen you with your hair down?"

"Not in front of a young man like you," she adds, meaningfully. "Dad's come hundreds of miles to check up on me and he finds me like this!" She gives another tug at her hair as she speaks.

I begin to say, "So what?" and then I realize she's talking about more than her hair. I open my mouth to say something to console her, but I don't have time. A tall, well built man of about fifty is making his way towards us. We both dismount and lead our horses towards the stables.

I can see Cherry's father clearer now. His eyes are fixed on his daughter's face. I'm not sure he's even conscious of my presence. My, but he looks stern and unbending! No wonder his daughter seems scared of him. Then his features relax into one of the warmest smiles I've ever seen. If he was upset at first with the way his daughter looks, it doesn't seem to bother him now. I've seldom seen such love in a father's eyes as Cherry hesitates for just a moment and then runs into his outstretched arms. I know I should feel an intruder, but somehow I don't. Instead, I seem caught up into their private world, a world I know I shouldn't enter without their permission, but I can't help it. I feel the love flowing between them and hope that just a little reaches me.

And then it ends as suddenly as it began. Dennis, I remember Cherry once told me that was her dad's name, is whispering something into his daughter's ears. She pulls back from him and they stand staring at each other in silence. Both their expressions have changed now. He's stern again. She's reserved and just a little fearful. But it's Cherry who speaks first. "This is Angus, Dad," she announces in a remarkably cool voice. "I've already told you all about him."

"Yes, and that's exactly why I'm here," her father says, frowning, then recovers himself instantly, holds out his hand to me, and we introduce ourselves. Then standing with one hand on the fence, he fires about ten short, succinct questions at me, one after the other, which I answer as best I can and figure that by the time he's finished, he'll know almost as much about me as I do myself.

I breathe a sigh of relief as he takes his daughter's arm and begins to walk towards his car. Cherry shoots me a worried glance. The light has gone out of her face again.

"I'll drive my daughter to her apartment," her dad informs me. "I want some time alone with this girl of mine. But I'd like to meet you tomorrow, get to know you better. What about lunch after church?"

I nod. We arrange to meet at the Chinese restaurant at noon. It's all very normal, isn't it? I mean a dad wanting to check out his daughter's boyfriend? And yet it isn't normal, I tell myself, as they both get into the black Honda and drive slowly down the farm lane. This guy comes without warning and spoils what would have been a perfect afternoon. I can't forget the look on Cherry's face when she saw that car drive into the farmyard.

I shake my head as I go into the barn to take care of the horses. Cherry has a very strange relationship with that father of hers. One moment they're hugging and the next, well, I'm not sure I know what's going on between them, but somehow I feel as if I want to give Dennis McMann the biggest telling-off of his life. But I know I can't and probably never will. He's not the kind of guy you "tell-off." I think I'm already beginning to better understand this girl of his. So why did she think knowing Dennis might not help our relationship? It must be her pessimistic side. That must be why God has brought me into her life. I may be many things, but a pessimist is certainly not one of them!

I give a long sigh, as I make sure everything is locked up for the night. Cherry's dad has certainly upset the applecart all right. I had hoped to take her home again this evening. Now, instead, I've a lunch date with her father after church. But what church? Will they go together to St. Asaph's? Not likely! Then where? Maybe they'll both come to Pendleton Mission tomorrow night. I shake my head. No way am I going to sit and let that guy's eyes bore holes into me for forty minutes. No, if he comes, then he'll have to do the preaching!

Chapter Fourteen

Dennis: *Celebrating Angus!*

"Well, Dennis?"

Rachel pours me a cup of coffee and waits expectantly. I've just returned from my trip up north, a surprise trip, as far as my daughter was concerned. And now my wife won't be satisfied until I've told her every detail.

"Well?" I repeat.

"Don't keep me on a string, Dennis McMann, or I won't kiss you for a week."

For answer I take her in my arms. We're still lovers after thirty years of marriage. And we have no secrets between us. That's why, a few minutes later, we sit sedately opposite each other at the old oak table that nearly fills our kitchen and I begin to tell her all about the young man I went five hundred miles to check out.

"He's twenty-six, Rachel," I begin, holding her hand tight in mine. "He's five feet nine and on the stocky side. Hair a light brown and rather unruly, eyes gray, chin rather protruding. Let's see, anything else? Oh yes, his father is dead and his mother is a recovering alcoholic."

"Oh, dear," Rachel interrupts. "So he didn't come from a Christian home?"

"No, doesn't seem like it, but then, neither did I," I remind her, smiling. "He was brought up Episcopalian and lived a wild life until he was converted while in Vietnam two or three years ago."

"And is he genuine?" my wife wants to know. "I mean, is he worthy of our Cherry?"

I pause and think over that one for a moment. Then I say slowly, "Well, can anyone be worthy of her, Rachel? She's not where she should be spiritually; I'm the first to acknowledge that, but she's one in a million."

Rachel's eyes shine with pride. "I love to hear you say that, Dennis. Sometimes I wonder if you appreciate our daughter for who she really is."

I stare at her in unbelief. How on earth could someone who knows me as well as my wife does even question such a thing! Rachel sees my expression and adds hastily, "And Angus, tell me more about him, Dennis."

I sit back and fold my arms. "Want to know the truth?" I ask. "The real truth?"

"Of course!"

"The moment I saw him I thought to myself, 'He's God's choice for our girl.'"

My wife throws herself into my arms. I feel her tears on my cheeks. "Mind you," I go on, feeling I've got to be completely honest, "he's still new in the faith and pretty raw in many ways. He's brought a lot of baggage with him into the Christian faith that I hope he'll soon lay aside."

"What do you mean?" she wants to know.

"Oh, the way he talks. It's a bit too modern for my liking. And his hair could do with cutting."

"Is that all?" Rachel seems to be laughing at me now.

"And he's still officially an Episcopalian but I think that'll soon change. Main thing is, he seems very genuine. And something else," I add, stroking her graying hair. "He's going to Africa!"

My wife sits bolt upright. "A missionary! He's going to be a missionary! That means...."

"Not so fast," I interrupt. "He's only going for a year, to Ngavi, the Stanton's mission. He made that quite clear. I think Cherry is the pull on him. He's very fond of her, very. But talking to him, I became convinced that he's got a call on him. And Cherry has too, only she doesn't realize it. But, oh, Rachel, isn't God wonderful! Our daughter goes to college and begins to kick the traces. But God, as it were, throws her into the arms of this precious young man."

I break down now. After all my prayers for Cherry, it's just too much. "And he's coming on a visit at Easter," I inform her. "So you'll see him for yourself."

"But Cherry," my wife wants to know. "You haven't said anything about how she feels about him."

I laugh out loud. "She's very fond of Angus," I assure Rachel. "You can see it in her eyes. And she seems the happiest I've seen her in months. No, Rachel, they're a perfect pair. Just give them, and God, time. Now was that my favorite apple pie I saw you take out of the oven a few minutes ago?"

"It was," Rachel says smiling.

"So let's celebrate with pie and ice cream and a time of praise and prayer."

"Celebrate?" my wife repeats.

"Yes, Cherry has met the man of God's choice. Isn't that worth celebrating?"

"But is it the man of *her* choice, Dennis?"

Her eyes meet mine. "Don't be a wet blanket, wifie," I tell her. "Have I ever been wrong when I've felt something was of God, really of God?"

She shakes her head. "Not that I can remember, husband, at least, not about something important like this."

"Thanks for the qualification," I say grinning. "Now, a huge serving of apple pie, please, and my favorite ice cream!"

Chapter Fifteen

Cherry: Church-hopping.

It has been six weeks since Dad sprang his visit on us all. I suppose I should be thrilled that he and Angus hit it off so well, but I'm not. Somehow, deep inside, I rather wish the two men in my life had argued, found flaws in each other, or something like that. Now I know what it will be. Dad will push me towards Angus, tell me he's the man of God's choice and all that. And then, if things work out between us, I won't know if I have chosen Angus or if Dad has. And I'm not sure I could live with that all my life.

When I'm with Angus, though, I forget all my worries. We're both very fond of each other. Even Allie can see that. And Angus does me such a world of good. He's so full of life, so optimistic, so joyful in everything he does. And we seem to fit together like hand and glove. I suppose it's only natural when we spend nearly every Saturday afternoon and Sunday morning together to say nothing of special occasions. There's only one problem, and it could become a pretty big one for both of us. For three-and-a-half months, we've attended nearly all the churches in Pendleton and Blackmore and so far, haven't found any that we both really liked. The Presbyterian came the closest for me, but Angus said he couldn't agree with their Calvinist Doctrine. For his part, he said he could be Methodist, but I told him that I'd rather have the real thing at St. Asaph's than putting up with a watered-down version of the liturgy at First Methodist Church of Pendleton.

April arrives and Easter is nearly upon us, and so we find ourselves heading south. We're spending the weekend with my parents.

"Why don't you read out our comments on the churches we've attended," Angus suggests, after we've stopped for a bite to eat. "I guess we need to come to some conclusion, don't we? Otherwise we're going to be accused of becoming 'spiritual gypsies.'"

"Spiritual gypsies?" I repeat, fumbling in my bag for the notebook in which I have kept a detailed record of our discussions and conclusions.

"Yes. Surely you've heard that expression?"

I nod. "I have, and that's the last thing I want to be. I really don't like this 'church tasting,' Angus."

"Me neither. So go ahead and read our comments, Cherry."

I open the notebook and begin to read. I hadn't realized I had written so minutely.

"We haven't found that 'middle ground' yet, have we?" Angus comments when I finish.

"No, and time is running out. When do you leave for Africa?"

"In August. But we can continue this when I come back, I suppose."

"I suppose, but what do I do in the meantime? Twelve months is a long time, Angus!"

"Sure is," he agrees. "Feel free to go back to St. Asaph's, if that's where you feel most at home."

"It is. But what will we do when you come back?"

"Let's cross that bridge when we come to it," he replies cheerfully. "We may need to strike a compromise."

"Meaning?"

He grins. "That we go to St. Asaph's in the morning and attend a home fellowship or mission in the evening. Would you be willing for that?"

"Yes, Angus," I answer slowly, "if that is the best we can do. It does worry me, though, that we can't agree on this."

"Me, too," he admits reluctantly.

"And that might be difficult in the future."

"I don't think so," he counters. "The happiest marriages are often where husband and wife can air their differences openly. When it is all 'Yes, Yes, dear, whatever you say, dear,' I get very suspicious of what goes on behind the scenes."

I move uneasily in my seat. I'm not ready to talk about marriage right now. "But not seeing eye-to-eye about worship and doctrine is pretty serious for two Christians, isn't it?" I ask pointedly.

"I suppose so, if those differences go deep," he admits.

I give a sigh and put my notebook back into my bag. "You still have to try Dad's home fellowship," I remind him.

"I know, and I'm looking forward to it," he says with a smile. I don't return his smile, but stare out the side window and into the driving rain.

"You're not looking forward to this visit, are you?" Angus asks, reaching for my hand, something he's never done before. Then he withdraws it suddenly.

"Sorry," he says quietly.

"You needn't be. I like it," I tell him honestly.

"And so do I. That's the trouble."

"Isn't it natural, Angus, for us to like holding hands?"

"Yes, very," he mutters. "But you don't know me, Cherry. You think I've got great restraint. But I haven't. Not really. And...."

I reach for his hand and hold it tight. I know I'm being bold but I feel we need to do this, somehow. "I trust you," I say softly.

This time he doesn't withdraw his hand. "That's the biggest compliment you could pay me," he tells me. "But Cherry, we really do need to decide."

"Decide what?" I ask, though I know very well what he means.

"If you and I could go through life together."

"I'm still so young, Angus," I begin slowly. "I'm not ready for marriage, yet."

I let go his hand as I speak. He gives a long sigh. "That's what I was afraid of," he mutters. "And that's why I don't hold your hand. I made up my mind when I became a Christian that I'd keep such intimacies for the woman who agrees to be my wife."

"But it's only holding hands, Angus," I protest. "Do you call that intimate?"

"Your dad would."

"So you're showing this marvelous self restraint to please my father?" I try to keep the sarcasm out of my voice, but I don't succeed very well.

Angus reddens. I see he wants to take back his words. "I shouldn't have mentioned your dad, Cherry. I'm sorry," he apologizes. "No, I'm doing it because of who I am," he protests. "You don't understand. When I became a Christian, everything became new, including the way I interacted with girls. Once we're engaged, as I hope we'll be one day, then, well, it'll be quite different, I promise you."

We say nothing for a very long time and then I remark in a rather small voice, "You'll be away a whole year, Angus?"

"A whole year," he repeats solemnly.

"We'll write, and by the time you come back, I'll know my own mind. And I'll give you an answer then. I really will."

His face breaks out into his usual sunny smile. "Agreed! Now, I really mean to enjoy this visit, Cherry."

"Good!" is all I say.

"You're worried about it, aren't you?" he wants to know.

"Yes," I admit, looking out the window. Only five more miles now and we'll be there.

"Worried about your parents' reaction when they get to know me better?"

"No, it's not that."

"Then what?" he asks gently.

"It's your reaction I'm worried about, not theirs."

He looks surprised but doesn't ask what I mean. And I'm glad, for I'm not really sure what I mean myself.

Chapter Sixteen

Angus: Cherry or Africa?

"Sleep well, Angus."

I catch Cherry's eye as we say goodnight. She smiles a little, turns on her heel, and makes for her bedroom. She hasn't been herself since we got here. I can see that she's even more on edge than when we had a meal with her dad in Pendleton six weeks ago. And when Dennis asked me, over supper, to give my testimony at the fellowship on Sunday, she squirmed in her chair, fidgeted with her napkin, and did anything but look at me.

It's only when Dennis isn't around that she relaxes. Of course, no one could be nervous for long in her mom's presence. She's one of the kindest and most hospitable ladies I have ever met. And she pretty near idolizes her daughter. But then, so does Dennis, in his own peculiar way. I see it in his eyes when he looks at her. I wonder if she knows how much her dad adores her. If she doesn't, she needs to pretty soon, before... well, before what? I'm not sure, only I know she can't go on like this. Sooner or later, she'll take some step to show her dad she's her own person. And when she does, I hope I'm around to help her through. I might not be around, though. I could well be clearing the jungle, or fording swollen rivers, or taking treks into the bush.

The thought of leaving Cherry niggles me terribly. Why do I need to go to Africa at all? Maybe I've made a mistake. Maybe my redhead needs me more than the natives of Malawi, or Reg Stanton and his farming project.

It's well past midnight before I drift off into a fitful sleep. The next morning, at breakfast, Cherry looks as if she's slept even less than I have. So far, this visit hasn't been much of a success. She's on edge and I'm frustrated. I want to make her relax like I always do—to talk, and laugh, and argue, and I simply can't.

"You two are very silent," Dennis comments as he hands me the toast for the third time.

"Sorry," I apologize. I know I'm not being civil. I'll have to shake myself out of this. "I didn't sleep that well," I confess. "Too many things on my mind, I suppose."

Dennis and Rachel exchange knowing glances while Cherry looks more worried than ever. "I suppose that goes for Cherry, too," Rachel says, giving her daughter a sly smile. "Well, well, what it is to be young again."

That breaks the ice. Soon Dennis and I are deep in "farm talk," and when the meal is over, he offers to show me round the farm. I think it is on this walk that we really get to know each other. The more he talks, the more I like him.

"I'm worried about Cherry," he tells me as we stroll back to the house.

"Really?"

"Yes. She's more worldly than she used to be and so terribly independent!"

His words take me completely aback. Cherry—worldly? The thought has never crossed my head. Maybe that's because I was brought up Episcopalian.

"She is pretty independent," I agree. "But I like that about her. And why shouldn't she be? She's over twenty, isn't she?"

"She's got you wound round her little finger, Angus," Dennis warns me with a smile.

"Maybe," I agree. "I'm certainly growing very fond of her."

"I can see that."

"But about her being worldly—well, compared with all the other girls I know, that's not at all how I think of her."

"I don't compare her with other girls," Dennis says proudly. "Cherry is unique. We dedicated her before birth to God's service, you know. And we've brought her up with that in mind."

"But she'll have to decide for herself, won't she?" I dare to ask.

"Yes," he agrees. "She will. But the Bible does say that if we train up a child in the way it should go...."

"And even when it is old it will not depart from it," I interrupt.

"Exactly! So I've a lot of faith that Cherry will do just that."

"But she's trying to find her own feet spiritually," I tell him after a few moments silence.

"I suppose so." He gives a long sigh. "But oh, Angus, how I want that girl of mine to love my Lord with all her heart, soul, mind, and strength! That's my ambition for her."

His face is drawn and tight. He may be mistaken in some things, but he's the most sincere Christian I have ever met.

"I love that girl as life itself," he goes on in a low voice. "And what it cost me to give her completely to God, you will never know."

His words make me respect him more than ever. They also make me extremely uneasy. What if God asked *me* to give Cherry completely to God? What would it mean for me, I wonder?

"What church is she going to?" Dennis asks abruptly, as we approach the farmhouse door.

"Right now, we are searching for one that suits both of us," I reply evasively.

"And?"

I hesitate a moment. "So far, we've not really succeeded."

Dennis looks relieved. Our walk is over and we join the ladies in the living room. That afternoon, Cherry takes me for a drive. She insisted on that. "And we'll be back after supper, Dad," she announces. "I want to take Angus to our favorite Amish restaurant."

Dennis grunts something I can't make out but, for once, his daughter gets her way, probably because she asked in front of me, at least, that's what Cherry tells me later.

For a few short hours, I watch her relax. She's laughing again, and arguing too, just as we did back in Pendleton, but by the time we return to the farmhouse, she has gone back into her shell, a shell I didn't even know she possessed till this visit.

"I'm dying to hear your dad preach tomorrow," I tell her as we say goodnight. Cherry says nothing and seems uneasy. I don't understand. It almost seems as if she's upset that I'm fitting in so well here.

In the morning, we decide to attend the Wesleyan Methodist church in a nearby town. Her dad is at home preparing for the evening service. It seems that his fellowship only meets on a Sunday evening. Cherry is unusually silent as we drive back to the farm.

"What's wrong with you?" I ask, concerned. "Spit it out, Cherry. I really need to know why you're like a cat on hot bricks when you're with your parents."

"Oh, it's just how I often am at home, Angus," she tells me, her eyes sad and unsmiling.

I shake my head in frustration. She's got a wonderful family. Oh, her dad is a bit too strict, perhaps, but how he loves her! I'd give the earth to have had a father like hers.

"I told you meeting dad might not help you understand me better," she reminds me, smiling faintly.

Yes, she did tell me that and I didn't understand. Now, maybe I do, just a little, but I'm not going to tell her that. "I did defend you, Cherry," I tell her defensively, "when he said you were getting independent and more worldly. I told him you needed to find your own feet spiritually."

"You defended me to Dad? Bravo you!"

"Didn't you expect me to do that?"

She shrugs her shoulders. "I never know what to expect when I introduce someone to my father." Then her expression changes. "But, Angus, how on earth can I find my own feet, as you put it, when they're chained to my father's? First step would be to find a key that'd fit the padlock, and if I couldn't do that, then, well, what's the alternative? Cut both our feet off and leave each of us maimed for life?"

I cringe at the metaphor. "You make it sound pretty awful."

"It is awful, Angus, and completely out of the question. Now, I hope you're hungry because Mom's Sunday dinners are out of this world."

She is right. Rachel McMann can cook like no one else. After lunch, Cherry excuses herself. She has a headache, she tells me. She is still looking pale as a ghost this evening as we trudge up the gravel path to the building the McManns have built for their home fellowship.

"You know we can't sit together," Cherry warns me. "Men on one side, women on the other."

"Anything else I should know?" I ask with a grin.

"Have your Kleenex ready. There's going to be a lot of high-geared emotion let loose, so be prepared."

I'm not quite sure I like her tone, but don't have a chance to comment. We soon join a stream of people headed to the service. Cherry stops to introduce me to several families who eye me up and down curiously. I notice nearly all the women have long hair and long skirts to match. I understand now why Dennis thought his daughter was growing worldly! She doesn't fit in, somehow. I do, though, with my tweed jacket and brown pants. All the guys are dressed pretty much like me. I think that's kind of odd and a bit unfair. Why should women be judged as worldly by their dress and yet men seem to escape the same sort of judgment?

The singing has already begun as we enter the building. Cherry points to an empty seat on the men's side, gives me a smile, and disappears into the crowd. There must be a few hundred present at least. I pick up my hymnbook and turn to "And Can it Be." I look around. I'll say one thing—everyone seems to be singing as if they believe every word of this glorious hymn. It's pretty overwhelming for me and before we've reached the last verse, I feel I'm already next door to Heaven.

Soon it's time to give my testimony. I'm nervous at first but soon my audience is pulling the words out of my very soul. I've never had an experience like this before.

I sit down amid a shower of "Amens." I glance at Cherry, who has found a seat just across the aisle from me. She's looking straight ahead, her face totally without expression. I feel hurt. Isn't she supporting me in all this? Or does she think I'm playing to the galleries? I try to catch her eye but it's no use.

Now it's time for Dennis to give the message. As he begins, I realize who he reminds me of—Father Andrew Price of St. Asaph's. Very strange, isn't it? But both men are extremely eloquent, and impassioned, and knowledgeable. There's one main difference, though. Dennis, for me at least, is more convincing. He speaks as if he has lived his message. His words reach into my spirit and move me profoundly as he talks on the resurrection and the necessity of being buried with Christ and then raised in His likeness. Cherry must be terribly proud of a dad like this. I know I would be.

I glance at her and note that her face shows neither pride nor admiration. She's wearing that same uneasy expression she has worn ever since we arrived here. I turn my eyes back to the platform. Dennis is making an appeal. A man walks past me to the altar. Something inside urges me to follow. I glance once more at Cherry. I wonder if she can read my thoughts. We lock eyes for a brief instant. I can't stand her gaze. It's reproachful, pleading, mournful. What is she afraid of? Doesn't she want me to become a better man? Does she think…?

I force my eyes away. The urge to go to the front increases with every second, but still I sit transfixed. The appeal is ending. Dennis is returning to the platform. The last hymn is being sung and then, suddenly, and before I fully realize what I'm doing, I get up from my seat and literally stumble my way to the altar.

"Africa, Africa, Africa!" The words bombard me from every nook and cranny of the building and from far beyond. I know why I'm here. God wants me to spend my life in Africa. I grip the altar rail and so begins the fiercest struggle of my entire life. Facing the enemy in Vietnam seems like child's play compared with this.

"But I'm going to Africa for a year, Lord," I argue. "Isn't that enough?"

A vision of a girl with a halo of red-gold hair and a smile that makes me buckle at the knees rises before me. Cherry and Africa? They don't mesh, somehow. Now, kneeling at this altar, I know I have to face the whole question head on.

"But I can farm for You in America, Lord," I argue.

"Africa!" comes the answer. "I want you in Africa and not just for a year."

I feel a hand on my shoulder. It's Dennis. He kneels down by my side and pours out his heart. It's quite obvious he's been down this same path himself—giving Cherry up to God, I mean. And as he prays, everything except the glory of serving Christ fades away. It reminds me of how I felt when I came to Christ that night in an army camp in faraway Vietnam. Then it was Heaven or hell. Now it's Africa or Cherry. I didn't refuse Christ's demands then. So how can I now? He has already brought me such a long way. I can't stop halfway, not even for the most perfect woman on earth!

"I'll go to Africa, Lord," I breathe, "if You'll give me the strength to do it." In an instant, it's all over. Heaven invades my soul.

It is only then that I realize the service has ended. I feel myself gripped in an immense bear-hug and hear Dennis whisper words of encouragement in my ear. I can see I have made his day. We walk together up the long aisle to the door of the building. Someone asks to speak to Dennis and I walk alone into the still night air.

"What happened to you in there?" a girlish voice asks in my ear. I give a start and turn around. I was so carried away I did not see Cherry standing waiting for me on the steps. I must have walked right past her.

I take a gulp of air as we begin to walk towards the farmhouse. "I told God I'd spend the rest of my life in Africa, Cherry." That's all I say, but it's enough.

"It was Dad's sermon that did it, wasn't it, and his prayer?" she asks in a low voice.

I shake my head. "It was much more than that, Cherry. God spoke to me Himself. Don't blame your dad for this, please."

We're under the security lamp now, just outside one of the cow sheds. I can see the expression on her face and like a flash, I know my worst fears have come true. She meets my gaze and for the second time that evening, seems to read my soul. Then she shakes her head as if to say, "It's all up with us, Angus," turns on her heel, and makes for the house.

"Can't we talk?" I call after her. But she doesn't turn back. Instead, she opens the door and disappears.

"I've lost her," I tell myself as I hesitate on the doorstep. A knife pierces my heart. I bow my head. The tears are falling fast now. I place my hand on the doorknob.

"That you, Angus?" I hear Mrs. McMann's voice calling me from the kitchen. "Come in. Please come in! Supper is ready when you are!"

I hesitate again and then put one foot over the doorstep. That's how I'll have to go through life, one step at a time. I push the door wide open and the light streams about me. I leave the darkness behind and enter into the light.

Chapter Seventeen

Cherry: Good-bye, Angus!

I shudder as I open my eyes and sit up in bed. I can't face today, can't face Angus, or Dad, or anyone. Why on earth did I bring my boyfriend home and why did it have to be at Easter! I should have known Dad's Easter Sunday sermons would bowl him over.

I slip on my clothes and run a brush through my hair. "And now what?" I ask myself as I pack my clothes ready for the journey back to college. "A ten-hour trip with Angus?" A few days ago I was looking forward to having so much time alone with this very special guy who is like no one else I know, but now?

"A lifetime in Africa!" I repeat to myself in dismay as I glance around my room to make sure I've not left anything important behind. "Of all places, it had to be Africa!"

"I'd like a word with you alone, Cherry," I hear Dad's voice outside my bedroom door. My heart sinks. Another lecture? Or more likely a reminder that at last, his dreams for me will come true. But he's in for a shock, a real shock.

But Dad does not lecture me as we walk outside together. And there is no word of Africa or any other far-away mission field. Instead, he's propelling me in the direction of one of the barns. He's opening the door. He's pointing to a shiny, little green Honda, parked in one corner of the huge building.

"Like it?" he asks, as he leads me towards the car and opens the driver's door.

"Like it?" I repeat, puzzled.

"It's not new," he apologizes, "but I know the owner—and it's in excellent condition."

"It's for me?" I stammer, totally unable to believe my eyes or my ears.

"It's for you," he repeats, smiling broadly.

"But I've got a car already," I murmur.

"Call that a car? It's only fit for the trash heap," he tells me grinning. "I've meant to buy you a decent vehicle for years but, well, my finances wouldn't allow it until now. But I figure it's better late than never."

I'm speechless. Then I throw my arms around my father and he holds me tight. "Thank you, Dad," is all I can manage to say.

"You deserve it, Cherry," he murmurs, stroking my hair as he used to do when I was a child. "Now you can sell your wreck of a machine for scrap. That's all it's worth."

"This is wonderful!" I mutter, still in shock.

We stand like that for an age. I relish every moment of this closeness, sensing that it might be the last I'll have with my father for a very long time. Once he knows I'm breaking up with Angus, then, well, to put it mildly, it won't be pleasant.

That was this morning. Now it's late afternoon. I'm pretty tired after six hours of steady driving and need a break. I pull into a gas station. It's not often I've driven so far. I'm glad Angus is following me. It makes me feel safe, somehow.

I jump out of the car and begin to pump gas. Angus drives up behind me and rolls down his window. "Doing OK?" he asks, concern written all over his face.

"Fine," I mutter.

"You don't look fine," he counters. That is probably true. I didn't sleep much last night! "Hungry?" he asks as I screw the lid on the gas tank.

"Not really, but I do need a break and I could do with a drink."

I follow him into the restaurant adjoining the gas station. He brings me an orange juice and sits opposite me. Then he takes the plunge.

"I told you last night that I know I'm to spend my life in Africa," he begins slowly. I nod but say nothing. "You're pretty sure you could never share that kind of life with me, aren't you?" I see worlds of tenderness in his gray eyes and feel the tears beginning to trickle down my cheeks.

Angus draws a Kleenex from his pocket and hands it to me. If this conversation doesn't end soon, we'll both be bawling our eyes out, right in the middle of this gas station.

"Well, I promised God I would follow Him whatever that might mean or wherever that would take me," Angus goes on.

"But you've told God that before, haven't you?" I ask in a small voice.

"Yes, but it didn't have the same significance as it did last night."

"Why not?" I ask in spite of myself.

He clears his throat and looks away for a moment. "Because I was not in love with you before," he mutters huskily.

My heart rises to my mouth. So I have been right after all. "You see, Cherry," he goes on sadly, "I know that there's no way you're prepared to go as a missionary to Africa, and God made it plain to me last night that that is exactly what He wants of me, no ifs or buts."

Suddenly, I feel as if I would do anything not to lose Angus. Sure, I'm not ready to go as a missionary right now, but I'm still young. Maybe I'll come to terms with it if he'll give me time. I open my mouth to tell him then I see that he's not finished yet.

"And then," he goes on slowly, "I promised God that I would not compromise my convictions even for the most wonderful woman in all the world."

He looks at me now and there is anguish in his grey eyes. "Compromise?" I echo.

"Yes. I realize that what your father believes is only too true. The churches in general, especially the mainline churches, are apostate, Cherry. I can never be a part of them, even to please you."

I feel his words are sealing our fate. Maybe eventually, I could embrace the idea of missionary life in Africa. Maybe God would call me as he had Angus. But this! I can never agree on this!

"I never dreamed that your fellowship was just what I've been looking for," he goes on, his face shining now. "We have been searching for a church that was right for us. Well," he said firmly, "I have found mine."

"Then it's 'Good-bye,'" I tell him mournfully.

Angus looks deep into my eyes for a very long time. "You're making a mistake, Cherry," he says tenderly. "A very big one!"

My eyes flash. "And don't you think you could be making one as well?"

His eyes still look very sorrowful but his voice is firm. "Not in this, Cherry," he tells me. And," he continues, looking at me again so earnestly that I can't stand his gaze, "you don't realize what a wonderful family you have. I would give anything to have a father like yours."

"But, Angus," I say in a low voice, "you told Dad I need to find my own feet spiritually."

"Yes and you said...."

"I remember what I said," I interrupt hurriedly. "You don't need to remind me."

He leans forward and tries to fasten me with his gaze, but I drop my eyes. I can't stand the look in his. "Are you trying to tell me that you've found the key, Cherry, or...."

"That's maybe the silver lining in it all," I say softly, tears raining down my cheeks now. "If all this hadn't happened maybe there'd have been a worse tragedy. But you, Angus, maybe you yourself are the key!"

"You mean...."

Suddenly, I'm utterly exhausted. "I don't know what I meant right now. Just forget it!"

"I can't forget anything you say," he tells me softly, reaching for my hand and holding it for one brief moment. "I can't forget anything about you and I never will."

What have I done to this wonderful guy! I rise abruptly from the table.

"We need to get going," is all I say as I head for the car.

Part Two

Chapter Eighteen

Cherry: Joining St. Asaph's.

"I want to join this church," I tell Father Andrew after the mid-week service. It has been three days since I got back from Easter vacation— three miserable, interminable days. And Dad's phone call yesterday didn't help matters. As if it wasn't enough for him to bring Angus under his spell, he made me feel as if I am spurning the man God has pre-ordained for me. That was the last straw!

"Angus spurned me by choosing Africa," I exploded. I was being unreasonable, I knew that, but I didn't care.

"He had to choose between you and the Lord," Dad retorted.

At that, I had hung up on him and, as usual, I've felt terrible ever since. If Dad knew the mountains of guilt he lays on me every time we contact each other, he'd be utterly shocked. And I find it impossible to tell him how dreadfully I miss Angus, even though I'm also very angry with him. When will I grow up? Why are the men in my life so obsessed with doing God's will that they usually end up hurting those they love the most? I ought to be used to it by now, but I'm not. Instead, I bottle it up and take it with me to St. Asaph's. But now, as I stand on the church steps and shake the priest's hand, I feel a lot better.

"You're really sure about being confirmed?" Father Andrew asks. His eyes probe mine as he speaks. He has very compelling eyes. Allie would call them mesmeric. I call them the eyes of a man of God— prophetic, maybe? Actually, come to think of it, they're not unlike Dad's eyes.

"Yes, Father, I'm very sure," I answer, meeting his gaze. I try to drown out Dad's warnings and Angus' fears. This good, kind man is someone I want to be my spiritual guide. "I've tried other churches," I go on. "I've not decided on the spur of the moment."

"No, you certainly haven't," he agrees.

"And I am nearly twenty-one," I add significantly. "I think I'm old enough to make up my own mind!"

He gives me one of his brilliant smiles. "You certainly are, but I didn't know you were so ancient."

"No, you probably thought I was about fifteen," I find myself saying. He laughs merrily. I like his laugh. It's not as loud or as hearty as Angus' but just as contagious.

"We'll have to have a celebration for you, Cherry," Kathy interrupts. She's standing just behind me.

I say nothing. I'm not in a partying mood these days. "I suppose your parents know of your decision?" Father Andrew goes on, as if Kathy had never spoken.

I blush scarlet. "No," I mutter, lowering my eyes. "They don't know."

"And you're not sure if they would approve?" he probes gently.

"They wouldn't approve at all," I blurt out. "But you just agreed with me that I'm old enough to choose where I worship, so that's exactly what I'm doing."

Father Andrew raises his eyebrows a little. "But you don't want a permanent rift with your family, Cherry, do you?" he asks gently but directly.

His question goes deep and brings the tears to my eyes. "No, Father, I don't," I whisper softly. "And I've tried for several years to avoid this, but I'm trying to follow God the best I know how and, well, it seems to be leading me in a totally different path from the one my parents have chosen."

Father Andrew nods sympathetically. "But your paths will eventually merge, Cherry," he tells me.

"Are you sure?"

He smiles his brilliant smile that makes me feel warm and safe. "If what I've discovered about God is true, then He is bound to bring you all back together in His own good time," he assures me.

"But until He decides to do that?" I ask dejectedly.

"Until then, this church is your home, Cherry, and we are your family. Don't forget that."

Father Andrew's words are still ringing in my ears as I unlock my apartment door several hours later. The phone begins to ring. To my surprise, I hear Madeline's voice on the other end. Strange, she has never ever called me before. In fact, I haven't seen her since that weekend by the lake.

"You're all right?" I ask in concern.

"No, I'm not," she tells me frankly. I can tell that something has upset her terribly.

"What's happened?"

"Your brother broke it off with me last night and I'm devastated."

"Broke it off?" I repeat. Inwardly, I'm not surprised. I saw it coming after that last trip home. At least he's taken four months to think about it.

"Yes. He says...." I hear her sobbing but I don't know what to say. I'm rather confused. Part of me feels that Paul has done the right thing and part of me is downright mad at him.

"Please come to me," she pleads. "This weekend, if you can. Mom and Dad are away. I'm all alone and I can't stand it. I know you don't know me that well, but you're Paul's sister after all and, well, you just might be able to make me understand why he's done this. I love him so much." She ends her sentence in a wail that goes straight to my heart. What else can I do but tell her that I'll come?

A few moments later, I find myself phoning Paul. I want to hear his side of the story. "I had to do it," he says obstinately. "I could see where I was going—downhill fast. Dad was right. He...."

"Don't!" I shout into the receiver. "You've just broken a girl's heart. Leave Dad out of it for once, can't you?" I stop abruptly, shocked at my own words. "Well, maybe you had to do it," I admit reluctantly, "but at least you could show a bit of pity for Madeline."

I hear the receiver click on the other end of the line. I shake my head in despair. Everything seems to be going wrong.

"What's up?" Allie wants to know as I make myself a drink of hot chocolate.

I don't want to tell her but I do. "Paul's broken it off with his girlfriend."

"That glamour girl?" she asks. I don't like the sarcasm in her voice.

"Yes, that glamour girl," I retort, my eyes flashing. "But I'm sure Dad's behind this. Paul wouldn't do it on his own."

Allie raises her eyebrows but says nothing. I can guess what she's thinking though—that my wonderful brother is free now. But he won't look at her. He never has, even though they've known each other for years.

I study my roommate for a few moments as she tidies away the dishes I've left around. She's not pretty. She's too angular for that. But she's extremely bright. And she plays the piano like a pro. I do wish I took to her more. She's all I ought to be, or at least all Dad thinks I should be. Well, I'm not so sure I think that any more. Her moods are scary at times and getting worse. Strange, Allie never did seem the moody type.

I go to bed very depressed and I'm still depressed when I ring Madeline's doorbell a few days later. I don't really know why I'm here. I'm not the right person to cheer anyone up. And yet, somehow, that's just what I seem to do. I think I make her understand a little why Paul has done this. At least, I do my best to explain. At any rate, by Sunday night, Madi tells me she feels a heap better. And, believe it or not, she has managed to persuade me to go with her to California for the summer.

"My aunt has a large shoe store and needs some help," she tells me. "It'll be a chance for you to see California and make some easy bucks into the bargain."

I have mixed feelings as I drive back to my apartment. The prospect of a summer job is very appealing. But spending ten weeks with Madeline Cummings? I'm not sure what that will mean—distraction at least, and that's what I need right now. But what will Paul say, or Dad, or Mom?

I shrug as I park the car and trudge up the familiar stairs. I've chosen my own path now and I'll have to do what I feel is right for *me*. Is that so awfully wrong for a twenty-one-year-old to feel?

"Your dad's not going to like it, Cherry," Allie warns as I tell her the latest.

"I know." I agree reluctantly. "But for goodness sake, Allie, don't lay more guilt on me. I've enough to cope with as it is. You and Dad just have to stand back and let me find my own way. I've got to one day, you know."

"Angus was good for you, Cherry," Allie remarks suddenly.

"You didn't think so when I was spending every Saturday with him, did you?"

"No, because you do everything with such a bang. You go from one extreme to another. But you haven't treated him right. He deserved more. He's a great guy. I've always liked him."

"Good. Go ahead liking him! I like him too, but he's determined to spend his life in Africa and I...."

I pause and fight back the tears. Where am I bound for exactly? California, at any rate! I give a faint smile. Madeline Cummings and Cherry McMann—who would have thought it! Two opposites spending the summer together! Oh well, they say opposites agree, so maybe it'll be OK. I smile again. Maybe it'll be more than OK—much more!

Chapter Nineteen

Angus: Africa, here I come!

"Congratulations!" I turn around and find myself gazing into the face I've tried so hard to forget for weeks. The rays from the chandelier highlight the gold tints in her hair. She's wearing a green pantsuit. Green always suits her, though I'm not sure what her dad would say if he could see her right now.

Cherry holds out her hand to me. I shake it and then drop it quickly. I graduated *summa cum laude* today and now Mom is hosting a celebration party at our house. She made sure Cherry received an invitation. I've told her what has happened between us, but she's still convinced that her future daughter-in-law will be the girl with the red-gold hair.

"Thanks for coming here tonight," I say when I finally find my tongue.

"Well, we are old friends, aren't we?" She flashes me one of her special smiles.

I smile back. "Of course!"

"Dad tells me you're spending the summer on our farm," she comments, pushing back a stray curl from her forehead.

"Yes," I answer, attempting a smile. "Can you blame me? I need a bit of practical farming before I go abroad." I wonder if she realizes that I'd waited until I heard that she would be spending her summer in California before I accepted Dennis' invitation.

"So I'd better say 'Good-bye' and wish you God's blessing," she murmurs. "I suppose you'll be leaving before I get back from the West Coast."

"Yes," I answer again. "I leave mid-August."

She raises her eyebrows. "So soon?"

"Yes. Ngavi Mission desperately needs someone to supervise their new farm and as I'm self-supporting, I don't need to make the usual deputation rounds."

She looks a little surprised but says nothing. Then Mom comes and propels us to the table which is loaded with goodies. It's only when

Cherry makes for the door an hour later that we finally say good-bye. I want to take her hand in mine. I want to tell her that I can't face my life without her. Her presence tortures me and reminds me of what I might have had if only.... I stop abruptly. The girl is bewitching me again. I almost wish she hadn't come tonight.

"I'll be praying for you, Angus," she says simply as she turns to go. "I'm sure that your mother will keep me in touch with what's happening to you."

"I'm sure she will," I agree. "And my prayers will be with you, too," I add softly.

"I'll need them," she replies, and then adds in such a low voice I can hardly distinguish her words, "especially yours, Angus."

I stand on our front porch, waving her off. I watch until the taillights of her car vanish into the darkness, a darkness I can actually feel. It's in my eyes, my throat, and worst of all, in my heart.

It's at least half an hour later before all the guests have left. I go to my bedroom, toss my jacket on a chair, kick off my shoes, and throw myself onto the bed. Is Africa worth it? Is anything worth losing a girl like Cherry? The darkness grows thicker every minute. I'm floundering in a world I thought I'd left forever—a world in which nothing really matters but satisfying my desires. And Africa? I feel right now as if I could sacrifice that and everything else as long as I can hold the girl I love in my arms—forever!

I turn on the radio for distraction. It's not long before I'm swept up in the music I once made my idol. My body rocks to the rhythm. My thoughts wander in forbidden and almost forgotten paths and then, suddenly, I come to my senses. I lean over and switch off the music. I'm in a sweat. Darkness is everywhere! Is my love for a girl worth this— worth losing—well what exactly am I losing? I panic for a moment as I frantically search in vain for the peace and joy and light that have filled my life for three whole years! They've gone! And God—my God—the God Who saved me, changed me, and made me the happiest guy alive— where is He now?

"Come back!" I cry. "Please come back to me!" And in a flash the light returns. It enfolds me in its comforting rays. It warms and cheers me. Life isn't over for me, after all. No, it's really only beginning. So Africa, for better or for worse—here I come!

Chapter Twenty

Cherry: Christmas at home.

It is only two weeks before the Christmas holidays. I'm in my senior year now and snowed under with term papers. I'm sharing an apartment in Pendleton with Madeline Cummings. She has gotten a job as head librarian in our college library. After spending the summer together in California, we decided we'd make ideal roommates. Madi says we're a good balance. I'm not sure of that. I think she tips the scales each time! But she's a lot of fun to live with. She's so alive and just herself. I'd like to be myself, too, only I still don't know what that is.

Allie was very upset when I told her I wouldn't be living with her during my last year at Blackmore. I would have thought she'd have been relieved. I wasn't really her type and we were always falling out with each other. But when I began to move my things out of the apartment, she went to pieces and started to cry as if her heart would break. I told myself it was just another of her mood swings, but somehow, I think she was getting rather fond of me. I wonder if I've done wrong to keep her strange behavior a total secret. She keeps promising she'll see a doctor but never does. I really worry what will become of her. I'm glad that another girl from our fellowship has begun college here and has decided to share Allie's apartment. I only hope it works out well.

Dad was furious with me when he found out I was living with Madi. Sometimes I worry that maybe I am on the wrong track. I feel guilty doing anything that displeases my parents. But I can't live like that forever, can I? Anyway, one thing is clear. Madi and I are really good for each other. She gets me to relax like no one else can. Oh, I admit I let my hair down a lot more these days. Paul thinks we're both going to the dogs. That's because Madi is constantly buying me fashionable clothes and because we laugh a lot together. But apart from that, I'm still very much me—Cherry McMann. And I think I've taught Madi a few things, too. She has begun to attend church regularly—the Catholic church in Blackmore. She goes to mass twice a week and occasionally comes with me to St. Asaph's which, she admits, isn't half as boring as her own church. She thinks Father Andrew's sermons are out of this world. I've asked her why she keeps on going to St. Mary's. "Once a Catholic, always a Catholic, I suppose," she answered with a shrug. "Dad would have a fit if I became Protestant. Besides, who knows, maybe one day I'll become a nun."

I started to laugh and then realized she wasn't joking. "I don't think I ever will, though," she added after a long pause. "I haven't the guts."

I thought about that one for a long time and wondered if Paul had anything to do with Madi's ideas about convents and nuns and all that. But then, I wonder about so many things these days. For example, I wonder what my first Christmas at St. Asaph's will be like—the anthems, the Christmas Eve sacrament, the candlelight carol services, and the feeling of belonging—the connection to Christmases past and Christmases to come. This is why I am very disappointed when Father Andrew meets me at the door of the church one Sunday morning and says in his gracious way, "Well, Cherry, I suppose you will be going home for the Holidays."

I can't believe my ears. I stare at him incredulously for a few moments, toss my head a little, and reply firmly, "I don't think so, Father. My parents are pretty upset with me right now."

"So I gather, but I don't get the impression that they've banned you from ever setting foot in their home again."

I look startled. "Why, of course not!" I reply hastily. "They wouldn't do that."

"Exactly! Just what I thought," Father Andrew says, smiling. "So then, don't you think that they will be expecting you home this Season?"

I shrug. "I'm not sure. But I'd feel so uncomfortable, Father, after all they've said about this church, *my* church now," I remind him proudly.

He nods. "Yes, but maybe you should show them that as an Episcopalian, you have not forgotten how to love God or your parents."

I stare at him for a few moments. I didn't expect this advice. "I'm saying this because I care for you, Cherry," he says slowly.

"I know, Father, you care for all your people," I find myself replying.

I see a peculiar look come over the priest's face and hear him mutter something under his breath which I can't quite catch. Then a woman coughs behind me. I turn round, and there stands Kathy. I guess she has overheard most of our conversation; Madeline has, too, and gives me a wink, which seems to me totally uncalled for.

I think a lot, though, about Father Andrew's advice and have a long talk with Paul on the phone. In the end, I decide to go home for a week if, that is, he will let me ride with him. I can't face going alone. He comes to pick me up and I notice that his eyes never leave Madeline's face. She's looking especially attractive today in what, for her at least, is a very modest two-piece outfit that brings out the deep blue of her eyes and shows off her gorgeous figure.

I throw my arms around her. "Have a wonderful Christmas, Madi!" I whisper.

"Same to you, Cherry," she whispers back. Then she turns to my brother, blushes, and says softly, "And to you, too, Paul."

"Thanks," he mutters, reddening as she catches his eye.

"You were right, Cherry," he comments when we are alone in the car, speeding southwards. "Madeline has changed quite a bit."

"Yes, she really is trying to follow Christ," I answer. "And she still loves you."

My brother says nothing for a while. "We nearly went too far," he blurts out suddenly.

"You mean…?" I gasp.

He nods, blushing to the roots of his hair. "Yes, I couldn't trust myself around her. And when she sensed I was backing off from her, she put on the charm full force. That scared me. I realized that we had already gone further than we ought to have and felt awfully ashamed. After all, I knew better."

"I don't think Madi has any idea how much a temptress she can be at times," I comment.

He gives a bitter laugh. "Oh yes, but she does, Cherry. You judge others by yourself. You're completely taken in by her. She deliberately tempted me, more than once."

"But you admitted yourself that she's changed, Paul," I say, defensively.

My brother shrugs. "Maybe, but it's too late now."

"Too late?"

"Yes. It's all over with us, Cherry. Just accept that, will you?"

He sounds frustrated but I press ahead. "Maybe, some day, you'll come to love her, Paul."

His expression changes. "I love her already, Cherry," he says simply.

Those words shock me. "Then why on earth don't you…," I begin, but he cuts me off.

"And I could ask why you broke it off with Angus Campbell when it was obvious you were very fond of him? You were going in different directions, weren't you? Well, that's how it was with Madeline and me."

I flush scarlet. He's turning the tables on me, something I always resent. "It's not the same," I protest hotly. "God was leading him in a direction I couldn't follow and be true to myself. So that was that. And another thing, I'm not sure I really do love him, Paul. If I did, well, maybe it'd be different." I cringe when I say these words. I think Angus meant a lot more to me than I like to admit.

There's a long silence and then my brother says the words I'd expected all along. "When I marry, it will be someone who can fit in with our family," he tells me firmly. "Madeline never will, no matter how much she changes."

"Then shame on our family!" I blurt out.

"Not shame on Madeline?"

I don't know what to say. Personally, I'm pretty convinced Madi would do nearly anything to please Paul, and maybe that's not right either.

The minute I enter our farmhouse door, I feel sure I'm doing the right thing to come home for the Holidays. Mom gathers me in her ample arms and I feel safe and secure. Not that I'm very comfortable in my father's presence. He is still stiff with me, but I can see that underneath, he is glad I've come home, even if he has to give me a lecture or two about the apostasy of Christendom at large and of Episcopalians in particular. Such lectures always seem to relieve his conscience. And, in a strange way, I feel more comfortable in our Sunday fellowship than I've done for years.

"Life's not quite complete without Dad's lectures and his down-to-earth preaching," I tell my brother on the long drive back north. "I am really glad I came home," I go on. "I never want to lose my parents' love and respect. Maybe if I keep steady and show that I'm not straying from the narrow path too much, they'll come to accept me as I am, Episcopalian and all."

Paul says nothing for a long time. Then he gives a long sigh. "Maybe," he repeats rather doubtfully. "With Dad, anything can happen. But accept you as an Episcopalian, Cherry? Isn't that just a bit too much to expect?"

Chapter Twenty-One
Angus: *Christmas in Africa.*

My first Christmas in Africa! I glance around the room. Bare, is what Mom would call it. I call it comfortably practical—a square wooden table, four hard back chairs, one old sofa that looks terrible but feels great, a homemade desk in the corner, and that's it.

It's Christmas Eve. Tomorrow, all the missionaries on the station are having a communal dinner, but tonight I've been invited to the "big house" for the evening. The "big house" is where Mr. and Mrs. Stanton and their two sons and one daughter live. I suppose they feel sorry for a guy like me. No one seems to know quite what to make of me. I can't blame them. I'm a farmer, not a preacher or teacher; I've never been to Bible School or seminary. Most of the other missionaries have been Christians for years, so I'm still a novice in their eyes and not quite fit for the mission field! Then, too, I support myself. That scares some people and confuses others.

Another thing, I'm the only bachelor on the station. That makes life interesting to say the least. There are six spinsters, or I should say, unmarried ladies in the mission, four of them under forty, the other two as old as my mother or older. And then there are three married couples including the Stantons.

I wipe the perspiration from my forehead. I'm still not quite used to the heat here, especially in December!

"*Odi, odi?*" (May I come in?) a familiar voice calls outside my door.

"*Odini!*" (Come in!) I call back.

The door opens slowly and a plump, jolly looking African lady of about sixty-years-old enters the living room followed by her ten-year-old granddaughter.

"*Monire, wa dada!*" (usual greeting used when addressing a man) the lady intones, bowing slightly.

"*Monire wa mama!*" (usual greeting used when addressing a woman) I reply.

"*Muli uli?*" (How are you?)

"*Nili makola,*" (I'm fine) I answer dutifully. "*Kwale imwe?*" (How about you?)

"*Nili makola.*"

Greetings in Malawi seem endless to me, but I am fast discovering that they are as indispensible as food and sleep.

"You speak our language fine, Uncle Angus," the little girl pipes up as she settles herself on my sofa.

"Think so?" I ask, grinning.

Her grandmother frowns a little. Her granddaughter has just committed a breach of African etiquette. After all, our greetings have barely begun. We haven't yet inquired about each other's immediate and extended families, naming them person-by-person. Then, gradually, her face relaxes into one of her wonderful smiles. I suppose she reckons she doesn't need to stand on ceremony with someone as new to African ways as myself.

"Yes, Dada Angus. You speak very fine," she echoes. Her knowledge of English is just a little less than my knowledge of ChiTumbuka, the language spoken in Northern Malawi. Communicating with Rhoda, whom Reg has appointed as my cook and housekeeper, is a challenge to say the least. I spend hours every day in language study and am making good progress, or so I'm told, but I still find it almost impossible to express myself. And that's where Rhoda's granddaughter, Joy, comes in. She's my interpreter everywhere I go. She takes to English like a fish to water. Maybe it's genetic. Her father was an Englishman who deserted Joy's mother when he discovered she was pregnant and disappeared, no one knows quite where. Two years later, an epidemic of smallpox swept through this part of Malawi. Many died including Joy's mother. Since then, the child has lived with her grandmother in a small brick hut just up the dirt path from my cottage.

Rhoda is the best thing that's happened to me since I came to Africa. She's fast becoming a sort of mother to me. She makes sure I eat well; she washes and irons my clothes, lectures me on African etiquette, and best of all, joins me each day for family prayers. And when she prays, Heaven comes down into my tiny living room and glory fills my soul!

"Here, Dada," Rhoda tells me as she hands me a spotless white shirt.

"*Tawonga chomene*," (thanks very much,) I tell her smiling. Then I turn to Joy. "Tell her that my mother is very happy that I've got someone to look after me in this wild land, as she calls it. She thinks there are lions in the garden, snakes under the chair, and scorpions in my shoes."

Rhoda looks enquiringly at Joy who is cutting out paper dolls from some colored paper I gave her last night. She thought it was her Christmas present!

Joy puts down her scissors and interprets every word I've said. Her grandma places her hands on her ample hips and laughs until her sides shake. She waggles her finger at me. "You look out, Dada Angus. You laugh at your mama but she knows. And Rhoda, she knows."

Rhoda pauses, not able to go any further. "She knows," Joy continues in a businesslike tone, "that there are lions and snakes and scorpions in Ngavi. You just not been here long enough to see them, Uncle Angus."

I pretend to quake with fear. "So is it safe to walk up to the big house tonight?" I ask. "Maybe you'll need to come with me, Joy, to chase away the wild animals."

Joy jumps from her seat. "I'll come," she says, her pretty little face wreathed in smiles. "I will go anywhere with you, Uncle Angus." Now that's trust for you! I wish a certain young lady had said those same words to me last Easter!

But Rhoda shakes her head, and I can see that she understands more English than I had thought. "You not go," she says decidedly. "Dada Stanton not ask you, child."

"I know," Joy pouts. "But Uncle Angus asks me. So I can go, Grandma."

"And Dada Stanton not ask me, child," she reminds Joy gently.

"No, but I'm half white, Grandma," Joy says with dignity. She runs over to where I am standing and puts her small, well-formed hand on mine. "Look, Uncle Angus, I'm almost white like you, not black like Grandma."

"Almost white" may be an exaggeration, but her skin is certainly nearer the color of mine than of her grandmother's. I see something pass over Rhoda's face. I can't quite tell whether it's anger or sadness, or maybe a little of both.

"Why didn't God make me all white like you, Uncle Angus?" Joy asks me suddenly. "I'm not black and I'm not white."

"He made you very beautiful, Joy," I hedge, wanting very much to say that she should blame her parents for her color, not the Almighty.

Joy's face brightens. "That's what Guy Stanton says," she tells me proudly. "He says I'm a lot prettier than all the white girls at his school. I know he wants me to come to his house tonight. He says I've got the best of both worlds. What does that mean, Uncle Angus?"

Rhoda obviously doesn't understand every word, but the mention of Guy Stanton acts like a red flag.

"That boy no good!" Rhoda warns. "He be too old for you."

Joy tosses her head and says decidedly, "He's only thirteen, Grandma, but anyway, I like Uncle Angus a whole lot better."

I smile at the compliment, but inside, I feel like screaming. I've only been here a few months and already I'm pretty upset. I didn't expect it to be exactly Heaven, but I did think that blacks and whites would sit together, play together, and worship together more than they do. Oh, the mission church is for everyone, they say, and technically that's true. But most of the missionaries worship at the English speaking church in Mpongo when they're not needed to help out in the service here on the station.

Reg warned me just last week that I was getting too familiar with the natives and would live to regret it. And by familiar I suppose he meant that I prefer to spend my evenings praying and reading with Mama Rhoda and helping Joy with her homework instead of socializing with my fellow missionaries. But, someone please tell me, why exactly am I here? To join a "missionary social club" or to make friends with the people I've come to serve? That's what I ask myself every day.

"What does 'best of both worlds' mean?" Joy persists. "Please tell me, Uncle Angus."

"I'll tell you some day," I promise. "But not tonight. Your grandmother is right, Joy. Guy is too big a boy to be your friend right now."

"Promise you'll tell me when I'm as big as he is?" she asks as she goes over to the sofa once more and bends over her dolls.

"I promise. Now, I'd better get this shirt on or I'll miss my supper."

"The best of both worlds," I repeat to myself as I make for my bedroom. Guy Stanton hit the nail on the head all right. The child has got those soulful, liquid brown eyes that only the natives possess and her hair is jet black. But it's not short and woolly like her grandmother's, but long and glossy, and waves right down to her slender little waist. When I saw her that night on the slideshow several years ago, I couldn't get her out of my mind. And no wonder. There's something about little Joy that tugs at your heartstrings.

And another thing. Joy has inherited all the airs and graces of an English lady. But she's not an English lady. She's just a little girl of mixed race who doesn't quite fit in anywhere. I'm thinking of sending her to the best boarding school in this part of Malawi. It's in Mpongo, a town sixty miles from here, high up on the African plateau. Of course, Rhoda might object. I've a feeling she'd rather keep her one and only granddaughter nearby in the local mission school, but Joy deserves more than that. I'll probably never have a daughter of my own, but this precious little colored girl is becoming a very good substitute.

"You look very handsome, Uncle Angus," Joy exclaims when I emerge from my room ten minutes later.

"Love is blind!" I think to myself as I smile down fondly into the child's dark eyes.

"Aren't you going to give me my good-night bear hug?" she asks wistfully as I make for the door.

I swoop her into my arms and hold her tight and think again how good God has been to give me a daughter like Joy. She puts her arms around my neck and whispers in my ear, "I love you so much, Uncle Angus. And I hope you'll love me forever and ever."

I set her down gently on the ground and turn to go. "Of course I'll love you forever and ever," I assure her. "You're like my own little girl, Joy."

"Watch out for snakes, Uncle Angus!" she warns, as I take my flashlight and make for the door.

"I will," I assure her.

She stands on the doorstep and waves till I'm out of sight. I wonder, as I walk up the dusty path to the mission, what Mom would think of this child. If anything happens to Rhoda, maybe I should adopt her. Then my mind wanders across the ocean. What will a certain redhead be doing this Christmas? I try not to think too much about her. Long busy days on the farm, language study in the evenings, and then church nearly all day Sunday, keeps me without much time for moping. But tonight is Christmas Eve, and I can't help but think of the friends I have left behind.

"Cheer up, Angus!" Reg tells me as he welcomes me into his home. "You look a bit glum. Glenda, take care of Angus tonight. I think he's a bit homesick."

Glenda, a slender nineteen-year-old who tries to look twenty-nine most of the time, smiles coyly as she takes me by the arm.

"Dad's worried about you, Angus," she whispers confidentially as she steers me into the living room where our mission family have already gathered. "You spend too much time on your own."

I shake my head. "I'm fine," I assure her. "I'm kept terribly busy and don't have time to feel lonely. Still, I'm glad you invited me tonight. It's my first Christmas in Africa, you know."

Glenda nods understandingly. She's a nice enough girl, but I'd enjoy her company more if I didn't have a strong suspicion that Reg has already determined I'll be his son-in-law.

"This is no place for a single man," he told me not long after I landed in Africa. "You'll soon find that out."

Now, as I sit opposite Glenda Stanton while we share homemade gifts and nibble on Christmas candy, I think of her father's words and know he was right. I remember the first time I nearly bumped into a woman, totally bare from the waist up, on the path that connects the farm to our mission station. Somehow, I wasn't quite prepared for it, though I suppose I should have been. It's just the custom here, and maybe I'll get used to it. But right now, it's pretty off-putting. However, with plenty of prayer and a lot of good, hard work, I'm managing pretty well. I must say, though, that I often think a wife would be rather handy at times. Problem is, I've been terribly spoiled when it comes to young ladies.

After we've sung carols to our hearts' content, I study Reg's oldest son, Guy, as the maid, Lena, brings in the Christmas pudding. He's very charming when he wants to be, but I don't take to him nearly as much as I do to his younger brother who isn't half as good-looking. And I don't like the idea of this Stanton boy hanging around young Joy Mkandawire. I just don't trust him.

"There's a letter for you," Reg tells me, as I get ready to leave. "It came yesterday."

It's from Mom, just as I thought. I stick it in the pocket of my khaki shorts, grab my straw hat, thank everyone for a pleasant evening, and head for home. Home! I sigh and think of our two-storey house in the woods, of my book-lined study, my favorite recliner, Mom's home cooking—a house where no mosquitoes pester me all night and where the night sounds are peaceful and comforting.

I hear the drums beat in the village a mile or so away. A hyena barks in the distance. Two red eyes peer at me from a tree above and make me quicken my pace. I shine my flashlight on the path ahead and see a snake scurrying into the grass. Maybe I shouldn't have laughed at my mother's fears. At any rate, I ought to have driven to the Stantons' tonight. It's not really safe to walk anywhere after the sun goes down.

Mama Rhoda has lit the kerosene lamp and left it in my window. Its warm rays light my steps as I near my little house. Soon I'm undressed and ready for bed; I curl up under my mosquito netting and read my letter in the light of the lamp. Mom is missing me terribly and rambles on about all the news; I say rambles, but every word is precious. If only my friends knew how I treasure every letter, maybe they'd write a lot more often.

"I've started to go regularly to St. Asaph's," she writes. "So I see a lot of Cherry McMann. She's changed quite a bit since she spent the summer in California. That Madeline Cummings seems to be rubbing off on her. But it'll take a lot to spoil Cherry. She still looks and sings like an angel. Father Andrew seems pretty taken with her, in his reserved way, of course. I notice his eyes on her especially when she sings a solo as she often does. Others have noticed it too, though the girl seems totally oblivious. I wonder what will come of it. Probably nothing at all."

I let the letter fall onto the bed and lean back on the pillows. I swat at a stray mosquito that has found its way through a tiny hole in my netting, and then squash it mercilessly between my fingers. Father Andrew and Cherry! I laugh at the thought. He's nearly old enough to be her father. Oh, he's probably attracted to her all right. Who wouldn't be? But Cherry? I smile to myself. I know that one day I'll probably hear the news that she's engaged to someone or other, but I don't think it will be to Father Andrew.

I keep telling myself this during the next few days, but I soon give up. I know deep inside that Father Andrew is an extremely handsome man and holy too; respect is next door to love so it's not impossible that....

"*Odi!*" a voice calls outside the window. It's the new boy I've just hired. I give a long sigh and turn my thoughts to the present, to Africa with its demands, its dangers and its joys.

Every day, I see the farm shaping up that little bit more. The rains have come at last. I think we'll have a bumper crop of corn and yams to say nothing of peanuts. I've put my heart and soul into this project and it's paying off. Everyone is fascinated with it. Missionaries and government employees come from Lilongwe nearly two hundred miles away to look it over.

I hear Rhoda humming in the kitchen as she makes my supper. Then the door bursts open and in bounces Joy. "Uncle Angus," she begins excitedly, "can you help me learn more English words? I have a spelling test tomorrow."

I sit beside her on the old worn sofa. She looks up at me smiling. "I'm glad you came here," she tells me softly. "I want to live with you forever!"

Tears come to my eyes. I feel just the same about her and her grandmother. It doesn't seem to matter now that their skin is different from mine; I only see their warm smile and their happy, joyous ways. And, yes, I lap up the attention they give me. What guy wouldn't? It doesn't matter to them that I'm not like the other missionaries around. They accept me just as I am! So I'm not lonely any more, or at least, not often. God may take away with one hand, but I'm discovering every day that He gives with the other!

Chapter Twenty-Two

Cherry: Kathy drops a bombshell!

"Valedictorian!" my mother exclaims proudly as we congregate outside the chapel after my graduation ceremony.

"Well done, Cherry!" Dad tells me, giving me a bear hug just like he used to do.

"Yes, congratulations!" I hear Father Andrew's voice saying at my elbow.

"Dad, Mom, this is Father Andrew from St. Asaph's." The moment I have dreaded for months has come. Dad tenses, coughs, and then extends a hand. Mom does the same, and introductions are over.

"Now, everyone is invited to a celebration in Cherry's honor," I hear Madeline saying. My parents exchange glances.

"We probably ought to be off," Dad says, avoiding my eyes as he speaks. My stomach knots. I know that he and Mom are on their way to a camp-meeting in New York State and haven't much time to spare. But still, I don't graduate *summa cum laude* every day.

"Please, Dad," I beg. "Come, even if it's just for a few moments. You've not seen my new apartment. Besides, Madeline has put on a real spread with help from some of our church members. And I want you to meet my friends."

After what seems an age, Dad's face relaxes ever so little. He nods and then makes for the car. Half an hour later, I introduce my parents to the other guests as we all crowd into our small apartment. Besides my parents, I have invited Mrs. Campbell, Kathy, and the entire choir from St. Asaph's. Allie is here, too. She graduated at Christmas and will be studying for her Masters in music. A strange coincidence that she's chosen the grad school where my brother is studying, don't you think? Maybe it's good Paul was so sick with the flu he couldn't be here today. It just might have been rather awkward for Madi, at least. She still loves my brother and hasn't dated anyone since he broke off with her.

I watch, contented, as Mom and Madi chat with each other. Dad looks on, rather confused. He's probably trying to reconcile Madi's unaffected charm and grace with her rather skimpy, knee-length, black dress and sparkling diamond necklace.

"Look at Father Andrew," Madeline whispers as we refill glasses and dish out the ice cream. I peek through the kitchen door. My dad is in deep conversation with the priest. I long to eavesdrop but have to be content with trying to read their faces. Father Andrew is pleasant and gracious as always. Dad is obviously very ill-at-ease. But as they chat together, I see him relaxing. Now he's actually smiling. Someone puts their hand on my shoulder. It's Angus' mom, wanting, as always, to talk about her son.

"Angus is settling in fine," she tells me smiling. "The farm is really doing well and he's managed to hire some pretty reliable workers. It seems, too, that he's preaching on a Sunday in one of the small, village churches nearby and loves it. Only he's worried about me. I've been having chest pains," she confides in a low tone. Then her face brightens. "And there's an elderly African lady who acts as his housekeeper and mother all in one and her darling little granddaughter. I think her name is Joy. He never stops speaking about them and what they mean to him. I'm so glad, because I do worry that he must be terribly lonely at times."

Joy! That name rings a bell, somehow. Then I remember two large brown eyes and the cutest smile you've ever seen. I remember, too, how that child pulled at my heart for weeks after I'd been to Pendleton Mission. Well, now she's got a very good man's love showered on her. "But not a mother's," my heart reminds me. I feel a pang or two. I was fond of Angus, very, and I know that he'll make the best of husbands for some brave woman. She probably will be devoted and saintly, not redheaded and impetuous like me⁻ someone who'll make him happier than I ever could have done.

Mrs. Campbell gives me a long look and I know what she's thinking. I smile but say nothing and finally she leaves me and begins to putter around the kitchen. I know she longs for a daughter-in-law, but I'm afraid it will never be me.

At last, my parents and all the guests have left. Madeline and I are alone. Exhausted, we flop on the settee and drink in the quiet of the balmy, spring evening.

"Thanks Madi for a beautiful afternoon," I say affectionately.

"You deserved it. I think even your parents enjoyed it. I'm not sure about Allie, though. Why do you think she doesn't like me, Cherry?"

"She's nuts on Paul, that's why," I blurt out. "He hasn't showed any interest in her up until now, though."

Madi's face clouds. "Up until now," she repeats gloomily. "But they'll be at school together. So who knows what will happen."

"She'll be in the music department and he's in law," I remind her. "Besides, he's nearly finished. And anyway, Madi, you don't need to worry. He and Allie will never hit it off." Inwardly, though, I'm worried. I've noticed that Dad is constantly trying to pair them together. When we were home at Christmas, he made sure that Allie and her mother came over for a meal.

"I'm trying to put it all behind me," Madeline says in a small voice, "though it's hard, very hard. But your parents, Cherry, do you think they liked me?"

"Mom fell in love with you on the spot. That was obvious. And you completely bamboozled Dad and that's saying a lot. Do you think he liked Father Andrew?"

"Yes, in spite of himself. But who wouldn't like him!"

"Not many," I agree.

"You almost worship him, don't you?" Madi asks, her eyes twinkling.

"Of course I don't worship him," I splutter, "but I do respect him a lot. After all, he is my spiritual advisor, isn't he? I mean, that's what a priest or a pastor is meant to be."

"But I wonder what he really thinks of you, Cherry."

"That I'm a naïve country girl who needs counseling and instructing in the ways of the Lord," I answer quickly.

"You don't realize your charm, do you?"

"Charm?" I laugh. "If you call my red mop my charm, then, of course I realize it. But...."

The phone is ringing. Madeline picks up the receiver. Then she hands it to me with a smug smile. It is Father Andrew wanting to know if Madeline and I will join him and his family for lunch after the service tomorrow. It is to be a sort of church affair. Kathy and the organist will be there also and a few others from St. Asaph's. "My kids will be with me," he adds. "You don't really know them, do you, Cherry?"

"No, that is, I've said 'Hi' once or twice, but when they're home for the holidays, I'm usually away."

"I know. That's why I want you to meet them."

When I hang up, Madeline shakes her head. "I expected something like this, but not so soon," she says, grinning.

"What do you mean?" I ask, curious.

"Nothing that you won't find out for yourself, sooner or later," she tells me significantly.

I can see the conversation is closed, but I can't forget her words. I'm still mulling them over when we file into the room reserved for us at the Chinese restaurant the next day. I think of my Sunday lunches with Angus in this very place, and for one brief moment, I have nostalgia for days gone by.

I am about to take my seat next to Moira, our choir director, when I see Father Andrew motioning me over to his table. "As I mentioned over the phone, I'd like you to get to know my son and daughter," he says smiling.

I glance uneasily at Madeline. "There's room for your friend, too," Father Andrew tells me. I ignore Kathy's frown and sit down beside him.

"This is Gloria," Father Andrew announces, nodding at his daughter. Gloria's dark eyes meet mine for a moment and then she smiles warmly. "And that individual over there," the priest continues, "is Peter, my son and heir."

"Hi!" Peter says, eyeing me up and down.

"Hi!" I return. I seem to be tongue-tied and nervous. I feel all eyes are on me.

"You're about the only teenager here today," Gloria begins.

"Yea," Peter echoes. "It's a change to talk with someone that isn't ancient."

I hear Madeline suppress a giggle. "Cherry's not exactly a teenager," their father explains, catching my eye as he speaks.

"No, I'm twenty-two," I tell them.

"Twenty-two!" Gloria exclaims. "I thought you were about seventeen at the most."

"Me, too," said Peter. "Or maybe eighteen," he concedes.

"I'm always taken for younger than I am," I say, smiling. "And now, what age are you both?"

"I'm thirteen and my brother's sixteen," Gloria informs me. Then she adds, as she helps herself to a roll, "And I do like your hair. I wish mine was luminous like yours instead of plain, ordinary brown!" she goes on enviously.

I sense Father Andrew's eyes on me. He is smiling and seems to be enjoying everything tremendously. As for Peter, he says nothing, but continues to stare at me in a very disconcerting way.

"And this is Madeline Cummings," Father Andrew tells them, smiling.

I anticipate some "wows" from Peter as he glances casually at my friend, but none are forthcoming. I don't know what to make of it. This is the first time I have eclipsed the gorgeous Madeline and it totally confuses me.

I glance at Kathy who looks like a thundercloud. Then I abandon myself to the joy of the moment. It's rather a delicious novelty to be in the limelight. I find myself telling all about being raised on a farm, about my horse and the adventures we have had together. Peter and Gloria seem transfixed. Then the meal is over and we file out into the warm May sunshine. I feel a tug at my arm.

"We're going on a walk by the river," Gloria tells me, her eyes dancing with fun, "and then we're going home to play board games. I've just told Dad I want you to come, too, and your friend, if she likes. It's so boring at home in the summer."

"You go, Cherry. It'll do you good," Madeline advises. "I'll go on home. I've got a book I want to finish this afternoon."

I hesitate. Do I really want to go with them, alone, without Madeline?

"Oh, come on, Cherry," Gloria pleads. "Don't spoil my afternoon."

"Yes, why don't you join us?" I hear Father Andrew's voice in my ear. "My kids need some younger company once in a while."

A few moments later, we are sauntering down the path that leads to the river. "Race you to the water," Gloria suddenly challenges me. "You, too, Peter!"

Her brother grins. "I'd better give you two girls a start," he says, condescendingly.

"OK!" I say, accepting the challenge. "And I don't need a head start," I add.

Father Andrew laughs, gives the signal, and off we go. I soon leave Gloria far behind, but I'm running neck and neck with Peter.

"It's a draw," Peter concedes, giving me an admiring glance. "You run pretty well for a girl."

"For a young lady," his father corrects.

"Oh, I know you want to think of her as a young lady," his son says, grinning, "but to Gloria and me she's a girl. And she's great fun."

Later that afternoon, after we have played several games, Gloria tells me the same thing. "You're cool, Cherry, and yet you're different from other girls."

"Maybe it's her red hair," Peter suggests.

"No, I don't mean that," his sister counters. "She seems so innocent and sort of pure, doesn't she, Dad?"

Her father seems totally taken aback by her question. As for me, I blush scarlet to the roots of my hair. Teenagers can be so embarrassing at times. But Father Andrew soon regains his composure and answers calmly, "Yes, Gloria. You've hit the nail on the head as usual."

"But she's also great fun," Gloria adds. "Can she stay with us while you're at work, Dad? It gets so boring here."

Their father looked at me questioningly. "Well, how about it, Cherry? But you've got a job now, haven't you."

"I haven't heard for sure yet. It looks as if I might have a job at the *Pendleton Times* but I won't know for a week or so and even then, I can't begin till next month, I was told."

"Well, but maybe you have other plans."

"Not really."

"Well, that's settled then," Father Andrew says. "And I'm really grateful to you, Cherry. I'll pay you, of course."

Before I leave, I agree to go over to the parsonage tomorrow and take Gloria and Peter out with me somewhere, or occupy them at home till Father Andrew returns from his afternoon visiting. I don't want payment, but I am keen to get to know these kids better. I feel angry at a mother who prefers drugs and men rather than taking responsibility for her two precious children. But when I tell Madi over supper about this unexpected turn of events she stares at me unbelievingly for a few moments and then bursts into a fit of laughter.

"What's the joke?" I ask, impatiently.

"I never thought Father Andrew was so subtle," she tells me, "or that you were so naïve."

"What on earth are you driving at?"

"I'd better not say, just in case I'm wrong," she replies, rising from the table. "But you need to know, Cherry, that whatever Father Andrew's intentions are, he's going to stir up a hornet's nest in the parish. But maybe that's exactly what he wants to do."

"Oh, stop it, will you," I burst out angrily. "You're always insinuating things about Father Andrew and I don't like it. He's a holy, upright man and doesn't do things with double motives. I think you judge others by yourself, Madeline."

Madeline grabs a plate and disappears into the kitchen. Of course I've upset her, but she's made me terribly confused. I don't agree for a moment that Father Andrew is subtle, but I do see that tongues might start to wag. Where will it lead to, I wonder?

That night, before bed, Madi and I make up. "Don't worry about it, Cherry," she advises. "The kids need you and so does Father Andrew. And you need them, too. They'll bring you out of yourself. So go for it, and whatever will be, will be."

I'm not quite sure what she means by that, but I must say that the priest's kids are great fun and seem to really want my company. And I see a lot of Father Andrew, much more than I expected. Sometimes he even joins us in a game, or sits and listens while the kids chatter away to me, a curious smile on his handsome face. Yes, he is very handsome. I often wish he wasn't. It would be easier to think of him as my spiritual advisor if he was about sixty and losing his hair.

"I don't understand you sometimes," Gloria tells me when we are at the pool one very hot Saturday afternoon.

"Why not?"

"Well, one minute I think you're the coolest girl I've ever met, and the next...."

Gloria hesitates and looks dreadfully embarrassed. "I say or do something that doesn't fit in with being a cool girl, right?" I suggest.

"Right!"

"I take that as a compliment."

"Well, that's what it was meant to be. I've just never met anyone like you, Cherry."

"I suppose I am a bid odd," I admit, grinning.

"I like odd people," Peter interrupts, coming up behind us. "And so does Dad. I notice he admires you a lot. Maybe a bit too much."

I blush scarlet. Gloria looks daggers at her brother. "I don't blame Dad for liking Cherry. Who doesn't?" Then her expression changes. "Maybe you'll become our mom some day," she adds wistfully, her large dark eyes scanning my face for my reaction. "I'd really like that."

"She's far too young. Dad's thirty-six, nearly old enough to be her father," Peter protests hotly. I'm glad I don't have to reply. I'm nearly dying from embarrassment.

"He's not too old," Gloria counters. "And I'd like Cherry for a mom."

"Well, I wouldn't," Peter says firmly. "I could never think of her as a mom. She's too near my age. And there'll only ever be one mother in my life. And if she can't come back, I don't want another. No offense to you, Cherry," he adds quickly. "I like you a lot. In fact, if I was just that little bit older, I wouldn't let Dad get a look in at you." He gives me a wink as he speaks.

"That's enough," I tell him sternly, finally coming to my senses. "Now, let's get out of here and back home before your father thinks I've drowned you."

This is only one of the many conversations I have with Gloria and Peter. Sometimes we talk about creation and evolution, sometimes about whether there really is a God after all. I am amazed how deeply these kids think about so many things and mention it to their father one day, shortly before they are to return to school.

"They do think a lot, Cherry," he agrees. "Most of my friends don't see that side of them. But you do," he adds gently. "You don't know how pleased I am that you get along so well with them."

I blush scarlet but remain silent. "And, Cherry," he adds in a low voice, "don't pay any attention to gossip." I know what he is thinking. As Madeline had predicted, tongues are buzzing, speculating as to why I am spending so much time with the priest's kids, and why their father encourages it. "Because," he goes on, "I'm afraid you'll have to get used to it, to gossip, I mean."

He doesn't say any more, but he's set me thinking. And when Gloria and Peter leave for boarding school, I am determined that I will get my life back to normal. And then a knock comes on my door one evening. I'm alone; Madeline is visiting her parents. I open it gingerly, wondering who it might be, and there stands Kathy. She hardly ever visits me these days so I'm a little apprehensive as I invite her in and serve her coffee and ice cream.

We talk about the weather, about the Bishop's coming visit, and about her garden. Then she draws her chair closer to mine and lowers her tone to a confidential whisper. "You know I think a lot of you, Cherry, and that is why I've come tonight, to offer you some advice."

"Go ahead," I say calmly, trying not to betray the agitation I feel.

"Well, I suppose you know that tongues are wagging," she begins.

"Yes," I interrupt. "I'm not deaf, Kathy. Everyone seems to think it is very suspicious that I would want to spend so much time with Father Andrew's kids."

"They don't blame you, dear," Kathy says gently. "You're young and naïve and always mean well. No, it's our priest they're blaming."

"But why?" I ask, dreading the answer, yet needing to hear it at the same time.

Kathy clears her throat. "Father Andrew seems to have lost his senses. It's quite obvious that he used his kids as an excuse to spend time with you. It's very unwise of him to say the least," she says in a low voice. "It looked very much as if he was sounding the waters."

I stare at her uncomprehending. "How naïve can you be, Cherry!" she exclaims impatiently. "Haven't you seen the way he looks at you, and has been doing so for months now?"

I feel uncomfortable. Madeline has hinted the same thing. "Of course, it's only a passing infatuation," Kathy says with a short laugh. "Everyone knows that, but it's causing gossip. And Father Andrew either is unaware of it or determined to ignore it."

"But you said 'infatuation'?" I remind her. "Are you trying to say that the priest of St. Asaph's is infatuated with a girl like me?"

"Well, you do adore him, Cherry. Admit it. And any man, even if he is a priest, loves to be adored by women."

I rise from my chair. I know my cheeks are flaming. "I respect him a lot," I tell her indignantly. "And as for Father Andrew, well, he treats me as a daughter, or almost," I add, trying to be absolutely truthful.

"Oh, come on, Cherry; the way he looks at you is far from fatherly. Come to grips with yourself. Father Andrew is made of flesh and blood after all. And though you seem not to do it intentionally, you've been pretty nearly throwing yourself at him recently."

I collapse into my chair again and cover my face with my hands. I'm ashamed, embarrassed, and very angry. Then I come to my senses. Maybe she is right about me. Maybe I have gone rather overboard in my attitude to our priest. But Father Andrew? How dare she talk like that about a man of God!

"I think you're very mistaken about Father Andrew," I tell her indignantly. "You said he was infatuated with me. I just don't believe it."

"Well, what else could it be? I mean you don't seriously think that a man of his intelligence and maturity and spiritual stature would think seriously of marrying a young thing like yourself, do you?"

"Marry me? No, of course not, Kathy! The thought's never entered my head. And anyway, I'm not half good enough for him or suitable and prepared to be a priest's wife. I don't think of him in a romantic way, and I never have."

Kathy shakes her head in disbelief. "I think you're deceiving yourself, child, but I'm glad to hear you say it all the same. Now, the point is, what are you going to do about the situation? Only you can diffuse it. Father Andrew is in no mood to do that right now."

I think hard for a moment and then I get the message. Kathy wants me to clear out for good. I look at her steadily for a long time and then say slowly and deliberately, "You want me to leave, Kathy. You think that if I'm out of the way, you and Father Andrew will get married." I know I shouldn't have said those last words, but the temptation was too strong for me.

Kathy stands to her feet, her face a brilliant red, her eyes flashing. "Cherry McMann, how can you accuse me of such a motive! No, I want what's best for St. Asaph's and for our beloved priest." There was a catch in her voice as she went on, "I admit I love him, always have, and I admit also that I have thought he cared for me, before you came along, that is. But I really think that you are too young to get embroiled in all this. You need to find a young man your own age. So...."

"I've gotten the message," I say very quietly as I see her to the door. "You won't see me in St. Asaph's again, at least not until Father Andrew is married. Now, if you'll excuse me, I need to be alone. What you have said has come as a terrible shock. I am very fond of our church and...." The tears are falling fast now but Kathy has gone. She has done what she came to do, and is content.

I'm glad Madeline isn't here right now. I need to think this thing out. I know that it's considered somewhat beneath their dignity, maybe even unethical, for priests to date one of their parishioners, so I can't imagine that he's really serious about me. But there is no way I can face the church at the moment. Then what can I do?

I long to call Mom and ask her advice but I can't, not about Father Andrew. And if I talk to Madi, I know she won't keep quiet but probably go to the priest himself. That won't do either. Then I remember the two letters which came in the mail today. The job I thought was all sewn up has fallen through, but one I applied for in Chicago looks hopeful. I'll go and stay with Paul a week or so, and see where to go from there. I don't want to leave Madeline or St. Asaph's or...." It's too much. I cry into the pillows and wish I'd never met Father Andrew. No, that's not true. He's one of the best things that has happened to me, spiritually, I mean.

I finally sleep and dream and wake and dream again. At last, the light is streaming through my window. I know I'll have to tell Madi eventually. I can't keep anything from her. But oh dear, what a mess I'm in. What a huge mess!

Chapter Twenty-Three

Andrew: A priest's dilemma.

"Good Morning, Father. Isn't it a glorious day!"

The voice is vaguely familiar. I put a can of tuna into my shopping cart and turn around. A tall and very shapely blonde is standing a few feet away, obviously waiting for me to recognize her.

"Good Morning!" I mutter, smiling to camouflage the fact that I can't remember who she is.

"I'm Madeline Cummings, Cherry's friend," the blonde informs me.

At the name "Cherry" I come to life immediately. "I haven't seen you at church lately," I begin. "Or Cherry," I add, trying to sound more casual than I feel.

"No," Madeline admits, blushing slightly. "Cherry's spending a few weeks with her brother, and I don't usually go to St. Asaph's without her. But I'm sure she'll be back next week."

I have at least a dozen questions on the tip of my tongue and then I remember who I am—Father Andrew Price, priest of St. Asaph's and responsible for the spiritual well-being of several hundred parishioners.

"Tell your friend we all miss her," I find myself saying, making sure that I emphasize the *"we"* in an appropriate manner.

Madeline gives me a knowing look from under her long eyelashes. "And please know you're welcome with or without your friend," I add hastily.

"Thank you, Father, but I usually go to St. Mary's on a Sunday morning."

"I see."

"But I admit your preaching beats Father Thomas' any day. I didn't believe Cherry when she kept telling me you were the best preacher she had ever heard, but once I heard you, I had to agree."

"Cherry said that?" I want to ask but bite my tongue just in time. Something in the way this young woman is looking at me brings me to my senses. She seems to read my mind in a most disconcerting way.

"I am glad you enjoyed my sermons," I assure her in my most priestly manner. "I always pray that God will use something I say to bless my hearers. Now, if you'll excuse me, I need to finish shopping and get back to work."

We say "Bye!" and go our separate ways, but as I push my cart to the checkout, I wish for the thousandth time that I was married. That way, I wouldn't get embarrassed so easily. And anyway, I never did enjoy shopping. Now I have to do it all, except when my mother comes to clean out the manse and make sure I'm getting enough to eat to survive. Or when my daughter Gloria comes home for the holidays. She loves to shop, just like her mother did.

Her mother—another blonde and the popular cheerleader I fell headlong in love with in my junior year at high school—the girl I got pregnant and then married six months later—the spunky rebel who helped to draw me away from the straight and narrow—the popular, intelligent, feisty Mary who couldn't understand when one day, out of the blue, I saw the Light, and changed my lifestyle overnight. Yes, there is no doubt about it. Becoming a priest ruined our marriage. But I had no option, did I? It was all or nothing. I was only following in the footsteps of St. Paul, or trying to, at least.

I give a long sigh as I load the groceries into my car and set off for home. Not that this spacious house with three bedrooms ever feels like home, except, maybe, when my kids spend their vacations with me. I park the car in the garage, and let myself in through the side door. Soon, I make myself a cup of strong coffee, put on some soothing music, and settle in my chair. What was I thinking about? Ah, yes, my kids. My daughter told me before she left for school a month ago that she had decided I should marry Cherry McMann.

"If I'm ever going to have another mom," she said wistfully as we said good-bye, "please let it be Cherry!" Strange, she didn't know it, but that's pretty nearly the exact message I've been sending to God for months now.

I reach for my Bible and lectionary and settle down to prepare for Sunday's message, but that pure, sweet face interrupts my thoughts and intrudes into my prayers. I'm carried back to the first Sunday I saw her. I remember it well. I had gone through a tortuous week, finding myself in several awkward situations and asking God to please lighten my pathway if he wanted me to continue in the ministry. And He sent my angel to me. I call her that because that's what she's been to me. And now she's gone.

Every Sunday for a whole month I've looked for her; every Sunday I've entered the pulpit hoping that, miraculously, I would hear her clear soprano soaring above all the other voices and reaching deep into my spirit. But no, I never hear her, never see her, never get a chance to welcome her, or even to say good-bye to her.

"What are you doing to me, God?" I complain. Yes, I'm actually complaining to the Almighty, or maybe complain is too strong a word. "Questioning" may be a better way to put it.

The phone rings. "Father Andrew speaking," I say mechanically.

"I wasn't up straight with you this afternoon, Father," I hear Madeline Cummings' voice on the other end of the line. "I ought to have told you that Cherry is looking for a job in Chicago. You caught me by surprise and, well, I told you what I know you wanted to hear and what I hoped would happen, but...."

"It's OK," I tell her. "We're all caught out like that some time or another. Thanks for being honest with me. And let me know if you hear anything further, please."

"I think she'll let you know herself, Father," comes the reply. "And one thing more."

"Yes?"

"I'm thinking of joining her if she succeeds in getting a job."

"Is that so?" I say politely. "Well, I wish you all the best."

I hear her put down the receiver and go back to my coffee, my prayers, and my melancholy. Then, the very next day, I find a letter postmarked Chicago in my mailbox. I know it is from *her*. It is short and to the point, well, not exactly, for it leaves too much unsaid.

"Dear Father Andrew," Cherry writes. "You must be wondering why I haven't been to church for a month or so. I am up in Chicago with my brother. The job in Pendleton fell through so I came here looking for a job. I've found one at last, a good one, so I'm moving here permanently. I really am so grateful for what St. Asaph's has meant to me."

I let the letter fall to the ground. "Has meant," I repeat. Looks like she's finished with us for good! I make myself pick up the notepaper and continue to read: "You will never know the effect your sermons and your life have had on me. I will always be grateful to you and to St. Asaph's, but it seems that circumstances are leading me away from Pendleton, so it's not likely I'll be back at your church again. I know I left without giving you warning, but maybe it's best that way. I'm not good at saying good-bye."

I put the letter back in its envelope, then rise and pace the deck. It's only when I realize she won't be back that I know how much this redhead has wormed her way into my heart. And I suppose I let it happen. After all, wasn't she an answer to my prayer? But now, how can I preach without her eyes on my face? How can I sing without hearing her sweet soprano blending with my bass? How can I...? I stop abruptly, put my head in my hands and groan aloud.

I watch the sun setting behind the steeple of St. Asaph's. I get out my pen, sit down at my desk, and begin to write. For the next hour I write nonstop. The first letter is a declaration of love, simple, honest, tender, just what any man would write the girl who has captured his heart. But it won't do. She's twenty-two; I'm thirty-six, nearly thirty-seven! I'm too old and too experienced in the ways of the world even though I am a priest and she's naïve, and very trusting. And besides, I'm divorced with two kids. Dear God! What can I be thinking!

I screw the letter up in disgust and toss it into the trashcan a few feet away from my desk. I begin all over again. This second letter could be read by anyone, even the bishop, but if this girl cares for me at all, then she'll see between the lines and understand my heart. So? Then what?

I shake my head in despair as I wad the letter into a ball and send it the way of its predecessor. I pick up my pen for the third time. "Dear Cherry," I write. "Your note came as a bit of a shock to me as you had not intimated that you might be moving to Chicago. I'm sorry that you have not given either myself or my parishioners a chance to personally wish you God's blessing, but I trust you know that our prayers will go with you. Thank you for your kind words. I'm so glad I have been of some little help to you along the Christian path. And never forget that you have meant a lot to us, too. You have left a hole in our little church that no one else can fill. I wish you all the best. Father Andrew."

I read it over three times. Yes, it's the only letter a priest like myself can write his parishioner. Of course, it doesn't say a fraction of what I'm feeling. But I can't tell her that, ever. Maybe it's for the best. Marrying a divorced priest would be a hard pill for her parents to swallow. No, God has stepped in before I ruin her life.

I get out my prayer book and Bible. I can't and won't let this slip of a girl distract me from my high calling. Now, what are the lectionary Scriptures for next Sunday? There, that's better. After all, I managed before that redhead stepped into my life, didn't I? So I can surely carry on without her.

Well, that's about all I do for the next few weeks—carry on, I mean. And then, one Sunday, I see Madeline sitting on a back pew. "I came to tell you I'm moving to Chicago tomorrow," Madeline tells me as I shake hands with her when the service is over.

"You'll be living with Cherry, of course?" I can't help asking.

"Yes, Father. I will."

"Whatever made her do this?" I blurt out suddenly. I know I'm not being professional but I can't help it.

"I think you should ask her that yourself," Madeline murmurs, avoiding my eyes.

"Ask her myself?" I repeat. The idea has never even crossed my mind.

"Yes, Father." Madeline looks over her shoulder uneasily and then whispers, "Go after her, for goodness sake. If you think as much of her as everyone says you do, then isn't that the only thing to do?" Madeline throws me a meaningful glance and then trips down the steps and is gone.

"Go after her!" I repeat to myself all that afternoon. No, I can't do that. Madeline doesn't understand. I'm not just any guy in love with any woman. I'm a parish priest, called of God. I have a dignity to preserve. I have my calling to pursue, without distraction.

One month later, I still have no answers. A page in my life has closed. And I've told God that if it is to be reopened then He'll have to do it Himself.

Chapter Twenty-Four

Angus: Mother, I miss you!

"Dust to dust, ashes to ashes," I hear Father Andrew's voice intone. I shiver slightly even though it must be at least eighty degrees in the shade. I'm still in shock. And no wonder! Only five days have passed since I received the life-shattering telegram that my mother had passed away suddenly after having had a massive heart attack.

I'm standing in the little cemetery behind St. Asaph's church. Mom left clear instructions about her funeral. Father Andrew was to conduct it, and Cherry McMann was to be the soloist. It has been an extremely moving funeral—everything about it—the liturgy, the brief sermon, and of course, Cherry's solo; I completely lost it when she began to sing.

Everyone is leaving the cemetery now. I watch as the last shovelful of dirt is spread on the grave. I feel very, very alone.

"I'm terribly sorry, Angus," I hear someone whisper. I give a start and turn around to find myself staring into the eyes I have seen so many times in my dreams and the compassion I see in them makes me lose it all over again.

"Please excuse me," I mutter, reaching for my handkerchief.

"It's OK to cry, Angus," Cherry says gently.

"Thanks," is all I can say.

We walk slowly back to the church together. "And thanks for fulfilling Mom's wishes," I add as we approach the church door.

"I couldn't do anything else," Cherry says softly. "I was very fond of your mother, Angus."

"I know you were. And she was fond of you, too."

"How long will you be in the States?"

I shake my head. "I really don't know. It's been suggested that I take a seminary course, but I haven't decided yet. Everything is hazy right now."

"I understand. I'll be praying for you, Angus."

"I will need it, Cherry," I answer.

Just then, an old college friend comes up behind us and begins to offer me condolences. Cherry slips ahead of me into the fellowship hall where refreshments are being served. A few minutes later, I follow her just in time to see her deep in conversation with Father Andrew. He's bending towards her and saying something very earnestly. Maybe he's blessing her, or advising her, or saying something else very priestly. Really, it doesn't matter what he's saying. What does matter is that suddenly, and only for an instant, their eyes meet. They hold each other's gaze for a moment longer and then she catches sight of me standing a few feet away, blushes a deep scarlet, and disappears into the kitchen. The priest sees me too. He reddens a little, looks rather embarrassed for a few moments, and then recovers himself. He gives me one of his warmest smiles, a smile which, temporarily at least, eases the jealousy that has suddenly threatened to swallow me up.

"I remember how it was when my father died," Andrew says kindly as he comes over to where I am standing and places his hand on my shoulder. "I was a grown man but when they lowered his body into the grave, I felt as if I were a naked child being reborn into a cheerless and loveless world."

"That's exactly how I feel right now," I mange to mutter as he leads the way to a table at the other end of the room, "and yet I know that God's love is all around me, whether I'm conscious of it or not."

The priest nods. "Yes, and that love will see you through the coming weeks, Angus. And the love of family and friends. That will help a lot, too."

"I have no family now," I reply sadly, gulping back the tears.

Father Andrew looks rather surprised. "Well," I correct, "I do have friends who are becoming like family, back in Malawi, that is. I'm rather losing touch with folks here in the States."

"You will need Christian friends in the coming days, Angus," the priest goes on kindly. "I realize that you don't know me very well, but if you ever feel in need of company, just give me a ring. By the way, coffee or juice?"

"Coffee, please."

Soon everyone is offering condolences. I thank them mechanically. After three whole years in Malawi, America seems like another planet. All I want to do is to be alone with my grief.

I'm walking to the car when I hear footsteps behind me. It's Cherry again. "I'm leaving, too," she tells me and then she begins to chat as if we did it every day. I learn that she has a wonderful job in Chicago and is living with Madeline. As we reach the parking lot, she turns and I can see there are tears of sympathy in her large brown eyes. "Good-bye," she tells me gently.

"Good-bye," I tell the woman I love; yes, I still love her, unfortunately for me. I watch as she pulls onto the main road and disappears out of sight.

My mind is full of questions as I drive homewards. How can I ever face life on the mission-field now that I have no mother at home to write me, to send me parcels, and of course to love me as only a mother can? Why can't I marry like all the other missionaries? What I really mean is—why can't I marry the girl with the red-gold hair?

And as I swing up the familiar drive to Mom's stately home, I find myself wishing that I were back in my sparsely furnished, two-room brick house in Ngavi, and long to feel Mama Rhoda's motherly arms around me. "Don't forget you have Joy and me, Dada," she had reminded me when I had just shared the news about Mom's passing.

I walk up the familiar path to the front door and turn the key in the lock. The house breathes of my mother. The tears begin to flow as I realize what I've lost. She's gone forever, no not forever. But being in Heaven, while it's wonderful for her, doesn't help me right now.

I flop into my favorite recliner but it doesn't feel right. It's too soft. I wander into the kitchen and begin to make myself a hot drink but I can't make up my mind what I want. The choices are too many. I go into the study but feel overwhelmed by the rows of books staring at me from each wall. I wander into the garden but it seems bland and uninteresting. What is happening to me? Am I becoming incapable of living anywhere else but in the African jungle?

I flop into the recliner once more. This time, it feels good. Then I think of my faraway friends and of their smiling faces. My destiny is bound up with Africa and with my new family there. Then I hear Reg Stanton saying as he drove me to the airport a few days ago: "Bring back a wife. You need one, Angus."

I pick up my pen to write the love letter of my life. Then I drop it in disgust. I need to be a realist. Cherry was wonderful to me this afternoon, but I'm no fool. I saw the way she and Father Andrew looked at each other. I'd give anything if only she'd look like that at me. Anything! Or would I? Would I give up my calling? Would I, really and truly? Of course I wouldn't—couldn't is more like it. No, it's Good-Bye again to my red-haired angel. And really, if she has to marry anyone besides me, who deserves her more than Andrew Price?

I lay my head back and close my eyes and the tears begin to flow. "Oh, Mother," I sob. "I miss you so much."

Chapter Twenty-Five

Cherry: God or Satan?

One warm summer's day about three weeks after Mrs. Campbell's funeral, Madeline announces suddenly: "I'm going home for the weekend. Sorry to leave you, but you do have Paul nearby, don't you?"

I nod, noticing the wistful look on her face. She and Paul have a strange sort of relationship now. Sometimes, when he comes to visit me, which is seldom, he never takes his eyes off of my friend's face. And yet, that's as far as it goes. Madeline is frustrated and hurt. She's never had another boyfriend though she could have had twenty.

Madeline packs her bag, gives me a hug, and is gone. The doorbell is ringing. I open the front door and there, standing large as life, is Gloria Price. She has grown several inches in the past two years and matured a lot. Of course, she must be fifteen now, I remind myself, as I give her a hug and invite her inside. She glances quickly at the car in the driveway. I follow her gaze and see that someone is at the wheel, who exactly, I can't quite tell.

"I'll only be able to stay a few minutes," she says as I lead her into the front room. "Dad's in the car so I don't want to keep him waiting."

"Tell him to come in," I say, blushing a little.

"He won't," she replies shortly. "He wants you to know that this is completely my idea, my calling in like this, I mean."

I smile and tell her it is a pleasant surprise. "And I've come to invite you to spend the weekend at Grandma's house by the lake," she tells me, beaming. "We're spending the night in the city and can call back tomorrow to see what you've decided, once you've had time to think it over. I've been dying to see you."

I can't believe my ears. "But what do the others think?" I falter. "I mean your grandma and...." I pause a moment, my cheeks burning.

"And my dad?" she asks, laughing. "Oh, of course he wants you to come with us as much as I do. Anyone can see that, a mile off, though he keeps reminding me that coming here today is completely my idea and that I have to take the consequences."

"And what does that mean? That I'll get thrown out by your grandmother?"

"That's not likely," Gloria says, smiling. "I'm not sure what he means. He's just not himself these days. But I want you to come, so please think it over."

"I will. But you can phone me to save yourself another journey," I suggest. "It'll be a waste of gas if you come all the way out here and find I'm not going with you."

"You can't refuse as easily if I'm right in front of you," Gloria says mischievously. "But where are you going?" she asks, as I push past her towards the door and out into the hot July sunshine.

"To be civil, of course, and invite your dad in for a cold drink."

"He won't come. He's in a bad mood," she warns me.

"I've never seen your father in a bad mood," I say, as I walk towards the car, my heart beating wildly. Gloria has no time to reply. Her father sees me coming and opens his car door. Then the old smile creeps over his face as he reaches out his hand to me.

"Well, Cherry, I hope you're not mad at my daughter for insisting on dropping in like this?"

"Mad?" I repeat as I shake his hand. "Of course not! You both are old friends and you must come in for a cool drink. It's very hot."

He hesitates just for a moment and seems to be debating something in his mind. Then his face clears and he says lightly, "I'd like that, and so, I'm sure, would Gloria."

As we sit sipping ice-cold lemonade and munching on Madeline's homemade peanut butter cookies, Gloria keeps the conversation rolling. She tells me all about school and about her brother who is now eighteen and has a steady girlfriend.

"You've lost a lot of weight, Cherry," she comments suddenly, eyeing me up and down. "Hasn't she dad?"

"Yes," Father Andrew agrees. He has been speaking in monosyllables ever since he has entered the house.

"But it suits her, doesn't it, Dad?"

"Yes," he says again, as he drains the last drop of lemonade. Then he rises and makes for the door. "We have to go, Gloria," he tells her abruptly.

"I need the restroom. I won't be long," she tells us. But she is long, so long that I begin to suspect she is delaying on purpose. Her father obviously thinks so too and smiles a little.

"What's this about me going with you tomorrow?" I venture. I have to know what he thinks of his daughter's wild scheme.

"Oh, this is Gloria's idea," he tells me lightly.

"But what do you think of it?"

He hesitates a moment and then grabs my arm and pilots me into the hallway and out of earshot of his daughter. "Cherry, I'd like it very much, but I'm afraid," he says, his hand tightening on my arm as he speaks.

He's looking at me so steadily now. No one in all my twenty-four years has ever looked at me like this. My heart nearly stops beating. What is happening to him? What is happening to me?

"Afraid?" I repeat when I get my breath.

"Yes, afraid of the love that's been bottled up inside of me for three years—that it'll explode and frighten you away—forever!" His words startle me and shock me. I can hardly breathe, or think, or move.

Then I feel myself being led gently into the sitting room and onto the sofa by the window. He sits down beside me. "For at least three years," he begins slowly, "I've fought against my feelings, tried to beat them down, stamp on them, throw them out the window. I've fasted and prayed. But it's no use. I still long to hold you, to take you in my arms and ask you to be my bride. But then I remind myself that I'm divorced, with two nearly grown kids and a church to take care of."

I'm about to answer, well, I really don't know quite what, when we hear Gloria opening the bathroom door. He takes away his hand from my arm. "Please come tomorrow, Cherry, that is, if...." He stops abruptly. Gloria has come into the hallway. But it's OK. I have gotten the message.

It's night now. Madeline and I have talked for hours. If I went by her, I'd marry the priest tomorrow. Yet I'm very confused. What exactly is love? What I felt when Father Andrew took my hand this afternoon? What I feel now when I think of him?

Alone in my bedroom, I hear Dad's voice in my ears: "This is a no-no, Cherry! Father Andrew's divorced! You know what the Bible says about that."

"The Bible says different things to different people," I retort, as if my father were standing by my bed.

Then I remember what I told Angus on our first real date: "If Father Andrew ever marries, then it'll be a different story." I give a start. Have I changed that much in three years? I wonder what Angus would think of this new Cherry? Well, it doesn't matter what he thinks. He's gone out of my life for good.

But no, I can't go tomorrow. I can't let myself fall in love with someone like Father Andrew. He's too old for me, too good for me, and just, well, too different. Then I begin to shake as the reality hits me. I know, deep inside, that I fell in love with this wonderful man two years ago. That's why I ran away from St. Asaph's. That's why I've been so unhappy ever since.

I throw myself on the bed. I'm afraid if I spend this weekend with Father Andrew and his family, that'll be the end of it. And do I really want to become a divorced pastor's wife? And what's more, am I willing to lose my family, maybe for good, for it could easily come to that.

"I don't think I'll be coming," I say hesitatingly when Gloria rings the next morning.

She groans. "I was afraid of that."

"Let me speak to her," I hear her father command. "So you're not coming?" he asks in a flat voice.

"I can't," I burst out. "You're divorced, and you're a priest."

There's a very long silence at the other end. "So that's it?" he asks calmly.

I suppose I ought to say, "Yes, Father. That's it." But I can't. I can't throw away this very precious something that possesses me when I even hear his voice.

"I'm just not sure, Father." My voice trembles. "It depends on you," I finally stammer.

"What do you mean?" I can hear the tension in his voice.

"I mean that I'll come if…." I hesitate. What am I really trying to tell him?

"If what…?"

"If…if…you don't take my coming as a sign I'm halfway to the altar already," I stammer.

I didn't mean to say that. It just came out, somehow. I hear a laugh at the other end. "So, Cherry, you're not the meek and mild little girl everyone thought you were in St. Asaph's?" I hear him asking.

"You mustn't know me very well, or you wouldn't even ask that," I retort. "I'm not meek and certainly not mild, Father," I assure him. "Ask my family. But I'm serious," I protest. "If this weekend is just a chance to get to know each other better, then yes, I'll come. But I'm afraid...."

"So am I," he whispers. "Very."

"Then why...," I begin. I stop abruptly. I already know the answer.

"Then you'll come?"

What on earth can a naïve, twenty-four year old, falling in love for the first time in her life do but say in a very small voice, "Yes, Father, I'll come."

"See you in half an hour," I hear him say quietly.

"Whoopee!" I hear Gloria yell.

"Whoopee!" Father Andrew echoes joyfully.

"See you soon," is all I can say.

I place the receiver in its cradle and slowly make my way to my bedroom. My hands tremble as I pack my suitcase. I pull the zipper shut and lift the case off the bed. For a few brief seconds, a vision of Angus Campbell's sad, worn face rises before me. He seemed so changed at the funeral⁻ so grave and serious and so unlike the Angus I used to know.

And then I hear Father Andrew's words: "I long to hold you, have you in my arms, take you for my bride. Angus never told me that, did he? And isn't that what every girl wants to hear?

"Yes," I shout to an imaginary audience, "I know he's divorced. I know I'll have to think that one out. But God is opening a door! Would He open the wrong one?"

"Maybe it's Satan opening the door?" a voice suggests.

I roll my eyes in disgust as I pull my prettiest top out of the closet. "Satan and Father Andrew don't go together," I tell myself firmly, "any more than Dad and Satan do. Come to think of it," and I find myself smiling now, "it's going to be a fabulous weekend. I can feel it in my bones."

Chapter Twenty-Six

Andrew: Heaven on earth.

I can't believe it's happening. I'm sitting on my mother's front porch and my angel is sitting beside me.

"She's good, isn't she, Dad?" It's my daughter speaking. It's hard to get Cherry alone. Gloria follows her everywhere like a faithful sheepdog.

"Who's good at what?" I ask absent-mindedly.

"Cherry is good at swimming, of course," his daughter says impatiently. "What do you think we've been doing all afternoon?"

"Of course she's good," I answer at last. "She can dive and swim like a fish, or, I should say like an enchanting mermaid."

Cherry blushes scarlet. I shouldn't have said that, probably. But, for goodness sake, she'll have to find out that priests are very human, especially when they're in love. And, watching her swim this afternoon, I realized that maybe angels were human too.

I glance at her. The sun is setting and its soft rays catch the gold-red of her gorgeous hair. It's twisted up on top of her head and it makes her look regal, just how a priest's wife should look, I think to myself, and give a wicked grin.

"What are you grinning at, Andrew?" my mother asks. I'm glad she likes Cherry. I knew she would.

"I'm just happy," I answer evasively. "Very!"

I glance at Cherry as I speak. She's still not used to me in the role of a suitor. It seems to overwhelm her.

I put my hand over hers protectively. It's been so long since I held a woman's hand that I suppose I'd forgotten just what it feels like. I hold it tighter. She's blushing scarlet now. I see my mother and daughter exchange knowing glances.

"Let's go for a walk before the sun sets," I whisper.

We walk off down the path to the lake hand in hand. She says nothing. We stand and watch the sun sink lower in the western sky. The evening is balmy and still. I'm in paradise, well almost.

"You're making me very happy," I whisper, as we stroll along the lake's edge.

Still silence. "I've dreamed of this day for months, Cherry," I continue.

"For months?" There that's better. She's found her tongue at last.

"Maybe for years is more correct."

She shakes her head in disbelief. "I still can't get used to this, Father Andrew," she begins.

"Andrew," I correct. "Just Andrew, remember. You've got to learn to drop the 'father,' Cherry.

"Yes, Father," she answers, then she laughs her clear, silvery laugh. "Sorry, but this is all so strange to me."

"You mean it's strange to walk hand in hand with a priest?" I ask smiling.

"I mean it's strange to walk hand in hand with a man," she answers shyly.

I stare at her. "So you've never...?" Goodness, so she really is an angel after all!

She blushes again. "Well, I had crushes on several boys in my teens. They would come to our farmhouse to visit me, but Dad saw to it we were never left alone."

"But," I persist, "surely you didn't go through college without dating anyone? What about Angus Campbell? I remember you brought him to church once and made me so jealous I could hardly preach."

She stares at me in shocked silence. "But that was right at the beginning. I hardly thought you had noticed me at that point."

"Not noticed you! The very first morning you entered the doors of St. Asaph's I noticed you so decidedly that I told God I was sure you were an answer to my prayers."

"I don't understand," she murmurs.

"No, I'm sure you don't. Well, I was feeling that I needed a wife if I was to continue in my ministry and, well, looking down into your face that morning, I realized that God had perhaps answered almost before I asked Him."

I've overwhelmed her now. "So because I did feel that way," I go on, "I noticed Angus Campbell that first, no, second time you attended St. Asaph's. You did date him, didn't you?"

She blushes furiously. "Yes, for about six months."

"And you're telling me that you never once even held hands?"

"Well, only once. He didn't think we should have much physical contact until we were engaged."

I groan inwardly. I know I fail daily in a life of self-discipline. And then this missionary farmer comes along and beats me at my own game. "I marvel at his restraint," I comment eventually. "I really do."

"Angus had lived a wild life before he became a Christian," she explains. "So he determined to be very careful with girls."

"Admirable!"

She says nothing. "And what happened when you did hold hands?" I ask relentlessly.

She looks at me just a little surprised. "You do ask a lot of questions, Andrew," she says lightly.

"I know I do. I've often acted the role of father confessor, you know."

There, I've shocked her good and truly now. "But you're not a Catholic priest," she protests.

"No, but we Anglicans practice confession, too, not quite in the same way as our Roman Catholic brothers and not as frequently, but, in some churches at least, it is done."

I'm not quite sure what she's thinking right now. She looks puzzled, that's for sure. Well, she may as well know everything there is to know about me and my calling before we go any further.

"But I haven't come to you to confess, Father," she finally comments, giving me what I think is rather a sly smile.

"No, of course you haven't. But we're not going to have any secrets between us, are we?"

"Eventually, no," she admits.

"Eventually!" I repeat, grimacing a little. We have reached a bench under the trees. We sit down together, very close. I reach for her hand again. "So are you going to tell me more about this Angus?" I ask smiling.

"There's not a lot to tell," she replies quickly. "We were very good friends. We got on very well together though we did argue a lot."

I raise my eyebrows. I'm not sure I like what I'm hearing. She sees my expression and smiles impishly. "I don't think I'll have the nerve to argue with you, Andrew," she says softly.

"No? Do I frighten you that much?"

She nods. "Right now, you do."

"I'm not too worried," I say laughing. "I think you're pretty feisty when you want to be. Now more about this Angus, please."

She blushes, sighs a little and then tells me how Angus really loved her, but that they both discovered that their life journey was taking them in different directions.

"So he loved you. I thought he did." I mutter.

"Yes, Andrew, but I don't love him; at least," she pauses and lowers her eyes as she speaks, "at least," she repeats, "I never felt the same way when I was with him as I feel when I'm with you. Never, ever!"

She looks as if her own words have scared her to death. I squeeze her hand tighter. Then I feel her wrench it out of my grasp and before I know it, she's off like the wind. I run after her, but she's too fast for me. I shake my head in frustration. Why can't I approach things more casually? She's so young and inexperienced and I come along and frighten her away the first time we are really alone together. Oh well, there's always tomorrow. I can redeem myself tomorrow and the next day. A whole weekend with Cherry! Surely by Monday she'll come to terms with who I really am—a full-blooded, passionate man under a priest's clothing, no more, no less, but a man who does his best to love God with all his heart, soul and strength.

Chapter Twenty-Seven

Cherry: The innocent party.

I can't sleep. I still feel the touch of his hand, the look in his eye, the tenderness in his voice. Father Andrew actually loves me. I never imagined love would be like this. It's far beyond my wildest dreams!

I sit up in bed. I'm glad no one is sharing my room, especially not Andrew's sister. She's a perfect lady, but not my type at all and not a bit like her brother or her mother.

I run my fingers through my hair and go over the events of the day one last time. Yes, I'm over the moon with happiness but also scared to death; that's why I ran away from Andrew this evening. He absolutely overpowers me. I didn't know being in love felt like this. I slip down between the sheets once more. Right now I couldn't care less that he's divorced. Someone like Father Andrew is not going to violate Scripture even to marry me. Not ever! Then why can't I just trust his judgment? He's older and wiser than I am and a lot more holy. And he's in love with me! I'm crying for joy now. I'm in Heaven and I don't deserve this bliss. I know I don't.

I am still floating on air when we meet for breakfast the next day. An hour later, we all go for a boat ride on the lake. Andrew never takes his eyes off of me, I notice, and so do the others.

After lunch, he corners me in the parking lot. "Now you're coming with me, young lady," he says firmly. "I want some time alone, you know. And I need to know what I did to frighten you last night."

He pilots me into his car as he speaks. Andrew really is very commanding at times. Actually, he reminds me of my dad in many ways. Maybe that should worry me, but it doesn't. I've always been commanded by someone or other, so this is nothing new. Well, that's not true. This is so startlingly new that I'm really scared to death.

Now we're off, I'm not sure where but I don't care. I'm ready to go through life with this man, so where he takes me now doesn't matter a bit. He repeats his question once we're on the highway.

"You overpowered me," I murmur. I feel his eyes on me but I keep mine on the road ahead.

"You do the same to me, but I think we're perfectly safe with each other, don't you?"

I nod but say nothing. We drive around the lake for several miles. Then we pull into a scenic lookout and sit in silence for some time, enjoying the view.

"I need to talk to you," he says at last, breaking the silence.

"I need to talk to you, too," I tell him with a faint smile.

"Then that makes two of us. Well, as you already know, I'm a divorced man. And I'm a priest as well, so that makes it more complicated for you, right?"

"I suppose so," I admit reluctantly.

"I don't want you to go against your conscience," he tells me, and there's a world of tenderness in his voice. "But I think you need to hear my story." He takes my hand in his and draws me closer.

I pull away and he frowns slightly. "I can't concentrate when..." I mutter, avoiding his gaze. He drops my hand.

"Sorry," he apologizes with a wry smile, and then his voice changes. "Now for my story. I was heartbroken when Mary divorced me."

"She must have been crazy," I interrupt.

"No, she wasn't crazy," he counters. "She was cool and rational when she made the decision. She simply decided that she wasn't cut out to be a priest's wife. But I need to begin at the beginning. You see, we were high-school sweethearts. And we had a lot in common—we liked the same music, read the same books, and shared the same views on lots of things. Her dad was a Methodist minister, a very devout man, but she had found his religion too restricting, just as I had mine. One difference though—she had been brought up more strictly than I had so her rebellion was more extreme than mine. Well, having found our freedom, we began to party; we both loved dancing and Mary was the heart and soul of every gathering. She was a real beauty and I didn't want to lose her. So before I knew it, she was pregnant. She was nineteen and I was twenty—both of us mere children. Well, I married her right away—four months before Peter was born.

"The first few years we were extremely happy, or thought we were. We were involved in nearly every social activity in the neighborhood yet very seldom attended church. But, all the time, I knew my mom was praying for me. And one evening in my own room, I had my Damascus road experience. You've heard all about that often enough in my sermons and know how it totally revolutionized my life. It wasn't long before I felt a call to the ministry, or priesthood as we Episcopalians call it. Well, Mary was not pleased with my transformation. I wouldn't go to parties anymore and would spend hours reading and praying.

"At first, she tolerated my religious fervor but gradually it got too much for her. Then we moved to be near my seminary. I was away a lot, and looking back, realize that I was partially to blame for what happened. While I was studying, she was making friends of her own. And finally, she gave me the ultimatum: she would divorce me if I insisted on continuing in my vocation. She could never, she told me emphatically, become a priest's wife.

"Well, I thought I had no choice. My call seemed irrevocable. So she kept her word and I found myself a divorced man. I was heartbroken, Cherry. And if you've never gone through a divorce, you can't know the agony I went through. The day the papers were signed, it seemed as if I was walking in a desert. And for months, I wandered around like a man out of his mind. I kept praying for my ex-wife and had some sort of wild hope that she would walk into the house one day and tell me that she had come back to God. She had custody of the children, but I saw them every weekend. Then, when Peter was about seven and Gloria four, my son told me that his mother was having different men in the house and from what I saw of Mary from time to time, I suspected that she was on drugs.

"In the end, things got so bad that the court gave me custody of the children. Mary disappeared suddenly. It was rumored that she had run off with someone to California. That happened ten years ago and I've never heard of her since, nor have the kids."

Andrew lies back in his seat. I can see that telling his story has exhausted him emotionally. "Is this why your hair is prematurely white?" I ask gently after a few moments of silence.

"Yes," he says slowly. "It went that way almost overnight."

"It makes you look very distinguished," I tell him, my eyes fixed on his face.

Andrew smiles tenderly. "I'm glad you think that," he murmurs. "And I won't say how you look."

"That's enough," I warn him, blushing scarlet. "Now, have you finished your story?" I ask to change the subject.

"Not quite. When Mary disappeared from our lives, I was priest at a small country church north of Chicago. Soon after that, I was called to St. Asaph's," he went on, staring out at the water and beyond. "My children became restless and unruly. I had my parish to take care of and so when Mother suggested they stay with her during the school year, it seemed the only thing to do. You may have noticed that Peter and I are not that close. I think he partially blames me for losing his mother. He told me not long ago that if I hadn't been so set on being a priest, we would still be one united family, but I find that hard to believe. Gloria, on the other hand, is always begging for another mom, a real one, one who will never desert her. I'm beginning to see God's heart of love and realize He doesn't want the children to suffer all their lives because of Mary's sin." He hesitates and then reaches for my hand.

This time I don't pull it away. "I've learned to control my desires through prayer and fasting. But it hasn't been easy. And working in a parish such as St. Asaph's, I realize that I need a helpmeet. Women such as Kathy are always hovering around."

"Kathy!" I interpose. "She gave me the impression that if I got out of the way, you and she would probably marry."

Father Andrew gasps. I put my hand to my mouth in dismay. "I didn't mean to tell you that," I exclaim.

He holds my hand tighter. "What else did she say?" he demands firmly.

"Well, she said you were infatuated with me and that if I went, I would save myself and you and the parish from a lot of problems. She hinted that I wouldn't make a suitable priest's wife."

Andrew mutters something under his breath. "And she's right," I go on, pulling my hand away. "I won't. I'm too young and naïve and not half sophisticated enough. I'll spoil your life."

"That's an absolute lie!" he explodes. "As for being young and naïve—that's why I love you. And not sophisticated enough? Well, let me be the judge of that." Then his face clouds. "So Kathy is the reason why you disappeared?"

"Yes."

"I thought it was because of the gossip. Kathy said it was too much for you."

"That wasn't true. It was the feeling that I was messing up your congregation that made me leave," I confess.

"You could never mess up my parish," he tells me tenderly.

"And something else," I add, blushing scarlet.

"Yes?"

"I think even then I was falling in love with you and it scared me to death."

That does it. Next thing I know I'm in his arms. "But I can't ask you to live with a violated conscience all your life by marrying a divorced priest," he murmurs.

"But you are the innocent party, aren't you?" I murmur back.

"Yes," he agrees. "And I've studied Jesus' words and feel that there is a loophole given to those whose partners have been unfaithful."

"To marry again?" I mutter.

"Yes. I know it's controversial but, oh blow it, Cherry!" he exclaims in a rather un-priestly way. "How on earth do you expect me to discuss Scripture with you in my arms?"

"I need to think about all this," I say softly. "I'm already in love with you, I admit, so...."

But he doesn't let me finish my sentence. "I said I need to think about all this," I repeat when he finally releases me.

"Don't keep me waiting too long," he murmurs.

"I won't," I whisper back. "I certainly won't!"

Chapter Twenty-Eight

Dennis: *Losing our daughter.*

"Mr. McMann!" I see the utter surprise in Madeline Cumming's face.

"I'm sorry to drop in without warning," I apologize. "I thought I'd stop by for a few minutes as unexpected business has called me to Chicago. Is Cherry in?"

Madeline seems very embarrassed, I'm not sure why. "Yes, she's in the garden. Just a moment and I'll call her."

"That's OK. I'll find her myself. I love giving surprises. Now which way do I go?"

Madeline hesitates a moment, then gives a shrug. I follow her around the back of the house and then I stop stock-still. There, on a swing under a tree, is my daughter. But she's not alone. She's in the arms of some man or other. It can't be Angus. He's on the other side of the world. I take a few steps closer. Well, if it isn't that priest from St. Asaph's! Aren't looks deceiving! I thought he was a gentleman even if he did call himself "Father." But what can you expect from Episcopalians, especially priests!

Madeline gives a cough. Cherry looks up and sees me standing a few yards away. The priest sees me, too, and rises from his seat. They are both taken aback and very embarrassed.

Then Father Andrew, I think that's his name, rises and clearing his throat, begins to speak. "I was just asking Cherry to marry me," he announces as he draws my daughter to her feet. "And she has accepted. I certainly hope that we have your blessing."

My mouth falls open. I have imagined this day for years—the day when some good, Christian gentleman would ask for my daughter's hand. The day has come and I am not prepared.

Cherry leaves Andrew's side and throws herself in my arms. "Oh, Dad, I'm so happy!" she whispers. "I never thought I could be so happy."

She lays her head on my shoulder just as she used to do. I stroke her thick, wayward curls and say nothing for a very long time. Madeline has left us alone and so has Andrew. Cherry leads me to the swing and we sit down, side by side. I'm still thunderstruck. The happiness in my daughter's face is unmistakable. This fellow has certainly won her heart.

"Andrew is such a wonderful man, Dad. He really is. I know what you think of Episcopalians, but he's a genuine Christian."

"How long have you two been dating?"

"Six months."

"And you haven't told me?"

"You haven't asked, Dad."

That's true. I've tried to stay out of her life lately, let her find her own feet, as she keeps telling me she needs to do. But I did expect she'd be more open with me. She always used to be, in the old days, that is. I give a sigh. How I wish those days were back!

At last, I find my tongue. "He's a lot older than you, isn't he?" I ask, hedging for time.

"Yes, fourteen years."

"Isn't that a bit much?"

"Not when two people are in love as we are and share so many things together."

"So he's thirty-nine and never married, or maybe he's a widower?"

Cherry stiffens. I hear her take a gulp before replying: "He was married when he was very young, before he became a Christian. Then when he got converted, his wife divorced him and is now on drugs and living with another man."

I blink to be sure I'm not dreaming and then stare at her for a very long time. Then, as her words sink in, I feel angry, disappointed, shocked, and yes, betrayed. I stand to my feet, my eyes flashing. "So he's divorced, and a professed man of God and a preacher!" I exclaim hotly. "What can you be thinking of, Cherry? Are you in your right senses?"

My daughter has risen, too. Her eyes are pleading and her lips trembling. "I've thought a lot about it, Dad," she says falteringly. "I've weighed all sides of the question. Andrew is the innocent party. He's been single more than ten years. He's called to the ministry and needs a wife to help him fulfill that calling. We've both prayed a lot about it."

"Prayed a lot about it!" I echo. I don't think I've ever been so upset.

"Yes," she repeats. "A lot! And I feel sure it is God's will."

"Much you know about God's will!" I explode. "You've been living in rebellion for years."

I hear footsteps on the gravel behind me. This Andrew fellow has come back, probably to defend his girl. I turn to him and say more quietly now, "And what do you have to say for yourself? What excuse do you have for breaking God's laws, not so much by divorcing—that may not have been your fault, but in daring to enter the pulpit in that state and now to actually think of getting remarried, and to my daughter, a mere child, who is overcome by your looks and eloquence, I've no doubt?"

Andrew meets my gaze and holds it. "In the first place, Mr. McMann," he says clearly, "I can't see how you can call your twenty-five-year-old daughter a child. And secondly, I am the innocent party in the divorce. No, please, let me go on," he begs, as I am about to interrupt. "Jesus did speak about that in Matthew nineteen, didn't He? Yes, I know that there is a lot of controversy over the subject of remarriage, but the Bible says it is better to marry than to burn. I came to the point where I knew I could never continue to be a pastor without a helpmeet. I was so desperate that I asked God, if he wanted me to continue in the ministry, to send me someone. And He has answered my prayer."

"Satan can do a pretty good job of counterfeiting," I interrupt.

Andrew's face goes white. "I have agonized over this whole question, Mr. McMann," he begins again calmly, "but I feel that if God called me to the ministry, and I know that without a doubt, then it is not in His character to deny me the one who will, with His help, of course, enable me to fulfill His calling in a way that is honoring to Himself. You may see it all as a ruse of Satan. Cherry and I see it as a loving provision of our Lord and Savior. Only time will tell which of us is right."

I listen to Andrew, almost spellbound; he does seem sincere and certainly has the gift of the gab. Then my anger returns full force. "You are very plausible, Mr. Price, but don't talk about prayer and my daughter being God's answer. As the Bible clearly states, she will be causing you to live in adultery if you marry so I cannot give my blessing. Until she returns home, without you, then she is not welcome in our house. God has told me that she will return to us one day so, for both your sakes, it is better she returns single than breakup your marriage to do so. Now, I think it best if I leave. May God have mercy on your souls and forgive you both for what you are doing."

How I make it home I'll never know. When my wife hears the news, she is as heartbroken as I am. We talk until the small hours of the morning and then, exhausted, we kneel down together by the sofa and ask God to step in. We've done all we can—we've brought Cherry up to love and obey God; we've dedicated her to God's service. We can do no more.

We rise from our knees and then hug each other tight. Our tears are flowing fast. We feel as if we have lost our daughter. And it hurts; oh, how it hurts!

Chapter Twenty-Nine

Andrew: Almost in Paradise!

Mr. McMann has gone and we both know the worst. Cherry's parents will never agree to our marriage. We sit together in silence for a long time.

"You need to take time to pray over this," I finally find myself saying.

"I already have," she replies in a low voice. "I knew Dad would react like this so I've already faced losing my parents if I married you."

"You have?" is all I can say.

"Yes, Andrew."

"And you love me that much?"

"Yes, that much."

When she speaks like this I'm always undone. And then a thought strikes me. Is she really in love with me or with her newly found freedom? And when she's used to being her own person, will she discover too late that she's made a mistake.

"What's wrong, Andrew?" she asks, looking full into my eyes.

"You're young," I murmur. "Awfully young to face all of this. You need to be very sure that...."

Cherry rises from her seat and stands facing me. I've never seen her look so upset. "I'm twenty-five, Andrew. I just heard you tell my dad I was no longer a child. You were married and divorced by that age. And if you think I don't know my own mind by this time, well then it's obvious that you don't really know me."

I take her onto my knee but she pulls away. "Maybe it's you who should pray about it," she tells me hotly. "Maybe you should be very sure you want to marry a 'child' like me. Maybe Kathy is right and you're just infatuated with me."

That does it. We're both upset now and so we have our first quarrel, ever. It lasts a week. And it does us both good. I spend the time fasting and praying. After all, do I want to be the cause of splitting up a family when one of my main roles as a priest of God is a peacemaker? And Cherry means so much to me, maybe too much. Is she taking the place of God in my life? But no, God sent her to me. Of that, I'm absolutely certain. And, anyway, I find, and she finds, that one week apart from each other is too much for both of us. So how on earth can we spend a lifetime apart?

"I will marry you, Andrew Price," Cherry tells me as we sit together on the swing in her back yard. "I know what it will mean, but like Ruth I can say, 'Where you go, I will go,' and say it with all of my heart."

I draw her to me and hold her tight. I love this woman more than life itself, more than.... Oh no, God, not more than you! I'd give her up if You told me to, wouldn't I? But You sent her to me. She's my salvation.

"My angel!" I whisper. "My poor angel! And you've done it for me, Cherry!"

"But look what I get in return," she reminds me, laying her hand on mine.

"You get a worn-out priest who feels pretty much a failure right now," I say a little sadly.

"And you get a naïve young wife who knows little about parish matters, or bishops, or convocations."

"I know enough about all these matters for the two of us."

"That's true! But I do want to be a help, Andrew."

"A help!" I exclaim as we enter the house together. The sun is setting and the air is chilly. "You're my rescuing angel. Now, Madeline has prepared supper for us. We'd better go to her."

"I don't feel like eating," she murmurs.

"Nor I. But we'd better make an attempt for Madeline's sake."

We've reached the kitchen door when Cherry turns and puts her hand on my arm. "One more thing," she says. "Please don't forget you will be my husband not my father or mother when we marry. I may be a child in your eyes in many ways, Andrew, but I want to be a true wife to you."

"Oh, you will," I assure her. "And don't worry; I'm not feeling very fatherly right now, young lady."

"Not in public, Andrew," she protests as my lips meet hers.

"Just proving I don't think of you as a child, that's all."

"Point proven," she assures me, blushing furiously as Madeline gives me a sly smile and orders us to take our seats at the table.

"What must she think of us?" Cherry whispers, pulling away.

"That we're madly in love!"

"If only Mom and Dad approved, it would be like paradise," she murmurs, as we take our seats.

"We are not promised paradise on earth, my dear," I say a little sadly. "But life with you will be as near a paradise as any man could hope for."

Chapter Thirty

Cherry: *Father Andrew's fiancée.*

"Cherry, will you come and stand by my side?" I hear my fiancé saying. I blush scarlet as I feel all eyes turn my way. Andrew had warned me that he would announce our engagement this morning.

Yes, I am back at St. Asaph's at last, sitting in my usual pew and dressed in a pale blue two-piece that Andrew bought for me last Saturday. I rise slowly and make my way to the front, my eyes fixed on his face. That way, I'll have the nerve to go through with this.

He draws his arm through mine as I join him. I'm sure at least half the audience are thinking that I'm too young to be a priest's wife, that I'm not half sophisticated or experienced enough, that Andrew has gone out of his senses, that....

But for the moment at any rate, all I hear are murmurs of surprise and delight all around. "I saw it coming," one lady tells me as we shake hands at the door some minutes later.

"You dark horse!" someone else tells Andrew. "You certainly sprang this one on us."

Kathy, of course, is noticeably absent. I say "noticeably" because she has already let us both know that she thinks we are making the mistake of our lives and that she would no longer be attending St. Asaph's. That perhaps is the only cloud that shadows this glorious day. It has been like Heaven to hear Andrew preach once more. I've missed his sermons terribly. I've been attending St. Martin's Episcopal Church in Chicago every Sunday morning. It's just a stone's throw from where I live. So it's pretty overwhelming to be back at the church I love best of all after two-and-a-half long years.

As I listened to Andrew preach this morning, I felt so proud to be marrying this handsome, holy, man. Yes, I still think he is holy even though his holiness is a lot earthier than I thought it would be. At first, that bothered me a bit. I'd see Dad's frown when I was in Andrew's arms as I often am, or when I felt his lips on mine.

"God made us to love and be loved," Andrew reminded me, "and that means physical love as well as spiritual."

"I know," I agreed, "but before marriage, Andrew? I mean...."

"Before marriage we have boundaries," he interrupted. "And neither you nor I have overstepped those boundaries. And we do trust each other completely, don't we?"

"Of course we do," I assured him. "It's just that Dad...."

"We can't have that father of yours intruding into our private lives after we're married, Cherry," Andrew had interrupted, frowning again.

"Of course we can't," I had whispered. "I need to give Dad a good telling-off, but I can't seem to do it even in my imagination."

"You will, one of these days," he had assured me. "You wait and see. Meanwhile, we'll pray about it." And we did pray, there and then. That's the thing about Andrew. He's kissing me one minute and praying the next. I guess that's what the right kind of love does—makes you feel like praying, I mean. Just one thing seems a bit strange. We don't have many "in between" conversations. We're either kissing or praying. What I mean is, we hardly ever argue or talk about what we've been doing the past week, or politics. But then we agree in most things, not like Angus and I. So we've nothing to argue about.

After church, we have lunch and then drive out to see Andrew's mom and tell her the wonderful news. My future mother-in-law is thrilled, just as I expected her to be. As for Gloria, as soon as she sees my ring, she hurls herself into my arms.

"Dad's done it at last!" she exclaims, half laughing, half crying. "I've prayed every day for two years or more that this would happen."

I stroke her glossy dark hair and feel the tears falling on my fingers. "You won't need to call me 'Mom,'" I whisper. "I'm only nine years older than you."

"I know Peter won't call you that, but I will, the minute you're married," she says decidedly. But when is it to be and where and...."

"We will be married in the spring, Gloria," her father interrupts. "And it will be a wonderful day for us all."

I look over at Peter. He avoids my eyes, says nothing, then turns and leaves the room. Andrew's sister, Alice, is also silent.

"They'll both come round in time," Andrew assures me as he drives me home that evening.

I wonder about that, especially about Peter, but keep my thoughts to myself. This day has been marvelous. I feel queen of the whole wide world.

"I've never seen you look so happy!" Madi exclaims, as I make us both a cup of hot chocolate that evening.

"Who wouldn't be?" I whisper. "I'm on cloud nine!"

And then she tells me what her wedding present will be. "I'm going to buy your gown," she announces, whirling me around on the kitchen floor. "It's pretty obvious those parents of yours won't pay a cent and...."

She stops abruptly as my face falls. "Sorry," she murmurs. "Trust me to put my foot in it."

I shake my head. "No! You're right. They've made it pretty clear they won't come to our wedding," I murmur, "or Paul."

Madeline looks shocked. "Every day he seems more on Dad's side," I explain. "But Andrew's brother is going to give me away. That's one comfort."

The ceremony is to be at St. Asaph's, of course. Where else could it be? And the Bishop will be officiating. Not having my family present will be the one blot on what I'm sure will otherwise be an absolutely heavenly day. No, there is another cloud in the sky—Peter! He's not pleased his father has decided to remarry. He just can't face the idea of anyone taking the place of his own mother. He will come to the wedding, though, for his dad's sake.

"What if Mom makes a turnaround, Dad?" he asks Andrew as we sit together one evening on Mrs. Price's verandah.

Andrew looks a little confused, as if he'd never thought of that. I can't say I hadn't, though I've always pushed the thought away as soon as it came.

"If she does, then Cherry and I will bless the Lord," Peter's dad replies simply.

His son frowns. "But wouldn't you feel that you'd done wrong by marrying someone else when you could have gotten back with Mom, assuming she had changed, of course?"

Andrew's face darkens. "I've waited fourteen years for her to change, Peter. And if she does, then I can only say that God would have seen that she did it before I met Cherry, if He'd wanted us to get back together. And after all, legally, I'm single now, and free."

"But," Peter protests, "if you do find out before the wedding that she's changed, what would you do, both of you?" He's appealing to me now.

I swallow hard and meet Andrew's eyes. He smiles comfortingly. "We'll take that one if and when it ever comes, Peter," he says lightly. "Now, I don't want to hear any more of this. It's hurtful to both Cherry and me."

When we're alone, I ask Andrew what he would do if Mary got converted before we tie the knot. He draws me very close and holds me for a long time. "I don't think that will happen, darling," he whispers. "God wouldn't let it for your sake. I mean, I can see you feeling you should run away and leave me to her, but what good would that do? I'd only end up a sour old bachelor who probably would have to give up the ministry and I don't think that would be God's will, do you?"

Put that way, what could I say but, "No, I don't think it would." And yet, Peter's question troubles me, when I'm alone, that is. When I'm with Andrew, I'm in very heaven! I'm just glad the wedding is only two weeks away now. Dating for twelve months is about all we can take. I'm still in a dream. Cherry McMann marrying God's priest! How good He is, how very good!

Chapter Thirty-One

Angus: In Africa for keeps.

"Cherry's getting married in a few weeks, Angus. Did you know that?"

I nearly jump out of my skin. Dennis and I are walking through his fields, looking at the cattle and chatting about farming, about my life in Africa, and about the fellowship. I've finished a two-year seminary course and have just spent the weekend with the McManns. I spoke at their fellowship yesterday, but my words seemed to fall flat, probably because I found myself rather critical of the service. The women seemed to be copies of each other and that irked me. And everyone simply worships Dennis McMann. I suppose I did too, once, and that's what bothered Cherry. Now he seems more human, more fallible. But then, I've matured a lot. I'm learning that I shouldn't be so afraid of compromising my convictions that I toss love out the window. Is that what I did with Cherry?

"Angus, did you hear what I said?" Dennis asks, tapping me lightly on the shoulder.

I give a start. Dennis has just told me something I've expected for months and yet it still knocks the feet from under me. "Yes, I mean, no. I didn't know it was all arranged," I mutter when I can find my voice.

"I've shocked you, haven't I?"

"Yes, you have, actually, although I shouldn't be. I saw it coming. I just hoped...." My voice breaks. I am dying a hundred deaths with no possibility of resurrection.

I feel a hand on my shoulder. "You still love her, don't you?"

I nod. "Yes," I admit after a few moments. "I realized that when I saw her at Mom's funeral."

"I don't know what's gotten into my daughter," Dennis says hotly. "I came across her unexpectedly in the arms of that priest-lover of hers six months ago. I went off the deep end when I learned that he is divorced as well as being an Episcopal priest. In fact, I told her not to come here with him, ever."

I stare at Dennis in dismay. "You told her...what?" I can't believe my ears.

Dennis reddens a little. "I told her she wasn't welcome in our home unless she breaks it off with that priest of hers."

I have never really differed with Cherry's dad before but now I have no alternative. "I can understand your disapproval, given what you believe," I say slowly, "but to pretty much disown her, Dennis. Isn't that going too far?"

Dennis stares at me for a few minutes in disbelief. Then he recovers himself and says hotly, "Going too far? Is that what you call being faithful to God and His Word, Angus?"

"You can be faithful to God without being cruel to your daughter," I protest.

"Cruel?" He gives a short laugh. "So that's what you think of me? I'd never have thought I'd hear this, coming from you, of all people."

The recriminating look in his eyes unnerves me. "But you can forgive her, Dennis," I say as gently as I can.

"Forgive?" he splutters. "Of course I would forgive her if she asked for it. But that means admitting she's done wrong and that she'll never do."

"It takes two to make a quarrel!" It's out before I can help it. Dennis stares at me uncomprehendingly for a long time. Then his face blanches.

"I'm disappointed in you, Angus," he tells me, trying hard to control his annoyance. "No matter how much you love the girl, I didn't think you'd look on my differences with Cherry as a simple quarrel."

"You're both human!" I explode. He has thoroughly riled me now.

"Yes, but she's rebellious and stubborn. And while I know I make mistakes, I've never said 'No' to God, Angus."

"Never?" I don't know what's gotten into me, arguing with this saintly man, but I can't help it.

"No, never, not willfully, I mean."

"I don't think Cherry has, either," I reply hotly.

"That girl of mine has completely hoodwinked you!" His voice is sad now. He's pacing back and forth, and I detect anguish as well as anger written all over his features.

Just then, one of his farm hands calls him from the milking parlor. I'm glad to be alone for a while. I need to digest what I've just heard.

Supper is a rather strained affair and I feel relieved when I'm alone in my bedroom. But soon it dawns on me that I've lost the only girl I've ever loved forever and forever. Oh, I know I've thought that before, but there was always some faint ray of hope lurking somewhere in the background that maybe some day, it would still work out between Cherry and me. But now she's going to be someone else's wife! I sob into the pillows, glad no one can hear me. This finishes me for America. What or whom have I got in this country now? Nothing! No one!

"I'll never be coming back to the States," I tell Dennis as we say good-bye the next day.

He looks startled. "But your friends?" he protests.

"Friends?" I try to keep the bitterness out of my voice.

"Well, you have got us," he goes on mildly.

Our eyes meet. "I'm grateful for all you've done for me," I begin slowly. "But I don't think we can be very close friends as long as you treat the one girl I still love the way you do." I see his expression and add quickly, "Oh, I know she's out of my life now for good, but I can't help it, I still love her and will defend her till the day I die! She's marrying a very good man and deserves your blessing, Dennis."

Dennis looks at me pityingly, then shakes his head sorrowfully and mutters, "God bless you, Angus. You'll certainly need it." And then, without looking back once, he strides away, leaving his wife to see me off.

"He's terribly disappointed that it's not you Cherry's marrying," Rachel explains as I make for my car.

"But that's in the past, Mrs. McMann," I remind her. "His anger against Cherry frightens me."

"Me, too," she mutters in a very low voice. But when I attempt to say something more, she turns on her heel and escapes into the house.

I give one last look at the farmhouse. "It was where she was born," I think sadly, "and where she grew up and played and studied." I get in the car, roll down the window, and give one last wave.

"Good-bye, Cherry," I murmur through my tears. "God bless you in your new life. Andrew is a man in a million. May you be blissfully happy!"

I roll up the window and steer my little car down the bumpy farm lane. "And now," I say through my teeth, "Africa, here I come. I'm yours for keeps now, for better or for worse."

Chapter Thirty-Two

Cherry: My father's daughter.

"Will you take this man to be your lawful wedded husband?" I'm standing in white, facing my handsome groom, about to say the word that will unite me forever with the man I adore.

"She won't take him as long as she has a father in this world to stand up for what is right," a deep bass voice booms in my ear.

It's Dad! I know it without looking round. Andrew's face blanches and then flushes with anger. I let out a long, low wail. Andrew's arms are around me but he can't keep me from falling...falling...falling into....

"Cherry! Wake up! It's only a dream. Wake up, for goodness sake!"

I open my eyes and see Madeline bending over me. I blink as she turns on the bedside light. Then I sit up, and stare wildly around. "Where am I?" I mutter and sink back onto the pillows.

"Here, safe in your own bedroom," my friend whispers softly. "You had a nightmare. Another one! That's two in one week. What's going on?" she wants to know.

I hesitate. I don't want to tell her my dream. Yes, she's right. I've had it twice now in the last seven days.

"Want to talk about it?" she asks gently.

I hesitate again and then it all comes out. When I finish, she takes me in her arms and holds me close.

"You poor baby," she murmurs, pushing back my disheveled mop from my face. "I'm so glad you'll be married in two weeks. How dare that father of yours treat you the way he's doing! Of course it gives you nightmares. Now come to terms with it, Cherry. He won't be at your wedding, but I'll be there, and all your friends will be there, and best of all, the only one that really matters in your life now will be there. So face your dad. Tell him...." She stops abruptly. It's probably better she doesn't finish her sentence.

But after she has gone and the light is off and I'm alone with my thoughts once more, I do as she says. I give my dad the biggest telling-off in his life. Of course he doesn't hear it. But I feel better and for the rest of the night, I sleep like a baby.

"This time next week you'll be a married woman, Cherry," Madeline tells me several days later.

I blush scarlet. I have just been thinking the very same thing; in fact, next Sunday evening, we will be on our way to the Rockies where we are going to spend our honeymoon. Andrew spent his childhood there and he wants to show me all his old haunts. Tonight, as we are eating supper together, I tell him about my nightmares.

He is very upset at first. "You'll have to deal with this, darling," he tells me firmly. "I've told you already that I'm not going to have that dad of yours intruding into our marriage."

"I know," I agree. "And he won't. I let him have it after my second dream and he didn't like it. At least, I've not had a repeat nightmare in almost a week."

Andrew's face relaxes. "That's good. I know it is hard for you, Cherry. You're losing so much to marry me."

I put my hand on his mouth. "I'm gaining so much more," I tell him.

"There must only be one man in your life, you know," he goes on, his eyes probing mine as they often do. Andrew is becoming increasingly possessive, I've noticed lately.

I nod. "There will be, Andrew. I promise."

I think over this conversation as Madeline and I speed towards the Wesleyan church. It is the Sunday before my wedding. I hope to see Paul tonight. We always do when we go to this church. I wish he'd change his mind and come to my wedding. Maybe I can persuade him yet. He's been softer lately, for some reason or other.

We have just slipped into a seat at the back of the hall when Madeline nudges me. "Look, Paul's got a girl with him," she whispers. I hear the tension in her voice.

I follow her gaze and give a start. "It's Allie Jordon," I whisper back.

"I thought you said...," she begins then she stops abruptly. Allie is snuggling close to my brother who has just put his arm around her shoulder.

"I just can't believe it!" I mutter half to myself. "Paul has always given Allie a wide berth. He thought she was terribly stuck up. She's scary bright, though. Maybe that's the attraction. Are you all right, Madeline?"

Madeline has gone white now and I see her hand is shaking. "I'm not feeling good, to be honest. Mind if I go home? Paul can drive you back, can't he?"

"And Allie?" I ask wryly.

Madeline shrugs as she rises from her seat. I see she's terribly upset and no wonder. Paul hasn't dated anyone since he broke it off with Madi. I keep my eye on my brother. He still has his arm around Allie and is whispering in her ear.

The service begins, and I soon remember that it's youth night and we're having a special speaker, someone who's been on drugs and who has a marvelous testimony. I think that some kids from the streets have been invited. Should be interesting!

The place is packed. An usher is placing some extra chairs at the very back of the hall. The guest speaker has already been introduced before I can take my thoughts away from Madi and Paul.

I study the speaker as she walks up to the platform. She is about forty¯ a tall, willowy blonde. I can't see her face too well from where I'm sitting. She has been converted for about a year. As I listen to her testimony, it rings a bell somehow. Where have I heard a story like that? But then, I figure, it is pretty common—brought up in a Christian home, rebelled, a divorce, then drugs, other men, living on the street, invited into a rescue mission, taken to a Christian rehabilitation center where after two or three attempts at going off the drugs, she had at last been overwhelmed by the love of those around her and capitulated to their message of hope and love.

Her talk is followed by question time. "Will you be able to get back with your family?" one girl asks.

The woman hesitates for a very long time and then begins slowly: "I would like to tell you 'yes,'" she says sadly, "but I'm afraid I'm reaping what I've sown. You see," she pauses again, and even from where I am sitting, I can see the pain in her face as she goes on, "my husband got converted a few years after we married. He stopped partying, turned over a new leaf, and in the end, felt called to be an Episcopal priest."

I give a gasp and grip the seat in front as the speaker continues her story. As she goes on, I find I already know nearly every detail off by heart.

"Have you contacted your family since your conversion?" is the next question.

"Well, I live with my parents," the speaker replies. "I asked my father's forgiveness right after my conversion."

"And your ex-husband?" someone else wants to know.

My pulse quickens and I lean forward to catch her answer for she has dropped her voice and I can see she is struggling with her emotions as she answers slowly, "I intend to phone him after he gets married."

Her words bowl me over. It *is* Mary. I feel myself falling. I grip the seat again and force myself to listen. "So he's getting married again?" someone asks.

"Yes, to a beautiful young Christian girl, or so I've heard. They're getting married next week, my dad tells me. He saw it in the papers."

In that instant, my world turns upside down. I sway, and the next thing I know, Paul is by my side. "Sis," he's calling, "Sis, wake up." Several women are standing around me, one feeling my pulse, the other wiping my forehead with a cool cloth.

I sit up and try to speak. "I'm all right now," I stammer.

"You don't look it," Paul tells me. Allie is standing by his side, looking totally nonplussed.

The next thing I know, I'm in my brother's car and being whisked homeward. Paul asks no questions.

"Take care of her," he tells Madeline as I stumble into the living room half an hour later. "She's had a shock. I'll check in on her tomorrow."

The door closes and I'm left alone with my very best friend. I collapse onto the sofa. Madi bends over me. I close my eyes and murmur, "I saw Mary Price tonight. She...."

I can't speak. I can't think. And then I hear Dad's voice speaking from somewhere deep inside me. "It's an answer to prayer!" he's saying, and I can hear the triumph in his voice.

"No, it isn't!" I shout, forgetting that Dad is hundreds of miles away.

"Isn't what?" my friend demands, her blue eyes wide with concern.

"It's not an answer to prayer. I won't let it be. I'll fight to the end. Andrew is mine, not hers. She gave him up years ago."

I slump back onto the cushions, exhausted. "Of course he's yours," Madeline says soothingly. She's very concerned now. Then she turns and disappears into the kitchen. A few moments later she returns with a cup of steaming chocolate in her hand. "Look, Cherry, what you need is a good night's sleep. Drink this first and then to bed with you."

I drink the chocolate. I take some Tylenol. I stumble into the bathroom and reach for the toothpaste. I feel the fight draining out of me. I'm no match for Dad. What I really mean is that I'm no match for God.

"Maybe we should call Andrew," my friend suggests, as I pour myself a glass of water and make for my bedroom.

I shake my head. "Please," I plead. "Not tonight, Madi. Let him have a good sleep. And I'm too confused to know what to say right now."

"Confused?"

I shake my head in exasperation. "Yes. Can't you understand? Mary Price has appeared like a ghost from the past and our lives can never be the same again!"

Madeline looks blankly at me. "Oh, come on, Madi," I say irritably. "It changes the whole scenario, doesn't it?"

"Not at all," she replies sweetly. "Mary is Andrew's ex-wife and that's that. I'm sure Andrew will be glad she's converted but that'll be all. Not a thousand ex-wives could drag him from you, my dear."

I feel more frustrated than ever with my friend. "Don't you understand?" I'm shouting now and making for my bedroom as I speak. "It's not Andrew I'm worried about."

"Then who else on earth is there to worry about? Peter?"

"No," I yell. "Not Peter, you dummy! It's me, conservative, fundamentalist me! Me, my father's daughter, me my father's clone, me my father's wonderful, saintly, dedicated missionary. I'm worried about ME, ME, ME!!!"

Chapter Thirty-Three

Joy: I want to be like you, Cherry!

"Do you think he'll see a change in me, Grandma?"

"Sure he will, Joy," my grandmother reassures me. "Who wouldn't? You were a child when he left and now you're...."

"A woman," I interrupt.

"Not quite," Grandma counters. "But nearly."

We're expecting Uncle Angus any moment now. He's been away an age—two whole years! I run my hands through my long, glossy, jet-black hair as I stare for the hundredth time this evening at my image in the mirror. I know I'm the prettiest girl on this mission station. Even the white girls are envious, especially of my hair. It's wavy and thick, and reaches down to my waist. It wasn't that long when Uncle Angus left two years ago. I was thirteen then, and Grandma had just cut it quite short. Now I'm not a child anymore. So I do what I want, or pretty near. Grandma is too old and too sick to keep an eye on me like she used to. She has no idea of all the boys I flirt with, especially Guy Stanton. Well, he's really my boyfriend, only we have to meet in secret. That's a challenge, and lots of fun. He's eighteen but that doesn't matter. Everyone says I look seventeen at least though I won't be sixteen till November. Guy is madly in love with me. At least that's what he says. I think, though, that he nearly worships me. He says girls like me are made to be worshiped. I've thought about that one a lot.

But now I'll have Uncle Angus back again. He's always been like a dad to me and dads are terrors for discipline. So...? I'll just have to wait and see!

I twirl around, and face my grandmother. "Dada Angus is blind if he doesn't notice you've grown into a very beautiful young lady," Grandma tells me, smiling proudly.

I give a shrug. Of course I'm beautiful. Everyone tells me that! Then I catch sight of a small picture frame Uncle Angus keeps on his dresser. I go over and take it in my hands.

"Looking at that photo again!" Grandma mutters.

"I can't help it, Grandma," I admit. "It's Uncle Angus' girl, or was. I think she gave him up when he decided to come here. He told me all about her before he left. I look at her because I want to know what he sees in her. She's not half as pretty as I am," I go on. "Her nose turns up, her eyes are too big for her face, and her hair is too frizzy."

I can't look into Grandma's eyes, because I know I'm lying, and she does too. It's true that the girl in the picture has a pug nose and that her eyes do seem a bit on the large side, but she's got the most gorgeous hair I've ever seen. That's not the main thing, though. She seems to have— I'm not sure what exactly, but something I don't have.

Grandma comes over to the dresser and peers at the picture for a very long time. "Maybe she's not as pretty as you are, Joy," she replies slowly, "but she's special; I knew that the first moment I looked at her."

"Special?" I repeat. "How?"

"She looks pure, just like an angel must look," Grandma says softly. "No wonder Dada Angus loves her more than anyone else in the world!"

"More than us?" I want to know, frowning.

"In a different way than he loves us," she explains patiently. Grandma is one of the most patient people I know. She has to be, living with me.

"What do you mean?" I want to know.

"Well," Grandma begins slowly, "there's a love we have for family and a love we have for the person we want to be our husband or wife."

I think over that one for a while. "So we're family and she's, well, she's someone he wants as his wife?" I want to know.

"That's about it, Joy," she says beaming. "You're such a smart girl."

"But that was years ago," I go on impatiently. "She mustn't have loved him like he loved her or he would have brought her here as his wife."

Grandma's eyes twinkle. "I think he just might be bringing her back as his wife one of these days."

"Well, he's not told us about it in his letters," I tell my grandmother with a toss of my head.

"Maybe it's to be a surprise," Grandma says smiling. "Wouldn't it be wonderful to see Dada Angus married? He certainly deserves it. And if anything happens to me, Joy, she'd be like a mother to you.

But I don't smile back. I don't want a mother anymore. Or a father. I want…. Suddenly, I remember that this kind of wanting can get you into a heap of trouble. It did with my mother, so Grandma tells me.

I put back the photo on the dresser with a sigh. I'm not sure right now I know what love is. I thought it was what I felt when Guy gave me that kiss last week. That was something else! I still remember it. Well, actually, I remember a lot more than his kiss. If Mr. Stanton hadn't walked in on us I don't know what might have happened. No, I don't think what I felt for Guy right then was the kind of love I need. That kind of love brings nothing but trouble, especially to colored girls like me. I do like it, though. Very much!

"They're here, Joy!" Grandma shouts from the window.

I look again in the mirror. Then I give my hair another vigorous brush, retie the bow at the back of my white, Sunday dress, and rush to the door. Mr. Stanton's jeep is pulling up in front of the house. I take my grandmother's arm and lead her onto the front porch. She stumbles a little. She doesn't seem as strong as she used to be. I'm very worried about her. Maybe she'll be fine now that Uncle Angus is back.

We stand together, arm in arm, watching as a man jumps out of the jeep. He sees us and waves. Then, a few moments later, one suitcase in each hand, he walks briskly up the short path towards us, sets down his luggage, and before we know it, Grandma and I are in his arms. I don't know abut the other two, but I'm crying and laughing for joy. It's just like it used to be, but wait, it isn't quite. Hugging Uncle Angus feels very different now. I wonder if he finds it different, too?

"Oh, it's so good to be home!" he exclaims, as we lead him into the house. He looks the same as he always did except he's put on quite a bit of weight. All that rich American food, I suppose. I notice that he seems worried when he glances at Grandma as she takes his arm for support. She has hardly enough strength to reach his favorite chair by the window. Then he stands absolutely still and gazes around the room in wonder.

"I can't believe it!" he exclaims. "This place has been totally transformed!"

"Joy did most of this," Grandma tells him proudly. "And just look at her, Dada. Hasn't she grown? She's quite a young lady, now."

He does what Grandma says and looks at me for a very long time. I hold my breath. I wonder what I look like to him now—his little adopted daughter as he used to call me, or does he see me as Guy Stanton sees me or as all the other boys at Ngavi see me?

I'm looking at him too. He seems sadder than he used to be, but his smile is just the same, and his eyes are tender as they always are when they look at me, I mean tender as in "father," or "brother." But maybe there's something else in them too? I'm not sure. It's just that he seems under some spell or other and can't take his gaze away from me.

Then, suddenly, he makes a sort of bow and the spell is broken. "You have grown into a very charming young lady," he tells me. He sounds awfully polite—not at all like he used to sound when he talked to me.

I put on my most dazzling smile and try to curtsey. "Thank you, sir," I murmur, trying to sound very grownup.

Then an awful thought strikes me. Has Mr. Stanton told him about Guy and me? I don't think so, I tell myself, otherwise he wouldn't smile at me like he does. We eat supper together and have family prayers just as we always did. It seems as if he's never been away.

We clear away the dishes and I know it's time for Grandma and me to go home. "So you didn't bring her back with you after all?" Grandma asks as she points to the picture on the dresser. "I was almost sure you'd come back married, Dada Angus."

"Were you, though! I hope you're not too disappointed?"

"I'm not disappointed," I interrupt. "Grandma and I want you all to ourselves, don't we, Grandma?"

My grandmother smiles at me fondly. "Well, in a way, dear," she admits, "but I really think Dada Angus needs a good wife."

"Did you ask her to marry you, Uncle Angus?" I persist.

My question seems to hurt him. "She's marrying someone else," he says in a low voice.

I ought to feel sorry but I don't. Instead, it seems like a load of a hundred years is taken off my chest.

"I'm sorry, Dada Angus," Grandma says sympathetically. "I'm very sorry! You do need a wife."

"That's what Reg Stanton keeps telling me," Uncle Angus says impatiently. "But with you and Joy as family, what do I need with a wife?"

"He's right," I tell Grandma. Then, suddenly, I feel so terribly happy that Uncle Angus has come back to us. Before I know it, I throw myself in his arms just like I used to do. I feel him stroke my curls and murmur. "My little Joy! How I've missed you."

I look up and see Grandma looking at us curiously—not pleased, not angry—just curious, as if she's thinking a lot but doesn't really know what she's thinking.

"I've missed you, too," I murmur. "Please don't ever go away again, Uncle Angus. I can't be good without you."

He pushes me away gently and looks me full in the eyes. "It's God who helps you to be good, Joy. I won't be with you forever, you know."

"Why not?" I want to know. "At least you'll be with me till I'm grown and able to look after myself."

He smiles gently. "Yes, I can promise that, Joy," he assures me.

It's then that I think of *her* again. I walk over to the dresser and take her picture in my hands. "Can I have it?" I ask, before I know what I'm asking. "You won't want to look at it anymore will you, now she's marrying someone else?"

Uncle Angus looks a bit shocked at first. Then he smiles his old smile. "Of course you can have it. But why do you want it, Joy? You don't even know the girl in that photo."

I look at the picture for a long time and then look back at him. "I want to be like her," I tell him suddenly. It's the first time I've ever thought like that. I don't know what's come over me.

"Like her?" he repeats. "But Joy, you have grown into a very sweet young woman, too."

I shrug a little. If he only knew! Then I feel a tear run down my cheek. "Maybe, Uncle Angus, but I'm not like *her*." Suddenly, I feel I want to be alone. "Good Night," I mutter. "I'd better get Grandma home now."

"Good Night and God bless both of you," I hear him call after us as I push open the screen door, the photo clutched tightly in my hands.

I help Grandma into bed and then get undressed. I don't feel like sleeping. The night is filled with what Uncle Angus calls "the sounds of Africa"—frogs croaking under my window, a hyena barking in the distance, an owl hooting from a tree at the bottom of the garden. I hear a mosquito humming near my nose. If it is humming, then it won't be a malaria carrier, but still, I'll be full of bites by morning.

I switch on the light. Thank goodness we have electricity now! Uncle Angus bought a generator just before he left for America and it serves both of our houses. And he put up fly screens at every window and door! Now I don't need to sleep beneath those wretched nets anymore. And, well, what hasn't he done since he first arrived at Ngavi, nearly five years ago?

I'll never forget meeting Uncle Angus for the first time. I was only ten. I liked him immediately. His gray eyes seemed so kind and he talked to me as if I were a little white girl. He didn't see me as half black, half white, not like most people do. And right away, he seemed to take the place of the father I have never seen. Grandma has told me about my father. I know he's an Englishman and has lots of money. Then why doesn't he send us some? Or why doesn't he write now and then? Doesn't he even know he's got a daughter?

I climb into bed as the clock strikes eleven. Really, I don't think of my father much anymore. Uncle Angus' coming changed all that. I smile as I remember what it felt like to be in his arms this evening. Oh, I know Grandma was there, too. For right now, that's the way it's going to be—Grandma, Uncle Angus, and me. But one day Grandma won't be with us anymore, and then what? I smile to myself, not because I want Grandma to die, but because I suddenly decide that I'm going to make Uncle Angus love me. Oh, I know he loves me to death already, but Grandma's right. There's family love and then there's—well the kind of love he had for his redhead. The kind of love that makes you worship someone enough to die for them. I think he'd do that for his Cherry, only she isn't his anymore. And one day he's going to be mine, only mine, forever and for always.

I clench my fists together as I speak. I usually get what I want, one way or another. And I'll get this, too, if I have to wait till I'm thirty. Right now, I know I'm not good enough for Uncle Angus and probably never will be, and yet, if God will give me one more chance, I'll work ever so hard at being like *her.* I'll never look at Guy again. I'll tear up all his love notes and put away all the paperbacks he gave me. I'll never say bad words again not even to myself. I'll read my Bible every day and pray. And....

My eyes fall on the photo of the redhead. So I take the picture in my hand and say slowly almost as if I'm praying: "I want you to help me be like you, Cherry, so that I can marry your Angus when I'm a bit older. I want God to make me look like an angel just like you do, if it's possible for a colored girl like me to look like an angel. Maybe angels are only white. But no, I'm sure there must be colored angels, too. And maybe if I am very, very angelic, then Uncle Angus will one day love me like he loves you now."

I put the picture on the table by my bed so I can see it first thing when I wake in the morning. I've heard that if you look at something enough you become like it. And as I pull the sheet over me and settle down to sleep, it seems as if God is listening though I've not spoken directly to Him, and I fall asleep soon after, feeling happy and peaceful, just like I did before Uncle Angus left us two years ago. He seems to bring happiness wherever he goes. And I want to spend my life making him happy. Yes, that's all I want forever and forever!

Chapter Thirty-Four

Andrew: Mary again!

It's Sunday evening, my last Sunday as a single man. Both Cherry and I have set apart today for fasting and prayer. We both want our marriage to be hallowed and blessed. Sometimes I worry that I love Cherry more than God. I know the answer is to love God more. Cherry wants that, too. We've shared our fears about becoming idols to one another. We both are so madly in love. But it was God Who brought us together so that makes us both feel safe.

Tomorrow, my fiancée is going to my mother's house to try on her wedding gown and take care of a thousand and one things that a bride-to-be has to think of a few days before her wedding. I begin to wonder what she's doing right now and reach for the phone. Madeline answers.

"Can I speak to Cherry?" I ask. "Or is it too late?"

"She's gone to bed," Madeline tells me rather abruptly, which is not at all in character.

I know Cherry has a phone by her bed so I ask, "Do you think she's asleep yet?"

Madeline hesitates a long time before saying slowly, "I don't know if she's asleep or not, but she indicated that she doesn't want to be disturbed.

"Not even by me?" I persist.

Another long pause. "Not even by you, Father."

I put down the receiver, very upset. I sense something is dreadfully wrong and hardly sleep a wink. The next morning I call again to check if Cherry is OK.

This time Madeline is more co-operative, but what she has to tell me by no means quells my fears. "Cherry fainted in church last night," she begins. "I told her I would tell you that when you phoned again."

"Fainted?" I ask, concerned.

"Yes, fainted," Madeline repeats.

"Whatever caused that?"

"I'll let her tell you when you come," Madeline says hastily.

"Come? But that wasn't in our plans," I begin.

"No, but her fainting wasn't planned either. You'd better come, Father. She's in no state to travel or see to wedding arrangements today."

"Maybe you should call the doctor," I suggest.

"I'll leave that up to you and Cherry. Just come, Father, as soon as you can."

Madeline sounds urgent. I phone Mom and Alice and tell them plans have been changed, and then I speed towards Chicago. A dozen possible scenarios rush into my mind. "She's got cold feet and can't face marriage. No," I tell myself, "that's not like Cherry." "Maybe she's discovered she's got some serious illness," I wonder. And on and on it goes until at last, I pull up to the familiar gate, jump out of the car, and stride up the garden path.

Madeline meets me at the door and leads me into the sitting room. She looks troubled. "What is wrong with Cherry?" I ask, as I take off my jacket and hang it in the hallway as I've done scores of times before.

"I promised not to tell," Madeline mutters, avoiding my eyes.

"Then I'm sure she'll tell me herself," I say confidently.

"She won't see you, Father, and is upset that I told you as much as I did."

My face flushes. "Are you sure?"

"Positive. She's locked her door and won't come out."

I have risen to my feet in my agitation but sit down again and scratch my head. "You say she fainted in church?" I ask. "The Wesleyan church?"

"Yes. I came out early for private reasons," Madeline says looking embarrassed, "and so wasn't there when she fainted. Paul brought her home."

"And it was a regular service?" I ask, feeling like a detective.

"Not exactly. They had a special speaker, a woman who was on drugs and then got wonderfully converted." Madeline is trying to sound casual but not succeeding very well. And she avoids my eyes as she speaks, which she seldom does.

My stomach begins to churn. "Did you catch her name?" I ask, not really wanting to hear the answer.

"Yes, it was Mary Pri..., I mean Mary Mahoney," she stammers.

My heart comes into my mouth. I stare at Madeline in disbelief. It makes sense now. I try to speak but can't. Madeline waits patiently until at last I manage to whisper, "Mary Mahoney is my ex-wife."

Madeline nods. "At least you found out about her for yourself," she says weakly.

"So now, what do I do?" I ask, feeling I'm drowning fast.

"Pray!" Madeline suggests without hesitation. I blush in shame. I'm a priest and it takes a young woman whom I've castigated as worldly and sensual to suggest that I appeal to the God I profess to serve for strength and guidance!

We both kneel down and we both pray but I get the feeling that it's Madeline's prayer that reaches Heaven. Mine seems to go no higher than the ceiling.

"Knowing Cherry," Madeline says softly as we rise from our knees, "I'd let her be alone today, Father. She's thinking all this out and praying too, I'm sure. She knows she can't stay in that room much longer. But she's in shock."

"I am, too," I grunt. "But doesn't she know that she has nothing to fear from me?"

"I told her that last night," Madeline answered. "She said she knew that. I asked if she was worried about Peter's reaction and interference and she lost her cool with me, something she rarely does. It seems she's worried about her own reaction to all this, not anyone else's."

I lay my head back on the sofa and begin to weep. At least I know what I've got to cope with between now and Saturday. I'm up against twenty-odd years of brainwashing.

"Oh, God," I breathe, as I walk out to my car, "if ever I need You it's now. Our whole world is falling apart. Why did Mary have to step into our lives just now? Why not a week later?"

I think I know the answer, though I don't hear it shouted from Heaven. But I can't accept it, not yet, and maybe never ever!

Chapter Thirty-Five

Cherry: I have to do it!

I can't believe that I'm sitting opposite Mary Price, well, Mary Mahoney as she calls herself now, five days before my wedding. I snuck out of the house while Madeline was at work. Mary is staying for a week with the pastor of the Wesleyan church and has very graciously received me. I have been quizzing her about her conversion and her recovery from addiction, but I find that I've run out of questions. Right now, she's looking curiously at me with those big sky blue eyes of hers. She's been a beauty once upon a time, that's for sure, but up close, I can see traces of her past life. Or can I? Maybe I want to see them. Maybe I want to prove she's no saint. Maybe I want to make her cry, make her pay for turning up like this and ruining everything.

Any moment, now, I'm going to spring my true identity on her. Cruel? Maybe, but a desperate woman can be cruel sometimes, and wasn't she cruel to Andrew and to her own precious children all those years? Even if she has been changed, she can't undo the past.

"Why, exactly, did you want to see me?" Mary asks curiously. "You don't look as if you have addiction problems yourself. Maybe you have a loved one who needs help, or maybe you're interested in joining a ministry such as mine?"

I shake my head. It's now or never. If I don't take the bull by the horns, then my visit here will simply be a waste of time for both of us.

I take a gulp and then blurt out: "I came because I am Andrew Price's fiancée." There, it is out! My heart pounds as I watch her reaction. That's why I'm here, isn't it? To see if she's genuine? To discover if she's worth sacrificing my whole future happiness for?

Mary catches her breath and goes white. She sits without moving a muscle for what seems an eternity as my words sink in. I watch her, hardly daring to breathe. Then she covers her face with her hands. Her whole frame is shaking with emotion.

I can't stand to watch her agony. I rise and make for the door. I put my hand on the doorknob, but Mary has risen, too, and is stumbling across the floor towards me. She reaches out her hands. I grab them in spite of myself.

"Please forgive me," she stammers, raising her tearstained face to mine. "It's just that you caught me off guard. I wish you every blessing. Andrew deserves all the happiness he can get."

I stare at the woman in disbelief. Then I find my tongue. "You still love him, don't you?" Maybe it's not a question I should ask my fiancé's ex-wife, but I have to know.

The tears are stealing down Mary's cheeks as she nods her head and gives a faint smile. "Yes. I still love him."

"Then," I probe relentlessly, "why did you desert him and leave your children just when they needed you?"

She flushes and bites her lips as she sinks into the nearest chair. I'm sure my bluntness has hurt her but I'm not here on an errand of mercy. "My love was selfish in those days," she admits, sitting down again. "It wasn't true love. I see that now. But in my own way, I have loved no one but Andrew. Oh yes," she adds, seeing I am about to protest, "I did live with two different men and then the drugs took over and my life revolved around the narcotics I needed in order to survive. But since my conversion, my love has come back full force, even although I know it will never be returned. I don't deserve Andrew's love. So as I said before, I wish you God's blessing."

I think she wants me to leave, but I haven't finished yet. "What would you do if I decided to cancel our wedding and leave Andrew to you?"

Mary stares at me blankly as if she hasn't heard correctly. Then, as she realizes my meaning, she sits up very straight and looks me full in the eye. "I would continue to serve God as He has called me to do." Her voice is full of grace and dignity. "I don't love Andrew because I hope to get him back," she says simply. "I've lost him forever. I love him because I can't help it."

She really means it, I think to myself as I watch her. But still, I have to ask at least one more question. "You will contact Andrew, won't you, if I leave? I mean, what about your children?"

Mary smiles at me and I fancy I detect pity there. She senses what I'm suffering. "I had intended not to contact Andrew till after you both were married. Then I just wanted permission to see my children. I didn't expect or think it wise to see him myself."

I rise from my chair. But now it is her turn to ask questions. "Why did you really come?" she probes.

I sit back down again and begin to weep uncontrollably. "You don't understand," I burst out. "My parents are praying that I'll never marry Andrew. He's Episcopalian and divorced and that's a no-no for them. And I had to go against them to get engaged to him. I prayed a lot about it and felt I was doing right. But now you've come on the scene and I'm confused."

I stop. She's crying too. Our eyes meet, and, in that moment, my decision is made. I force myself to speak words that will probably seal my doom. "No, I'm not confused any longer," I say. "Everything is suddenly clear as day. I know I can't marry him. Before God, you are still his wife."

I can't go on and yet I must. I came here today to check her out, but God knows she's checked me out instead. I feel an arm around me and in spite of myself, I cling to her as I would to my own mother. I try to speak again, but the words won't come.

"You don't need to say any more, Cherry," Mary is telling me.

"But I have to," I manage to splutter. "God has allowed all this to happen when it did. A week later, it would have been too late. The only decent thing I can do is to step out of Andrew's life now."

"But...," she begins.

I stop her. "No, don't protest. Please help me to do what I feel is right." I raise my eyes to her face. "You are not the same woman who walked out on Andrew years ago. You are his age; you'd make a better priest's wife than I would ever make. And you are the mother of his children." I rise to go again, but the next moment, I feel her arms around me again and we are crying on each other's shoulders.

"You brave, brave girl! No wonder Andrew loves you." Her voice is full of an admiration I know I don't deserve.

"I'm not brave," I sob. "I'm not really doing this because it's right, though I made it sound that way a moment ago. And I'm not doing it because I'm convinced it's Scriptural. I'm doing it because I can't do anything else. 'Train up a child...' and all that?"

Mary strokes my hair as my mother would do. "Go and pray about it with Andrew," she advises. "I'm afraid all this will hit him very hard. And don't do this just because...."

I pull away and run to the door. I put my hands to my ears. "Don't, don't! I have to do it! I'm not good, or brave! I'm angry that I feel this way. I love him. I adore him. My life is ruined and maybe his, too, but I can't do anything else. Don't praise me. I don't deserve it; pity me if you like and pray for me."

I bolt out the door, seize my jacket from the peg in the hallway, nod to the pastor who stands, perplexed, in the kitchen doorway, and run down the driveway to my car. I turn on the engine, put my foot on the pedal, and zoom onto the highway. I whizz past the turnoff to our house. I'm going straight to Pendleton and to Andrew.

"Get it over with!" I keep telling myself as I speed along the interstate. The speedometer reads eighty miles an hour but I don't care. I'm reckless; I'm desperate; I'm angry; I'm determined. Anything else? Oh yes, how can I forget! I'm desperately, terribly, and irrevocably in love!

Chapter Thirty-Six

Andrew: Left in hell!

It's three in the afternoon. I'm about to call Cherry again. I have to contact her. I'm nearly crazy with worry. And I'm angry! In a rage, is more like it! No, I don't think it's with God, though who knows right now! I suppose it's my ex-wife I'm mad at. Well, who wouldn't be? And I'm angry with myself for feeling angry with her. I ought to be praising God for her conversion. I've prayed for that long enough, and now when God answers my prayer, I'm plain mad—no state for a priest to be in. And that makes me feel so guilty and ashamed. When, or how, will this all end?

I hear a screech of brakes and look out of the window. My heart nearly stops beating. There, slamming the car door behind her, is the love of my life. Her gorgeous hair is tumbling all over her shoulders. I open the door and she barges in, pushes past me, and makes for a hardback chair by the window. I come in and stand near her, not knowing what's coming next.

"I've seen her, Andrew!"

"I know."

"I mean today."

"Today?" I can't believe my ears.

"Yes. And she's genuine."

"How do you know?" I retort. "You can't judge by one or two meetings with the woman."

"Yes, I can. I tested her out and she passed with flying colors."

"OK, she's genuine," I concede. "So what? She's still my *ex*-wife who tried to ruin my life. Thanks to you, she didn't succeed in the end, at least not yet. And another thing—why didn't she transform herself ten years ago? I'll tell you why!" I'm raising my voice now for I see Cherry is about to interrupt. "God wanted you to be my wife, that's why," I conclude, conscious that my words are bouncing back to me.

"Then why did He allow Mary to step into our lives six days before we get married?" she wants to know.

"To see if we are strong enough to go ahead and do what's right?" I venture, conscious that she can easily refute that one if she wants to.

To my surprise, Cherry says nothing. Instead, she puts her head in her hands and weeps uncontrollably. Of course I put my arms around her, but she shakes me off.

"No," she protests, raising tear-filled eyes to mine. "It's no use, Andrew. You can twist Providence one way. I can twist it another. But it won't make any difference. Mary's back. She's genuine and she still loves you, and she loves without any demands. She loves because she can't help loving."

Cherry lays her head on the nearby table and weeps as if her heart will break. I suppose it's already broken, though. Mine certainly is. I have to step closer in order to catch her words. "I have no other option but to cancel the wedding. I...."

I lose it now. I grab her; I'm kissing her passionately—lips, cheeks, hair. "I'll never let you go," I murmur. "Never! If you run away, I'll follow you to the ends of the earth. I can't live without you!"

The passion and desperation in my tone scares her. I'm scared too. I seem careening out of control like a high-powered car in the hands of a madman! She tries to escape my clasp, but I hold her in an iron grip and raise her face till she's looking into my eyes. I speak a little calmer now. "Listen," I mutter, "can you really imagine that I'll go back to Mary now? Can you think that her coming makes one iota of difference to me?"

"But she's more suited, Andrew. She'll make a wonderful priest's wife. And she's the mother of your children."

"Stop it!" I yell, interrupting her words with kisses. "If you leave me now, I'll give up St. Asaph's forever! I can't live without you. And I could never ever face living with Mary again no matter how much she has changed. She's killed something in me forever."

Cherry looks into my eyes, and I see that she believes me. I press my advantage. "Do you think it is God's will to ruin my ministry? Do you think He's brought us together, blessed us so abundantly, only to thrust us apart so cruelly at the last minute. Think carefully, darling; it's just not like the God I know."

She says nothing for a long time. Then her head droops onto my shoulder. She stands there, passive in my arms. I hold her tight. She makes no resistance, and I think that the battle is won. Then she raises her eyes to mine and struggles to speak.

"It may be like God or it may not be," she whispers. "I don't know anything right now except that you overcome me, Andrew. What I do is up to you! Your passion is too much for me. I'm no match for it."

"I've won!" is my first thought. I clasp her tighter. She makes no resistance. But as I look down into her face and see her eyes are closed and her lips are moving.

I bend down and catch her words, or think I do. "Forgive me, God!" she's murmuring. "Please forgive me!"

Suddenly I come to my senses. This girl in my arms is praying for forgiveness and all because of me. How can we begin a secure marriage on the shroud of her violated conscience? I slowly, very slowly, release her, take her arm, and set her in the nearest chair.

"Thanks, Andrew," she murmurs. Her head is still drooping, but I sense that strength is beginning to return to her body. I fold my arms tight so that I won't throw them around her again, and say just two words, "Explain yourself." They sound abrupt, even cruel, but they're all I can manage.

She gives a very faint smile, takes a gulp of air, and begins slowly and hesitantly, "I'm so terribly sorry, Andrew. But I can't marry you. It's how I think; it's how I've been programmed. I'm angry at myself; I'm angry at my dad for bringing me up this way. But I have no other choice."

Our eyes lock. For what seems an eternity, we stand motionless, knowing that our destinies hang in the balance, hang on me, I should say. I've fought many battles in life but none so terrible as the one I fight now. And yet, I have no choice but to win. Cherry's training has led her to her decision. Mine leave me no alternative but to say in a voice that I hardly recognize as mine: "I accept your choice, Cherry."

That's all I say. That's all I need to say. My words seem to be like an electric current that propels her towards the door. I'm after her, but she is too quick for me.

"Tell your family I'm dreadfully sorry," she pants. Then she jumps in her car and is gone. I watch till she disappears from sight and I know she's gone forever. I throw myself on the floor and weep for hours. God may be with me, but I certainly don't feel Him. All I'm conscious of is a dark despair creeping over me until it reaches my heart. My tears stop flowing. I stumble to bed and stay there until my mother arrives at eleven the next morning and makes me get up.

She brings me a cup of strong coffee. I can't face anything else. And then she talks—slowly, calmly, reasonably. I know, though, that she's terribly upset. I can hear it in her voice when she phones Cherry and insists on seeing her. I see it in her distraught face when she returns late afternoon and throws herself into the recliner.

"Why did you fall in love with that redheaded angel?" she asks me abruptly.

"'Why has my angel left me in hell?' you should be asking," I reply caustically.

Mom's face changes and her voice softens. "Maybe she's really just pointing the way to Heaven, Andrew," she suggests gently. "At least, let's look at it like that."

I feel Mom's arms around me. She stays with me for the next five days. Then, on the day when I should have left for Colorado with my beautiful bride, I board the plane and go to the Rockies on my own, go over my childhood haunts once more, imagine what it might have been like with my one and only love, and then I return a broken man. I hand in my resignation to the Bishop, stumble through four more weeks at St. Asaph's, tell my kids they're free to contact their mother, and then head for God knows where. First stop is Alaska. And after that? What does it matter! Oh yes, I'll come round in the end. I have to. I'm a Christian still. I don't blame God. I don't blame Cherry. And I don't even blame Mary any more. Or do I? I struggle for weeks to forgive her and finally give up. I'll have to in time, but it's too soon, far too soon.

I leave Alaska and return to Indiana but not to St. Asaph's. I can't face ministering to people ever again. But then, I can't face anything except the moment in which I am now living. And that, I suppose, is a sort of grace, isn't it? After all, I haven't committed suicide, though I felt like it several times. I haven't abandoned the faith either, though I came near doing so. I still have my kids. Gloria needs me especially. Peter is over the moon that his mom is back on the scene, but my daughter is devastated, at least temporarily so. Her dreams of a new mother have been shattered, and she needs me.

And Cherry? I've heard that she's planning on attending medical school next year. She's going to be a doctor. She never goes home. Madeline says she can't forgive her parents. I pray for her every day without fail. I think I'll always love her till the day I die. I wonder if her love is like that. Or will she eventually go to Africa, marry that Angus fellow, and live happily ever after?

No, I haven't seen Mary. I still try to forgive her, but I'm not God. I can't forget what she's done to me, to Cherry, and to my kids. For weeks I can't pray and then, slowly, as a child learning to walk, I stumble my way back to His throne and lie before Him, prostrate. I've been an idolater. I've put the creature before the Creator. My sin is great. Word's don't come but God doesn't need words to know that I'm throwing myself on His mercy. It is the lifeline that will eventually bring me into the light again. There has to be a light at the end of the tunnel, doesn't there?

Chapter Thirty-Seven

Dennis: Please, Lord, give me back my daughter!

I let the receiver fall from my hands. I can't believe my ears. The wedding has been canceled! Our prayers have been answered! Our daughter has been saved from disaster!

"What is it, Dennis?" Rachel asks, coming into the kitchen.

I place the receiver in its cradle and run towards her. Tears are streaming down my cheeks. "There will be no wedding this Saturday!" I exclaim. "God has heard our prayers."

We stand, locked in each other's arms, for a very long time. Then my wife raises her face to mine. She's crying, too. Suddenly, she pulls away and flops into a chair. "But Cherry!" she moans. "Oh, my poor child! She'll be devastated."

"But she had the courage to do what was right," I say exultantly. "Just think, Rachel, our teaching stood by her in the end."

"But what a blow to Andrew!" my wife moans. "And...."

I go up to her and grab her hand. "What on earth are you saying?" I ask heatedly. "Here we've prayed for months for this to happen and when it has, your sympathies are with...."

My wife bursts into a flood of weeping. Of course I comfort her, and soon she is telling me that she knows it's for the best, only she is human and can't help feeling for her daughter. As she speaks, I reach for the phone and begin to dial my Cherry's number.

"Don't!" Rachel cries out. "Don't call her right now!"

"But why?" I want to know. "She needs us now more than ever, doesn't she?"

"But wait until she tells us herself," Rachel begs. "She confided in her brother, but not in us." But it's too late. Cherry has already picked up the phone.

"Yes, Dad?" Her voice is cold, abrupt.

"I want you to know how...."

"How glad you are that I did the noble thing?" Cherry explodes. "That I am, after all, a chip off the old block, that I have not turned my back on my upbringing, that I've had the courage to do what is right?" I try to interrupt but it's no use. "No, I'm not getting married," she goes on, her words tumbling over each other. "Well, your prayers may have been answered, but in the process, you've lost a daughter. Good-bye, Dad. And please, don't call again."

The line goes dead. Rachel sees my expression of shock and rushes to me. I put my head on her shoulder, something I rarely ever do. She strokes my hair and murmurs, "Now then, Dennis. Give her time!"

"But how much?" I sob. "I'm getting old, Rachel. How much time can we afford?"

"Remember reading the other day, 'My times are in Thy hand'?" she asks in her gentle way.

I nod. "Well then, let's just leave them there. God has answered one prayer. Now let's thank Him and ask Him...." She stops. She can't go on.

We kneel together on the tiled floor of our farmhouse kitchen. The kettle is singing on the stove but we let it sing. I hear our farmhand outside the window and know it's milking time. But still we kneel in silent prayer. At last I rise and go outside.

"Is answered prayer always so enigmatic?" I ask myself as I enter the milking parlor and reach for my overalls.

And then it strikes me. Cherry blames me for the breakup of her marriage! She blames me for having power in prayer. She blames me for her broken heart. And what I consider as a glorious victory for truth and virtue, she regards as one more piece of evidence that she is, in the truest and most negative sense of the word—"her father's daughter!"

I watch the containers fill with milk. What will it take to bring her back into the fold? "Do it, whatever it takes, Lord!" I cry as I walk back to the house. "But please, give me back my daughter."

Chapter Thirty-Eight

Angus: I won't ever be your daughter!

Rhoda Mkandawire was buried four weeks ago today. That means that I've lost two mothers in a couple of years. That's a lot for a lone bachelor to bear. I feel orphaned all over again. This time, though, I'm not the only one who's grieving. Young Joy is nearly eating her heart out. And comforting someone else, makes my grief easier to bear. And that's what I'm doing, this sultry evening in late January.

"I miss her so much," Joy says suddenly, putting her head on my shoulder. We are sitting on her grandmother's porch trying to adjust to life without the loving, gracious woman who had become so central to both of our lives. I have another housekeeper now who is also Joy's companion at nights. Her name is Sarah. She's a good cook, but a terrible gossip. I'm glad she's taken the day off. We could never share our grief like this with her around.

I pat Joy's hand affectionately. "But think how happy she is," I remind her gently. "Remember the funeral? It was more like a wedding, wasn't it?"

She nods. "That's the way she wanted it to be," she says through her tears.

"Yes. And she would want us to go on with life, too, Joy."

"It's hard," the girl mutters. "I can't face a new school next week. I just can't, Uncle Angus."

I watch as the fireflies dart around us and say nothing. "Do I have to go?" she asks. She's clinging to me now as if I were the only thing she has left in the whole world. Her large black eyes meet mine. Rhoda practically insisted that I become Joy's guardian. After all, she only has me now, only me!

"Yes," I reply firmly. "Of course you do. You'll get nowhere without a high school diploma, Joy. You know that. And you'll love being at boarding school," I say, much more confidently than I feel. I've wanted her to go to Mpongo Girls' School for years but Rhoda couldn't bear to have her even that far away. Now I don't see any alternative.

"I suppose I'll have to go," she admits reluctantly, "but what will you do without me?"

"I'll muddle along," I reply smiling. "And I'll visit you regularly."

"How regularly?"

I think a moment. "Once every two weeks?" I suggest.

Her lip drops and tears fill her eyes. "Two weeks is a very long time, Uncle Angus. And no one else will visit me but you."

I stroke her long glossy hair and think what a beautiful daughter God has given me. I don't think I could love this girl more if she were my biological child. "Then I'll come every week," I tell her. After all, an hour's drive each way is nothing out here in Africa.

"Thank you!" she says smiling.

Joy has a beautiful smile, something like Cherry's, actually. I told her that once and she started to cry. "I'm not a bit like her," she had protested, "but I'm trying hard to be," she had added wistfully.

"Just be yourself," I had advised her. "I love you for who you are, you know."

That made her cry, strangely enough, but then, I'm discovering that women are the strangest, most enigmatical creatures on earth. And I suppose, taking care of Joy without Rhoda to guide us both will be the biggest challenge I've faced yet. When I returned from the States, her grandmother told me she was getting more and more difficult to control. But I haven't found her that way at all. Everyone here says she's like a different girl now I'm back.

I study her again as she thumbs through the Bible lying on her lap. How on earth am I to keep my word to Rhoda without a woman to help me? Then a thought strikes me. But maybe being her guardian isn't the way to go. I've often thought I'd adopt her if anything ever happened to Rhoda. And now it has...so? I can't help thinking that's what her grandmother would really have preferred, adoption, I mean.

"I've just thought of a wonderful idea," I say suddenly. "I'm thinking that being your guardian may not be enough, Joy."

She gives a start. "What do you mean, Uncle Angus?"

"Well, we're like father and daughter anyway, so why don't I adopt you?"

I don't know what I'd expected—a "Whoopee!" or "That's great!" or something like that. Instead her lips go into that pout she puts on when she's not pleased with something I've said. I frown as she draws away from me and stands to her feet.

"Please, never talk about adoption again, Uncle Angus," she pleads, her eyes looking so pathetic I can't stand it.

"But why not?" I ask, totally puzzled. "I thought you always wanted this—to feel you had a real father, I mean."

Joy flops back down beside me and buries her head in my chest. "I did," she mutters through her tears. "I did want this and I still do."

I lift her face so her eyes are looking into mine. "Then what's the problem?" I ask, now totally at sea.

She clings to me as if she never means to let me go. "I do want a father," she mutters, "but I don't want you to be that father. Never ever! And I'll never be your daughter!"

Now it's my turn to be hurt. I push her gently away and rise to my feet. "I just don't understand you, Joy. I thought this is what you wanted more than anything else. You'd better do some explaining and do it now!"

She sees I'm really upset and grabs my hand. "Just become my guardian, Uncle Angus," she pleads. "I can't explain now or maybe ever. Though," she adds, looking up at me through her long eyelashes, "I think one day quite soon you'll understand yourself, without my explaining."

I put my hand to my head. It's throbbing something awful. Why on earth did Rhoda have to go to Heaven before this granddaughter of hers was at least eighteen? Then a thought strikes me. "Don't you think your grandmother would have wanted me to adopt you?" I ask, pretty sure what the answer will be.

Joy sits bolt upright. "She never discussed it with me in the open," she admits, "but from hints now and then, I'm absolutely sure she wouldn't have wanted you to become my official father, Uncle Angus."

Her words stab me like swords. Some gratitude! Then it dawns on me that the dear old soul probably thought it would be too much of a responsibility for me. Being a guardian was only to last until the girl was eighteen. Being a father would be, well, the job of a lifetime. Joy probably thinks that way, too.

"I think I understand, Joy," I assure her, smiling. "Now, let's have a drink of good English tea."

But Joy is not smiling. "I don't think you understand at all, Uncle Angus," she says mournfully. Then she brightens. "But someday, maybe quite soon, I'm sure you will."

That sets me thinking again. If I'm to survive the coming three years, I'm going to have to take a lot of what this young lady says with a pinch of salt. After all, she's only fifteen, and just lost the dearest person on earth to her. She's emotionally upset a lot of the time these days. So I only mutter as I put the teakettle on to boil, "I think I understand already. But who knows? You women are a real puzzle to old bachelors like me."

"Good!" she exclaims, her eyes dancing. "I like being a puzzle. It's great fun!"

Mood swing again! I give a sigh and settle down to sip my tea.

The next day, I take a trip to Lilongwe, the capital of the North, and make myself the legal guardian of Joy Maria Mkandawire. The guardianship is to end at age eighteen, a little too soon, I think to myself, but that's what her grandmother wanted. I'm still to keep an eye on her until she's twenty-one, which sounds sensible.

The night before Joy begins her new school, I bring up the subject of Guy Stanton. Reg had mentioned to me soon after I got back from the States that he caught them kissing and cuddling about a week before I returned to Africa. I find that hard to believe. Joy hardly looks at Guy or any other boy, though they look plenty at her. Unless she's doing it behind my back. I find that hard to believe. Still, I promised him I would talk to her about it. But then Rhoda got worse and the doctor told me she had only a few months to live, so that put everything else out of my head. I'll have to keep my promise though, especially now that I am officially responsible for the girl.

We are sitting opposite each other at the kitchen table. "You're nearly a woman now, Joy, and changing fast," I begin, wishing I didn't sound so much like a preacher.

"I'm glad you've discovered that at last, Uncle Angus," Joy comments coyly, fluttering her eyelashes at me as she does quite often these days. If I didn't know her so well, I'd think she was actually flirting with me sometimes.

I clear my throat. She's certainly not making it easy for me. "I've been away two years, and have lost touch with a lot of things," I begin slowly, ignoring her comment. "Is there anything I need to know about you so that I can be sure we're on the same page?"

"We already are, Uncle Angus," she replies quickly.

"Well, we ought to be. We've been through a lot together. But to keep up a good relationship, Joy, we need to be open with each other."

Joy can't meet my eye. "What do you want to know?" she mutters. Then she tosses back her long hair and changes her question. "I mean, what do you know already?"

I see that she's got the message. "When I came back from America four months ago," I begin, "Mr. Stanton told me he had caught you and his son together. Is that right?"

"Yes, but you know that Guy and I have been friends for years." She still won't meet my eye.

"I know, but according to Reg Stanton, you were kissing each other and not exactly like...." My face is burning. I don't like this part of being a guardian. It's horrible!

Joy's face changes. "We were kissing like boyfriend and girlfriend kiss, Uncle Angus, if that's what you're trying to say," she admits defiantly.

"Not in my world, they don't," I retort, angry now. "Christians don't do like others, Joy. You know that!"

Joy tosses her head again. "But Guy Stanton kisses lots of girls!" she informs me. "And he's a missionary's son!"

"He's no model to go by, Joy, and you know that!" I remonstrate. We're getting nowhere fast.

"He says he can't resist me," she goes on in a tone I definitely don't like. "And I'm the only non-white girl he's kissed," she says proudly. "He told me so himself. That's why his dad was so mad."

I'm furious now. "He had every right to be mad," I retort. Then I see her expression and add quickly, "not because you're not white but because you're so young, Joy, and from what Reg hinted, you were doing more than kissing. I'm just glad nothing more happened."

The defiance is gone from her face now. She hangs her head and I see tears falling onto her clasped hands. "I'm glad, too," she whispers. "And I'll never do it again, Uncle Angus. I promise."

My heart softens. Her tears always have that affect on me. Problem is, she knows it only too well.

"I don't mind you being friendly with boys," I go on gently, "or even inviting them to my house where I can act as chaperone. And maybe...."

"You don't need to chaperone me," she sobs. "Now you're back, I'll not let any boy kiss me or cuddle me again." I reach for a Kleenex and hand it to her. "I've almost given up trying to be like *her*," she murmurs.

I don't have to ask who "her" is. "You are not Cherry, or ever will be," I remind her, "but you are equally important to God." I pause, "and to me."

"Really?" Her eyes tell me she can't believe my words.

"Yes, though in a different way, of course. But to get back to Guy Stanton. What kind of a relationship do you have with him, Joy?"

"None, now."

"But before?"

"Well," she stammers, "he's liked me since I was about ten and used to hang around me whenever he was home from boarding school. Then the last year or two, we have snuck out once or twice and went for walks and things like that."

I'm not really sure what "things like that" might mean, but feel I have asked enough questions for one day. "But since you came home four months ago, I made up my mind I'd stop chasing boys," she goes on quickly.

"You don't need to chase them," I say dryly. "They flock round you like bees to honey. But I take your word for it, Joy. And as I said, liking a boy is not a sin so if you...."

She shakes her head vehemently. "No, Uncle Angus. I'm going to study hard and forget boys. It's just that I was so lonely when you were away. Grandma was wonderful but spent most of her time singing hymns and praying and she kept to herself a lot, and so I got bored. But now I have you. You love me and don't think of what color I am. Boys do— both black and white."

There it is again—color prejudice! "I know it's hard, Joy. But some day, someone just like you, someone who can understand and share your problems, will come along," I say reassuringly, "someone who...."

She jumps to her feet and comes over to where I'm sitting. "Don't you ever say that again," she explodes. "Promise me, Uncle Angus? Never ever?"

Why oh why did Rhoda put me in this situation! What on earth has come over the girl? Now if only I had a wife.

"If I ever marry, it's going to be a white man!" she begins again, not waiting for my answer. "Not someone like me. I decided that ages ago."

Now, somehow, that bothers me a lot. Joy sees my confusion and adds softly, "It's all right, Uncle Angus. I'm far too young to think about that. And right now, I'm trying hard to be good, I really am."

I hardly hear her last sentence. The words, "It's going to be a white man," hammer at my consciousness and I wish for the thousandth time that God had made us all one color. America, Africa—it makes no difference—I can't get away from racial barriers. Then I look at the girl I'm responsible for and say slowly, "I really miss your grandmother, Joy." Somehow, thinking of Rhoda makes things seem right again.

"Me, too," she whispers.

Chapter Thirty-Nine

Cherry: Tell me who I am, Dad!

My luggage is packed and I'm ready to board the plane for London first thing tomorrow morning. Oh dear, there's someone at the door. I peek out the window and my heart reaches my mouth. It's my mom and dad! I haven't seen them or spoken to them for eighteen months at least. I feel sick as I go to open the door, and yet I feel glad. I need to get some things out of my system once and for all.

I open the door and my mother falls into my arms. She's lost weight and looks a lot older—all my fault, I tell myself, as I let her stroke my hair as she always used to do and mutter, "Oh my girl! My dear girl! How I've longed for this moment."

I look over her head and see Dad smiling at me. I cringe and then hate myself for doing so. How many times I've longed to see his smile and yet now I would rather he yell at me, tell me I've broken their hearts, anything but smile. He still makes me feel so terribly guilty.

Dad gives me a hug which I barely return, and then we all sit down and talk about sweet nothings until, at last, Mom turns to me and asks reproachfully, "Do you really have to leave us like this, Cherry?"

"Leave you?" I repeat. "You told me to go nearly two years ago. Remember?" I know that wasn't quite fair, as they have repeatedly invited me home since I broke it off with Andrew and I have refused every time. I see the look in her face and add hastily, "I'm leaving the States because I want to start all over again, Mom."

"But you can do that here," Dad butts in. "And we'll help you all we can to find your feet. It's only normal that you're reacting to all that has happened. You've been through an awful lot, Cherry."

"You were praying that I wouldn't marry Andrew, weren't you, Dad?" I ask abruptly.

"Yes, of course we were and...."

"Don't say it," I interrupt. "Don't tell me it's all an answer to your prayer. Maybe it was and maybe it wasn't. I'm confused. That's why I'm going to England. I need to find out what I believe and what I don't.

Right now, I'm my father's daughter, but Cherry McMann? Tell me please, somebody, who exactly is she?"

My parents stare at me in consternation. "And," I go on, determined to get it out of my system, "I admit I'm bitter as well, but hopefully, that will pass with time and I'll be able to come back home and behave as a normal daughter should."

Mom is weeping and I long to throw myself into her arms again. I'm sad and sorry and angry—all in one. I'm not at all sure what's going to happen next. Then the phone rings. It's my brother.

"Mom and Dad are here," I tell him. "Want to speak to them?"

"In a minute," he says. "But I want to say good-bye first and tell you some wonderful news."

"Oh," I ask. "And what news can that be?"

"Allie and I have just gotten engaged."

"Allie!" I gasp.

"Yes, Allie," he repeats. "You saw us together that night in the church, didn't you?"

"Yes, Paul, but to get engaged? And to her!"

"What's wrong with her?"

I sense that my parents are listening intently. "Let's not argue," I tell him. "I really do hope you are happy. You do love her, don't you?"

I could tell my brother was angry now. "Love her!" he repeats hotly. "Why on earth does a guy get engaged if he doesn't love the girl?"

"You're not answering me," I counter.

"Give me the phone, Cherry," Dad orders, coming up behind me. I go to protest. After all, it is *my* house and I am of age now. But then I change my mind and hand him the receiver.

"Congratulations, Paul!" I hear the joy in Dad's voice and cringe for the second time in half an hour. "It's an answer to our prayers!"

My stomach churns. I turn to Mom and whisper, "Did Dad have a hand in this, in Paul and Allie getting together, I mean?"

Mom hesitates a moment and then whispers, "Yes, he did a bit. But that's only natural, Cherry. He wants the best for both of you."

I rise from my seat. I'm angry now and Mom knows it. "This is serious, Mom."

"What is serious?" Dad has put the receiver in its place and walks towards me.

I gulp. "Paul's engagement, Dad."

"Of course it's serious," he agrees. "All engagements should be. But this is good news, Cherry. Paul has at last found...."

"Listen," I interrupt. "For once, listen to me, Dad," I beg. "I don't think either Paul or you know what Allie can be like at times. I've lived with her for a whole year. I know her inside out, or nearly." I'm practically shaking now. I've just got to make my parents understand.

"Calm down!" he commands as he leads me back to the sofa and pulls me down beside him. "Your nerves are on edge."

"Leave me out of it," I plead. "And please, listen to me! Allie has serious problems. She wasn't easy to live with."

"Neither were you," he counters, his eyes flashing.

I want to defend myself, but now is not the time. "Maybe I wasn't," I admit, "but Paul isn't marrying me. I'm almost sure this marriage won't work out, Dad. Allie is...." I stop mid-sentence, remembering my promise years ago. But what did I promise? To keep quiet about her problem if she agreed to get medical help? And she hasn't, as far as I know. And if this whole affair ends in some sort of tragedy, I'll never forgive myself for not speaking out.

My parents are waiting for me to go on. I take a gulp and say quietly, "When I lived with Allie, she was having dreadful mood swings. I am almost sure she is bi-polar."

"She can't be!" Mom gasps. "Not Allie Jordan!"

"And if she is, then why haven't we heard about it before now?" Dad wants to know. "If you were so concerned about it, shouldn't you at least have mentioned it to us so that we could pray about it?"

"Allie made me promise I wouldn't tell anyone. I told her I wouldn't as long as she got medical help."

"Well, she probably has," Dad interrupts. "She acts perfectly normal to me."

"You haven't lived with her. I've got to tell Paul, Dad." It's my turn to interrupt. Madeline will be home any moment now, and I've no time to lose.

"Let Allie do it herself, Cherry. Keep out of this, please. Besides," he goes on, "God told me she was the one for Paul. And I've never been mistaken when He speaks clearly to me, Cherry. Never!"

I shake my head in frustration. "That's between God and you, Dad," I tell him, my voice rising, "but I have a responsibility to Paul. He is my brother, you know!"

Perhaps it's fortunate for all of us that we hear a car door slam shut. I run to the window and look out. Yes, I thought so. Madeline has just driven up. What on earth will she think of this news?

Mom and Dad rise to leave. "Take care of yourself!" Dad whispers as he gives me a hug. "I still wish you wouldn't go."

"I've got to," I whisper back, "for all of our sakes. And, Dad, if you promise to tell Paul what I've said, then I won't say anything."

"I can't promise, Cherry," he says firmly, as he releases me and I turn to Mom.

"Then I'll have to," I say brokenly. I feel Mom's arms around me. She is sobbing now. We stand, and let our tears mingle while Dad waits impatiently at the door. In a few moments they are gone and I'm left alone with Madi.

"Paul's gotten engaged," I tell her as we prepare to go to bed.

I will never forget the look on her face as my words sink in. Madi has changed a lot lately. She goes to mass nearly every morning before work. I see her lips move. I'm sure she's praying. She does that often now. I watch as she crosses herself. Then she turns and goes into her bedroom and shuts the door. I go into mine and do the same, wondering if I should cancel my plans. But I can't. I've been accepted at Guy's in London to train as a doctor and I'm scheduled to begin next week.

I give a sigh. I didn't want my last night in America to turn out like this. I reach for the phone.

"Paul?"

"Yes?" His tonc is abrupt.

"About Allie, Paul."

"What about her?"

"I've lived with her and you haven't. And I need to tell you something very serious, Paul."

"That she's demanding, and a perfectionist? I know that already, Sis."

"It's more than that, Paul. She has terrible mood swings. I'm almost sure she's bi-polar."

I hear a short laugh at the other end. "I know you've never liked Allie. She's been terribly hurt by the way you've treated her."

I grip the receiver tighter. "Listen to me, Paul, please, for just one minute," I plead.

"I can't, Sis. I won't let you poison my mind. Besides, I've dated her for months. I'd have known before now if she had a serious problem. She'd have shared it with me."

"No, she wouldn't," I shout into the phone. "She's keeping it all a secret."

A long pause on the other end and then my brother asks in a very different tone, "So she's been diagnosed? You have proof of all this, Cherry?"

"I've proof enough, Paul. Her mood changes were terribly frightening. But she refused to go to the doctor."

"It's just as I thought, Sis. It's that fertile imagination of yours working overtime. And, anyway, what's the big deal? I know several friends of mine who are bi-polar and they lead pretty normal lives. Modern medication is pretty effective."

"Yes, but I'm afraid she won't be easy to treat, Paul. Apart from her mood swings, she's very difficult to live with."

"That's enough, Cherry. I'm able to cope with Allie. I feel pretty certain. Now, trust your big brother, won't you?"

"Then you'll ask her yourself?" I persist.

Paul does not answer for a long time and then I hear him say firmly, "I may or I may not. It'll make no difference. I've made up my mind, Sis."

"You mean Dad made it up for you!" I explode.

"Watch your words!" Paul warns. I know he's mad with me and I can't help but admire his self- control.

"But I can't go away without pleading with you to rethink the whole thing, Paul," I go on. Then I say something I know will be the beginning of the end between us but still, I have to do it.

"Madi still loves you Paul, and I'm almost sure you...."

"That phase of my life is over, Sis," he interrupts. "Now, aren't you going to wish me all the best?"

I can't stand the pathos in his voice. I know something's not right, but I've done all I know to do. Besides, I really do want the best for him and for Allie. "Of course, Paul," I say, my voice wavering as I speak. "I want the very best for both of you."

"That's all I need to hear," he assures me. "Now get some sleep. May God bless you as you begin a brand new life. Good-Night, little sister."

"Good-night, big brother."

I hear the receiver click. I climb into bed, turn off the light, but of course, I can't sleep. That's nothing new. For weeks after my wedding was canceled, I rarely slept at all. I lost pounds, hardly spoke to anyone, and was a pain to live with. Then, slowly, I re-entered the world I had wished to shun forever. As for Andrew, he's no longer in active ministry and looks years older. Gloria is still furious with me while Peter lauds me to the skies. What do I care! I did it, and that's that! As I told Dad, I seemed to have no choice in the matter.

I finally fall asleep as light is beginning to creep through the window above my bed. I dream that Paul and Allie are standing at the altar when Madi runs crying into the church. I brace myself for what will happen next and then my alarm rings. I reach over and switch it off, glad that at last this interminable night is over.

For the next few hours it is all go, but at last my luggage is in the car, and we're off to O'Hare. At first, Madi and I are silent, each absorbed in her own thoughts, which judging by our faces, are not very happy ones. Eventually, we begin to talk about my future, her future, and about our past. And then I pluck up courage and suggest that she follows me to London when she's able. With her qualifications, I tell her, I'm sure she'll get a good job anywhere.

It's then that she drops the bombshell, just as we're approaching the drop off area outside "Departures."

"I'm becoming a nun, Cherry," she says quietly as she brakes to a halt.

"You're what?" I gasp. I know we have no time to talk now. But as we give each other a final hug I manage to ask, "Why on earth are you doing this, Madi? Is it because of Paul?"

Madi's blue eyes are shining. I look at her in wonder. "No," she whispers as she releases me. "It's because of God!"

Part Three. Three Years Later.

Chapter Forty

Dennis: Good advice?

"Allie just threatened suicide, Dad!"

"Again?" I give a sigh and wait for Paul's reply.

"Yes, again. I know what you're thinking, but one of these days it'll be serious."

My son is probably right, although I also know that this wife of his will do anything for attention. "Bring her down for the weekend," I suggest. "I'll pray with her and with you, too, Paul. Are things still as bad as ever between you?"

"Yes, every bit as bad. But as for coming down, it won't work, Dad. You just aggravate the situation."

Now that hurts, not that there isn't some truth in it. I find it impossible to hear them fighting over anything and everything without intervening. Sometimes I have twinges of conscience over Paul's marriage, especially when I remember how Cherry tried to warn us about Allie before she left for England three years ago.

I'm still mulling over Paul's phone call as we eat supper half an hour later, just the two of us—Rachel and I. She's dreadfully upset over Paul's news. "Something has to be done," she says in her quiet way, "and done immediately."

"Such as?" I want to know.

"Counseling, Dennis. They both need a good Christian counselor."

"But they have us," I protest. "I've no use for counselors."

"Or medication," Rachel puts in dryly.

"Allie refused to take her medicine, Rachel. You know that."

"I also know what you advised her, Dennis," she answers quietly.

I wince. My wife has a knack these days of hitting the mark with uncanny accuracy. Six months after her marriage, Allie was diagnosed as bi-polar. She only took her medicine for several months. "Too many side effects," she told us. And then I...well, what did I do, really and truly? Advise her to trust the Lord? Of course! Good advice, wasn't it? Only it hasn't helped, has it?

I feel Rachel's hand on mine. "Look, dear. Let's face it." Her gentle voice soothes me as it always does. "Even if Allie had been perfectly normal, this marriage would have had serious problems. She insists that Paul doesn't really love her and it's eating her up."

"And doesn't he?"

Rachel gives a long sigh. "I think he does love her, Dennis, but not in the way she expects and needs. And I think you know why."

I shrug. "Many a man has loved a woman and gotten over it. He needs to forget that Cummings girl."

"He's trying, Dennis. As I say, both he and Allie need counseling."

I squirm uneasily in my chair. "They need prayer, that's what they need," I say firmly as I rise from the table. "Now, I'm off to the milking parlor."

That night, neither of us sleeps well. For the first time in years, I'm tempted to blame myself for Paul's marriage. I *did* interfere. I *did* tell him God wanted him to marry Allie. And I'm *still* interfering. So if I was wrong about Allie, then what about Madeline and Cherry and Andrew? And what about the fellowship and a hundred and one other things I've been so sure about?

I slip out of bed and drop to my knees. I have to stop questioning myself. God *did* lead me. I *did* hear His voice. It's my children who are wrong. They need to get right with God. And I need to do some fasting and praying for Allie, for Paul, and for Cherry—my precious Cherry whom I haven't seen in three years. God will hear me in the end, won't He? I've served Him for forty years. I know His voice. He knows mine.

"Come back to bed, Dennis." I hear concern in my wife's tone. "You know what the doctor said."

"Yes, I know," I grumble as I get up from my knees. "I need more sleep, more rest, more relaxation."

I feel her lips on my forehead. "I love you, Dennis," she says softly.

I smile into the darkness. With her love, and God's love, what more does an old man need!

Chapter Forty-One

Cherry: A prodigal daughter's love.

The phone rings in my small bedsitter, tucked away in the back streets of a London suburb. I can see from the caller ID that it's an overseas call. I pick up the receiver expecting to hear Dad's bass voice saying, as if he said it every day instead of only a few times a year: "Hi, Cherry, it's your father speaking." But no, it's my quiet little mother who's calling.

"Cherry?" Her voice is high-pitched and strained. I glance at my watch. It is eight a.m. British time, three a.m. Eastern Standard Time. It must be something extraordinary to make Mom phone in the middle of the night.

"Yes, it's me, Mom," I assure her after a moment's pause. "Is anything wrong?"

I hear a sob at the other end of the line. "Yes, a lot's wrong. Allie committed suicide last night."

My sister-in-law dead at thirty-two! I cannot believe what I'm hearing! "I'm so sorry!" is all I can manage, and then silence. I might have blurted out, "I told you so," but what good would that do? I have never been at peace about my brother's marriage and felt guilty more than once that I didn't go to his wedding even though it was in the middle of my exams. But death by suicide? How could I ever have been prepared for this?

Mom manages through her sobs to tell me the story, not that there is much to tell—Allie ran away and her body was found in the river. No note left behind, nothing to explain the tragedy.

"Your father blames himself, Cherry," I hear Mother say, quietly. I give a start.

"Blames himself?" I repeat. "I don't understand."

"Yes. He.... Oh, I can't talk about it right now, dear. Just come home, please, as soon as you can."

"Come home?" I repeat without thinking. I hear Mom give another sob and I say quickly, "Of course, I'll come home."

"Good girl!" She gives a sigh of relief. "Your dad needs you."

Now if she had said, "Paul needs you," I could understand, but Dad? My self-sufficient, resourceful, holy father—needing me?

"He has had a complete nervous breakdown, Cherry," Mom goes on sadly. "I'm practically running the farm. He needs your support right now."

"But why do you think he needs my help in particular?"

"You're his favorite; you always were, you know."

The words blow me away. I know they're not true. They're a fond mother's conception of reality. "I feel terrible for Paul," I blurt out, changing the subject. "He must be in total shock."

"He is, and *he* needs you, too."

"I have exams in three weeks, but I'll be home for Christmas, Mom."

"Just come when you can. And Paul and Dad aren't the only ones who need you. I do too, Cherry. Everything's changed, terribly changed!"

The words sound pathetic, pleading, and they melt the tiny core of resistance that I've been clinging to in an automatic act of self-preservation, something I've built up over the years when interacting with my parents.

"I need you, too," I sob. And I do. Three years away from home—well four-and-a-half if you count my last eighteen months in the States—have been far too long. I have never realized that I've been so homesick until this moment. And when I am actually in the air some weeks later, I am still in a daze. Where is my bitterness now? Do I still blame my father for what has happened to me? I look out the plane window and wonder if the clouds swirling around me have an answer. I'm not quite sure what I feel, but I'm certain it's not bitterness. Gradually, over the past months, I've been finding out who I really am, and that's been some discovery!

We are descending now. In twenty minutes I will set foot on American soil once more! I love England, but this vast land—this land of enigmas, this United States, not quaint, historic, fascinating Great Britain—is where most of my history has been written.

My thoughts drift to St. Asaph's and to Andrew. My eyes still mist over when I think of him. Loving him made me a better woman, though it has taken a long time to come to that conclusion. At first, I spent useless hours reliving the past. What had I really felt towards Andrew? Had I really and truly loved him, or had it been a sort of idol worship? Or maybe I had simply been overcome by his personality, his touch, his kiss? My parents thought it was the infatuation of an over-grown schoolgirl. Were they right? Or had it been the real thing—a woman's love for the man of her choice? I still don't fully know the answer. What I do know is that whatever this love was or was not, it has propelled me into womanhood and altered my entire perspective on so many things.

What still worries me, though, is what all this has done to Andrew. I know from Peter that his father has never been the same since I disappeared from his life. He has retired into a cocoon where not even his children can truly reach him and is totally absorbed in his studies. Poor Andrew, he sounds a far-cry from the gracious, kindly priest who captured my heart six long years ago. Remorse seizes me for a moment as it often does when I think of my former fiancé. And then a picture of a gracious blonde with a smile that warms you from the inside out rises before me. I no longer blame Dad for my decision. I couldn't have done anything else after I met Mary.

And Madeline? Will I see her on this visit, I wonder? She writes now and then. She's no longer a novice but a fully-fledged nun. I was rather hoping she'd change her mind before she took her vows but that hasn't happened. I read between the lines that she had a real struggle, at first, to fit into convent life. No wonder! Madeline the nun is still a conundrum to me.

The plane skids to a halt; we're on the runway, at the hanger, in the terminal, at the luggage checkout, and then in an instant, I'm in Paul's arms. We hug each other just as we used to do in the days when he called me "Carrot Top" and tossed me up on my horse like a feather, then had me gallop at top speed after him around the paddock.

I clasp his arm as we make our way to the car, but don't say anything. I can't. Allie and I never hit it off that well, but I did get fond of her in an odd sort of way. The tears are raining down my cheeks faster than I can dry them. I search for another Kleenex as Paul heaves my case into the trunk. Soon we are speeding along the interstate. Neither of us says anything for a very long time. Paul is first to break the silence.

"Dad's not well," he begins slowly. "That's why he didn't come to meet you."

"Mom told me he's had a breakdown."

"Yes. He blames himself for my wife's death."

I nod. "Mom mentioned something about that, too, but she didn't go into details."

"Well, after your call the night before you left for England, I had a long talk with Allie about these mood swings she was having. She was furious with you and said you hated her and were grossly exaggerating. I agreed with her. And anyway, I reasoned that even if you were right, it made no difference. After all, true love isn't put off by something like that, is it?"

I look at him closely. His features are distorted with anguish. "Do you mind if we don't talk about this, right now," he mutters.

The sadness in his voice is harder to bear than bitterness would be. If my brother would rise up and shout to the world that it's all unfair, that he's been the victim of circumstances, that.... I catch myself and shut my lips tight. Haven't I learned that acceptance of what God has allowed into our lives is the best way after all?

We don't talk much until we stop halfway for gas. Then, suddenly, Paul begins to tell how Allie and he never really hit it off after their marriage. She began to have violent mood swings, just as I had described them.

"You were right after all," Paul tells me sadly. "We all should have listened. But, well, I had made up my mind at that point. And so had Dad. Allie was brilliant, successful, and seemed to have it all together. And," there was just a touch of bitterness now in my brother's voice, "she fit into our parents' idea of a good, upright, reliable girl." His voice trailed off into a sob.

I take his hand. "So she was diagnosed as bi-polar?"

Paul nods sadly. "Yes, but that was not the real problem. Others have managed to cope; it was her refusal to accept it. After a few months, she refused to take her medicine. The diagnosis was just too shocking, too humiliating," he admits. "Here she was, teaching music in a conservatory, performing in concerts in the city hall, dignified, sophisticated and a huge success wherever she went, only to discover that she was the victim of something she couldn't handle without strong medication, medication that had side effects that she claimed altered her personality."

"And then Dad urged her to trust the Lord alone, right?" I suggest. I'm going out on a bit of a limb here, but by the slight smile on my brother's worn face, I can tell that I have hit the mark.

"Right!" he admits. "It seems that on one visit home, Dad had a private talk with her, prayed for healing, and advised her not to listen to the rest of us and trust God instead of her medicine. Of course, this is what she was already doing so Dad's advice really made little difference to her. She always declared that the problem lay in the fact that I didn't love her as a husband should, and had nothing to do with her mental state. But Dad thinks it might have been so different if he hadn't interfered as he did."

I stare out the side window. It's beginning to snow. I shiver a little and Paul turns up the heat. "And that's not all," he goes on. "I might as well tell you, Cherry, Dad stepped in when I wanted to get back with Madi."

"You wanted to get back with Madi?" I repeat in surprise. This was news to me.

"Yes. When I would see her at church, I longed to have her in my arms again. I knew I loved her as I loved no one else. But Dad persuaded me that she would ruin my life spiritually. He reminded me of my calling to be a preacher, and then gradually saw to it that Allie was at our house whenever I was home on holidays. Then, one day, he told me plainly that God had revealed to him that Allison Jordon was the woman for me. This is also why he's so devastated now."

I say nothing. It's all too sad, too unbelievable. "Allie was so demanding," Paul goes on. I nod understandingly. "Everything had to be perfection—from clothes to husband. And when I would object just a little, she would chide me for not loving her as I had loved Madeline." It was hard for him to get the last word out. "So her mom is blaming me for her death, well, blaming Dad even more so."

I listen in silence, light dawning on me gradually. I begin to see the big picture and it scares me. I'm going home to face a father I do not know—a scared, frightened, disillusioned father, who seems to be the victim of his own sanctity.

"How on earth can I help him, Paul?" I ask in a whisper when he finishes his story.

Paul smiles for the first time since he picked me up at the airport hours ago. "Just be yourself, Sis," he whispers back.

"I hope I know what being myself is, Paul. It might not be what Dad thinks it is, or what I want it to be."

"Show him you forgive him, Cherry," he says quietly. "That is, if you do forgive him."

"I think I do," I mutter. "But when I see him, maybe all the bitterness will rush back."

He shakes his head. "No, I don't think so, Cherry. Not as he is now."

I am still thinking over Paul's words as we drive up the bumpy road to our farm. We come closer. Everything looks exactly the same as it did four years ago, well, not quite. The fences need painting, the lawn needs mowing, and even the cows stare at our car in a depressed, mournful sort of way as we jolt past them. Fanciful? Of course it is. I always was fanciful.

But it's certainly not fancy that makes me stop and gasp as we come closer and I see Mom and Dad standing on the front porch, awaiting our arrival. I know it's been a long time since I've seen them, but that doesn't explain why Mom has lost thirty pounds at least, or why Dad hardly has the strength to stumble towards me, his face haggard and white. But it's his eyes that haunt me for days afterwards. The fire has gone out of them.

I make up my mind, however, not to let them see how shocked I am. Instead, I hurl myself into their open arms. Of course, I cry. And they cry. And Paul cries. Then Mom takes a step back and eyes me up and down.

"What a woman you've become!" she exclaims proudly.

Dad says nothing. He just lets his eyes feast on my face as we enter the familiar kitchen, sit at the same old wooden table, and drink tea from the same large china mugs with Cherry, and Paul, and Dad, and Mom written on them in large, faded letters.

Dad's still looking at me with those haunted eyes of his hours later as we sit around the fire in the living room. He has hardly said a word since I came home. But when I hug him before going to bed, he clings to me for a very long time.

I still feel his tears on my cheek as I say my prayers and pull back the patchwork quilt that Mom made for my thirteenth birthday. In fact, I think I'll always feel those tears, a sort of token that no matter how tough the future might be for all of us, our sorrow has brought us together again. Well, I can't speak for Paul. He's not exactly bitter—not exactly remorseful—just shut up in a world of his own, a world where his dreams have become nightmares. I understand how he feels. I used to feel that way. I'm glad I don't anymore. And most of all, I'm glad I'm where I've longed to be for years, nestled deep in my father's broken heart. And as I fall asleep, I pray that God might give me the tools to help repair that heart. The only tool I know how to wield is love, a prodigal daughter's love—forgiving love, hopeful love, joyous love and best of all, healing love.

Chapter Forty-Two

Joy: Becoming eighteen.

"I wish I wasn't eighteen today," I blurt out suddenly.

"What did you just say, Joy?" Uncle Angus sounds shocked.

"I don't want to be eighteen, because I'll be all on my own now," I mutter. I feel the tears beginning to fall. "You won't be my guardian anymore. And I'll be lost without you." I'm really angry with myself for being such a crybaby. I've so looked forward to this day. I don't know what's come over me.

Angus reaches across the table and puts his hand on mine. He hasn't done that for a long time, not since Reg Stanton told him I was too old for him to do things like that—that I wasn't his daughter in the first place and that I'm a young woman now—that the whole mission station was gossiping about us and lots of other rubbish. But today we're celebrating my birthday miles away from Ngavi, just the two of us, at the one and only decent restaurant in Mpongo.

"I might not be your guardian now," Angus says smiling, "but I'm still to keep an eye on you till you're twenty-one. I'm not about to step out of your life, Joy, dear. Surely you know me better than that?"

His voice is so tender I just can't stand it. I know he loves me a lot. We don't have anyone else really, Uncle Angus and I—only each other. I've tried so hard these past three years to make him happy and I think I've succeeded. He smiles and laughs just like he used to before his mother died and before that redhead deserted him for some priest or other. And I've done my best not to show him my bad side. I don't flirt anymore. Well, that's not true. I flirt with Uncle Angus sometimes, and he doesn't even realize it. And I read my Bible every morning. I don't read much, maybe a chapter or two at the most, which is a whole lot for a girl like me. Then I kneel down and ask God to make me like *her!* I'm not sure if I look very different, but I think I feel more like an angel than I used to. Uncle Angus is so happy that I'm teaching Sunday school, playing the piano at church, and taking food parcels to poor families. To be honest, though, when he looked at me like he did just now, I don't feel at all like an angel should feel. I suppose it's how my mother felt, too. I worry about that a lot. What if I do something that shocks Uncle Angus and he decides never to love me again?

But I'm not going to think about that right now. Here we are, having a special celebration together, just the two of us. I feel even happier than I did last night at the party Reg Stanton organized for me in the church hall at Ngavi. Nearly everyone on the station came, plus some of my school friends. And Guy Stanton was there with his girlfriend from South Africa. He couldn't take his eyes off me, but then, he's always been like that. I suppose it makes his girl mad. Everyone said I was looking absolutely fabulous in the pale pink dress Angus bought me for my birthday. I was afraid that becoming eighteen might change everything between us. But I see it won't. I think it'll only get better and better.

"Daydreams?" Angus wants to know.

"Yes, wonderful ones!" I answer.

"Share them with me?"

"Someday!" I whisper. "Someday soon, Angus!"

He gives a start and then he smiles again, that special smile I saw just a few minutes ago. "Dropping the 'uncle,' now, right?"

"Right," I echo. "I've waited for this for a very long time. You agreed that I could do it when I was eighteen, remember?"

"You've waited for this for years?" he repeats, puzzled. I puzzle him all the time and I like it a lot. Then he begins to look very mysterious, like he always does when he's going to tell me something special.

"There's something we need to discuss, now you're of age," he begins. "Something I'm sure you'll be very pleased about."

My heart beats faster. Pleased about? There's only one thing that would please me more than sitting like this—alone with the very best man in the world—one thing I've dreamed about day and night ever since he came back from the States three years ago.

"It's about England," he announces.

"England?" I repeat. "What do you mean?"

"How would you like to go to England when you graduate next summer?" he suggests. "I know you've dreamed about that for years."

"That would be fabulous, Angus!" I exclaim. It seems too good to be true. "Will you take me to see Buckingham Palace, and the Changing of the Guards, and the Tower, and the London Museum?"

Angus holds up his hand. "Hold it, Joy. I didn't say I'd be coming this time. I'm talking about your education—maybe at Oxford."

"If you don't come with me, I'm not going anywhere," I pout. I know I'm very pretty when I pout so I do it a lot.

"Of course I'll be coming to England eventually," he says smiling. "Then we'll see all there is to see in London and wherever you want to go. But I can't go with you next summer. I'm opening the new agricultural school, remember? But the Buchannans will take you. And their home will be your home for as long as you're in England. I know you're very fond of them, Joy. It'll be next best to having me there, won't it?"

"I'm not going," I mutter sullenly. "I'm just not going." He's right. I am very fond of Rev. Buchannan and his wife. And I really enjoy going to their church when I'm at school in Mpongo. They've been awfully kind to me. I don't know how many times I've enjoyed Minnie Buchannan's wonderful Sunday dinners. But not them, not anyone, is going to take me away from my Angus.

I feel tears coming into my eyes again. Angus puts his hand under my chin so I'm looking into his face. "Now, Joy," he says in the tone he uses when he gives me a lecture, "let's get this straight. You can't cling to my coattails all your life. You have to think about the future. With your brain and determination, there's no reason why you can't get into the best university in England. It's the opportunity of a lifetime and it probably won't come your way again."

"But I'm eighteen now," I remind him when he's finished. "That means I can choose for myself, right?"

"Right," he agrees reluctantly.

"Then," I say, taking a deep breath, "I definitely choose not to go to England to be educated; I choose to stay here, in the bush; I choose to…well, to do something like Ruth did in the Bible." I pause for breath.

"Go on," he urges.

"Ruth made a pledge, didn't she, to go where Naomi went and to die where she died? You preached about it a few Sundays ago. Remember?"

"Yes, I did preach on Ruth," he agrees. "I'm glad you were listening."

I toss back my hair. "I always listen to what you say, Angus," I tell him, just a little hurt. "Always!"

"Glad to hear it. So?" He looks at me as if he doesn't know where I'm going with all this "Ruth" business.

"So I'm being practical, like you always tell us to be. I'm applying it to me—well, to us."

"To us?"

"Yes. I'm Ruth; you're Naomi."

He chuckles as he often does when I try to interpret Scripture. He says I'm very unique in the way I think. And then, slowly, it dawns on him what I'm trying to say. Our eyes meet.

"It's your one chance, Joy," I tell myself. "Make him understand. Make him know what you've felt for years and years. Put it all into your eyes." And I do. I put everything into the way I'm looking at him—everything I've bottled up for ages. I hold my breath. Yes, he's gotten my message. I can tell by the red that's spreading all over his face and down into his neck. I've never seen Angus this way before. But he doesn't say anything. He tries, several times, but the words stick in his throat.

I know it's now or never. "I'm crazy about you," I murmur. I grab his hand and put it to my lips. "Don't you realize what you do to me every time I'm with you? I'd absolutely die for you, Angus Campbell!"

"Joy!" He's found his tongue at last. I sit absolutely still. Now his face is as white as a sheet. He looks shocked, absolutely shocked!

"I had no idea you felt like this, Joy," he tells me at last.

"No idea?" I simply can't believe it.

"No. I thought you loved me like…." He pauses. He's turning red again.

"Like a daughter or sister?" I finish the sentence for him.

"Yes, like a daughter or sister."

The waiter comes and places the bill on the table. Angus takes my hand as we head to the door. He pays the bill, leads me to his pickup, and starts the engine.

"Now what?" I ask, not knowing what's coming next.

"The park. We need to talk." I nod but say nothing. I can't. I'm terrified of what's coming next.

Ten minutes later, we are sitting side by side on a bench, neither of us saying a word. It's his turn now. I've said it all, or nearly.

Still he doesn't speak. I edge closer until finally, I'm clinging to him. I'll always cling to him. Not God, not the devil, not the whole wide world will ever tear us apart.

He doesn't push me away but says very slowly, "Of course I love you, too, Joy. More than anyone else in the world."

I give a start. "You really mean that?" I want to know.

"Yes." He's gone red again. "I know what you're thinking, but Cherry is out of my life now for good. You are all I have. You are my comfort, my joy, my sunshine. No, let me finish," he says gently as I'm about to interrupt. "You are my closest and dearest friend on earth. Right now, though, this love I have for you seems to be different from the kind of love you have for me."

"How could you think I love you just as a brother?" I interrupt. "Don't you see how I look at you when we are together? Don't you know why I read my Bible every morning, play in church, teach Sunday School? And don't you understand why I've not even looked at a boy for three whole years?"

He gets up and begins to pace back and forth in front of our bench. I watch him till I think I'll go crazy. "I've got no one but you, Angus," I say pleadingly. Then I get up and take a few paces towards him. The next minute, my arms are around his neck and my head is on his shoulder.

"Hold me, Angus. Hold me tight," I murmur. "And, please, never let me go."

For a few seconds he hesitates and then he does just what I asked him to do—he holds me very tight. I'm in heaven, in absolute heaven. I know he's going to kiss me now, not as a father, or brother kisses, but as....

"Don't do this to me, Joy!" He pushes me away, but I'm not going to let this end as easily as that.

I spring into his arms again. This time he grabs me firmly and sets me down on the bench. "Never do that again!" he commands. "Never!" His words are rough and hard and they make me afraid. What's happening to him? He's never spoken to me like that before.

Then the devil gets into me and I don't care what I do or say. "But you liked it, didn't you?" I ask . "You liked it a lot, Angus Campbell!"

Something's gotten into him too, though. "You know too well I did!" he shouts. "So now you've discovered I'm a man, after all. That's what you wanted, isn't it? Well now you know. And I hope you're satisfied."

He stops suddenly. I've risen from the bench and we're standing, facing each other. I take a step towards him. "No, Joy, please don't," he commands again. "I made a vow after I came to Christ that I wouldn't hold any woman in my arms unless I was going to marry her. I never even held *her* in my arms."

"I don't believe that!" I explode. I'd really think that he's telling me a tall story now, except that Angus is the most truthful person I've ever met.

"You know I wouldn't lie to you, Joy," he retorts. "And it wasn't because I didn't want to, either."

"Then you mean that *she* didn't want to?"

"Of course she wanted to? She's just as much a woman as you are!" He's absolutely mad with me now. "You call her an angel. Well, she is a very fleshly angel, I'll tell you that much. But I told her what I told you just now that.... Oh, bother you, Joy!" he explodes. "Why do you rake up the past like this? What good does it do? But if you must know, she wasn't sure about me."

"Then she was an utter fool!" I mutter under my breath.

"Don't you dare talk that way about her!" His eyes are flashing fire now. "She was honest with me. And I with her. There, that's all I'm going to tell you. Satisfied?"

I stand there petrified. What is there about this redhead that can change a man like Angus in a minute by just mentioning her name? I'd give the world to be able to do that. I feel the tears in my eyes again. This birthday is turning out to be a disaster.

Angus sees my tears and melts instantly. He takes my hand and leads me back to the bench. We sit down together and he begins again. "Sorry, Joy. I don't know what's gotten into me, or into you either, for that matter. I love you, as I told you, more than anything or anyone else right now, but I don't and can't give you the sort of love you crave. Liking you close, feeling passion for you and desire isn't enough to see us through the ups and downs of married life. And, Joy, you have to realize that, well, I don't think I can ever love you in the way I once loved. And anything else would not be fair to you. You deserve something better."

I'm crying now as if my heart would break. "What you are really trying to say is that you'll never ever marry me, isn't it?" I ask between sobs.

Our eyes meet again. "I can't marry you, Joy. I don't think it is God's will for us."

"So it's all been a waste of time!" my voice rises. "It's all been for nothing!"

"What has, Joy?" His voice is gentle now, but it's too late.

"Dressing modest," I explode, "studying when the other girls are out dating, praying, singing hymns, turning my back on Guy Stanton—it's all been for nothing!"

"Please don't say that," Angus pleads. "You did it for God as well as for me."

I rise from the bench. "I did it only for you, Angus," I call over my shoulder. "I've had enough. I'll do everything on my own now. I'm eighteen. I'm independent."

"Where are you going?" Angus calls.

"To the devil!" I shout back. "Coming with me?" I turn my back on him and begin to run. I hear him following. I'm nearly at the bus stop now. There's a bus for Ngavi sitting waiting. It'll leave in a few moments. I mount the bus, take a seat by the window, and stare down into Angus' sorrowful gray eyes.

"Come with me," he mouths.

I shake my head. I know that if I go with him, it'll be a sign I accept what he's just told me. And I don't. I never will. If I do, then I'll have to go on play-acting—being his little sister all my life—hiding my passion until it burns me. And it will one day. It almost did today. I know though, it will burn me anyway. But at least it won't be Angus who'll burn along with me. And I don't care what I do to anyone else.

I hear the driver start up the engine. Angus takes a step backwards. The bus begins to move away from the only one in the world I really care about. I settle back in my seat. In a way, I'm relieved. Now, I don't need to act anymore. I'll be myself—the colored, bastard girl. I should have known I could never ever be like *her.* Me, an angel? That's a joke! But I loved Angus so much I was willing to do anything. Well, if I can't be in *his* arms, there'll be plenty of other arms that will welcome me, I'm sure of that.

I turn and see him still standing by the bus stop. He raises his hand and waves. I wave back. "Good-Bye, Angus!" I mutter. "It's been nice knowing you, very nice!"

Chapter Forty-Three

Dennis: So right and yet so wrong!

My daughter has been home two days. She's like an angel to me. And yet I am totally ashamed that she should see me like this. I'm a complete wreck of a man in every sense of the word. Yet I must say that when I'm with Cherry, I see a glimmer of light at the end of the tunnel. It's very faint and intermittent. And when she's not with me, I revert to the darkness. Oh God! How dark these days have been! The doctor says I'm having a complete breakdown. Maybe I am. All I know is that my whole world has collapsed. As for the Almighty—He seems afar off. Oh I know, He's standing somewhere in the shadows. But I can't see Him; can't feel Him; can't touch Him. And without that, what is life to me?

Cherry and I are sitting alone together, sipping cups of hot cocoa. Rachel is having a shower. Paul, as usual, is in his bedroom. He keeps out of my way. And no wonder! If I hadn't told him I was sure Allie was God's choice for him, maybe she'd be alive today, maybe he'd be happily married to someone else, someone like that Madeline girl he was so crazy about. I give a shudder.

"Are you cold, Dad?" Cherry asks anxiously. "I can put more wood on the fire."

I shake my head. I don't speak much these days, even to Cherry. I can't. Words used to be my weapons, my tools, my indispensible friends. Now they've become my enemies. I'm scared of them. God only knows what trouble they've caused!

I see Cherry's eyes wandering around our large living room. A few Christmas cards here and there are the only tokens that tomorrow is Christmas Eve. In the old days, we always had our Christmas candle as a centerpiece on the table, a strand or two of lights festooned over the mantelpiece, and Christmas cards everywhere. As for carols! We could never imagine a Christmas without evenings of carol singing! But those old days have gone forever! Or have they?

Cherry finishes her cocoa and walks slowly to the piano. My eyes follow her every move. She sits down and puts her fingers to the keys. I stir restlessly in my chair but keep my eyes on my daughter. She begins to sing, very softly at first, but soon her beautiful voice fills the room. I hear the bathroom door open and shut and see Rachel come and stand behind her.

"You play," Cherry suggests. "I can sing better if you do."

My wife hesitates a minute or two, glances at me, and then nods. Cherry has just finished the last stanza of Silent Night and my wife is beginning to play "Oh little town of Bethlehem" when I hear another door open and shut and see Paul's tall form in the hallway. Cherry motions to him to join us. He enters the room slowly and sits down in a chair near the piano. I turn my gaze away. I can't bear to look into my son's eyes. I stare into the fire as Cherry sings those words I know so well:

> "How silently, how silently,
> The wondrous gift is given;
> So God imparts to human hearts
> The blessings of His Heav'n."

She knows how much I love this carol, especially the verse she's singing now:

> "No ear may hear His coming,
> But in this world of sin,
> Where meek souls will receive Him still,
> The dear Christ enters in."

As the last note dies away, I hear a sob coming from Paul's chair. The sobs gather momentum and I notice that his whole frame is shaking with emotion.

"Let it out, Paul," Mom advises. "It'll do you good."

"You know," he murmurs between sobs, "she thought I didn't love her, but now that she's gone, I realize how much I really did love her."

His words stab my heart like a thousand spears. I can't take this much longer. I'd love to cry as Paul is doing, but I can't. I simply can't.

Now there's a very long silence and then Paul mutters, "Sing 'Down from His Glory,' Sis." His voice breaks. "It was Allie's favorite."

There she is again—Allie—she haunts my dreams, follows me around my farm, points an accusing finger when I try to pray, laughs at me when I want to cry. But Cherry has stopped singing now. She's coming towards me. Now she has perched herself on the arm of my chair and is putting her arms around me.

"I love you so much," she whispers in my ear. "You taught me the real meaning of Christmas. In fact, you taught me the real meaning of many important things. Did you know that?"

Something in me snaps. "Stop it, Cherry," I command in a voice I haven't used for months. "You've manipulated this whole evening, trying to make me feel good, I suppose. Well, it only makes me feel a hundred times worse."

I rise to my feet and glare at her. I have to make her understand. "No one can make me feel good anymore!" I explode. "How can they when I can't forget, even for a minute, that I've ruined my children's lives? The worst of it is that I would do the same thing again, probably, if left to myself. I can't see that I was wrong in believing that holiness was the way to Heaven, that love of the world was a dangerous foe, that most of the churches around were backslidden. I was trying to lead you all in the way of truth and godliness."

There, I've shocked her now. I can see it in her face. She begins to interrupt, but I wave her aside. "Don't think that I'm not sorry for what I did. I'm terribly sorry." I flop back in my chair, cover my face with my hands and weep silently.

I hear her tiptoe out of the room, hear murmured conversation in the kitchen, but still I sit, gazing into the flickering flames. And, strangely enough, I feel better than I've felt in many a long day. And I sleep better too. I still can't face them all at breakfast, though, so decide to hose out the milking parlor. I've just finished when I hear footsteps behind me.

I turn round. It's Cherry. She greets me cheerily, but I'm thoroughly ashamed of my behavior last night. I grunt something about being busy, but she's not going to be put off.

"I don't think you should have let the fellowship break up like you did," she blurts out. "Is it fair to make everyone suffer for your personal failure?" She gasps a little as if she can't believe she's had the nerve to talk like this to her "revered" father. I can't believe it either.

"I had to do it." That's all I can say right now.

"But why?"

"Isn't it as plain as the nose on your face?" I ask dully.

"No, Dad, it isn't. Maybe I'm being awfully dense, but I don't see why this family tragedy should force you to give up the fellowship. I know Allie's mother blames you for her daughter's death, but...."

I hold up my hand and she stops abruptly. "It's not Allie's mother who made me quit, Cherry. I just can't preach or lead a congregation when I am so confused myself." I clamp my lips tightly together and quicken my pace.

We've reached the garden gate now. Cherry suddenly grabs my coat sleeve.

"Listen, Dad," she's says, trying to sound authoritative but failing miserably, "the days are slipping by. There'll soon be an ocean between us once more. We've lost too much time all these years, thanks to both of our stubbornness. Don't shut me out, as you're doing. It hurts. I am your daughter after all, or have you forgotten?"

"Shut her out?" "Days slipping by?" "Lost too much time?" Her words seep through the layers of confusion these past months have deposited in my once active brain. Then suddenly they hit a nerve. I swing around to face her. And then I ask the question that I have thrown in the face of the Almighty times without number. "How can I have been so right and gone so far wrong, Cherry?" I raise my voice and Rachel comes to the door, wondering what is happening. Then she catches my eye, gives a faint smile, and disappears into the house.

I swing open the gate and make for the kitchen door. I've said enough—far too much, but Cherry grabs me by the shoulders so that I'm forced to look straight at her. And then she says slowly and deliberately, "I don't know the answer to your question, Dad. I've asked it many times myself and have no answer."

"But why, child, why doesn't He answer me? I've served Him faithfully all these years," I wail. Yes, it's literally a wail. I can't help it. It comes from deep inside.

I see the look in my daughter's eyes. She's never been in this position before and she quite obviously hates it. She'd probably rather have a controlling dad, an angry dad, anything but this confused, disillusioned, broken man standing before her, shivering in the cold December wind.

"God didn't answer Job either, Dad," she falters. "Not for a long time."

I stare at her, unseeingly. No words will come. "But Job got his answer in the end, didn't he?" she reminds me gently.

My hand tightens on her arm. "Yes, Cherry," I manage to whisper, "he did...in the end."

Only a few stuttering words but they make her smile, her old smile, her "Cherry" smile. "Let's get inside," she commands, piloting me towards the house. "It's awfully cold. What we need, first of all, is a good hot drink, and then I need to wrap my presents."

"Presents?" I repeat, uncomprehending.

"Have you forgotten?" she asks whimsically. "It *is* Christmas, my first at home in years. And I'm going to celebrate it, even if no one else is." I smile faintly, very faintly, but still, it's a beginning.

"Make me a cup of good British tea," I command as we hang up our coats in the hallway. "And make it extra strong. I need some caffeine in me to cope with my redhead of a daughter."

Cherry almost runs into the kitchen and grabs the teakettle. A few moments later we drink some good old Typhoo tea. I, for one, have never ever tasted tea like it and, somehow, I think I never will again.

Chapter Forty-Four

Angus: Forgiven!

"Your fault! Your fault! Your fault!"

"Stop it!" I shout. "It's not my fault! I did my best! It's Rhoda's fault! It's Joy's fault! And oh, blow it, it's Cherry's fault!"

But the engine won't listen. Why doesn't it purr smoothly as it always does instead of spluttering and chugging and spelling out my doom with every chug it makes?

I pull into the side of the road and mess around with the spark plugs. That's better. Maybe I'll get home before dark. Oh goodness, there's that old bus again! I've passed it twice already. I'm sure that headstrong girl of mine is looking out the window and rejoicing. "Serves you right, Angus Campbell!" she's muttering. I'm almost sure she is!

I grab a cloth from under my seat and attempt to rub the oil from my hands. Phew! What an afternoon! I wonder what Rhoda and Mom are thinking up there where everything must look so different. I suppose they saw all this coming. I wish, at least, they'd been here to warn me where the wind was blowing. I needed someone to talk sense into my thick skull. I suppose Reg tried to, in his arbitrary way. And I thought I was being more cautious, I really did.

I stare into the darkness of the African night. An owl hoots above my head. It's eerie out here alone in the bush after dark. I'd better get going, though as I feel right now, I don't put much value on my life. Joy's the only one who'd miss me if a lion tore me to pieces, or a leopard pounced on me from that tree over there, or a snake slithered out and sank its fangs into my ankle. And I'd be better out of her life for good. I've made a mess of everything!

I give myself a shake get into the pickup and turn the key in the ignition. God-called missionaries shouldn't think thoughts like these. I'm here for better or for worse. Then, for the first time in hours, I find myself smiling, just a little. Women and Angus Campbell? They just don't mix, do they? When will I learn my lesson? My smile grows broader. What an absolute sucker I've been! Mom used to say I could never be in a bad mood for long. And she must be shaking her head at me right now. As for Rhoda...?

My smile fades. This really isn't anything to smile about, not even by an optimist like me. What if Joy really does go to the devil as she threatened? Then what do I do? And who will be to blame?

At last I chug through the mission gates at about ten p.m. I've had to stop at least three more times. The bus must have arrived an hour ago. I drive slowly past Reg Stanton's house, "the big house" we all call it, past the church, the school, the clinic. I turn right and yes, there's a light in her window. I need to be sure she's gotten home OK. But first, let me check my mail.

I open the box. There's a folded sheet of notepaper lying there, nothing else. I take it and unfold it. It's Joy's handwriting. I feel relieved. It's probably an apology. She never can be angry with me for long.

"Dear Angus," I read. "Yes, I got home safely. I haven't eloped with the bus driver or run off with Guy Stanton. So you can sleep in peace tonight, though I won't promise what I'll do tomorrow or the next day or the next. Things are going to be very different now. I'm eighteen; you're not my guardian anymore. Oh, I know. You've to keep an eye on me till I'm twenty-one. Well, OK, but do it at a distance, please. Anyway, you won't want to have much to do with the real me. You see, I'm not going to act any more. I'm going to show the world who I am—me, Joy Mkandawire—bastard daughter of an English no-good. Sorry, Angus. You did your best. I can't blame you. You are who you are and I am who I am. You have an angel in your heart. I have a demon. The two don't go together, do they? Thanks for all you have done for me. I still love you like crazy. Always will—till death—even when I'm in someone else's arms. And I will be. That's just the way I'm made. And you'll go on loving your redhead—till death. That's the way you're made. So may God, if there really is a God, have mercy on us both! Joy."

For a moment, I feel a fury rising in my chest I can't control. Before I know it, Joy's letter is in shreds. I'm still standing by the mailbox. I glance at the ground. Tiny pieces of white notepaper lie at my feet. Just like my life in Africa. Maybe I'll start again in India, or China. I can't go back to the States. Oh God, what a failure I've been! What must Reg Stanton and all the other missionaries think of me? They've seen what was happening all along. And on I went, blithely thinking that I was the best guardian ever.

I stoop and gather up the fragments and stuff them in my pocket. Why piece them together? I don't need any memento of this horrible day. I go to bed, but the clock by my bed is ticking: "Your fault, your fault, your fault." And my pulse beats in rhythm with the clock. And the crickets outside my window take up the chorus. Even the coyote in the distant hills barks the same refrain. I can't sleep. I get up and pace the floor. I cry; I stomp; I sniffle; I whine. But it's no use. And then I pray, pray till the light streams in above my head, pray till the cock crows in our farm down the road, pray till, finally, I can pray no longer but fall asleep on my knees and awaken several hours later, stiff, and sore. The clock is still ticking a message to me. What is it? And my pulse. And the birds outside my window. Only thank God, the message has changed. "You're forgiven, you're forgiven, you're forgiven!" rings in my head, my heart, my soul.

I go into the kitchen, make myself a cup of tea, and start a new day and maybe, who knows, a new life?

Chapter Forty-Five

Cherry: *Forgiving Dad.*

Only a week left of these wonderful holidays! I say wonderful, because, for the first time in years, I'm relaxed with my parents; not only that, but they really and truly seem to need me. I wish we laughed more together instead of crying. Dad dissolves into tears at the turn of a hat now, but that's better than the stolid silence that enveloped him just after my arrival.

And this morning, as we stroll through the fields together, I see something is on his mind. He stops abruptly and we stand facing each other. I feel a few soft flakes of snow on my cheek. My hair blows in the chilly, January wind.

"If only I hadn't been so sure of my holiness," Dad blurts out, "I might have made a much better job of fathering you and Paul."

I say nothing. This frank admission takes me completely by surprise. "I was the sanctified saint who thought that he was one hundred percent God's and wanted his family to be the same," he goes on, taking my arm as we begin to make our way back to the farmhouse.

"But you *were* one hundred percent God's," I protest. "That was obvious to all of us even when we got mad at you."

Dad raises his eyebrows. "But little good my devotion did either me or my family."

I lay a hand on his arm. "Don't say that, Dad. You know it isn't true. You were an example to all of us."

"Really? Then why on earth did my two children make sure they chose a completely different path from me, Cherry, if my example was so exemplary?"

I am silent, not sure what to reply. Whatever I say will either sound trite or cruel. "Can't answer that, can you?" he asks after a few moments. "Nor can I. Something went dreadfully wrong and I'm still stunned. I suppose I should have come to my senses when you took off to England three years ago. But no! You were always the rebel, or so I thought. But when Paul's marriage began to go awry, I suddenly woke up to the fact that I had been totally misguided regarding Allie. And if I made such a mistake once, where else had I gone wrong? That made me think of you, Cherry, and how hard I was with you and Andrew."

"I think it was all for the best, Dad," I say softly. "I was head over heels in love with him, but maybe God saw we weren't really suited."

"Maybe so," Dad agrees. "Anyway, you're here beside me, my own precious daughter. I only wish I had more time to spoil you silly. Instead, I've been preoccupied with my own problems and haven't been much fun to be with."

"Not much fun," I agree, smiling, "but wonderful to be with, all the same." Then my face clouds. "But what a price we have both paid!" I give a shudder. "Did it have to go the way it did?" I ask, choking back the tears.

"No, it didn't. Can you ever forgive me?" he asks brokenly.

"You don't need to ask," I say gently, as I open the garden gate. "I was more to blame than you were. You don't know how resentful I've been and how I've wished that I...." I stopped. I couldn't say it just like it was. It seems too awful and yet I know he is right. He is partly to blame. And, looking in his eyes, I see that he has not yet learned to forgive himself.

"But I controlled you," he interrupts. "I meant well, meant to protect you from the world and from yourself. But my zeal tripped me up. I became a tyrant for holiness, if there is such a thing. I can't preach anymore, Cherry. God seems so far away. I'm a total failure. And I've been thinking that I need to apologize to so many people—Andrew and Madeline for example, and Angus."

"Angus?" I ask, my eyes widening. "What have you done to him that needs apologizing for?"

He looks at me quizzically. "I quarreled with him about you."

"When?" I want to know, reddening a little.

"Angus and I fell out with each other the last time he was here, four years ago, I believe."

"I don't understand."

"No, I don't suppose you do," he comments dryly and much more like the dad of old. "But he told me in no uncertain terms that I was doing wrong to cut you out of our lives as we were doing."

"But...." I stammer, a host of emotions nearly overcoming me.

"Yes, I know, Cherry. I couldn't believe it either. He had just heard that the only woman he ever really loved was about to marry his rival and then he turned around and told me I was being too hard on you, that Andrew Price was a good man, that he deserved you etc., etc."

The tears are raining down my face now. I always knew Angus was out of the ordinary; now I think he's a positive saint.

"And," Dad adds, rather embarrassed by my tears, "maybe if I hadn't pushed you so hard that Easter, you and he would have sorted things out."

I shake my head. "No, Dad. We were already going in opposite directions. Oh, I admit that you pushed him along the path he would eventually have chosen for himself, but I don't think either of us were at a point where we could have made it together."

Dad thinks that one over for a long time. "And now?" he asks, with a slight smile, "What about now, Cherry?"

I've been thinking a lot about Angus lately, but Dad's question still catches me off-guard.

"He thinks you're married," Dad goes on. "We lost touch with each other after he went back to Africa, so I'm pretty sure he assumes that you're Mrs. Price, the priest's wife. Shouldn't you let him know that you're still Cherry McMann?"

"Maybe he's gotten married, Dad," I say, hedging. "I doubt if he gives me a second thought now."

"Knowing Angus, I think he gives you a lot of thought, but yes, he could be married." Dad admits. "It must be pretty tough on the mission-field without a wife to help him through. And I remember that he told me that he had consented to being the guardian of his old housekeeper's granddaughter, little Joy I think the girl was called. She was about fifteen when I saw him last."

"That makes her nineteen now," I calculated quickly. I've never forgotten the little girl with the large brown eyes that held you like a magnet. She must be a fabulously beautiful young woman by now.

"Yes, quite grown up, I suppose," Dad comments thoughtfully. "Angus seemed terribly fond of her and told me that he treated her as his own daughter. He was always talking about her and her grandmother."

I'm still thinking about this so-called daughter of Angus Campbell when I get ready for bed that night. There is that offer from the Presbyterian hospital in Malawi, begging for medical help—temporary and permanent. Well, I'm not about to commit to being a full-fledged missionary yet, but a month in Malawi this summer? Couldn't hurt, could it?

The rest of my vacation passes all too quickly and then I'm off to London again. "I'm thinking of spending a month in Malawi this summer," I tell my parents at the airport. Dad's face is a picture but he makes no comment.

"Well, that is a coincidence," Mom exclaims excitedly. "I think our old friend Angus Campbell is somewhere in Malawi."

"I think so, too," I say calmly, catching Dad's eye.

"Maybe you'll meet him," she goes on.

"Maybe I will," I reply, trying hard not to laugh.

"Write us all about it," she urges. "And give Angus our love if you do see him."

"Bring him back with you, Cherry," Dad suggests, grinning. "I'm sure he's overdue for a furlough."

"She can't do that, Dennis," Mom says, obviously shocked. "Unless...."

I stop her words with a kiss. "Drive home safely," I tell Dad. This is the first long trip he has driven since his breakdown.

"I will," he promises. Then he hugs me tight.

"Oh, Dad," I whisper, "this has been the best holiday in years."

"Even though I've been as grumpy as a bear?"

"Yes," I murmur. "Even though you've been as grumpy as a bear. Oh Dad, I love you so much!"

"I love you too, Ginger," he whispers back. Then he blows me another kiss and is gone.

Chapter Forty-Six

Angus: Saving Joy.

"I hate to have to write again, Mr. Campbell, but I need to inform you that you must do something about your former ward, Joy Mkandawire. Her grades are slipping, and at this rate, she is not going to pass her A-levels in six weeks' time. Her whole future is at stake."

I drop the letter on the table. It is the second I've received from Joy's headmistress this semester. It seems that Joy is flaunting rules left, right, and center. Just last week she was caught creeping in her window after midnight. And the problem is that she's no longer my "ward." I have no authority over her, no real authority, I mean.

"I can't understand what is happening to Joy," the headmistress wrote in her first letter. "Please, Mr. Campbell, do something, if you possibly can, for the sake of Joy's future."

"Do something?" I ask myself. I've tried to do just that for months. I began to try that first morning after Joy's eighteenth birthday. But she wouldn't look at me, talk to me, or listen to me. She changed completely overnight. I said I was sorry I'd been so naïve. She just laughed and walked away. The next day, I asked couldn't we start all over again? She laughed again and said, "Start what? Our little farce?" I got Roger Buchannan to speak to her. She was more polite with him, but hard as nails. So what more can I do? And it seems as if everyone, except maybe Roger and his wife, are blaming me for what is happening to Joy. Reg certainly is.

Oh, I know God has forgiven me. And I've learned a terrible lesson. But that doesn't help Joy right now. I've got to do something, and do it immediately, or the girl's life will be wrecked. For weeks I've walked around this problem of Joy Mkandawire. And I'm still walking around it. If I really face it, well, only God knows what I'll have to do. No, that's not being honest. The solution to all of this is not as complex as it is painful. And this indecision of mine could prove fatal. This letter tells me that time is running out. I'll follow my gut feeling and....

As always, just when I'm about to take the step which I probably will eventually have to take anyway, a vision of a redheaded girl floats before me. I groan and run my hands through my hair. I'm tired of visions that never materialize—tantalizing, forbidden visions. I wish sometimes that angels would stay in heaven and not disturb us mortals with their ethereal charms. And then it dawns on me. Maybe taking this step is my way of escape as well as Joy's!

"Be true to yourself and follow your heart," Roger Buchannan advised me the other day when I poured out my troubles to him. Following my heart is a bit tricky as it gets out of hand, and I'm not sure where it's going these days. But being true to myself? That's easier, much easier. I begin to feel brighter already. My old optimism returns full force. A bird in the hand is worth two in the bush, isn't it? Marriage will have advantages, won't it? Hasn't Reg told me for years that a bachelor missionary hardly ever makes it on the field? I've learned that the hard way. And Joy? Don't I want to make her happy, to protect her, to love her as a man loves the woman of dreams?

I stop abruptly. That's the problem. That's just why I've not taken this step sooner. I'm not sure I can ever love Joy Marie Mkandawire as a husband should love the woman he asks to be his life-long partner.

Three days pass, three long days and longer nights. By the time Sunday arrives, I know I've got to do something. I'm not preaching at our church this week, so instead, I get in my pickup and head for Mpongo. I arrive just before the service starts and slip in the back. The boarding-school students attend Roger's church every Sunday morning. I see Joy sitting on the right, a few rows in front of me. She's dressed in a bright red two-piece that leaves no room for the imagination. I notice the eyes of the boys on the opposite aisle wander in her direction during the sermon and it makes me mad. I notice, too, that she condescends to give them the odd smile and then rivets her eyes on the pulpit. But she isn't listening. I can tell that, even though Roger is preaching his heart out.

At last the service is over. The students file out, row by row. I wait until Joy comes level with my aisle and then slip out beside her. She looks shocked to see me. I put my hand on her arm.

"I've got to speak to you," I whisper.

"And what if I don't want to?" she replies haughtily.

I pull her to one side, aware of several pairs of curious eyes upon us. "Let's stop hurting each other, Joy," I say pleadingly. "I want to say sorry for the way I've treated you." I don't know quite what will happen to both of us before this day is over. I'm taking one step at a time, trusting that I have the guts to follow where His light is leading me.

"It's too late, Angus," she says, staring right past me. "I told you I'd go to the devil, and I have."

"It's never too late." Her eyes meet mine. Her lip trembles, but she says nothing.

"I've packed a picnic lunch," I tell her. "Will you share it with me?"

"What's the point?" she mumbles.

"What I want to tell you needs privacy, Joy. That's the point."

"More lectures?" she begins angrily.

"No," I interrupt. "No more lectures."

"Good Morning, Mr. Campbell!"

I give a start. Joy's headmistress is standing a few feet away watching us closely.

"Good Morning!" I reply, highly embarrassed. Then I pull myself together. "Could you give me permission to take this young lady out for the afternoon?"

"Of course. Any time, Mr. Campbell. We've missed seeing you around. Just bring her back before ten tonight. That's all I ask."

She gives Joy a very significant look and turns away. Joy's eyes are flashing fire. "I'm not going with you, Angus," she tells me hotly.

I sit down in the pew nearest to me. "Then what I have to say will have to be said right here," I begin, ignoring her expression. She glances around. Her roommate is standing by the door, looking as if she's about to intervene. I know she's very loyal to Joy, too loyal at times.

"OK," Joy agrees. "Maybe a short picnic—just this once."

"Then let's go," I say, rising and offering my arm.

She takes it, looking absolutely nonplused. "Why are you doing this?" she stammers as we exit the church and head towards my pickup.

"Because I have to," I tell her soberly. "Just trust me."

"But I've always trusted you, Angus," she retorts. "Even when I was mad at you and I've been very mad, you know. I still am."

"I know," I reply grinning.

"And I've been very naughty, too," she adds defiantly.

"I know that, too, but I'm at least partially to blame, you know."

She looks as if she doesn't believe what she's hearing. Then her lip crumples. "I know," she murmurs, as she climbs in the passenger seat of my old blue pickup. "You are a lot to blame, Angus Campbell. You broke my heart. You broke it in a thousand pieces!"

I go to start up the engine and then I stop. I know I've hurt this girl, but broken her heart into a thousand pieces? Girls exaggerate, though, don't they? Then I see the expression in her eyes and know she is telling the truth. I lay my head on the steering wheel and weep. What else can a man do but weep his heart out when he knows he's broken something tremendously precious that can never be fully repaired again?

Chapter Forty-Seven

Joy: Getting my way at last.

I've never seen a man cry like this before and I just can't stand it. Angus is sitting, hunched over the steering wheel, bawling his eyes out. Well, bawling isn't the word to use. He's not making a sound. That's what's so hard. I feel terrible. It's me who should be weeping like that, not Angus.

I put my arm on his shoulder and whisper, "Please, don't, Angus. I shouldn't have put it like that."

He raises his face to mine. I can't stand to see him like this. He looks absolutely shattered. "But it was the truth, wasn't it?" he mutters.

I wish he hadn't asked that, but I'll have to be honest with him. "Yes, it was the truth, Angus, but I could have said it more kindly."

"No, I needed to realize just what I've done to you, Joy," he says sadly.

"But I used it as an excuse to...." I can't get the words out. Do I really need to tell him everything?

"I know," he replies, as if I had finished my sentence. "But I've been doing a lot of thinking, Joy." He fumbles in his pocket as he speaks. He puts a small box into my hand. "Open it," he orders.

My heart starts beating out of control. My hands are trembling. I guess what might be in that box. I lift the lid and look inside. Yes, it is a ring, a ring with one diamond on it.

Angus lays his hand on mine and says very softly, "It was my mother's, Joy. Do you think you could take it from me?"

I want to fling my arms around his neck but I can't. There's something between us—something big and dark and black.

"You don't know how bad I've been," I stammer. I close the lid and lay the box on his lap.

"Yes, I do," he says gently. "I know all about it. Your headmistress has told me."

"About going out the window at night?"

"I know all about it," he repeats. "You don't need to tell me more."

"But about Guy?" I stammer. "You know about Guy Stanton?" Angus' face goes white.

"No, I didn't know about Guy." He's sad again, very.

"I met him three times," I admit, hanging my head.

I feel Angus' arms around me. "Thanks for telling me, Joy, but it's in the past. I don't want to know anymore."

I open my lips to speak, but I feel his lips on my forehead. "And whatever you did, I forgive you," he says gently. "After all, I drove you to it. I was so insensitive."

We sit like this for a long time. I'm still in one wonderful dream. Then Angus pulls away a little. "One thing, though," he begins slowly. "Do you love Guy Stanton? I need to know that."

"Love him?" I explode. "Of course I don't love him. All that I've ever felt for him is passion, and as you told me once, that's not enough, is it?"

He draws me close again and strokes my hair gently. "No, it isn't enough, not by a long way, Joy."

"After our third meeting," I mutter, feeling I have to tell him just a little bit more, "Guy had to go back to South Africa. He wanted to take me with him. I told him right out I didn't love him. I loved only you. He was mad. I tried to apologize, but he left in a rage. And that was that. I never want to see him again. Never! And I'm sure he's had enough of me to last a lifetime. He's gone back to his girl, I suppose. But Angus, I was terribly naughty with Guy."

"It's all right, Joy." His voice is gentle now and breaks me up completely. "I was naughty, too, before I came to Christ. We all are, without Him. So you don't need to tell me anything else. Tell it to God, instead."

"Please forgive me, Angus," I sob.

"That's easy to do, Joy," I hear him say quietly. "Now let's ask God to do the same."

So right there in the church parking lot I pray, and Angus prays, and then he takes the ring out of the box and slips it on my finger.

"Now I'm hungry as a wolf," he announces as he puts the truck into gear and roars off towards the park. And we sit on the very same bench we sat on last October when all the trouble began between us.

"I've talked to Roger Buchannan," Angus begins when we've finished our sandwiches. "I know that the last time we discussed your going to

England with them, it ended in an explosion; but we do need to talk about it, Joy."

I don't understand. Why is he talking about this England business again? "I'm marrying you, Angus, not going to England. If not, what does this ring mean?" I look from him to the diamond glinting in the sunlight and then back to him again. Then my lip crumples. Has the last hour been some dream? "I don't want to go to England," I pout. "I only want to be with you, forever."

"I know," he says, patting my hand. "But you're still very young," he reminds me. "I don't want you to wear that ring in public until after you've finished your studies."

"Please, Angus, let's get married right away. That's the only thing I want."

"That's what you think now, Joy," he says drawing me to him, "but you may change your mind. You need to meet new people, stay in new places, learn new things, and then, if you still feel that I'm the only man for you, you can slip on that ring and declare to the whole world and to me, that we are engaged. So, I don't want my answer yet."

"You know it's 'yes,'" I burst out, tears streaming down my face.

"But I insist that we give it time. I'm very good at waiting, you know."

"But you *will* marry me in the end?"

"If you still think I'm the man for you," he says smiling.

"I won't change," I pout. "It's you who will change."

"I won't change, Joy. I promise. And you know I always keep my promise. There's just one thing."

"Yes?"

"You'll have to be patient with me. And you need to understand me. Right now, I'm not sure the love I feel for you will satisfy you when we're married, or before, for that matter. My love for you is changing, but it'll take time."

A few months ago, his words would have bothered me terribly, but right now, with his mother's ring on my finger, I'm not bothered at all. He's right. It'll take time, but not as much as he thinks. He has already come a long way in a few hours.

"Just let yourself love me," I whisper. "And I'll do my best to help you."

"I don't doubt you will," he says with a funny little smile.

"And I'm sure that eventually, you'll love me just like you loved *her.*"

He puts his hand on my mouth. "Don't say it," he commands. "Our love will be unique, Joy. Let's not compare it with past loves." And then he stoops over and kisses me tenderly, not passionately, like they do in movies or like Guy Stanton kissed me, but maybe I don't want that kind of kissing till we're married. I'm sure Angus doesn't.

"I wish we could get married tomorrow, Angus," I tell him, suddenly feeling a bit afraid. "So much can happen in three or four years."

Angus smiles. "A lot of wonderful things can happen, Joy. Now study hard. Make up for lost time, and meanwhile, I'll come and see you as often as I can till you graduate, if you want me to, that is?"

For an answer I throw my arms around his neck and whisper, "I've missed you so much, Angus."

"I've missed you too, Joy."

"Can't I tell anyone about the ring?" I ask.

"Just the Buchannans. But you can tell all your friends that we're dating, because from now on, that's what we'll be doing. Our engagement isn't official till you come back from England, so I don't want you to wear the ring till then, for your own sake, that is."

I really don't understand why he's doing it this way, but I trust him. I always have and always will, forever and forever.

Chapter Forty-Eight

Andrew: Better friends than enemies!

"Dear Andrew, I'm very sorry for the way I treated both you and my daughter when I discovered you were engaged. It was totally unchristian." I give a gasp as I glance up from my letter.

"What's wrong, Dad?" Gloria wants to know. She's spending a few days with me before returning to Chicago where she lives with her mother when she's not at college, studying to be a French teacher. She will be twenty-one in a few weeks which is hard for me to take in.

"Dennis McMann has written me a letter of apology, Gloria," is all I can manage to say.

She looks as surprised as I feel. "Well, that's great, Dad," she finally manages to say; "though," she adds uncertainly, "it won't make much practical difference to you now, will it?"

"That would depend on Cherry," I answer after a long pause.

A few years ago, Gloria would have given anything to see Cherry and me back together; but since she was reconciled to her mother, she looks at it very differently. "You were more a father figure to her, Dad," she told me not long ago. "She worshiped you, but maybe that wasn't what you needed."

I had disagreed of course, violently disagreed. And now I'm not sure how to answer her question. I daren't tell her that for the first time since Cherry stepped out of my life, I feel a spark of hope kindle somewhere deep inside me.

Gloria's face darkens. "I don't think Mr. McMann was writing this to get you two back together, Dad."

I shrug and then pick up the letter, remembering I haven't finished reading it yet. "I still feel the same about divorce and remarriage," Dennis writes, "but you and Cherry were sincerely trying to serve God. You didn't deserve to be treated like criminals." I smile wryly. Gloria is probably right, though the letter doesn't say specifically what the writer would do if I tried to renew contact with his daughter. "So please forgive me, Andrew. I know I caused you a lot of pain. God has been overhauling me lately and it's very painful, but, hopefully, I'll come out a better man on the other side."

"Overhauling!" I smile wryly. That's just how I feel right now, though "the other side" as he calls it, seems light years away!

I finish the letter and look up to find Gloria's expressive dark eyes fixed on my face. I can't stand the sympathy I see there and I jump up from my seat. "I've got to go to town on business," I say lightly.

Gloria says nothing more about the letter, not then, nor when she rings me and asks me to come to her twenty-first birthday party. Of course I refuse. How can I go when Mary is organizing the whole thing?

But I've been thinking a lot since then. That letter has raked up the past as I thought it would, and for days I am gloomier and more depressed than usual. I think of what might have happened if Cherry's father had been in this frame of mind four or five years ago, and it's driving me crazy. But recrimination is deadly, especially of other people. Not that I don't recriminate myself even more so. And that can be deadly too.

And then one morning as I have my devotions, the word "forgive" jumps out at me from several passages of Scripture. I kneel down, open my heart to the One Who has forgiven me so very much, and simply begin to forgive Dennis McMann for what he did to Cherry, and to me, and I feel so much better for it, that I begin to wonder what would happen if I actually forgave Mary, too. So, three days before her party, I surprise the life out of my daughter by announcing that I am coming to her celebration after all. Her joy is worth all the agonizing I've been going through to reach this conclusion.

"Mom will be over the moon," she tells me, her voice very unsteady.

"I know I need to meet her again, for your sake," I go on, "but don't get your hopes up, Gloria. Your mother destroyed any love I had for her, destroyed it absolutely. But at least I can be civil to her for your sake and for Peter's. I need to meet her privately, though, before I go to your party. We probably both have some things to say to each other if we're going to be...." I pause, not quite knowing whether I should continue. "Friends," I finish. "I can never be more than her friend, Gloria. You need to accept that."

"Friends sound a whole lot better than enemies, Dad," she tells me quietly. And what can I do but agree?

Chapter Forty-Nine

Cherry: The longest night ever!

I am sitting on the jumbo jet waiting for takeoff. I'm on my way to Africa and so excited I can't concentrate on anything. I try to read a book that I've bought specially for this flight, but the words aren't making sense. I pick at the meal the flight attendant places in front of me but have no appetite. In the end, I let my emotions do what they want with me. I lean my head back on the inflatable cushion I take with me wherever I go and, for the first time in months, maybe years, I let myself dream about my future. I'll see Angus at last! What will he look like? Has he still got that lock of hair that hangs down over his forehead? Does he still laugh until everyone around is laughing too? And, what is the most important thing of all—does he still love me?

Anyway, when I see him, I'll know the truth. I mean, I'll know if what I've been feeling about him lately is really love. It's not what I felt for Andrew—not some overwhelming feeling that made me incapable of wanting nothing else but to be in his arms. No, it's a feeling that I've never ever had a friend like Angus Campbell—that I need his happy smile and infectious faith to help me be a better woman—that I'd be the happiest person on earth if I could only spend my life making him happy. So if that's true love, then I'm in it up to my neck!

Something else, too. When I see Angus, I'll know the truth about him, also. Maybe he's forgotten me. Maybe he's in love with someone else. Or just maybe he still holds a special place for me in his heart. Well, whatever the truth is, I need to know it.

We land the next day in Blantyre, the capital of Malawi. I'm in a daze. Cherry McMann in Africa! Mabel, a doctor from Queen Elizabeth hospital in the city, comes to meet me. I met her at Guy's when I first went to London. I'm spending the night with her. Then she's taking me to the Presbyterian Hospital near Lilongwe where I'll spend a month helping out. They are desperately short-staffed and hopefully, I'll profit from the experience. There is a smaller hospital at Mpongo, an hour's drive from Ngavi, where I'm hoping I can visit as an excuse to make contact with Angus. I only need to see him once, and I'll know....

"You OK?" Mabel asks me.

"Just terribly excited," I reply. My friend looks at me curiously and a few hours later, over a cup of hot tea, I tell her my secret.

"How romantic!" she gasps.

"I hope it ends well," I say with a sigh. "It's been years since I've seen Angus. "Anything may have happened."

"The sooner you find out about this guy the better," my friend tells me the next morning. "You look as if you haven't slept a wink."

I hadn't slept much. My first night in Africa was unsettling. And it wasn't just Angus who drove away the sleep from my eyes. It was Africa itself. I thought of my parents' prayers for me before my birth and wondered if they had anything to do with my being here. Dad's prayers again! But I'm not afraid of them like I used to be. And if this trip ends in my commitment to a life-long missionary career, then it will be because I know deep inside that this must be God's will for my life.

"I'll drive you up to Mpongo," Mabel announces over breakfast. "If you're going to spend a month here, this Angus should know it as soon as possible."

"But that's a long drive, Mabel," I protest. My stomach is churning. I'm not sure if I am ready for this.

"Yes, but we'll stay overnight in Lilongwe, in a rest-house."

"Rest-house?"

Mabel laughs merrily. "Yes. Somewhere to rest your weary head— a simplified guesthouse you could call it, very simplified."

My head whirls. Jetlag is catching up with me. I go to protest, but before I know it, Mabel has rung the Presbyterian minister at Mpongo and arranged for me to spend a few days at his manse.

"He'll probably know Angus and arrange a meeting for you," she tells me brightly, very pleased with herself.

The journey to Lilongwe is hair-raising. Only one lane of the main highway north is paved. That means that when two cars approach each other, one has to give way to the other. But which? Mabel seems to think it's always the other driver who should give way.

And dust! Both of us are soon covered in powdery red dust! It's the dry season and Mabel tells me that traveling is much safer now than when the rains come and the roads are slick as ice. Our car has no air-conditioning so we have to drive with the windows open.

"You'll need a warm sweater in the evenings," Mabel tells me as we speed northwards.

I'll need more than a warm sweater, I'm thinking, still unsure if I want to meet Angus so soon. I'd rather adjust to this strange land first. But Mabel is going hundreds of miles out of her way to chauffeur me and if I don't take this opportunity, I might not get another.

Very late that evening, we reach Lilongwe. We locate a rest house, where I spend another restless night and then we're off again. It's a five or six hour drive to Mpongo and what a journey! Our narrow winding road climbs steadily upwards. We see an elephant in the distance. Several buffaloes cross the road just in front of us.

"I feel as if I really am in Africa now," I say excitedly.

"You haven't seen the half," my friend replies coolly. "We're going through lion country right now." She frowns as she glances at the radiator gauge. We've climbed steadily for miles and the engine is overheating. We pull in by the side of the road.

"There's a slow leak in the radiator," Mabel announces, as if she were telling me it was time for supper.

"What on earth will we do?" I ask anxiously. "We haven't passed a gas station in two hours."

"It's OK," she reassures me. "I never drive without several gallons of water in the back. By the way," she adds casually, "just keep your eye on the bush on both sides of the road, will you? As I said a few moments ago, we are in lion country now."

My heart starts beating wildly as I watch her lift the hood and peer into the engine. My eyes focus on the undergrowth a few yards from our car. I breathe a sigh of relief as the moments pass by uneventfully. Mabel has just poured the last drop of water into the radiator when I stiffen. Two large green eyes are staring at me from the bush.

I open the door slightly and in a shaky voice I say in a loud whisper, "Something's watching us, Mabel. "I think it might just be a lion."

Mabel screws on the radiator top, glances to where I'm pointing, nods, then slips quietly into the driver's seat. With a huge sigh of relief, she closes the door and window and starts up the engine.

"Was it a lion?" I ask tremulously.

My friend shrugs. "Who knows? It might have been a leopard. They're everywhere." She puts her foot on the accelerator. "Now, Mpongo, here we come!"

I shudder. She laughs merrily. "You're fortunate today. You've seen more wildlife in a few hours than most visitors see in months. By the way, Cherry, it's snakes you really have to watch out for. Never go into long grass. Never go out at night without a flashlight. Never...."

"Stop!" I say laughing as I put my hand to my ears. "You've told me enough for today. But slow down, Mabel, please."

"You have to go fast," Mabel says defensively. "We're on a dirt road now and these corrugations pull the car to pieces. You have to ride on top of them and to do that you have to go at least forty miles an hour if not fifty."

It is noon before we pull up at the Presbyterian manse. Mabel only stays long enough to greet the Buchannans and then she's off again to spend a few nights with an old friend who runs an orphanage on the outskirts of Mpongo.

"Pick you up the day after next," she says with a wink. "Behave!"

I like Roger Buchannan and his wife the moment I meet them. When Mabel has gone, they show me to my bedroom which I'm to share with some girl who is working in the hospital until she goes to college in the UK. The Buchannans are taking her back with them. I would have preferred to be alone, but then, I'm in Africa now, not in my old home in North Carolina, or my one-roomed apartment in the London suburbs.

"Don't worry if people stare at you, Cherry," Roger warns, as we walk over to the hospital.

"I'm getting used to that," I reply, grinning. I put my hand up to my hair. "Being a red-head in Africa is quite an experience!"

"I'm sure it is," Roger agrees.

I'm not quite prepared, though, for the curiosity I excite as I enter the low, red-brick building which looks more like a barracks than a hospital. Black faces peer out of doorways and mouths fall open as we walk down the long corridor that leads to the main office. I peek into several of the wards. Everything is spotless. I hadn't expected this in a bush hospital.

Half an hour later, Roger leaves me and I begin my first day's work in this vast land. I'm fascinated with everything. I can't imagine how the staff manages to maintain such order and efficiency with so little equipment! And everyone is so glad I've come. By the time the sun has set, I've delivered three babies, injected a score of people for various complaints, and treated child after child with conjunctivitis. I tell myself that I'll have to get used to the poverty and malnutrition I see everywhere. And yet those large, liquid brown eyes, curly mops, and welcoming smiles make up for everything else and capture my heart before the day is over.

At last, I go off duty and make my way to the parsonage. "I'll have to bring up the subject of Angus tonight," I tell myself, as I near the garden gate. "I've only one full day here before I have to go back to Lilongwe." Then I stop abruptly. I hear voices and notice a couple sitting on a bench some feet away. I have no idea who the girl is. She's tall and slim with light brown skin and long, black wavy hair. I glance again at the man sitting close beside her and smother an exclamation of dismay. It's Angus Campbell! I couldn't mistake that mop of light brown hair anywhere. I can't see his expression from where I'm standing but I can see the girl's. She's looking adoringly into Angus' eyes. He's talking in a low voice and they're sitting very close. Lovers! I'm sure of it.

I wrench myself from the scene and tiptoe through the back door and into the house. Suddenly, I forget about how I felt a few moments ago. All I know is that I want to leave this wretched land of lions and leopards, of dusty roads, and hot mosquito-infested nights. Most of all, I want to run into my mother's arms and lay my head on my dad's chest as I used to do when someone made fun of my hair at school, or when my favorite horse died, or when I found out Grandma had cancer and only three months to live.

"Finished for the day?" Mrs. Buchannan greets me. "We'll have supper in a few moments once Angus has gone."

"Angus?" I ask tremulously, trying to sound surprised.

"Yes, the missionary farmer from Ngavi. He's visiting in the garden with Joy. He...." She stops abruptly. I look around and see her husband has entered the room. "Joy is rooming with you tonight so she'll tell you all about it herself," she goes on hurriedly. "Angus is taking her back to Ngavi for supper, but you'll see her tomorrow if not tonight."

Her voice seems a very long way away. "Are you ill?" Mrs. Buchannan asks anxiously. "The heat's been too much for you. You may need to cut that hair of yours. You'll find it a lot cooler out here if you wear it short."

I shrug. Normally I would have reacted violently to such a suggestion. My thick mane is my only glory. But right now I couldn't care less.

"I'm going to take a quick shower," I mutter.

As I pull on a clean blouse and skirt, I decide that my host and hostess will never know about Angus and me. As for the girl.... I stop short. Joy—the name is familiar. Of course! She's the girl I saw on those slides long years ago. I've never forgotten her. Angus is her guardian, has been for years. It all makes horrible sense! He has fallen in love with his ward. It's natural and it's awful at the same time. I begin to tremble. I'll have to call Mabel and ask her to come for me tomorrow evening when I finish work. I simply can't face two nights with the woman who has obviously stolen Angus' heart.

I will never know how I get through supper. Fortunately, no one thinks it strange when I excuse myself as the clock strikes eight. Jetlag, my first day in the bush, and five hours' work without air-conditioning—all these seem ample reasons for the dark rings round my eyes and my monosyllabic answers to Mrs. Buchannan's well-meaning but endless questions.

It is ten before I hear my roommate tiptoe into the room. My eyes are closed tight but sleep is miles away. Tomorrow, I'll have to meet her—in the morning when the light is streaming through the window and the birds are chirping outside. It always seems easier to face truth in the daylight. And maybe she'll sleep late, and I can slip out before she's awake.

Eventually, I hear her measured breathing and know she's asleep. I pull the sheet over my head, stuff the corner of the pillow in my mouth, and battle with my tears. I haven't even seen Angus, but I know the truth already, well, two truths really—first that I am terribly and irrevocably in love with him, and secondly—that he definitely has forgotten me. So maybe I should go home right away. What does Africa mean to me without Angus?

If I could only cry, but I daren't. That's the torture of it. If I could really shout my anger and frustration to the Almighty and then maybe shake the girl in the bed by the window and ask her how she could do this to me, then I'd feel better, wouldn't I? But I can't cry, can't shout, can't even pray. All I can do is concentrate on controlling my emotions. If I can get through this one night, there's hope I'll get through tomorrow, and the next night, and the next day. It can't get worse than this, can it?

Chapter Fifty

Joy: Is she really an angel?

"Had a nice evening, Joy?" Minnie Buchannan asks, as she opens the manse door and lets me in. It's nearly eleven.

"Sorry I'm late," I apologize. "And yes, I've had a fabulous evening. Time just flew by." Actually, it's flown by for weeks now. Cramming for exams, graduation, application for universities in England—all have whizzed by me so fast, I've been almost dizzy. And, of course, dating Angus has been more than I could have ever hoped for. Time always flies when you're content.

"I'm glad to see you and Angus so happy," Minnie whispers.

"That's all I want to do forever," I whisper back. "Make Angus happy, I mean."

"That's a wonderful goal, dear," Minnie says smiling. "Now just be quiet as you go upstairs. I'm sorry, but you'll have to share your room with a young woman from the States. She's a doctor, or will be soon, and is helping out in the hospital for a few days. I thought she'd be more comfortable here at the manse than anywhere else. It's her first time in Africa."

"I'll be quiet," I tell Minnie. "Very! She's probably tired out from her journey."

"Yes, she is. And she's been working all afternoon. Take good care of her, dear."

"I will," I say brightly. I've had such a wonderful evening with Angus, I don't mind sharing my room with someone else. And I'm so tired, I know I'll go right off to sleep.

I open the bedroom door and tiptoe over to my bed. It's dark and I'm afraid to switch on the light. I glance over at the other bed, but it's too dark to see much. I'm real curious. I don't get to meet many people from America. I wonder what she's like.

I fall asleep almost as soon as my head touches the pillow and wake up at the usual time even though I've not set my alarm. The other girl seems to be still asleep. Strange that she's not up by this time, if she's supposed to be on duty this morning. Day shifts begin at seven. I know, because I've worked as a nurses' assistant now for several weeks. Maybe I ought to waken her.

I walk across the wooden floor, and bend over her bed. I give a start as I catch sight of something glinting in the rays of light streaming in the window opposite. I stare at a mass of gold-red hair, scattered all over her pillow. I've never seen hair like it, not in real life that is but.... I bend down closer. No, it can't be! But I'd know that nose anywhere, and that smooth, creamy-white complexion I've been envious of for years!

I turn away quickly as she begins to waken. She rubs her eyes for a moment and then sits up. I panic. What do I do? I feel as if the world has come to an end, my world, I mean. I ought to have known she'd turn up sooner or later. But right now, I suppose I can pretend I don't know who she is and see what happens. After all, she won't know who I am, will she?

I force myself to turn around. "Good Morning!" I tell her. I sound much brighter than I feel.

"Good Morning!" Her words are just as forced as mine are. Our eyes meet, and I know that she knows that I know who she is. I take a long gulp and sit down on my bed.

"I'm Joy Mkandawire," I tell her, trying to smile.

She opens her mouth several times and then closes it again. I can see she wants to bolt out the door. I do, too, but I won't. I've the advantage. She's not engaged to Angus Campbell; I am! And, anyway, she's married, isn't she? I can't see her hand from where I'm sitting. Maybe she's divorced.

I sit and watch her struggle for words. I'm not going to help her out one bit. But wait, how on earth does she know about me? Maybe Minnie told her. Yes, that's it. Well, she's messed everything by coming here and she'll have to pay for it.

At last, after what seems an age, she mutters in such a low voice that I wouldn't be able to make out the words if I didn't know them already: "I'm Cherry McMann." That's all she says, but it tells me everything. Angus' old sweetheart is still single and has come chasing after him.

"Don't pretend you don't know who I am, Joy," she goes on, sounding just a bit annoyed. "I could see it in your eyes a minute ago."

"And I could see that you know me, too," I retort, "though how, I've no idea."

"About nine years ago, I saw you on some slides a missionary was showing at a mission near my college."

"And you remembered me?" I ask incredulously.

"I couldn't forget you, Joy."

"But I've changed a lot in nine years," I protest.

"Well," her voice falters, "I saw you with Angus last night."

I rise from the bed and take a step towards her. "You saw us last night? Then you saw...him...too?" I can't speak his name to *her.*

"Yes," she murmurs, "but just from behind. I couldn't see his face."

This is absolutely crazy. What's happening right now would make a good movie, only neither Cherry nor I know how it's going to end. That's the wild part. I suppose it'll be in a tragedy for one of us, that's for sure. Problem is, for her or for me?

"But how did you know who *I* was?" Cherry begins after a long time. "Did...." She stops and can't go on.

"Angus had your photo on his dresser for years," I tell her as calmly as I can. Inside I'm raving mad. My worst nightmare is coming to pass. So why am I sitting here letting her quiz me. I'm not the guilty one. And Angus promised that he would stick by me, and he never breaks a promise. So I've not a thing to worry about after all, have I?

"Go on," she mutters. "I want to hear it all."

Well, if she wants to hear it all, then I'll tell her it all. "When Angus came back from the States," I say slowly, "he said you were marrying someone else." The tears are trickling down her cheeks now. "So, I asked for your picture," I continue, determined to be honest with her.

Cherry finds that one hard to believe. "Whatever for?" she asks, her eyes opening wider.

"So that I could become like you. Then, I thought, maybe Angus would come to love me some day just like he loved you."

I watch her face closely. She doesn't know what to think about what I've just said. Then, after several minutes, she smiles. I can't believe it! I'd think she had nothing on earth to smile about. And she's got a wonderful smile. No wonder Angus couldn't resist it! "I don't think you needed to do that to make him love you," she tells me. "You're about the most beautiful young woman I've ever met."

This is maddening. Of course I'm glad she's noticed how beautiful I am, but I don't want *her* to compliment me. I want her to lose her cool with me, to shout, and rave, and wish me in hell. Oh, I know she won't do any of that. She's too holy! But she doesn't need to be so sickly sweet with me.

"And what's the use of being beautiful?" I shout. "What good will it do me now? You've spoiled everything! Just when I thought you were getting out of my life for good, and I'm making Angus finally forget you, you turn up from nowhere and act the saint."

Cherry's face is crimson. Her eyes are flashing. So she has got a temper after all! Great! I'll try to make her madder still. "And anyway, why did you come here?" I demand. "I'm Angus Campbell's fiancée and I deserve to know."

"Fiancée?" she repeats. "So you're engaged?" She's turning white now, awfully white. I hope she doesn't faint on me.

"Yes, we're engaged," I repeat proudly. "Only it's still a secret between us. But I think Angus would want *you* to know." The devil is getting into me again. But I don't care. This girl has made me suffer for years. Surely I have the right to pay her back just a little?

I toss back my hair and take off the gold chain that is hanging round my neck. I've put Angus' ring on this chain so that it'll be next to my heart, always. "Here's the ring he has given me," I tell her. "It was his mother's. Isn't it beautiful?"

I slip the ring on my finger and hold it up to the light. The diamond sparkles as it catches the sun's rays. I gaze at it for a long time, hold it to my lips, and then put the chain round my neck once more.

Our eyes meet again and the pain I see in hers sends me crazy. I yank at the chain with all my strength. It feels like a noose. I pull it over my head and toss it onto the bed.

"It's no use," I pout. "I know he doesn't love me like he loved you. And as soon as he sees you, he'll love you all over again."

"It's all right, Joy," Cherry says very quietly. "I'm leaving Mpongo tonight and won't ever come back."

I can't believe her! "But you did come here to meet him, didn't you?"

"Yes," she admits, blushing crimson. I've never seen anyone blush like that before. "I wanted to know if Angus still loved me before I move on with my life. And now I know he doesn't."

"But he will once he knows you're still single!" I shout. She stares at me for a very long time.

"If what you say is true," she says very quietly, "then he shouldn't be engaged to you. But that's his business, not mine."

Her words stab me like knives, but I won't let her know that. She slips on her dressing gown and makes for the bathroom. "Wait!" I call after her. "We need to talk this out. You don't understand."

Her hand is on the doorknob. She hesitates a moment, then turns round and faces me. "Meeting you has already half killed me, Joy. I can't take any more!"

She slips out into the hallway and into the bathroom opposite. I dress and decide to wait until she comes out. Half an hour ticks by. I finally knock on the bathroom door. "You OK?" I ask.

"How on earth have you the nerve to ask that?" she asks irritably.

"She's human after all," I think to myself. "She's not the angel I thought she was, but then, red-headed angels aren't typical, are they?"

"What will I tell them downstairs?" I ask through the keyhole.

"That I'm not well and won't want breakfast," she mutters. I shrug. What else can I expect?

I can see that the Buchannans are worried about their guest when I pass on Cherry's message. "She wasn't well last night," Minnie tells me. "She's too delicate to be working here."

I eat my breakfast in silence, make my way over to the hospital, and begin another day. Only it's going to be the very worst day in my life. Well, it's already been the worst day in my life. Maybe tomorrow will even be worse, because if Cherry does keep her word and leaves here tonight without seeing Angus, he'll know anyway. I'll need to tell him. I can't act a lie, can I?

I see Cherry from a distance several times during this horrible day. She avoids me and I avoid her. Six o'clock strikes at last and we're ready to go off duty. She meets me in the hallway and slips me a folded piece of paper. I go to say something, but she has gone.

I sit down on a bench and begin to read: "Joy, I'm sorry I lost my cool with you this morning. But you did upset me, a lot. And I know I upset you, too. But please, let's forgive each other and pray for each other. I've been doing a lot of thinking today. Whether you tell *him* or not that I've been here is between you and God. You may not be able to

do anything else but tell him everything and be true to yourself and to
him. But I will understand if you don't tell him. What good can it do?
He'd never break his word to you for a thousand Cherry McManns if I
know Angus Campbell. And even if he did, I couldn't marry him now. It
wouldn't be right. I want to get as far away from him and Malawi as I
possibly can. Yes, I'm very upset right now and very jealous. I'm no
saint, and, to be honest, I can't face meeting you again. Hopefully, soon,
I'll be able to pray for you and for Angus. After all, I really don't deserve
his love any more. I broke his heart once. You've won that heart fairly
and squarely. Take it and heal it, Joy, with your fabulous beauty and
love. Sincerely, Cherry McMann.

"You won that heart fairly and squarely!" The words yell at me from
the page. They dig into my heart. I give a groan. Is that the way it was
and, anyway, have I really won his heart? I don't know. I really don't.

I thought, this morning, that she was as human as I am, but now I
know I'm wrong. So, will I tell him she was here, or won't I? Who
knows right now what I'll do, only *she* said herself what good would it
do? And angels are usually right, aren't they—even redheaded ones?

Chapter Fifty-One

Andrew: I truly forgive you!

I'm standing on my ex-wife's doorstep, my heart beating like crazy. I want to be anywhere in the world but here. And I wouldn't be, except that I feel God-propelled—as if I couldn't do anything else and still lift up my head before the Almighty and call myself "His servant." Not that I've been much of a servant these last few years. Still, if His calling is without repentance, then in His sight, if not in the sight of others, I'm still His priest! And that comforts me and also frightens me to death!

I put my hand out, ring the doorbell, and wait. I'm here to say "I forgive you" to Mary, to say I want to be friends for the kids' sake, to....

The door is opening and she's standing there. I haven't seen her in almost seventeen years. We are both staring at each other in complete silence. She's still a tall, willowy blonde, still has those same sky blue eyes; and yet, of course, she's not the same. I can see right away traces of the life she led for many years, but they are just that—traces.

And Mary? I'm wondering exactly what she's thinking about me as we mutter some sort of greeting, shake hands, and she leads me into a small, simply furnished sitting room. My hair has turned white since I saw her last. Actually, I think the years have done more damage to me than to her which surprises me.

We both sit down, avoid each other's eyes, talk about the weather, and then follows the longest conversational pause I can ever remember. I stir uneasily in my chair, thinking of a hundred things to say and discarding each as quickly as it pops into my head.

"I want you to forgive me, Andrew, for what I have done to you and to the kids." This unbearable silence is broken at last, but Mary's words hit me between the eyes. I knew she would say this when I arranged to see her this morning. She is a Christian now, and Christians always ask for forgiveness. But the way she asks is, well, convicting. But I don't think I can give her the kind of forgiveness she needs. I hesitate. Her lip trembles and tears fill her eyes.

"Of course I forgive you," I assure her, but the words bounce back at me like a rubber ball.

Mary's lip trembles again. "Can we be honest with each other?" she asks me timidly.

"Of course!"

"Well, after you first got converted, I was utterly shocked. The change in you came so rapidly it bowled me over."

"As a conversion should do," I mutter.

"Yes, but I was not prepared for it, or for the new lifestyle you adopted so suddenly. One night you were partying with me; the next, you were on your knees or in some church service or other."

"I remember you poured water down my neck once while I was praying," I remind her, with a wry smile.

"I remember too. That was an awful thing to do, but I did it and a lot of other things because I was jealous."

"Jealous?"

"Yes. A third Person had come into our marriage—Someone you loved more than me. I couldn't stand it."

"Why didn't you tell me?" I demand.

"I did try, several times; but you didn't understand, or if you did, you thought it was a terrible thing, which it was, very terrible—to be jealous of the Almighty. And yet it did prove something which I think you didn't realize."

"What?" I ask, knowing the answer before I asked it.

"That I loved you more than I loved life itself. In fact, you were my idol. And so I was jealous of your love for Christ."

I'd need to think about that one a long time. But she was continuing: "In the end, I figured I'd have to put up with this third Person, and that maybe one day, you could teach me how to love Him too."

I stare at her. I had never known that flighty Mary Price had thought like that. "And then you dropped another bombshell," she goes on. "You told me you were going to be a priest. That infuriated me at first, but then I thought I'd be able to put up with it because I loved you so much."

She paused. "Go on," I urge.

"But the old jealousy came back as I saw you so absorbed in your religious life. I'd be alone most evenings so I began to make my own friends. Finally I laid down the law to you—give your seminary training up or I'd divorce you." She's on the verge of tears now. "It was the mistake of my life," she admits with a sob. "How many times I'd have given the earth to take back that decision! From then on, I went from bad to worse."

I listen intently. "So you didn't have other men in your life before the divorce?"

She looks at me, surprised. "Of course not! And I didn't divorce to get another man. I divorced because I was mad at God and mad at you. But it wasn't long before I had other men in my life. I lived with two during the next eight to ten years, but I never remarried. Somehow, I had a faint hope that we might get back together again. But the drugs ruined everything until I met some people who cared and showed me the love of Christ operating in their lives."

Somehow, her story makes me uneasy. I had relayed it to Cherry and others rather differently. But Mary is right. That was exactly how it had been. Then it strikes me that while I've come to give forgiveness, I maybe should begin by asking forgiveness instead.

"Please forgive me, Mary," I begin, and with that comes a release of spirit that is overwhelming.

"Forgive *you*?" she exclaims, tears pouring down her face now. "Anything I need to forgive you for is miniscule in comparison with what I've done to you and Gloria and Peter. Oh, Andrew, can you ever forgive *me*?"

Her words make me cry, no, bawl is more like it. I cross the room and kneel beside her chair. "Of course I forgive you," I sob. Then I begin to pour out my heart to God.

When I'm through, I look up. Mary is still crying, but I'm almost sure her tears are tears of joy. "So you do forgive me, really and truly?" she whispers.

"Really and truly," I assure her, smiling through my tears. "I should have done it years ago."

"Better late than never," she says lightly as I rise from my knees. "And now for a bite to eat. What shall it be? Your favorite apple pie or lemon meringue?"

"You have baked both?"

"Of course. I've got a long memory. Now which, Andrew?"

"A slice of both, please."

I watch as she cuts both pies, places them on a plate, and hands it to me. "Can you come to Gloria's party?" Mary asks as we munch our pie.

"Yes," I answer without hesitation.

"Good," she says, smiling broadly. "We have invited a motley crowd, though, so be prepared."

"Meaning?"

"Meaning that some of the kids I work with will be there. Gloria has grown close to them. She's a wonderful girl, Andrew. You did a good job with her." I feel embarrassed and fill my mouth with apple pie. Then I rise to go.

"See you at the party," she shouts after me as I drive off a few minutes later.

"At the party," I echo back.

By the time the next morning dawns, I feel years younger already, so much so that I go swimming with Gloria the next day.

"You're different, Dad," she tells me as we swim the length of the pool together.

"I sure am. I've forgiven your mother, Gloria, and it's released something inside, something that was eating me up."

She stops swimming and stares at me and then lets out the wildest war whoop I've ever heard. It doesn't matter that everyone thinks she's crazy. It doesn't matter that it isn't ladylike. And I whoop too. May as well! I've been forgiven; I have forgiven. Grace is over me, inside me, on top of me. It reminds me of my Damascus road experience those many years ago. And for the first time since Cherry went out of my life, I think wistfully of the ministry. Am I doing right to abandon it?

"Maybe you'll start preaching again, Dad," my daughter says suddenly. Sometimes her mind-reading ability seems uncanny. "You were a wonderful preacher, you know."

My smile changes to a frown. "Yes, but I think I'll do pretty well in the role of a professor, Gloria. I'm applying to Princeton," I say abruptly. "If I'm accepted, I'll take it as God's will that I keep on in the direction I'm going."

Gloria's face clouds a little. Then she shrugs. "Well, it's your life, Dad. And whatever you do or don't do in the future, this moment is a time to celebrate. I've prayed for this for years."

I look into her dark eyes and realize how I've hurt her. "Yes, daughter, let's celebrate. But how?"

"By taking the Eucharist together, Dad. Tonight. It's a date, right?"

"Right," I say, wishing all dates were as inexpensive, and thanking God that He had given me a daughter whose celebration centers around His church. I am truly blessed.

Chapter Fifty-Two

Cherry: Caricature or real?

Another sleepless night! Mabel and I are sharing a tiny bedroom in the nurse's quarters at Nkhoma Hospital. Whenever I close my eyes, I can see that girl's face. It's so utterly beautiful! I can't blame Angus for falling for her. And she's not just beautiful. She's earthy, real—like Eve in Eden. And that aura of pathos that hovers about her makes her all the more irresistible. I really think she'd die if she couldn't have Angus. She needs him more than I do. I have family; she has no one.

But all my attempts at the heroic fail miserably. I'm upset, disappointed, jealous, and utterly broken-hearted. I cry myself to sleep, waken with a splitting headache, and then, suddenly know what I have to do.

"You've got to cut my hair, Mabel!" I order, as we sip coffee together in the tiny kitchenette.

"I can't do it, Cherry. Please don't ask me to."

"Then I'll find someone who will," I say stubbornly. "I have constant headaches since coming to Malawi."

"Because of your hair?" she asks skeptically.

"Partly."

"And because of Angus?"

I nod and burst into tears. Mabel shakes her head and vanishes out the door. In ten minutes she is back with a pair of hair-cutting shears. Without one word, she sits me on a stool and wraps a towel around my neck. I've already combed out my hair. All is ready. She takes a handful of ringlets in her hand and then throws down the scissors on the table.

"I can't do it," she says decidedly. "I just can't!"

I reach over and grab the sheers. "Then I will," I say determinedly. Mabel covers her eyes with her hands as she hears the blunt scissors chewing away at my thick locks. But she refuses to help me. I begin to tremble, but at last it's done. The sun, shining in through the window, catches the golden tints in the mass of red curls lying at my feet. I suddenly feel completely detached. My hair—it's no longer a part of me, just like my past life. It's lying there, too, on the tiled, kitchen floor. Mabel puts her arms around me. We stand like that for a very long time. And then suddenly, I pull away, attempt a smile, and make for the bathroom.

"You look a fright, so be warned," Mabel calls after me. "You can't go on duty like that."

"My head will be covered anyway," I shout back. "And I'll go to the hairdresser's as soon as I can and get the odd ends evened out." Then I give a gasp.

Someone is staring back at me from the tiny mirror above the cracked hand-basin, but it isn't the Cherry I know. She seems a caricature of the real person. Wait, maybe that's not right. Maybe she is the real person and that other girl who usually stares back at me is the caricature.

Chapter Fifty-Three

Angus: Do I really need an angel?

"By the way, Joy, guess who we bumped into today at Nkhoma hospital?"

Minnie Buchannan sets a dish of our favorite chicken casserole on the table as she poses the question. She and Roger have just returned from a two-week holiday in the South and have invited Joy and me for supper.

I steal a glance at the girl beside me. She looks pretty fabulous in a pale pink blouse I bought her yesterday. I'm not sure I like the way men stare at her everywhere we go, but I suppose I'll have to get used to it. And I'll say this: Joy never gives any other man a second look. After all, she can't help being gorgeous. God made her that way.

Joy reaches for her napkin, places it on her lap, and wrinkles her forehead for a moment. Then she shakes her head. "I've no idea who you bumped into, Mrs. Buchannan," she tells her hostess smiling.

"It's that redheaded doctor you shared your room with the other week," Minnie says, as she sits down at one end of the table. "Remember?"

"Yes," Roger puts in. "I think she was called Cherry, wasn't she? Growing up in Scotland, I was pretty used to redheads, but I must admit, I've never seen hair like hers. It was something else, wasn't it, Joy?"

My heart leaps to my mouth. "Cherry was here, at Mpongo?" It's out before I can stop it. Roger and Minnie stare at me, perplexed. "There must be some mistake!" I add, wanting them to say both "yes" and "no" at the same time. I glance at Joy. She looks like a frightened rabbit, caught in a trap. Then, suddenly, she pushes back her chair, and makes a bolt for the door.

I'm after her like the wind. "No, you don't run away like that," I say firmly, grabbing her by the arm. "Look at me, Joy," I command. "Look at me and tell me the truth," I go on in the same tone. "You have her photo on your dresser. Was *she* here, in Mpongo and you didn't even tell me?"

I'm standing by the door so she can't escape. And I'm very, very angry. Actually, I'm absolutely mad! "Joy," I shout, "was this redheaded doctor the woman in the photo I gave you?"

Joy is shaking now. "Yes, Angus,'" she mutters and then wrenches herself free and bolts out the dining-room door.

"What's going on between you two?" Roger demands as he comes to where I'm standing.

I run my hand through my hair as I always do when I'm particularly distraught. "Cherry here in Mpongo and I knew nothing about it!" I finally exclaim, ignoring his question. I grab my pickup keys from the table and make for the door.

"What are you doing, Angus?" I feel Roger's strong hand on my arm.

"Doing?" I repeat wildly. "Why going after her, of course!"

"Take it easy, man," Roger says gently but firmly as he leads me to the sofa and sits me down. "Let's talk this over. You need to know that she's flying back to the States tomorrow."

"How do you know?" I demand.

"She told Minnie. She was only here for a month."

I jump up from my seat and make for the door once more. "Tomorrow?" I repeat. "Thank God you told me in time. If I start out now, I'll get to Blantyre airport by morning. I know flights to the States usually leave mid-morning."

Roger grabs me by the arm. "Have you forgotten Joy?" he asks. His voice is sterner than I've ever heard it.

His words make me come to my senses. Of course, there's Joy to consider. I've given her my word.

"Let's go outside," Roger whispers. "So we can talk privately."

I follow him mechanically into the garden. The sun has set. A few mosquitoes buzz about my face. "We won't stay here long, Angus, but I thought you needed a breather."

"I do," I murmur. "It's such a shock."

"This redhead—she's your former love?"

I nod. "I thought she was married," is all I say.

We stand staring up at the heavens for a very long time. Then I feel anger surging through me. I grab Roger by the shoulders. "Why didn't Joy tell me about Cherry?" I demand. "She's deceitful. She's sneaky."

Roger puts a finger to my lips. "Ask her why yourself," he says quietly. "But not as you are now. You'll have to pull yourself together for her sake."

I'm still fingering the keys to my pickup. What do I really owe Joy Mkandawire? Cherry's been here, looking for me, most likely. So I stand by and do nothing? I'm still single. Still free!

Roger's hand is still on my arm. It steadies me and brings me to my senses. Suddenly I wilt. No, of course I'm not free. "I know I can't forget about Joy," I murmur. "But it's awfully hard. Why has God timed it this way? Why did...." I stop abruptly. That's just the point. Cherry could have come to Mpongo a year ago, six months ago, but she didn't.

The tears begin to rain down my cheeks. "I need to go to Joy," I murmur. "And, please, Roger, pray for me."

I turn and re-enter the manse. I find Joy in the living room, lying face down on the sofa, sobbing her heart out. She hears my footsteps, springs to her feet, and throws herself into my arms.

"She said there was no point telling you, honest she did, Angus," Joy mutters over and over. "She said she wouldn't marry you even if you did break it off."

I take the distraught girl's hand and sit her gently on the sofa. "Now," I say as calmly as I can, though my heart feels as if it is going to thump its way out of my chest, "sit down and tell me all about it."

"But you've fallen in love with her all over again," the girl sobs. "I saw it in your eyes, when you heard she'd been here."

I can't dispute what she's saying. I'm so confused right now. Maybe Joy's right; maybe she's wrong. I only say quietly, "It was a shock. And yet you knew she had been here all the time!"

"But she said...," she begins wildly. "She...oh, you may as well read it yourself."

She fumbles in her handbag, the tears now falling thick and fast. Then she hands me a folded piece of paper. "Read it," she mutters, "and then tell me if you still blame me for not speaking. She gave that to me before she left."

I open the paper and begin to read. But when I come to the words, "I really don't deserve his love any more. I broke his heart once. You've won that heart fairly and squarely. Take it and heal it, Joy, with your fabulous beauty and love," something breaks inside of me and I put my head in my hands and weep silently.

"She's an angel, isn't she?" Joy mutters, her hand on my shoulder. I can't answer. I'm falling into a black hole that has no bottom.

"I'll never be an angel, Angus. Never, ever!" Joy wails.

I hardly hear her. I'm sinking, sinking. "Help me, God," I breathe silently. "Please help me!"

"I will never leave you nor forsake you," comes the answer.

"Not even in hell?" I ask for it seems I'm headed there directly. My lips are moving but my words go inward not outward. Joy can't hear them but she's staring at me, half scared to death.

"He brought me out of a horrible pit." They are the Psalmist's words and they are mine. I'm being lifted back to sanity. I feel my head clearing. And then I look into Joy's beautiful face. The anguish I see in it nearly bowls me over. I reach out and touch her hand.

"I said that I'll never be an angel," she repeats. "But you didn't hear me. I don't know what happened to you for a minute or two, Angus."

"I'm OK now," I say reassuringly. She's not ready for my explanation yet. Maybe someday she will be. And as for being an angel, maybe it's not an angel I need after all. Maybe what I need is some flesh and blood reality, like the girl sitting by my side, not some ethereal creature that flits in and out of my life, leaving me moping for some vision which never materializes.

"I don't think I need an angel, Joy," I finally say, managing a smile. "At any rate, God sent me you, Joy Mkandawire, and it's you I want for my wife."

"You really mean it, don't you?" Joy exclaims, smiling through her tears. "I can't believe it. You're telling me that you'll marry me, a no-good girl who has deceived you all these weeks?"

"You're not a no-good girl," I whisper, "though I wish you had been more up front with me."

"But she said...," she begins.

I put my hand gently on her mouth. "I understand why you didn't tell me. Now, let's put it all behind us and remember that whatever we've done, there is forgiveness with God, Joy."

"Pray with me," she whispers back.

I begin to pray for Joy, for myself, for Cherry, for Africa. And the girl beside me prays too, for forgiveness and for strength to do what's right.

"You're a saint, Angus," she whispers as I kiss her goodnight half an hour later. "Just like *she* is."

I shake my head, conscious that I've felt anything but saint-like during the past few hours and change the subject. "So you're having a thorough medical checkup tomorrow?" I ask, as she sees me to the front door.

Joy nods. "Yes. I'm as fit as a fiddle, so I'm not a bit worried." She does look a bit worried, though. But no wonder, after this terrible afternoon. Then an awful thought flashes through my mind. I brush it aside and say lightly, "Get a good sleep. You need it!"

"If I can," she says quietly. "It's been quite an evening, Angus."

Understatement of the year, I think to myself as I drive back to Ngavi. My old love has been so close and I never knew it! And the girl I've promised to marry has kept it from me all these weeks!

I am in an agony all night. I acted the hero in front of Joy, but now there's a pain at my heart that won't go away. I think of the "if onlys" in my life. If only I had not been so intolerant with Cherry those long years ago. If only I'd not let her father dominate me like he did; if only I'd not been such a naïve fool when it came to Joy; if only I'd taken the trouble to discover if Cherry was really and truly married before I committed myself to someone else.

All night I wallow in self-pity and in recrimination. I'm sinking into that pit again only this time I hear no voice of comfort or feel no hand lifting me out of danger. And I know why. This time, God wants me to climb out if I'll be willing to do it His way.

It is only when the cock is crowing, and the light beginning to steal in through my window, that I find myself on my knees. The one way out and up is the way of trust. It's true that I could have chosen differently, and so could Cherry. But we chose what we thought was the right path at the time. And we both loved God as much as we knew how. So can't I trust Him now? And can't I pray that Cherry, too, will find peace just as I am finding it? And Joy? Who knows what she's feeling this morning! Guilt? Forgiveness? Hope? Fear?

And as the new day dawns, the image of the redheaded girl that's haunted me for so long, fades away. In her place stands the girl I've pledged myself to marry—a broken, scarred girl—a girl who needs love and protection. After all, who has ever loved me like Joy Mkandawire? Even if Cherry loves me now, I was not her first choice, quite obviously. So maybe at last, then, I can truly say good-bye to the past and embrace the present.

I make my usual breakfast of paw-paw, eggs on toast, and a mug of steaming coffee and the day begins. I stroll over to the paddock nearby to milk our prize heifer. She moos as she sees me coming. I smile as I stroke her nose.

"Morning, Mafingosi," I say as she nuzzles my hand. Her large eyes look into mine. I almost envy her. She probably has never felt the kind of pain I feel right now. Then I look over her head at the rolling fields of corn and soya beans, stretching as far as the eye can see.

"Morning, Dada," my chief foreman shouts as he strides up the dirt path towards the nearest field.

"Morning, Samuel," I shout back. He gives me the widest grin.

"They're coming today from Lilongwe to interview us, remember, Dada?" he shouts again.

I grin back. I had almost forgotten. The article about our farm, recently published in the *Mpongo Times*, has made quite a stir. The pain at my heart lessens as I swell with pride. After all, this is *my* farm; and Africa is *my* country; and Joy Mkandawire is *my* future wife. And above and beyond all this, God is *my* God. So I'm not doing too badly, am I?

Chapter Fifty-Four

Cherry: Vows are vows!

It's been several weeks since I returned from Malawi. When Dad first heard about Angus, he had a terrible setback.

"It's all my fault," he kept muttering for days. But gradually, my love eased his pain, and together we prayed and cried and asked God to show us the way through the maze of our sorrow.

I've been spending a few nights with Paul in Chicago before I fly back to London. Madeline's convent isn't that far away, so I've arranged to meet her at a restaurant. I think it best not to tell Paul my plans, although I did tell my dad. I tell him most everything these days.

The very dignified lady in the nun's habit stares at me for a long time as I enter the restaurant. I stare back for a moment, and then we are in each other's arms. Several people gaze at us curiously but we don't care.

"What on earth have you done to your hair?" Madi gasps as we are ushered to a table in a secluded alcove.

"I cut it," I reply briefly. I could ask what she has done to hers, but I won't. It wouldn't be respectful.

"But why?" Madi persists.

"It was so hot in Africa so, well, I cut it!"

Madeline eyes me intently for a few moments. "You're not telling me everything, are you?" she wants to know, her blue eyes probing mine just as they used to do.

"How can I when we've only just met?" I hedge. "And what about you, Madi? How is convent life? You are happy in your calling, aren't you?"

"Yes, Cherry," Madi says quietly. I look into her deep blue eyes and know she's telling the truth. "And what about you?"

I squirm a little in my seat. "I've had ups and downs," I begin slowly, "but I really enjoy medicine. I feel fulfilled in helping to save lives."

"I'm sure you do. And your family? How are they?"

I squirm again. How much do I tell her? She probably knows nothing about Allie's death. "A lot has happened in the past year, Madi," I tell her, avoiding her eyes. "Dad's been through a lot."

"Did you have a death in the family?" she asks anxiously.

"Paul's wife committed suicide," I blurt out.

I see the horror in Madeline's eyes and wonder if meeting her has been a good idea after all. She tries to say something but can't.

"She was manic depressive," I explain in a low voice. "She refused to take her medicine."

"Poor Paul!" she whispers. "How tragic!"

"Yes, and this tragedy has so upset Dad that he's never been the same since. That's why he's written this note and begged me to give it to you in person."

I hand her the envelope. "Read it," I urge. "You may have some questions after you've read it."

Just then, the waitress comes to take our orders. When she's gone, Madeline slits open the envelope and begins to read. Dad read the letter to me so I know it nearly off by heart. It's short but to the point—a very humble apology for coming between Madeline and Paul and there's something more, something I begged him to omit, but he was adamant.

"It's my letter, not yours, Cherry," he had reminded me sternly. Yes, he still can be stern at times, and unbelievably stubborn! After all, his name is Dennis McMann!

"I know I can't make the past any different," he wrote, "but Providence has stepped in, Madeline. And I am sure that Paul still loves you." That's all he said, but I know my friend has caught his hidden meaning. I can see her blush scarlet, and two large tears trickle slowly down her smooth cheek. She wears no makeup now, but is as attractive as ever.

Madeline finishes reading and then folds the letter and hands it back to me. I look at her questioningly. "I can't keep it," she whispers. "It reminds me too much of the life I left behind me. I never intend to break my vows, Cherry. Tell your Dad that for me. But," she goes on, with just a trace of reproach in her voice, "I'm not made of steel, either." She turns her head away for a moment. When she looks at me again, she is serene once more. "Now," she says brightly, "you haven't really told me much about yourself. Africa, for example. I'm wondering what took you there in the first place?"

I'm not sure how much to tell Madeline. The waitress sets our plates in front of us. We eat for a while in silence and then, try as I will to stop them, the tears begin to flow and won't stop.

"Want to tell an old friend?" Madi asks softly. "At least I can pray for you, Cherry. Sounds strange coming from me, doesn't it? But that's what I do a lot of these days—pray!"

I smile through my tears. "It's Angus," I admit sorrowfully. "He's engaged to be married. I went to Malawi thinking...." I can't go on.

"I'm so sorry," my friend whispers. "I know at least a little of what you must be feeling, Cherry."

I nod. Of course she knows—knows every step of the journey I am now embarked on, a journey that never seems to end.

"I found healing in discovering God's will for my life," Madeline goes on. "That is the secret, you know."

I nod again. "Think I should put on the habit, like you?" I ask her with a half grin.

"I think there might be a Protestant equivalent for you," she replies, her eyes twinkling, just like they used to do in the old days. "I'm afraid your father might disown you if you follow in my steps."

I don't think Madi has any idea how much Dad has changed, but his only daughter—a nun? I grin again. "But seriously, Cherry, you do need to find fulfillment in serving Christ," she tells me. "It's the only way. And your heart will heal, in time."

"Like yours?"

"Yes," she says softly, "though your dad's letter made me realize that maybe the healing isn't quite complete yet."

"Maybe it'll never be in this life, Madi. That's what Heaven's for, isn't it? Isn't it meant to do for us what earth can't do?"

Madeline smiles her beautiful smile. We begin to talk about everyday things—she describes a typical day in the convent and then I tell her about Africa. The time flies. I glance at my watch and give a start. "Time to go," I say sadly.

We hug once more and then we part. I wonder about her as I drive back to Chicago. Did she really need to be a nun to find peace?

That night, when Paul has gone out for an hour or so to buy groceries, I call Dad. "Poor girl, she's tied for life," Dad comments sadly when I tell him of Madi's reaction to his letter.

"Not tied, Dad," I counter. "She's made a commitment to Christ. He is her heavenly Bridegroom. And she is content."

There's silence at the other end of the line. "Well, as long as you don't follow her example," he says, a trace of the old dad in his voice.

"Not likely," I assure him, "though there might be, as Madi calls it, 'a Protestant equivalent' that would be my solution."

"To a broken heart?"

"Yes," I murmur, the tears welling up again as they do so easily these days.

"I am sure there is, Cherry," Dad replies, "but I hope it isn't one that robs me of a brood of redheaded grandkids."

"Don't joke about it, Dad," I tell him curtly. "I'll never marry now."

"Never?"

"Never!"

"Mom and I are doomed then, unless that son of ours marries again. I had hoped that Madeline would...."

"Not a chance, Dad. Vows are vows. And I'm just thinking of taking one, too."

"Really?" Dad sounds anxious now.

"I mean," I explain quickly, "that I've decided to spend my life in Africa. In spite of what happened at Mpongo, I can honestly say my month in Africa made me fall in love with her people. And no one can accuse me of going there to get a man! That's one comfort."

"Our prayers answered at last!" he breathes. "But I'm sorry it took this, Cherry."

"No, don't be sorry," I interrupt. "It had to be this way."

"Maybe it did," he agrees, "you being the stubborn daughter of a still more stubborn father!" I hear both laughter and pain in his voice.

I don't contradict him. I can't, for he's right, absolutely right!

Chapter Fifty-Five

Joy: Two lost children.

"You are four months pregnant, Miss Mkandawire."

My stomach turns over as I stare into Dr. Milton's kindly eyes, hoping that he has made some mistake. "It can't be," I protest. "I didn't miss...."

He puts his hand on my shoulder and says in his fatherly way, "That sometimes happens. But your blood work shows clearly that you're pregnant."

This is terrible! Awful! Unthinkable! The doctor sees my distress and says kindly, "My advice is that you tell your family immediately. You look as if you've got a good family, Miss Mkandawire. Surely they'll understand."

Dr. Milton isn't a missionary, though he's white. But he does come to Roger Buchannan's church and I know he's a Christian gentleman. He also is the chief doctor at Mpongo Boarding School and he's probably had to deal with other girls in my predicament.

I nod miserably. "I'll tell them," I agree. "Right away!" But inwardly I'm panicking. I have no family but Angus. Of course I'll tell him, but....

"That's a good girl," the doctor says, as he goes back to his desk. "Now, let's schedule your next appointment."

"I'm going to begin university in England in a week," I blurt out.

The doctor shakes his head. "Dear me! That is a problem."

"I suppose I can't go now!" I say miserably.

"No, I'm not sure you can. Did your mother bring you here?" he asks. "Would you like me to tell her? Or your father?"

I shake my head decidedly. "No, a friend brought me, and I don't want her to know, not yet."

He smiles sympathetically. "Of course you don't. Well, I'll be praying for you, my dear. And let me know if I can do anything to help."

I get up and make for the door. "Thanks," I murmur.

I slip out of his office and head for the rest room. I can't face Minnie Buchannan just yet. She's brought me here today. Angus couldn't. His prize heifer is about to calve and he wanted to be at hand when she began labor. He spent the morning with me, though. I couldn't believe he was so loving and tender, after all that happened yesterday. What a twenty-four hours! First, Angus finds out that his old girlfriend has been here looking for him, and then this!

"Maybe I don't need an angel!" Isn't that what Angus told me last night? And this morning he had whispered just before I left for Mpongo, "God has sent *you* to be my wife, not Cherry. Always remember that!" Well, what good will remembering do now?

I enter the women's restroom at the end of the long, tiled hallway and lock the door. It's good to be alone, even if it is in the toilet! I need to think, need to blame someone, or I'll die here and now with shame. Why on earth did God let me get pregnant? I took precautions, or at least, thought I did. No, that's not right. I can't blame God. I'm sure He didn't tell Guy Stanton to look me up at Easter? He knew what we were like once we got together. No, I can't let Guy take all the blame, either. I flung myself at him at Christmas. Angus warned me to be careful. And, anyway, it takes two to make a baby, doesn't it? I put my hand on my stomach. I'm actually going to be a mother! Oh, God! What does Grandma think of me now?

Suddenly, something inside of me snaps. I turn on the water faucet so no one will hear me cry. I don't think I've ever cried like this.

After about ten minutes, someone tries the door. I'll have to go. I take some powder out of my purse and dab my face. Then I take a deep breath, open the door, and step out to face Mrs. Buchannan and the whole wide world!

Now, an hour later, I let myself into the little two roomed brick house that was home to Grandma and me for so long and throw myself onto the old faded sofa. I'm glad Sarah is at the church preparing for my going-away party. I just have to be alone for a while. I don't think Minnie Buchannan guesses my secret. For once, I was glad she is a bit slow on the uptake, sometimes, and totally unsuspicious. She did ask if I had a headache, I was so quiet. And I told her yes, which was the truth.

"Poor dear!" she sighed. "After what happened last night, I'd have a headache, too." And that was that!

One hurdle over! But the worst is to come! I put my hand to my head and groan. I want to cry but can't. I cried myself dry in the toilet at the clinic.

I glance at my watch. I have a few hours before I need to be at the church. I'd give anything to get out of this celebration! Funny how four or five words turned my whole world upside down! I suppose many women would give anything to hear those words, about being pregnant, I mean. Not me! They're like my death sentence. No more England, no more college, and what's far worse than everything else put together— no more Angus!

But I can't turn the clock back. So now what? Let's see. I'll be an unmarried mother at nineteen—following in my mother's steps exactly, except that the baby's father isn't a no-good English aristocrat, but a no-good missionary's kid from Ngavi. Well, Guy isn't exactly a no-good, at least, I won't call him that unless he does what my dad did. And maybe he will. Maybe that's what I want him to do! Then Angus can still marry me. I'm sure he would. That's the kind of man he is. But I can't let him do it, can I? And maybe one good thing about all of this is that the baby will set him free. I'm not good enough for him, never have been.

I can't sit still any longer. I walk back and forth across our tiny living room floor. How can I tell Angus? And Guy? I suppose he'll have to know very soon. Oh God, where do I go from here?

"Tell Angus right now," a voice inside whispers. "He'll help you do the right thing."

I make for the door, and then stop. I can't tell him now, not right before the party. Tomorrow, I'll let him know about the baby.

Then a terrible thought strikes me. Everyone on the station and at school knows Angus is officially dating me. So what will they all think? No, they can't think the baby is his! They know Angus too well for that, but they also know me! They already think I've got him wound round my little finger so who knows what they'll think now. I can't let him take the blame for this, or even part of it. Then what do I do? Oh God, what do I do!

I sit down again with a thump. There's only one way out of this and even that might not work but I'll have to give it a try, for Angus' sake. I get up again and go over to my desk. Soon I'm writing two letters, letters that will lead me to heaven or hell; I'm not quite sure which.

And tonight? How can I pretend I'm going to the UK when I can't now, can I? Or maybe I can. Maybe I can have my baby in England. Maybe I don't need to tell anyone—yet. Or maybe I can have a secret abortion. Plenty of girls do. I give a shudder. No, I could never do that, not with a grandmother called Rhoda and a fiancé called....

Now I lose it completely. For a whole half an hour I cry even harder than I did at the doctor's. When Grandma died, I cried a lot, but it was different. I cried on Angus' shoulder. And he cried too! That made it easier to bear. But he can't share this with me because it's more than sorrow. It's guilt and dread and desperation all mixed up together and making me feel like someone had put a giant weight on my heart, squeezing all the breath out of my soul and my spirit. I don't think I'll ever be happy again. How can anyone say there's no hell! I certainly can't, not after this.

I don't know how long I sit there. Then Grandma's old clock strikes six. I give a long sigh. Can't time have mercy on me for once and stand still, just till I can sort this whole thing out? Maybe I'll never ever sort it out. I'm reaping what I sowed, after all.

I shake my head as I slip into the bathroom. I don't use much makeup. Angus doesn't like it. But I can't go to my party looking like this. There, that does it. You can't tell I've been crying unless you look really closely.

Ten minutes later I walk slowly up the dirt road to the church. A tall slim young man is walking just ahead of me. He hears me coming and turns round. It's Guy Stanton. He waits until I catch up with him. "What's this about you and Angus Campbell?" Guy growls, as I come level with him and we walk slowly towards the church door together.

His words madden me. "*You* can't talk!" I splutter.

"Yes I can," he argues. "It's all off with me and my girl. And I did it for you."

Suddenly, I don't feel angry any more. After all, I am talking to the father of this baby inside of me. I say nothing. I can't. "I came home especially to see you before you go to England," he goes on.

"Thanks," I whisper. I reach into my purse and pull out one of the letters I've just written and hand it to him. Then I disappear into the crowd jostling around me.

Soon all my friends are hovering about me, wishing me the best as I leave for England. Some give a wink and whisper that they'll take care of Angus when I'm gone. Others tell me to be a good girl and come back soon so they can have a big wedding.

Then everyone clamors for a speech. I can't do it, I explain. I'm too emotional. They think they understand, but they don't really. I don't even understand myself. I see Angus enter just after Reg Stanton has given me an exhortation to not forget God or His people and presented me with a love offering. That's almost too much for me. If they only knew what I'm carrying inside, I'm thinking, they'd almost boo me out of Ngavi Mission. I'm crying. I'm thanking everyone, but really I'm thinking of nothing but the baby and Guy and Angus.

Roger Buchannan makes a little speech and says a wonderful prayer. Angus is standing beside me now.

"You all right?" he asks anxiously. "Did it go OK at the doctor's?"

"I'll tell you later," I whisper.

We sit down, Angus and I together. Guy is at the other end of the long table. He keeps his eyes on us the whole time. I think he's read my note. Yes, I know he has because the last hour or so has made him look ten years older. He's trying to catch my eye, trying to mouth some words when Angus isn't looking. But I look away. This isn't the time to discuss babies and, well, everything to do with them. I must say though, he doesn't seem mad with me, just confused, shocked, and I'm not sure what else.

We eat a sumptuous meal. Angus has literally killed the fatted calf for me. I can't eat much, though. I've been feeling sick for weeks now. I ought to have known why, but I wouldn't think about it. Angus senses there's something up with me, but before we have a chance to be alone, he's called back to his calving heifer.

"I'll see you first thing tomorrow," he whispers.

I nod, thinking of all the things that may happen before tomorrow. When he's gone, I look around for Guy. He's nowhere to be seen. That's strange. I'd have thought he'd want to talk to me. I don't know what I feel exactly as I walk home with Sarah and get ready for bed. Then I hear a man's voice below my window. It's Guy, of course; who else would it be? Angus never comes near my house at night. "It wouldn't look right," he has told me over and over again.

I open the window and lean out. I shine my flashlight into the darkness. It lights up Guy's face. "Don't worry, Joy," I hear him whisper. "I'll take care of you and the baby." Then he reaches up his hand and slips me a folded piece of paper. Before I can ask any questions, he has gone.

I tear open the envelope, my heart beating fast. I don't love this man, not in the way I love Angus, but he is the father of my child. And he says he'll take care of the both of us. Does that surprise me? It does in a way, and yet it doesn't. He said he has loved me for years. I didn't believe him. Now, maybe it was true after all.

I slip into bed, and begin to read Guy's note. It isn't long but says it all, far more than I ever thought it would say. I tuck the note under my pillow and turn off the light. And then begins the longest night of my life. I toss; I turn; I try to read; I pray; I pace the floor; I slip to the kitchen for a drink; and on and on, until I finally drift into a fitful sleep. An hour later, I awake with a start and look at my watch. It's four a.m.

Suddenly, I know what I've got to do. I haul down my large, black suitcase from the top of the dresser and begin to pack. I was going to pack anyway, in a few days' time, only now my destination has changed. It won't be England. In fact, I don't quite know where it will be. I only know that this time tomorrow, I will no longer be Joy Mkandawire, future wife of Angus Campbell, but....

My hands shake as I zip up my suitcase. Mrs. Stanton! How does it sound? Most girls in Ngavi would give the world to have a name like that. I start to cry. Am I doing right, I wonder? Well, I'm freeing the best man on earth so he can love the best woman on earth. And I'm giving the father of my child the chance to be a father and a husband. So yes, it seems like I am doing right.

I hear a knock on my window. I place my letter for Angus on the table where I'm sure he'll see it. I've rewritten it four times and it still doesn't say half I want it to say. Then I take my purse in one hand and my suitcase in the other, and slip out the door.

Guy is waiting for me. He knew I'd come. I stand on the doorstep for a few moments. He stands still too, right in the middle of the path. We're looking at each other, sort of giving each other the chance to back out of all of this. I'm not sure what he's thinking exactly. Maybe the same as me. Will we ruin each other's lives if we run off like this together?

I take a step towards him. He takes a step towards me. He looks frightened. I'm sure I do, too. Well, all we are is just two lost children, trying to get out of the tangle of our own sin. That's how God must see us, too.

Guy takes my arm. I'm stumbling now towards his bright red Jeep. "You OK?" he whispers.

I nod. Am I telling a lie? Not really, because suddenly I feel pretty sure that Grandma is looking down from Heaven watching me. I look up into the starlit sky. And I also think she's asking God to take care of the three of us—Guy, the baby, and me, and bring us all safely HOME in the end!

Chapter Fifty-Six

Angus: Free—for what?

"Joy has disappeared, Dada Angus."

I stare at Sarah for a long time. Then the words sink in. "Disappeared!" I repeat. I can't believe my ears.

"Yes, she was gone when I got up to make breakfast, but there's a letter on the table for you. That'll probably tell you everything."

I reach mechanically for the letter and slit open the envelope. As I unfold the notepaper, my hand touches something hard. It's my mother's ring! Joy is doing the unbelievable—she's breaking off our secret engagement!

I can feel Sarah's eyes on me, so I slip out to the verandah where I can be alone and sit down on the swing, the one I made for Rhoda those long years ago. I have not read far before my head begins to swim. The words, "I'm four months pregnant"; "you're far too good for me"; "I need to set you free to marry the woman you really love"; jump out at me from the white, lined notepaper I hold in my hand. But there's worse to come.

"I'm getting married to Guy as soon as possible," I read. "Please forgive me and love me still. And don't be too worried about me. Guy wants to take care of me and the baby. I think he really does love me. And maybe eventually I'll love him, too, though I'll never be able to love him like I love you. And, Angus, I often wish my father had been willing to do what Guy is doing. You don't know how I've always wanted a real father. And Guy is the real father of the child I'm carrying. So maybe it'll turn out all for the best.

"Don't worry about us. We'll contact you when we're married, which might be tomorrow. Please forgive me, dear Angus, and keep on loving me even though I don't deserve it. I know I'll love you forever and forever. Always, your Joy."

"Always my Joy," I repeat as I reenter the house, tears streaming down my face. "Yes, she has been my joy, a worrisome one at times, but a joy. And just when I was coming to think I could really love her as a man should love his wife, this happens!"

I stuff the letter in my pocket, mutter a few words to Sarah that I know must sound completely incoherent, and make for the Stantons. But Reg already knows. I find him pacing his verandah, hands behind his back. For the first time ever, he embraces me as a father does a son. We weep together and we pray together. And then, just when we've put the elopers in God's hands, knowing that there's not much more we can do, I hear an engine in the distance. A few moments later, Guy's red Jeep pulls up in front of the house. Out tumbles a distraught looking Joy who runs into my arms and sobs as if her heart will break.

I'm not sure what this means. Have they called their marriage off? I sit the girl down on a chair and then wait. Reg waits, too, very patiently for him. And the story comes out. They had thought they'd find someone to marry them in Mpongo, but on the way there, they talk things over. Both know that eloping isn't the way out—that it will hurt those they love and begin married life on the wrong footing. They have to face the music. And they do.

Although I've never been fond of Reg's oldest son, I almost admire him as he tells everything to his father and to me—how he had almost gone too far with Joy when she was only fifteen—how he felt guilty for years—how it made him stop playing with nearly every girl he met—how he couldn't erase the image of Joy from his mind or heart—and how he pled with his father to allow him to date her and how Reg had refused, absolutely and completely!

Here Reg shifts uneasily from foot to foot. I avoid his eyes as Guy continues his story. It seems he has always been obsessed with Joy, even when he dated another girl, a girl his father wanted him to marry. And when he came back last Christmas and found Joy was angry with me and only too willing and eager to be in his arms, well, his old passion returned full force.

"It was really my fault," Joy interrupts.

"It was both our faults," Guy protests.

"Of course it was both your faults," Reg agrees, a bit impatiently, "but what is done is done. Now finish your story."

And so Guy goes on to tell about his jealousy and anger when he found out Joy and I were practically engaged. He felt betrayed—

ridiculous, he admits, when he had been dating another girl for months. And then he found out about the baby. That did it! No one else would father his child. Not even Angus Campbell!

"And so, Dad," he concludes, looking into his father's eyes, "we're here to ask your blessing. If you can't give it, we mean to go ahead anyway. And we want yours, too, Angus," he continues. "And I'm willing to do anything—move to England so Joy can go to college as she planned—anything, only I won't give her up again, ever!"

He comes over to Joy and takes her hand. She's trembling like a leaf. What should I do? Step in and remind him that this girl is already engaged to me—that she simply can't do this to me, baby or no baby? And should I remind Joy that, just two days ago, I gave up Cherry for the second or third time in my life and all for what? To see my fiancée marry this scoundrel? What does she think I'm made of? Sawdust? Feathers? Well, she'll find I won't let her play with me like this.

Joy senses my mood change and stiffens. I take a step towards her. I sense Reg is holding his breath. Joy glances from me to Guy and then back to me again. Then she shakes her head sadly as she slips her arms around Guy as if to say, "I've chosen him for better or for worse."

Guy holds her tight—protectively, passionately. Then he raises his eyes to mine. "Forgive her, Angus," he murmurs. "Please forgive her."

Joy looks at me pleadingly. My heart melts as it always does when she looks at me that way. "Of course I forgive you," I say gently. "But I do need time to think about what's happened, to be sure I'm doing what your grandmother would want me to do before I can give my blessing."

Reg nods. "I feel the same way," he says firmly. "I need time, Guy, to come to terms with this."

I walk with Joy back to her house and we sit on the verandah, as we've done so many times before. She talks her heart out to me. I listen, but I'm in a daze. My emotions are on a roller coaster. I don't think Joy can understand why I'm tongue-tied. It just isn't like the Angus she knows so well.

And so I go to the lake for a few days where I fast and pray and pace the beach. Then I come back, compare notes with Reg, and then, together, we give our blessing to the marriage; the date is set; Joy's flight to the UK is postponed; and life returns to normal, or does it?

For me, it will never ever again be normal. I feel I've been a poor guardian and an even poorer missionary. And the two women God put into my life are lost to me forever. "You're free now," Joy has told me more than once over the past few days. I smile and say nothing. But inside I'm shouting: "Free for what?"

At least, Reg and I are closer than ever before. And the mission is prospering, and the farm, and the church. And, after all, I'm first and foremost a missionary, am I not? It's just that in the evenings, when darkness falls and threatens to invade my soul, I wonder why it has all happened. Then the Lord whispers peace to me, tells me I am not alone, that He is ruling the world not I, and that I must believe that all things do work for good to those who love Him. And I do love Him, don't I?

I ask this question many times and I always come up with the same answer: I may have a very feeble love, a very faltering love, but yes, of course I love Him, especially now, when all other loves have been snatched from me. And sometimes, when I feel His Spirit surrounding me with love and peace, I find myself saying, as I would say to the bride I will never have, "I love you...till death do us...." And then I stop. I can't put it like that, can I? This is a marriage that never ends.

And so I rise in the morning, able to smile once more, able to laugh with my workers, to tease Sarah when she burns my maize porridge, to write Joy and Guy in England that I am happy and content, to pray for Cherry and her family, and to enjoy this mighty land which is my only home.

And sometimes, on a Sunday morning when the church is packed and hundreds of voices sing in unison, I really think I'm tasting Heaven; and when my myriads of African brothers and sisters hug me and tell me I am their brother, their father, and their son, I don't only think I'm tasting celestial delights, I know I am.

Chapter Fifty-Seven

Andrew: Forgiving myself.

"Flight 489 to Newark has been delayed for at least an hour owing to engine problems."

I groan as I hear the announcement coming over the PA system at O'Hare. I decide to go to the nearest restaurant for a snack as I haven't eaten since morning, and it is now four in the afternoon.

I pass by a McDonald's and break over my resolution not to indulge in fast food. As I munch on a Big Mac, I fish in my briefcase for something to read. I pull out a pile of mail I didn't have time to peruse before leaving home this morning. A church newsletter catches my eye. An old friend has sent it to me for some reason or another, as if I hadn't read enough newsletters in my life to last an eternity. I groan and am about to toss it into a bin nearby, when I notice a paragraph marked in red ink.

"Isn't this the same Cherry McMann you were engaged to, Andrew?" my friend writes in the margin. "I thought you might want to know what's become of her, or maybe not. If not, please forgive my interference. I, for one, thought it interesting. Hope you do the same. I heard her speak at least twice at our church and was extremely impressed."

I frown a little. I don't need a reminder of what my ex-fiancée is doing. It's hard enough to keep her out of my mind for an hour at a time. But curiosity gets the better of me. I spread the newsletter on the table. A small, black-and-white photo of Cherry catches my eye. I look closer. The young woman in the photo has short, curly hair. Maybe it's not Cherry after all. But her smile! There's only one girl on earth with that smile!

My heart beats faster as I begin to read: "Cherry McMann, who has just completed training at Guy's Hospital, London, has been accepted by St. Luke's Hospital, Nairobi, as a full time medical missionary. Dr. McMann has spoken at our church several times, and we were impressed by her zeal, as well as by her magnetic personality. We rejoice that such a talented young woman is willing to devote her life to missions and wish to contribute to her support." Then follows an invitation to participate in this support.

I push the letter away from me in frustration. I see it all. Africa! Missionary doctor! She's marrying Angus Campbell; I'm sure of it. He's in Africa isn't he? But wait a minute! He's in Malawi, not Kenya, and this write-up doesn't speak of a husband in the offing.

I glance at my watch. I've just time to give Gloria a quick ring. She'll know all the latest about Cherry. A moment later, I hear my daughter's voice on the other end of the line.

"You OK, Dad?" she asks anxiously.

"Fine." I clear my throat. "I've just read in some mission newsletter that Cherry is going to be a missionary doctor in Kenya. Is this true, Gloria?"

"Yes, Dad. It's true. We get in touch from time to time, so I keep track of what she's doing."

I gulp hard and then take the plunge. "Is she going to be married?"

There is a long pause at the other end and then my daughter says slowly, "No, Dad. At least it seems highly unlikely from what I've heard, or, well...."

"Yes?" I want to know when Gloria can't seem to finish her sentence.

My daughter gives a long sigh and then continues reluctantly: "She went on a visit to Africa over a year ago and spent a month helping out in some hospital in Malawi. Well, she came back pretty broken-hearted. I know that, because I met her at the Wesleyan Methodist Church Mom goes to not long after she returned from Africa. We had a meal together afterwards. Cherry looked terrible and I wanted to know why." Another long pause. This time, I bite my lip and keep silent until my daughter goes on slowly: "Angus Campbell, I'm sure you remember him, Dad, well, it seems...?"

My stomach churns. "How could I forget him?" I interrupt. I'm glad Gloria can't see my face just now.

"Cherry discovered," she goes on, ignoring my comment, "that Angus was engaged to be married to some girl—a ward of his. She came back shocked and broken-hearted."

"Broken-hearted?" I repeat, not sure why I want to know all this.

"Yes. She really loved Angus, Dad. Sorry, but I'm sure she still loves him from what I can gather."

I hear my name being called on the PA system. "Got to go, Gloria. Thanks for the info." I bang the receiver down, grab my bag, and run for the gate.

"Why oh why did I have to read that newsletter?" I ask myself, as I board the plane and we soar into the summer night. I stare at the clouds swirling around me and force myself to come up with an answer. The same question still haunts me as I disembark several hours later and make my way towards the baggage claim. I'm headed to Princeton for an interview. Five long years of hard grind, and now, at last, I have my coveted PhD in New Testament Studies.

I pull my weekend case from the carousel. The very faint spark of hope that Dennis' letter had rekindled deep within me has been extinguished forever. Cherry McMann loves someone else. She, too, is broken-hearted, and yet she doesn't let that hinder her from fulfilling her calling. Then why can't I do the same? Or maybe I am doing the same? And anyway, what is my calling, really and truly? I've argued for years that I could fulfill that calling in a prestigious seminary such as Princeton, just as well as in some parish church like St. Asaph's. And can't I? After all, it isn't as if I'm giving up the priesthood, is it? Once a priest always a priest!

By the time I reach my motel an hour later, I'm still in a state of self-interrogation and I know it isn't over yet and won't be until I settle the question once and for all. Can I fulfill God's will for my life at Princeton? Is that what He wants for me?

I go to a nearby restaurant but I can't finish my meal. I return to my room, switch on the news, but I can't watch it. I pull out a book that I've been dying to finish for weeks, but I can't read it. I climb into bed, stack the pillows up behind me, and sit bolt upright, staring straight ahead at the blank television screen. I'm still in the grips of my own inquisition. Why didn't I accept the Bishop's offer to transfer me to another church when I said I couldn't face returning to St. Asaph's? And why did I suddenly decide that I wanted an academic career? Was I acting on the rebound? Sure I was, but why? Because the love of my life had exited as suddenly as she had entered it and left me bereft? Because I was bitter against her, and her father, and Mary?

My head begins to ache, but I force myself to answer my own questions. Well, I never was bitter against Cherry. It was her dad I blamed, but now I've forgiven him. I'm sure of that, and Mary! I can never doubt that I've truly forgiven her, too. Then maybe God is the problem, but I've never thought it was His fault in the first place, even though He sometimes seems to be working against me instead of for me. I owe too much to Him to ever question His love, even when I admit that it shows itself in strange and almost cruel ways. He put meaning and purpose into my life when I most needed it. And true happiness! I have never felt as fulfilled as when in the pulpit, or administering the sacrament, or praying with a dying parishioner. I give a start. Then what about the bliss I felt when my arms were around my fiancée and my lips were on hers? Wasn't that true happiness? Hadn't I told Cherry that she made me feel as if I were truly in Paradise?

I jump out of bed and throw myself on my knees. I begin to tell God what a hopeless failure I've been. I should have shown more restraint and less passion. I ought to have at least waited a few more years before entering into an engagement with a girl whose parents were so adamant against divorce. My love was overpowering, demanding, all consuming. And as for Mary, isn't she the answer to my dilemma? Why am I so determined never to remarry her? Why do I turn a deaf ear to my children's wishes, or harden my heart to the love I see in Mary's eyes every time I meet her?

My sins and failures seem to reach as high as Heaven's gate. "Forgive me!" I cry aloud. "Forgive me, Father!"

"I have already forgiven you, My child!" comes the answer, an answer any penitent longs to hear, but it does not bring me peace. Of course He has forgiven me! I've known that from the beginning.

The silence deepens with the shadows. It's midnight and I'm still on my knees. Then from the depth of my soul two words break into my agony and shatter my darkness. "Forgive yourself!" The words nearly bowl me over and I know their origin is divine. I know it because I don't need to answer verbally. The acknowledgment of the malady is immediate cure.

The next morning I make my way to Princeton, marveling at the calm that totally possesses me. I feel strangely indifferent as to whether posterity will remember me as "Dr. Price" or "Father Andrew," or even whether, in the end, I'll remarry my first sweetheart and work together with her as God's ministers of light, or instead, demonstrate to my family and friends that a celibate priest can be truly happy. Nothing matters right now except the peace that seeps into every pore of my being.

"Thank you, God," I breathe, as I pay the taxicab driver, grab my briefcase, and turn to face the future. "And," I add as an afterthought, "thank you...Cherry!"

Chapter Fifty-Eight

Dennis: *God bless you, Dr. McMann!*

"Blest be the tie that binds our hearts in Christian love." My voice chokes. I wish Cherry hadn't chosen this hymn. It always tugs at my emotions and now, when I'm about to bid farewell to my only daughter, it is a song I'm not sure I want to sing.

I look at her as she mounts the pulpit steps, opens her Bible, and begins to speak. This is the daughter I dedicated to God before birth to be a missionary, and now, after many ups and downs (sometimes more downs than ups), it is all coming together. But I'm not sure I can part with her. The last few years we've been so very close. I've watched her go through things that would have destroyed many young women I know. Yet there she is, telling in her honest, openhearted way how God has brought her to this point in her life.

I look over at Paul. His eyes are fixed on his sister's face. I see a smile playing on his lips at times; at others, I'm almost sure he's blinking back the tears. I glance at the woman by his side. She's a widow with three small children. They've been friendly for over a year now. I'm not sure what I think of their friendship. Paul needs someone, that's for sure.

Cherry is singing now and Rachel is playing the piano, the piano that hasn't been played in a very long time. In fact, this is the first service we've had in our old fellowship hall in some years. No, I'm not going to be the leader any more, but at least I can attend, preach occasionally, and acknowledge that God is slowly healing my heart. He hasn't answered all my questions, but then, I no longer demand answers as I used to do, because I'm coming to realize that He is answering them by the love He showers upon me every day.

I focus again on my daughter. And as she begins to sing, "We rest on Thee, our Shield and our Defender! We go not forth alone against the foe," I give a start. This is the hymn the five martyr missionaries to Ecuador sang before their last, fatal trip into the jungle. Why does she have to choose this particular song for her solo tonight?

Her eyes meet mine. I see they are filled with tears. She pauses for just a few seconds, takes a deep breath and then continues, her clear, bell-like voice filling the hall:

> "Strong in Thy strength, safe in Thy keeping tender,
> We rest on Thee, and in Thy Name we go."

When she comes to the last verse, I lose it completely:

> "We rest on Thee, our Shield and our Defender!
> Thine is the battle, Thine shall be the praise;
> When passing through the gates of pearly splendor,
> Victors, we rest with Thee, through endless days."

When she has finished, I run to the altar. I thought I was a consecrated Christian, but right now, I just don't want to give up this re-discovered daughter of mine to jungles, and natives, and untold dangers. I need her in my old age. Oh God, how I need her!

Someone puts their arms around me. It's Paul. "Cry it out, Dad," he whispers. We cling to each other. Then Rachel joins us, and finally I hear Cherry's gentle voice behind me saying, "It's OK, Dad. I'm safe in His will. That's what you taught me, remember? I'm only following in your steps."

"Following in my steps!" I want to say, "Don't do that. You'll go astray." But I don't. She believes in me with all her heart and if I don't yet believe in myself, what does that matter right now? I look into Cherry's face. It is radiant. She's gloriously happy.

"God bless you, Dr. McMann," I say, grinning through my tears.

"Thanks, Dad. And remember, that while I'll probably never give you the brood of redheads you've been longing for, I will still give you a host of grandchildren—all with black, shining faces, mops of curly hair, and eyes so large and so brown, they look like melted chocolate. How's that for a substitute?"

"Sounds like a mighty fine substitute, Ginger," I say fondly. "And you can count on me to be the best granddad on the face of the earth, you wait and see."

"I don't doubt it, Dad," she says lovingly as we walk back to the farmhouse. "You always were and always will be—the best of everything!"

Chapter Fifty-Nine

Cherry: Starting all over again.

"Is there a nurse in the Nairobi party? If so, please come to the reception area immediately."

I grimace at my roommate as I spring out of bed. I hadn't realized we had such an efficient PA system in the Mission guesthouse near Cape Town where I've been on a retreat with a group of Anglican missionaries from all over Kenya. We've been here nearly two weeks.

"There goes my afternoon siesta," I say ruefully. "And on my last day, too!"

"They asked for a nurse, not a doctor," Linda reminds me. Linda is a teacher from Nairobi. We hit it off the first time we met so agreed to share a room together.

I hesitate for just a moment. Maybe I should wait and see if the call is repeated. Then the doctor inside of me takes over. I grab my emergency case and make for the door. "Sleep well, Linda," I advise. "We have a long flight back to Nairobi tonight." Then I slip out the door and hurry down the winding staircase.

"You're a nurse?" one of the guesthouse staff asks questioningly, looking highly flustered.

"Well, I'm a doctor, actually—Dr. Cherry McMann."

The lady smiles a little. "That's even better. It seems that one of the men playing in the tennis tournament has sprained his ankle very badly. At least he thinks it's a sprain, not a break."

"We missionaries seem accident prone," I grumble good-naturedly. "We can't even play a recreational game without injuring ourselves."

"This is pretty high-geared, Doctor," the lady tells me with a chuckle. "Anglicans versus Presbyterians!"

I grin. I'd heard that a party of Presbyterian missionaries had arrived this morning and had challenged the Anglicans to a tennis tournament. "Where is my patient?" I ask.

"This way." I follow her into a large airy room and over to the window where I see a group of men gathered.

One of them comes up to me. "Nurse?"

"She's a doctor," the lady says.

"That's even better. Well, my friend here has done something pretty drastic to his ankle. He nearly fainted a few moments ago."

I go up to the sofa where I see someone stretched out. I hear him groaning softly.

"We asked for a nurse and got a doctor, Angus," one of the men tells him.

I nearly drop my bag. "I don't want a doctor or a nurse," I hear a familiar voice mutter. "I just want peace and quiet."

"He's out of sorts," his friend whispers in my ear. "Just when he was beating his opponent, he went and did this." The man shakes his head despondently. "He's the best on our team. Now we haven't much chance of beating you Anglicans."

"The Anglicans always win," says the same voice from the sofa. My hands are trembling but I mustn't lose my professional cool.

I put my bag on the table and take out my stethoscope and blood pressure cuff. I see that someone has already placed an icepack on the ankle.

I bend over my patient without saying a word. His eyes are closed now. "Just hold steady a moment," I say softly, "I need to examine your ankle."

I feel his body give a jerk and then stiffen as I touch his leg. He still keeps his eyes closed and stifles a moan. "It's a very bad sprain," I tell him a moment later, "but not a break. Now I need to take your vital signs."

I wrap the cuff around his arm and as I do so, the man on the sofa opens his eyes. They stare straight into mine. I see his lips twitch. I bend over to hear his heartbeat. "What on earth have you done to your hair!" he mutters in my ear.

His friends are looking out the window, watching the tennis match. No one hears his comment but me.

"I cut it three years ago," I say, trying to keep my voice calm. "All of us sacrifice something or other when we dedicate our lives to Africa, don't we? I sacrificed my hair." Our eyes meet. We both know that we are full of conflicting emotions. Then I remember.

"Isn't your wife with you?" I ask. "I mean, she ought to know about your accident."

Angus' friend is by his side again and has overheard my remark. He throws back his head and laughs heartily. "His wife? Angus has no wife. He's a confirmed bachelor, Doctor."

I blush scarlet as I see the man's amused expression. "I thought that she needed to know of his injury," I say hastily, "and how to tend his foot. But if he...."

"Then you'll need to tend it," his friend butts in. "Eh, Angus? A pretty doctor at your disposal? How's that for a substitute for tennis?"

"I'm leaving tonight," I say abruptly. "I've already been here nearly two weeks. Now let me see to this foot."

Keeping my eyes fixed on his foot, I proceed to bathe and bandage it and then go off to see if I can find some crutches. I can't stand to be with him, not in front of everyone. And I don't know how I feel or how he feels either. We've both thought we were pretty much dead to each other and experiencing a resurrection is pretty life-shattering for two down-to-earth missionaries.

I eventually locate some crutches and tiptoe back into the room to find my patient's eyes closed. He is alone. I sit down in a chair and watch him. He looks worn and haggard and very thin. His blood pressure is too low. I'll need to tell him that. And his heartbeat is very irregular.

I sit and look at him and remember. How I remember! "Which church do you go to?" That was the question he put to me and one that set us both on a journey of no return. I smile to myself. Now it seems that he has joined the Presbyterian ranks. I wonder if he's reconciled to predestination at last.

As old memories flood over me, old emotions follow in their wake. We can't seem to get rid of each other, Angus and I. I determined not to take a post anywhere near Mpongo or anywhere else in Malawi for that matter. I thought Nairobi was far enough away. And now we meet for a few hours in a seaside resort in South Africa.

I look at my watch. I need to go and pack, need to get a snack and then be off to the airport and away from Angus. How many times have we said good-bye already in our brief lifetimes—I mean a definite, final good-bye? Only none of them has been as definite or as final as we thought. Maybe this one will be different.

My patient stirs and opens his eyes. "Cherry?" he asks in a low but clear voice.

I bend over him. "I'm here," I say softly. "And I need to tell you, Mr. Campbell, that you must get medical attention when you return to Mpongo. Your blood-pressure is too low."

He grabs my hand and holds it tight. "You said you're leaving soon?"

"In an hour or so," I mutter. "And I have to go and pack immediately."

"So soon?"

I nod, choking back the tears. "You flit in and out of my life like..." he begins in a tremulous voice.

"A butterfly," I suggest, with an attempt at a smile.

"Or an angel, and a redheaded one at that!"

I blink back the tears. "But Joy, Angus. Where is she?"

His face grows sad. "She married the Stanton boy. She had to. She was pregnant."

His voice breaks. "He still loves her," I think to myself. I stiffen a little. But he still has my hand in his.

"Look, Cherry," he whispers, as he hears his friends approaching, "There's a lot of explaining I could do, but there's no time, so I just say as I've said before, 'Trust me.'" I nod. I can't speak. I'm too choked up.

"Let's start all over again," he murmurs, still holding my hand. "And see where it takes us to. Agreed?"

"Start all over again?" I repeat, half to myself. Then I look into his eyes and know there's only one answer I can give. "Agreed," I whisper back.

He drops my hand as his friends come up to the sofa. "Jim will get your address, Doctor," he says in a very matter of fact tone. "Won't you, Jim? Dr. McMann wants to know how my foot is doing and she's given me some medical advice I need to follow up on. So we have to keep in touch."

Jim laughs outright. "Don't fool me, Angus. You've fallen for the pretty doctor already. Who would have thought it!"

"Good-bye, Angus," I say, trying to sound as matter-of-fact as he does but failing miserably. Two large teardrops are rolling down my face.

"Good-bye, Doctor. I'll write soon." Then he smiles a typical Angus smile. I turn and bolt for the door.

"What's going on between you two?" I hear Jim asking curiously.

"I'd give anything to know that," I hear Angus reply wistfully. "But ask me again in a month or two and I'll be able to give you an answer."

"Well, I wish you success. She seems a real winner."

I'm eavesdropping now but I can't help myself. I linger in the corridor waiting to hear Angus' reply. There is a long silence and then I hear him say with a catch in his voice that tells me more than a thousand eloquent speeches could do: "What else can she be but a winner, Jim? She conquered me years ago. And anyway, didn't I tell you already that Anglicans always win?"

CONTACTS FOR TRUDY HARVEY TAIT:

www.harveycp.com
trudytait@gmail.com
www.facebook.com/trudy.harveytait

The Velvet Curtain

by,
Trudy Harvey Tait
336 page paperback
Size: 5.5 x 8.5 inches
ISBN: 1-932774-69-6
Retail price $11.95

Step back into the eighties when Communism still held deadly sway in Eastern Europe and imagine yourself with Esther, a Romanian teenager, coming to America, the land of freedom, for the first time and discovering that there is much more awaiting her than a mere change of cultures.

Her beauty and individuality attract the attention of handsome Ron Atwood and her talent as a singer soon opens up a whole new world. She rejoices in her new-found liberty and popularity but the "curtain" that her elderly friend, Hugh Gardner, warns her about in the plane is fast closing in. Will it completely smother her, or will she be able to escape its folds?

Behind The Velvet Curtain

by,
Trudy Harvey Tait
304 page paperback
Size: 5.5 x 8.5 inches
ISBN: 1-932774-70-X
Retail price $11.95

This book, a sequel to *The Velvet Curtain*, continues the story of Esther and Gabby, the two Romanian girls who escape the Iron Curtain, only to find themselves enmeshed in its Western counterpart. Esther takes drastic measures to stay clear of the Velvet Curtain while Gabby denies its very existence and calls it, instead, The American Dream.

And yet, behind this all-enveloping Curtain, the two girls and their friends, Len and Ron Atwood, discover that God can turn tragedy into triumph. The story will take unexpected twists and turns as His grace invades, transforms, and redirects the lives of flawed and erring human beings.

Escaping The Velvet Curtain

by,
Trudy Harvey Tait
271 page paperback
Size: 5.5 x 8.5 inches
ISBN: 978-1-932774-71-9
Retail price $11.95

Escaping The Velvet Curtain concludes the saga of Esther, her sister Gabby, and their friends. If, like myself, you often wish that life were less complex, then you will empathize with them as they make momentous choices, often not knowing where God is leading them. And all the while, God's grace is producing miracles in their lives, often however, upsetting the smooth flow of their earthbound existence.

Exploring the various ways in which each character seeks to escape the Velvet Curtain has made me retrace my own spiritual pilgrimage. I realize afresh that God puts us in a seemingly impossible position and then delights to deliver us when He sees that our trust is in Him alone.

by,
Trudy Harvey Tait
144 page paperback
Size: 5.5 x 8.5 inches
ISBN: 978-1-932774-74-0
Retail price $7.95

Three in Love

TRUE FAITH-INSPIRING ROMANCES OF THE FOLLOWING COUPLES:

Charles & Susanna Spurgeon
William & Catherine Booth
John & Madeleine Oberlin
George Bowen & Emma Morris
Jonathan & Rosalind Goforth
Tom & Iva Vennard
James & Ruth Stewart
John & Betty Stam
Edwin & Lillian Harvey

For more information go to: www.harveycp.com

CPSIA information can be obtained at www.ICGtesting.com
Printed in the USA
LVOW101259021212

309747LV00002B/4/P